"I CAN'T
CAM[

Cass was thinking that the little widow was remarkably adept at loveplay, but thought better about saying so.

He bent over to gather up the scattered snowdrops. Lightly, with feigned carelessness, he asked, "Don't you know what day this is? The Feast of St. Valentine, when any man bold enough may kiss a fair maid."

"You are no ordinary man," she protested. "You're the Earl of Bevington. And I'm not a maid. I cannot excuse what just happened except to say that I . . ." She glanced down at the flowers he'd returned to her, and her long black lashes shielded her eyes. "You see, it has been so very long . . ." As her head drooped, a lock of brown hair slipped down to cover one flaming cheek. "So very long."

His pulse stilled when he heard that wistful, haunting phrase.

While he'd held her to his heart, passionately kissing her, and receiving her kisses, she had been remembering the husband she'd lost. In that moment of comprehension, a bitter and wholly irrational jealousy was born. And with it, a desire so intense that he wondered how long he could bear to let it go unslaked.

Someday he was going to take Sophie Pinnock in his arms again. And next time, he vowed, she would yearn and sigh for him and no one else, living or dead.

Other **AVON ROMANCES**

A DIME NOVEL HERO *by Maureen McKade*
THE HEART BREAKER *by Nicole Jordan*
HIGHLAND BRIDES: THE LADY AND THE KNIGHT
by Lois Greiman
THE MACKENZIES: DAVID *by Ana Leigh*
THE MEN OF PRIDE COUNTY: THE OUTCAST
by Rosalyn West
A ROSE IN SCOTLAND *by Joan Overfield*
THE WILD ONE *by Danelle Harmon*

Coming Soon

HER SECRET GUARDIAN *by Linda Needham*
THE PIRATE LORD *by Sabrina Jeffries*

And Don't Miss These
ROMANTIC TREASURES
from Avon Books

AFTER THE THUNDER *by Genell Dellin*
DEVIL'S BRIDE *by Stephanie Laurens*
MY WICKED FANTASY *by Karen Ranney*

THE PROPOSAL

MARGARET EVANS PORTER

AVON BOOKS NEW YORK

AVON BOOKS
A division of
The Hearst Corporation
1350 Avenue of the Americas
New York, New York 10019

Copyright © 1998 by Margaret Evans Porter
Inside cover author photo by Pierre F. Durand/Chameleon
Published by arrangement with the author
Visit our website at **http://www.AvonBooks.com**
Library of Congress Catalog Card Number: 97-94316
ISBN: 0-380-79557-4

First Avon Books Printing: March 1998

AVON TRADEMARK REG. U.S. PAT. OFF. AND IN OTHER COUNTRIES, MARCA REGISTRADA, HECHO EN U.S.A.

Printed in the U.S.A.

WCD 10 9 8 7 6 5 4 3 2 1

Acknowledgments

Creating a novel is never a solitary achievement, certainly not for this author. Therefore I wish to acknowledge those people involved in the creation of *The Proposal*.

First and foremost, I am grateful to my husband, Christopher, with whom I discovered the splendid rooms and magical gardens of the Gloucestershire castle on which I modeled my fictional one. If he wearied of exploring so many other historic gardens, he was kind enough not to mention it. Our adventures in Jersey and Portugal, two places that feature prominently in this story, were an important source of inspiration.

Abundant thanks to Margot and Robert Pierson, who not only suggested that first castle visit but also accompanied us on a later one. I'm forever grateful to them for generously sharing the many delights of Clifton village, truly a home away from home. At last I've made good my promise to use it in a book!

I'm grateful to my mother, an indefatigable gardener and rosarian, and to my father for demonstrating all the patience necessary in a gardener's spouse. And to all those grandparents whose legacy to me was their passion for plants.

I am indebted to Diann Balser, a dear friend and talented "personal assistant," for her unfailingly cheerful encouragement. Many other friends followed my progress (you know very well who you are), in particular fellow writers Terry and Emma and Julie. A special thanks to Annie for providing such a vivid and memorable working title! And to my agent Robin Rue and my editor Ann McKay Thoroman—your enthusiastic support for this project made the writing process all the more worthwhile.

Susan Schnare, Ph.D., garden historian and landscape consultant, provided helpful information in the earliest stages of this book, for which I thank her. And I greatly appreciate the attentive staff at Westbury Court Gardens in Gloucestershire, Mottisfont Abbey Gardens in Hampshire, and London's Museum of Garden History.

Chapter 1

January 1797

Drumming her fingers impatiently on the windowsill, Sophie Pinnock surveyed the busy inn yard scene.

Below her a farmer wearing a smock unloaded cans of milk from his cart. A servant girl with a stick was driving a gaggle of noisy geese toward a water trough. The hostler and a postboy harnessed a pair of horses to the chaise that would carry Sophie on the final leg of her journey. All was in readiness for her departure, except that her traveling companion hadn't appeared and she couldn't leave without him.

His failure to join her for breakfast could mean he was still sulking after last night's quarrel. Riding in a closed carriage with an angry gentleman for a

1

further twenty miles was a dismal prospect, but she would endure. Sophie's impending interview with the Earl of Bevington marked a new direction. Before today, each prospective client had been a prospective victim. The years of deception had taken their toll, and she was eager to put the dishonesty of the past behind her.

The clock on the wall struck the hour of nine. Moving away from the window, she paced the length of the cramped parlor. Her trailing skirts swept the floor, gathering dust, but she didn't care.

Where was he, what was keeping him?

Another ten minutes ticked away before her partner in fraud entered the room. A gentleman of medium height, he wore his coppery hair in a short, smart crop. His dour expression warned Sophie that he hadn't slept off his ill temper, and his blue eyes bored into her accusingly.

Spying the portfolio under his arm, she breathed a small sigh of relief. While tossing and fretting the night away, she'd wondered if he might be spiteful enough to destroy its precious contents.

He placed it on the table and set his valise on the floor next to Sophie's *baheur*, the small leather-bound trunk that she'd brought to England as a bride.

"You look most fetching in green." His harshness sharpened the Scots burr. "It suits your dark hair and eyes."

"Compliments will gain you nothing, Fingal Moncrieff." She thrust her hand into her drawstring purse and felt for her silver card case, embossed with roses and engraved with her initials. She removed their trade card and held it up. "Remember, Pinnock and Moncrieff is a business partnership. It will never be anything more." Satisfied that she'd made her point, she replaced the card and shoved the case back into her reticule.

"But I've waited so long already. Your husband died over two years ago."

Did he suppose it had slipped her mind? Losing Tobias had been the one great tragedy of her life.

He seized her hand. "You're but twenty, too young a lass for this endless mourning."

Young she might be, and often lonely, but she preferred widowhood to becoming Mrs. Moncrieff. Her marriage had been based on mutual affection, dependence, and respect. The man standing before her inspired none of those feelings.

"I've discussed my intentions with the Pinnocks. They consent to the match."

"*Naturellement*," said Sophie bitterly. "My brother-in-law wants the partnership kept intact until his son finishes his schooling and apprenticeship. It's part of their plot to wrest control of the firm from me."

"I could prevent that. As your husband, I'd look out for your interests." He inched closer, until he was much too close for comfort. "Say yes. Don't be so stubborn, Sophia."

No one but Tobias had ever called her by that name.

"You know it's for the best." Moist lips nuzzled her neck. He placed his hand upon her breast.

"*Sécours dé grâce!*" she cried in annoyance, wrenching herself out of his embrace. "How many times must I repeat it until you understand? I told you yesterday—last evening—and I tell you now, I cannot be your wife." When he reached for her again, she darted to the opposite side of the table.

"Sophia—"

Picking up one of the rock-hard breakfast rolls, she flung it at his rusty head. "I never gave you permission to be so familiar!"

Furiously he smashed his fist upon the wood, rattling the crockery and cutlery. "Why will you not be reasonable? My expertise as an architect, coupled with your artistic talents, could make us the premier landscape designers in Britain."

"Us?" Sophie repeated incredulously. "If we married, you'd carry on pretending all my sketches were your own, exactly as you've done since the day Tobias died."

"You didn't object."

"I was grieving, and you took advantage of that. You swore it was a temporary measure, and I believed you. You were hoaxing me, as you've hoaxed all our clients."

"With your assistance."

Voicing the suspicion that had nagged at her all morning, she said, "When you received Lord Bevington's letter you promised this commission would be all mine, that in future I'd receive credit for my drawings. You never meant it, did you?"

Clenching his jaw, he retorted, "Now you'll never know."

"What does that mean?"

"If you won't wed me, there's no point taking on new business together. I'm resigning from the partnership." To underscore his statement, he picked up his valise.

Amazement deprived Sophie of her command of both the English language and her native patois—until he snatched up the portfolio. *"Non!"* she protested. "Those designs are mine. *I* created every one of them."

"Nobody knows that but you and me. They bear my signature," he reminded her.

Her heartbeat pounded ominously in her ears as she followed him out of the room and down the rickety staircase. *Bouôn Dgieu*, she prayed, don't let him take the drawings. This punishment was too severe for the necessary sin of deceiving their clients. No one had suffered from it, only herself.

Moncrieff, reaching the front door of the inn, paused on the threshhold and spun around to face her. "I'll ask you once more. Will you—"

"*Nou-fait!* Never!"

"Then our attorneys must decide which of us should keep these designs. In the meantime, they'll remain with me. After all, you've got the copies of the Blue Books."

She watched him cross the inn yard, stepping around the farmer's cart and scattering the geese. As soon as he climbed into the chaise the postilion spurred and whipped his horses, and they trotted off at a fast clip, hooves cutting up the mud and making it fly.

Overwhelmed, Sophie dropped onto the hall bench. This catastrophe far exceeded the many smaller disasters that had plagued her since arriving at the Royal Oak.

She'd been drawn to this inn by a notation Tobias had penciled in his well-worn gazeteer, linking it to King Charles II. All her life Sophie had heard legends about the merry monarch, for he'd taken refuge on her island early in his exile from England. But the peppery Scotsman cared nothing for its historic associations and had spoiled her pleasure with his persistent proposals of marriage, and his quarrelsome ways.

Now he'd taken her portfolio, and with it a significant portion of her past. Enclosed between its stiff boards was artwork that represented untold hours of painstaking labor. Her design projects were an important connection to her late husband; they had been her only solace in the aftermath of his death.

Her initial horror at being deserted—and robbed—was subsiding. She had no time to sit about and bemoan Moncrieff's treachery. She would have to act, and swiftly.

Hurrying out to the yard, she found the hostler and carter shifting the last of the milk cans. "Have you another chaise for hire?" she asked the hostler breathlessly.

"Nay, lady. Your gentleman has taken the only one."

"He's no gentleman," she contradicted. "And he'll never be mine!" Striving to be heard over his guffaw, she insisted, "I must reach Bevington Castle as soon as possible."

"That's near twenty mile from 'ere."

Said the owner of the cart, in a marked West Country accent, "It's not far off the Bristol road. I'll be traveling that way, ma'am, if it suits you to ride with me."

She could have kissed his leathery cheek. "It does," she assured him before rushing back to the inn to collect her belongings.

A heavy cart pulled by a single shire horse wasn't likely to win a race with a chaise and pair. But Sophie's driver, a man of few words, boasted that he knew the way as well as any postboy.

"If not better," he added.

"How much farther to the castle?" she asked when he diverted from the principal road. She worried that the narrow, twisting lanes confused him as much as they did her.

"Naught but two mile more. Don't fret, I'll have you there afore yon clouds open up."

The fog occasionally parted to reveal ragged hills, rocky vales, and remote cottages. But it was thick enough to obscure the distant view of the

Severn River and the Welsh hills so glowingly described by the guidebook in Sophie's *baheur*.

Whether or not she reached the castle before Fingal Moncrieff, she intended to transform this apparent defeat into victory. By convincing the earl to hire her as his landscape gardener, she'd bring her long and uncomfortable charade to its desired end. But could she manage it without showing samples of her work? The collection of Blue Books was at her house in Chiswick, too far away to be of use.

Clinging to the side of the cart as the wheels bumped over the ruts, Sophie thought back to the more comfortable journeys she'd known during the years as her husband's willing and enthusiastic assistant. With Tobias she'd traveled the country inspecting grand estates and modest suburban villas, taking detailed notes and making sketches. When drawing up his designs, he'd sought her advice. And each time their collaborations had been elegantly bound in indigo leather and presented to a client, her sense of achievement had matched his.

She understood why he hadn't publicly acknowledged her innovations, and she hadn't wanted him to. Her reward came in those private moments when he praised her for being as clever as she was comely. Unlike his junior partner Moncrieff, he'd never displayed any jealousy of her talent. Quite the contrary, he had nurtured it—purchasing the most expensive materials for her to work with, encouraging her to spend hours at the easel.

Despite the fact that statuesque, azure-eyed blondes were all the rage in artistic circles, not short, dark-haired females like herself, she'd been his favorite model. Their artistic life had been as rewarding as their domestic one—but both had been tragically brief. In the second year of marriage, they had learned about his illness.

As Tobias's health failed, his dependence on others increased. He relied on his partner to maintain contact with clients, and relinquished all design work to his wife. Whenever Sophie had watched his trembling hand scrawl *Tobias Pinnock* at the bottom of her sketches, she'd felt a sharp but fleeting prick of remorse.

Devotion to a dying husband had deafened her to the cry of her conscience. But Fingal Moncrieff, as ruthless as he was ambitious, had never deserved her cooperation.

The final mile of her journey was uneventful, apart from a near-mishap with a sheep reckless enough to push its way through a gap in the hedge. Sophie's farmer was as good as his word—no sooner had they passed through the quiet village of Bevington than the swirling mist transformed itself into the chilling, driving rain typical of January. He set her down near the church, too cautious to attempt the steep and slippery drive leading up to the castle.

"A gurt big pile, that," he commented. With a cluck and a light slap of the reins, he urged his horse to walk on.

To Sophie's eyes it looked like a larger version of Gorey Castle in Jersey, built from a similarly reddish stone. Studying that daunting expanse of crenelated walls and towers, she wondered what sort of man occupied this fortress.

In the course of her travels she'd encountered several marquesses, three dukes, and, on one memorable occasion, a royal princess—and all of them outranked an earl. There was no cause for nervousness, she need only summon up that calm confidence Tobias had always displayed when calling on prospective employers. But he'd been famous, his services had been in high demand. She had no reputation as landscape designer because she'd always used her talents to bolster her huband's.

And Moncrieff's.

The memory of his betrayal roused her courage. She shifted the *baheur* to her hip and brushed at the straw clinging to her green pelisse, telling herself that this Lord Bevington was about to become the first of her many satisfied clients.

She followed the long avenue of oaks to a plain stone archway similar in shape to the Norman ones common on her island. Farther on she passed beneath the breezeway of an inner gatehouse, and came to a spacious, stone-paved court.

Where was the main entrance? Perplexed by so many projecting towers with arched doors, Sophie halted. At last she settled on a wooden, nail-studded portal framed by a clinging vine.

At her approach, it swung open with a squeal of hinges. A young man stepped out, urging her forward with a welcoming smile. His complexion was exotically dark and his hair quite damp—he too had been rained upon.

"How may I serve, *senhora*?"

Handing over her trade card, she explained that she'd come at Lord Bevington's request.

"I tell him right away. Follow me, *por favor*—I take your box. *O carregador*, the carrier, he deliver these today," the foreigner informed her as they stepped around the collection of wooden crates cluttering the vestibule. "Senhorio worry his fine chairs and tables for the large drawing room take harm by coming so far in bad weather."

Sophie spied the legend *Ince and Mayhew* stamped on a large canvas-wrapped object. The earl had ordered his new furniture from the most fashionable—and expensive—of London's cabinet-makers.

"Has Mr. Moncrieff arrived yet?"

"Mon Creeve?" The young man shook his head. "No, senhora."

Her hopes for a successful interview soared. If her rival was lost somewhere in the wilds of Gloucestershire, she had a better chance of winning this commission for herself.

The servant led her through a great hall with a high ceiling supported by vaulted timbers, cathedral-like windows, and a stone fireplace at the far end. Beyond an arched opening lay a wooden staircase of unmistakable antiquity.

He ushered her up the stairs to a chamber decorated with tapestries and a worn Turkish rug. "I go find senhorio and leave you here in morning room—even though is now afternoon," he said, his parting grin showing his fine white teeth.

Although thankful to be indoors, she regretted the lack of a fire. Her limbs ached with cold. Five years in England, and still she wasn't accustomed to the chill of winter.

To warm herself she walked up and down the length of the room. She craned her neck to read the words inscribed on the painted wooden ceiling, and was surprised to recognize them as Norman French, from which her own Jèrriais language had evolved. She examined the allegorical scenes depicted in the wall hangings. Pausing before a mirror, she discovered that the raindrops had imprinted a haphazard pattern of dark spots on her pelisse. The sleek black feathers tucked into her bonnet were damp and sagging.

The sound of a male voice sent her to a more strategic position at the window. She stared intently down at the landscape requiring improvement, and at the first glimpse of terraced walks and walled gardens her optimism ebbed. There was a long central canal, *aussîn*, spanned by three little bridges, and a two-story structure with large windows for looking out over the gardens.

Closing her eyes to shut out the view, she pressed her forehead against one cold, diamond-shaped pane.

Nânnîn, she thought. No, not again. Not here, too.

"A dismal prospect, isn't it?"

Sophie turned away from the window. She'd imagined a much older, less attractive earl—this man couldn't be more than thirty and was outrageously handsome. His hair was black and waving, his eyes quite blue. He towered above her, and his figure was as well-formed as it was tall. Staring up at him in mute amazement, she couldn't remember if she was supposed to extend her hand or curtsy to a man of title.

"What has Luis done with the gentleman?"

"There is no gentleman," she blurted.

"Oh? I've been corresponding with someone called Fingal Moncrieff, and that can't possibly be you."

"Mr. Moncrieff recently resigned." She preferred not to reveal quite how recently.

He frowned down at the card he was holding. "And what of Mr. Pinnock?"

Her breath caught in her throat, then emerged as a sigh. "My husband died two years ago."

"Pray accept my belated condolences." It was a perfunctory civility, and to her ear devoid of true sympathy. Again he glanced at her card. "Did you come all the way from Chiswick to announce that the firm of Pinnock and Moncrieff is no more? A letter would have sufficed."

Head high, her shoulders squared, Sophie announced, "I am a landscape gardener myself. My husband trained me—in effect I was his apprentice. And his assistant."

The earl's sharply suspicious stare was a dagger slicing through her confidence. Sophie was tempted to claim sole responsibility for the many well-known designs attributed to Tobias in the months before his death, but she couldn't bring herself to betray him.

Choosing instead to sacrifice Fingal Moncrieff, she continued, "My partner—my former partner—has taken credit for the plans I've produced since my husband passed away. I'll not trouble you with the details except to say that when Mr. Moncrieff represented himself to you as a landscape artist, he did so falsely. He is merely an architect."

"I have no great need of him," he responded with a careless shrug. "All the top men have been round to look the place over. Humphry Repton. Samuel Lapidge. William Emes. John Webb. Some other chap, his name escapes me."

"Adam Mickle?"

The earl's dark head moved up and down.

She seized upon the valuable clue about the type of design he wanted. All the gentlemen he'd named were noted for their highly picturesque landscapes.

"You must not be altogether satisfied," she ventured, "or you wouldn't have sent for Pinnock and Moncrieff. After conferring with your lordship and touring the grounds, I shall devise a landscape in the most modern style. You'll receive watercolor drawings and other renderings, and a list of suitable shrubs and trees. All of which will be bound into a blue leather cover with 'Bevington Castle' and your title stamped on the front. In gold letters."

"I've already received a Red Book from Repton."

"Who, in fact, poached that idea from my husband." Modifying her acid tone, Sophie continued, "Mr. Repton has an instructive style. I say nothing against it. But I doubt he presented you with more than a few pretty aquatints. I can supply the more detailed information required by a contractor."

Displeasure had deepened the crease between his inky brows. "This debate is quite unnecessary."

"Because I'm a female?" She scarcely recognized the strained voice as her own.

He failed to respond to her question directly. "I intend to make extensive alterations. I also expect the person I employ to supervise the work. You cannot abandon your children for weeks on end."

"I haven't any children."

He looked down his nose at her for some time, then moved purposefully to the door and called for his servant.

Sophie rained silent *malédictions* upon the head of that *vilain* Fingal Moncrieff. If she could have shown her portfolio, the earl wouldn't be turning her away with such disheartening bruptness.

"Luis, this lady will take tea before she goes. Tell Mr. Searle that I'll join him in the library as soon as I'm able."

And she called upon *lé dgiâbl'ye*—the devil—to punish this coldhearted wretch of an earl for refusing to accept that her skill was equal to Humphry Repton's. He lacked the common courtesy, and the fairness, to consider her credentials or her merits. She was a woman, so he was offering her a cup of tea she didn't even want instead of the employment she so desperately desired.

The Countess of Bevington would probably have been a more sympathetic listener, for noblewomen had the leisure to study horticulture and often had strong opinions about the arrangement of their gardens. But it hardly mattered, for this proud and lordly fellow would never permit his wife's interference.

Lord Bevington's great height made her self-conscious about her lack of inches. Tipping back her head, she reminded him of his promise to reimburse her travel expenses.

"Yes, of course," he agreed, with a haste that told her he'd pay any amount just to be rid of her. "Tell Luis what you want, and he'll get cash from the strongbox. I must go now, madam. Another visitor awaits."

Sophie was determined to make her escape before Moncrieff arrived, wanting no witness to her humiliation. She retrieved her *baheur* from the chair where she'd left it and rushed out of the morning room. At the foot of the great staircase she nearly collided with the earl's swarthy manservant.

"Is for you, senhora," he said, holding up his tray. "Tea and cakes."

"I cannot stay."

"But you are wanting to see gardens, is why you come. I take you out, is no raining now." He placed the tray on a hall table shrouded in white cloth.

Reluctantly Sophie went with him across the courtyard and through the shadowed breezeway. Halfway between the gatehouse and the outer arch was a set of stone steps leading to the uppermost terrace. The grassy path was strewn with damp leaves; dead stalks littered the unkempt borders on either side. Here and there Sophie spied small green shoots of the earliest blooming bulbs, bravely struggling to rise from the debris.

"Your little trunk is safe here." Luis placed her *baheur* on a step. After pointing out the way to the

walled gardens farther down, he excused himself
to fetch her money.

Sophie was tempted to flee before he came back.
But curiosity won out over her eagerness to depart.

Another set of steps descended to a lower terrace
paved in stone and edged with lavender. A favorite
of hers, she brazenly plucked a silver-green sprig
and inhaled the familiar, soothing scent.

Farther down she found a rectangular lawn enclosed by a tall, unruly hedge on one side and an
ivied wall on the other. A long tunnel of mature
laburnums, their naked branches trained over an
arbor, brought her to the first of the three walled
sections she'd viewed from the morning room window. There was a shrubbery walk with large and
misshapen clumps of yew—neglected topiaries.

She followed a paved walk along the waterway
to an adjacent garden planted with shrub roses and
climbers. Bare, thorny canes rambled along the
stone walls or clung to supporting trellises. The
French influence was very strong here. In summer,
she thought, this would be a bower of blossoms
like the paintings of Fragonard and Boucher.

A dun-colored dog was frantically digging in a
border. She was a lean and leggy female with the
head of a greyhound and the rougher coat of a
herding breed. Obviously she'd scented a mole or
vole, for the many burrows and breaks in the ragged lawn indicated their presence.

"*Tu devthais aver honte,*" Sophie scolded.

The animal lifted her head.

"You ought to be ashamed," she repeated. When
the dog raced over to greet her, she stroked the
pointed muzzle. "On my island we would call you
un tchian mêlé—a mongrel."

Her explorations took her next to a series of intricate knot gardens, the patterns nearly ruined

from lack of attention. As she strolled the circular paths, her new friend trotted over to the canal to lap the murky water. Creeping under the open porch of the viewing pavilion, Sophie peered through a grimy window at an empty bathing pool within.

With the dog bounding and prancing at her heels, she retraced her steps. Luis was waiting for her in the shrubbery walk.

"Are no gardeners employed at Bevington?" she asked him. "Judging by their growth, these yews haven't been trimmed for two years or more."

"Since Senhorio come to live in England, he spend money for inside castle only. His sister, Senhora Fonseca, say is no reason to keep up gardens being soon destroyed. All here is to be made different." Shaking his head, he added mournfully, "I wish it not."

"That is the way of things," she told him, concealing her own regret.

"In England, *sim*. Would not happen in Portugal, my country."

"Nor in mine."

In Uncle Edouard's garden at Anneville Manor, the subject of her earliest sketches and watercolors, her childhood love of flowering plants had flourished. Even in her youth she'd admired formal landscaping, nowadays criticized as unnatural and undesirable.

Let someone else destroy this gem of the antique style, she thought bleakly. It was not a task she would relish.

"You are not *inglês?*" Luis asked as they ascended the terrace steps, the mongrel charging ahead of them.

"By marriage only." She was too weary and heartsick to offer a detailed explanation of Jersey's singular status as an independent possession of the British crown.

"Your *esposo*, he let you travel without him?"

"I'm a widow," she explained. "Does Lady Bevington approve of the earl's plan to alter the grounds?"

"Is no senhoria." When they reached the outer gate, Luis handed over a fistful of banknotes.

"You're very kind," said Sophie.

The sweetness of his smile cheered her a little when he said, "*De nada*. Stay," he commanded, his hand curling upon the dog's collar. "She no want you to go away." He bent down to murmur in the animal's ear, "Perhaps senhora come back to us soon."

But Sophie had no desire to return. Bevington Castle was a sad and gloomy place, and without flower gardens it would be far worse.

Retreating down the avenue of ancient, stately oaks, she mourned their inevitable demise. Humphry Repton would surely fell the lot of them.

Cassian Carysfort watched the tiny figure in green grow ever smaller. When it vanished over the crest of his sloping drive, he turned around to find his friend and tenant, Andrew Searle, sprawled upon a burgundy leather armchair.

"The lady must've been quite a charmer, Cass. If I'd known you were going to ignore me, I wouldn't have tramped across your deer park—in a driving rain, I might add—to call upon you."

"You didn't come to see me," Cass retorted. "You wanted to borrow one of my books."

The library was one of the few rooms that the late Lord Bevington had maintained in a style befitting his rank. Cass had made no changes here, apart from giving orders that the vast collection of calf-bound volumes be taken down from the shelves and dusted. He hadn't yet decided whether to remove the portrait of his predecessor, an overdressed chap in a curly wig serenely gazing upon a young gardener planting a rose tree.

"A beauteous widow," his friend continued, "unprotected and seeking your patronage. If you made no attempt to ravish her, you're a disgrace to your title."

With a laugh, he said, "I don't dispute that. I'm naught but an upstart earl, whose claim to all these dignities was so remote that it took more than a year for the lawyers to prove me the rightful heir."

Andrew ran ink-stained fingers through his shaggy, honey-brown locks. "Never did I guess when we were Bristol schoolboys that someday you'd live at Bevington Castle."

"Neither did I," Cass admitted. "But I don't live here yet."

Luis materialized in the doorway. "*Excelência*, is a gentleman here to see you. Senhor Mon Creeve."

"Moncrieff?"

The servant nodded vigorously.

Lifting his brows, Cass murmured, "An unexpected development. Yes, I'll receive him."

The gentleman whose abilities the Widow Pinnock had disparaged was most unimpressive. His bow lacked polish, and his Scots brogue was thicker than the fog outside when he said, "Lord Bevington, I pray my lack of punctuality hasn't offended you. I was misled by an unreliable postilion."

"I didn't specify an hour for our meeting, merely the day. Mr. Moncrieff, I present to you Andrew Searle, a poet of increasing repute." And decreasing sobriety, added Cass silently, troubled by his old schoolmate's bloodshot eyes and droopy lids.

The Scotsman nodded. "Honored, sir. Now then, my lord, I have here examples of my work. Shall I lay them out for you?"

"By all means."

Moncrieff opened his portfolio and spread several sheets across the desktop. "My designs for the Marquess of Gillingham's seat at Evensloe. In order to add picturesque features to the landscape, we chose to—that is, I personally advised him to eliminate the parterres and fill in the empty space with earth and turf. I also suggested planting these well-spaced trees in the near distance. His lordship was vastly pleased with the result."

Cass nodded absently.

According to the Widow Pinnock, Moncrieff had resigned from the firm. Presumably he'd traveled here to compete against her for the commission. A risky move indeed, if the lady was truly the artist responsible for all these excellent drawings. There was an endless supply, and Cass had ample time to look them over during his visitor's long-winded presentation.

"This is my plan for the grounds of Sir Antony Conway's Italianate villa near Roehampton. At my recommendation, firs and cedars were grouped to resemble the views painted by Claude of Lorrain."

"The designs bear your signature," he observed. "What contribution did your partner make?"

Moncrieff flushed. "I'm solely responsible for all designs. The late Mr. Pinnock," he said stiffly, "was merely a figurehead, whose taste and methods I oftentimes questioned." Abruptly gathering some pictures together, he uncovered a watercolor of a flower-filled border.

Cass picked it up. Drawn by a female hand—blunt, businesslike Moncrieff couldn't possibly be capable of such fine, delicate brushwork. The initials at the bottom confirmed his impression. Pointing at them, he asked, "Have you an apprentice, Mr. Moncrieff?"

"That sketch belongs in a different file." The Scotsman tugged at the picture so forcefully that it tore.

Definitely not his creation, thought Cass.

Moncrieff offered an architectural rendering in exchange, and said a shade too heartily, "You'll want to see this Temple of Adonis I created for Mr. Hamish Renfrew of Aberdeen."

"Exemplary. Now I have something to show you, sir." Cass opened a desk drawer and removed a thin, rectangular volume bound in red leather. "Humphry Repton produced this plan. Can you devise a better one?"

While Moncrieff paged through the Red Book, Cass exchanged glances with Andrew, who was evidently puzzled by his cavalier treatment of the landscape gardener.

"Mr. Repton," said Moncrieff reverently, "is a master. He prudently elects to fell the avenue of oaks, as any man of taste would do. I cannot argue with his choice to demolish the antiquated walled gardens and replace the canal with a meandering stream. Yet I believe my own firm will serve your lordship far better."

"Your firm," Cass repeated. "I understand your partner has passed away. Will the enterprise continue to bear his name?"

"Not for long. As soon as his widow becomes my wife, I shall make the necessary change."

Marriage? The lady had not only testified to a rift, she'd made clear her disdain for Mr. Moncrieff. Recalling her earnestness, the hint of vulnerability about her mouth, and the steady gaze of her fine brown eyes, Cass chose to put no faith in anything this man told him.

Andrew Searle's sleepy voice called him out of his reverie. "Cass, didn't you say the vicar was expecting you on the half hour?"

The words were no sooner out than the long-case clock in the corner chimed a single long note.

"Quite right," he said, rewarding his shamelessly untruthful friend with a smile. "Mr. Moncrieff, I wish I could review your past triumphs more thoroughly. If you leave your card behind, I'll inform you as soon as I've made my decision."

"I neglected to bring any cards with me. But I have many more drawings. I would most gladly return later in the day. Or even tomorrow."

"I'm off to London in the morning." It was no lie.

Unlike Mrs. Pinnock, Fingal Moncrieff accepted his dismissal without argument or demands for money. He gathered up the sketches and replaced them in the portfolio. With another bow, even stiffer than his first, he exited the library.

"I do believe," Cass commented to his friend, "that I'm now acquainted with every garden designer in the land. I've gazed at enough pictures to fill a gallery. But I'll be damned if I can say which one of these fellows is most capable of satisfying me."

"If it's satisfaction you crave, look to the lady."

Cass shook his head, in no mood to be teased.

He remembered the little widow's boast that she was more capable than any of the gentlemen he'd summoned to his castle. His difficulty in banishing her lively image from his mind—hair the color of darkest mahogany, almond-shaped brown eyes, a complexion like a lily, rose-petal lips—didn't mean he wanted her for his landscape gardener. And he refused to be swayed into a foolish decision by the fact that she was, undeniably, by far the most attractive of the many applicants for the position.

But elegance, chief grace the garden shows,
And most attractive, is the fair result
Of thought, the creature of a polished mind.

WILLIAM COWPER

Chapter 2

Cass wondered how soon he could wrest himself from Balthasar Prowdie's feeble clutch. When given a paper to sign, he scrawled his name in haste with the quill, and watched impatiently as the old man replaced it in an elongated black tin document box marked *Bevington*.

Closing the lid, the elderly solicitor quavered, "Now that our business is done, I'd be honored if your lordship shared my dinner."

Civility—and pity—forced Cass to accept the invitation. Poor old Prowdie lived alone above his Arundel Street chambers. His clients, every one a fossil, were expiring daily.

A doddering manservant, even more aged and infirm than his master, waited at table. After sampling the dishes that made up the first course, Cass discovered that his host was no epicure. He struggled with a single slice of tough beef, a pudding as tasteless as the bag in which it had been boiled, and a wine of middling quality. The attorney's dull and

23

pedantic conversation in no way compensated for
the unpalatable meal.

Eventually the butler shuffled out of the room,
leaving behind a bowl of fruit long past its prime.
Mr. Prowdie reached for an orange with a hand as
yellowed and wrinkled as the parchments he'd reviewed with Cass before dinner.

"Have I told your lordship about the late Lord
Bevington's attempt to interest me in gardening?"

Cass steeled himself for another boring tale
about the stranger whose property and title he now
possessed. "Not that I recall."

"His effort was wasted, for I'm a city-bred man.
But my good wife, when she lived, had a fondness
for flowers. Every day she sent a servant to Covent
Garden market to buy up great bunches of 'em.
They always made me sneeze." Hunching forward,
the lawyer fixed rheumy eyes upon him. "Whatever become of that Welshman, d'you know?"

"What Welshman would that be, sir?"

"Lord Bevington's gardener. Emrys Jones was
the name. Occupied a cottage *ornée* somewhere on
the grounds and may still, for aught I know."

"There's a new tenant now," Cass reminded
him. "I've never heard of this man Jones. But I visit
the castle infrequently."

"You surely recall from reading his lordship's
will that Jones received a generous annuity and a
dwelling in the village. A reward for services quite
unrelated to weeding the borders and filling 'em
with plants. I'll not go into the particulars except
to say that the relations between Lord Bevington
and this Welshman were, in a word, peculiar. They
were discreet, but I've no doubt whatever that their
intimacy was the sort which all men most abhor, a
gross offense against nature. If not for that stain

upon the earl's honor, I might have esteemed him greatly."

So old Bevington had been a molly. Cass had wondered about his predecessor's prolonged bachelorhood and lack of an heir. If Prowdie, sitting here in London, had guessed the shameful secret, the castle servants and the village folk probably knew it also. Yet none had given Cass any cause to suspect the truth.

When the solicitor continued his droning reminiscences about the late earl, his mind shifted from the subject of the Welsh gardener to his own search for a landscape designer. He was annoyed that the firm of Pinnock and Moncrieff was in disarray; it had a reputation for reliability and innovation. On his way into town yesterday, Cass had very nearly halted at Chiswick to find out if the pretty widow and her brusque Scotsman had patched up their differences.

After draining the last bitter drop of wine from his glass, he declared, "I've imposed upon your hospitality too long, sir."

"Must you go so soon?" Prowdie asked mournfully. "I have a bottle of port."

Cass barely repressed a shudder. The wine still tortured his tongue, raising doubts about whatever else lay in his host's cellar. His family associations and his years in Portugal made him extremely particular about port. "If I didn't have to leave London tonight—but I really must be on my way. My sister expects me tomorrow, and she's the sort to worry over any delay."

"Determined to hide yourself away in the wilds of Gloucestershire, aren't you? Ah, well, the last earl was much the same." The attorney shook his bewigged head in disapproval. "But he had much to fear from living in the world. You do not."

Cass could have refuted that assumption, but didn't care to.

Within minutes he was hurrying through the falling snow toward the Strand, where his carriage waited. The Bevington coat of arms had been painted on the door so recently that the colors were still bright: a quartered heraldic shield of gold and sable, supported by a pair of stags with collars of roses encircling their necks.

The driver, warming his hands over a street vendor's brazier, popped one last chestnut into his mouth and sauntered over to the coach. Still chewing, he reported, "I walked your lordship's horses up and down till their hooves nearly dropped off."

"You didn't tire them out, I trust. I mean to go as far as the Red Lion at Henley tonight. What has become of Luis?"

"I 'spose he wandered 'cross the way to water the side of a building."

Moving to the rear of the vehicle to check that his portmanteau was securely strapped on, Cass noticed three shadowy figures standing just beyond the street lamp. One wore a low-crowned hat, its round brim pulled down to hide his face. The second, a tall individual in livery, held a struggling Luis Costa by the arm and brandished a cudgel.

"Unhand him!" Cass commanded.

The man in the hat stepped into the light, saying, "Ah, Carysfort, here at last." An ugly scar puckered his right cheek.

Observing his handiwork, Cass could still picture the blood seeping from the fresh wound, the shattered bone visible beneath the torn flesh. He remembered the blustery dawn when he'd stood on Hounslow Heath, a smoking pistol at his side, uncertain whether Sir Michael Tait would live or die.

"But I ought to call you Bevington now," said the baronet. "Be not alarmed, I come in peace."

"Your companion carries a truncheon."

"Merely a precaution. There are footpads about."

"That's why my coachman is armed," said Cass as a warning. "Luis, on the other hand, is not so bloodthirsty, and poses no threat to you."

"James, let him go," Tait barked.

The Portuguese youth hurried to his master's side. "I sorry, senhorio," he panted. "They take me when I walk away from *coche*."

"You've done nothing wrong," Cass assured Luis. "It's all a misunderstanding."

In fact, this was something more sinister, but he couldn't be sure exactly what. He knew only that the meeting hadn't occurred by chance. Advising Luis to wait for him inside the vehicle, he turned to the baronet and asked, in a voice sharpened by mistrust, "How did you find out I was in London?"

"I spotted you walking along Bond Street this afternoon. Your appearance has changed very little these seven years. I'm hardly surprised by your failure to recognize me. My divorce was a greater scandal than our duel, and both have left me a wreck of a man."

Cass remembered when Sir Michael Tait's eyes had flashed with arrogance, and his body had been firm and muscular. Shocked though he was by his enemy's thin, wasted frame and damaged face, he had no sympathy to spare. "I don't give a damn about your misfortunes. You brought them on yourself."

"What of Cecelia, is she so heartless?"

The rage boiling in his veins spilled over. He lunged at Tait, thrusting him backward against the iron lamppost. The footman took a step forward and waved his stick, but Cass ignored him. "You aren't fit to speak my sister's name," he growled. "And you'll leave her alone. Let her mourn her husband in peace."

"Husband?"

"She married within months of our arrival in Lisbon." Cass took perverse pleasure in the baronet's dismay.

"I didn't know. I've had no news of her since you dragged her away to share your exile. Where is she now?"

"That's no concern of yours."

"I must see her."

"Trust me, you won't."

"I feared you'd be unreasonable," said Tait bitterly, reaching into his coat pocket. "You always were. That's why I've written this letter. Will you take it to her, and see that she gets it wherever she is? When she learns what agonies I've suffered—"

"Hand it over and be quick about it. My horses have already stood too long in the night air and the snow."

The letter was thick and heavy. It felt like a hot coal in his gloved hand.

Cass turned and went back to his carriage. He didn't hesitate to expose his back to his adversary; with so many witnesses, Tait wouldn't dare to slip a knife between his shoulder blades.

He climbed inside and sat down. Luis was still rubbing his arm. When Cass asked if he'd been badly hurt, he shook his head in vigorous denial.

"Tell me exactly what happened."

"I go to stretch my legs. Those men, they come up to ask questions—where the earl is staying, do he bring his sister? I no give answers. I speak only the Portuguese, senhorio, just as you tell me to."

"*Muito bem.*" As the carriage rolled along the broad thoroughfare towards Charing Cross, Cass leaned his head against the leather seat.

Although Sir Michael Tait had proved dangerous in the past, he'd detected no real menace in him tonight. Had their battle truly ended on the dueling ground?

He ran his thumb across the disk of red wax that sealed the letter. There was no writing on the outside to identify the intended recipient. "Luis, lower the window."

When the valet had carried out his impetuous command, Cass pitched the baronet's unopened missive into the icy street like the scrap of rubbish that it was.

Sophie touched a tiny star-shaped flower, leaning forward to breathe in the sweet, heady fragrance of the hyacinth. For weeks she'd watched the bulb as it took root and sprouted and sent up a stalk. Now it was in full bloom, pink and highly perfumed, a much-needed glimpse of spring in the midst of winter.

She untied the loose knot of her fichu and peeled it from her shoulders. Her ash-colored gown was made of wool, and the oil lamp on her worktable put out as much heat as it did light. After making a minor adjustment to the specimen in the hyacinth glass, she picked up her paintbrush and gently dragged it across her drawing paper to deepen the green of the stem.

Botanical illustrations were less profitable than landscape designs, but she could complete one in a matter of hours. In the peace and privacy of her own home. Without interference from a male partner.

The slamming of the front door and the thump of the bolt being secured shattered Sophie's concentration.

"Men!" sputtered her housekeeper, drawing the curtains. "They cannot do a thing without making a stir. If you mean to sit up much longer, ma'am, I'll nudge the coals a bit."

Briefly squeezing her eyes shut, Sophie answered, "I'll soon be done. You and William can go to bed now."

"Aye, and so should you," said the motherly woman before leaving the parlor.

One more leaf, Sophie encouraged herself. She pressed the tip of her brush against the green chip in her paint-box.

At last she finished, and with a defiant flourish signed her own initials beside her completed watercolor. Never again would Fingal Moncrieff lay false claim to her artistry.

Lack of employment had turned the blustering Scottish lion as meek as a Highland lamb. He'd called upon her yesterday, ostensibly to beg pardon for his behavior in Cirencester. His ulterior purpose had been to dissuade her from severing the partnership. She smiled, recalling how shocked he'd been by her decision to carry on without him. She'd taken great pleasure in pointing out that she wouldn't be the first widow to take over the management of her late husband's business. Had he ever, she'd inquired, actually counted the number of distilleries and printing presses and theatrical companies headed by a female proprietor?

For two years she'd lived quietly at the Chiswick villa she'd inherited from Tobias, producing plans for her associate to sign and present to clients. The time had come to prove that she, not Fingal Moncrieff, had absorbed the Pinnock genius and was the master's rightful successor.

When she finished washing out her brushes in a saucer of water, she closed them away in the shagreen paint-box Tobias had given her, with handle and lock and hinges of gleaming silver. She wiped her hands on a cloth, then pressed her fingers against her throbbing temples and rubbed hard. At last she rose from her chair—slowly and stiffly, for she'd scarcely moved in the past hour.

Before she extinguished the lamp she heard the unmistakable sound of horseshoes and carriage wheels churning the gravel drive. Moments later there was a rap on the door.

By the time she reached the entrance hall, both Redmonds had emerged from their room, Mary in her nightgown and stocking feet, a shawl draped about her stout person, and a barefooted William in his long shirt, chamber-stick in hand.

He peered suspiciously through one of the side-lights framing the door. "Who goes there?"

"Bevington."

Sophie drew a sharp, surprised breath.

"Shall I warn him off, ma'am?"

"Oh, no." Meeting Mary's astonished stare, she explained hastily, "He comes on business. You may both return to your room."

"We'll not slumber till we know he's gone," William grumbled. "Come along, woman." Hooking his wife's arm in his, he led her back down the corridor.

Sophie slipped the bolt and opened the door to find the earl's impressive figure looming tall in the darkness, draped in a gray garrick overcoat with gold buttons as big and bright as guinea coins.

"I had the devil's own time finding this place."

No apology for disturbing her so late!

Her temper flickered, then blazed high and hot when he strode past her, his long coat billowing behind him. Without being invited, he took it off and casually tossed it onto an upholstered hall bench. Fighting the urge to order him off the premises, she led him to her parlor.

Prowling the perimeter of the room, he reminded her of a great black panther she'd once seen at an exhibition. There was a tenseness about him, and he looked as though he would erupt into violence if crossed.

He paused before the oil portrait of Tobias. "Your famous husband? I imagined him to be an older man."

"He died at thirty-two." She went back to tidying her drawing table, intentionally repaying his rudeness in kind.

While he continued his exploratory circuit, she hoped he was noticing that her Chippendale chairs and settee were in the best taste, covered in rose damask to complement the dominant hue of the Persian rug. A gilt-framed chimney glass filled the space above the mantel, and landscape paintings in the style of Claude of Lorrain decorated the walls.

His long stride brought him to her table. "What have you been doing?"

She passed him her watercolor of the hyacinth. "It's still damp," she cautioned.

While he studied it, she was able to study him. Her artist's eye traced the chiseled lines of his face, moving downward from the broad brow to his lean jaw, ever so slightly shaded with a growth of beard. He had pleasingly sculpted cheekbones and his nose was perfectly straight. What a magnificent model he would make, she thought, provided he could sit still long enough for his likeness to be taken.

"You do have a gift, madam."

"I had an excellent master. When I began to study drawing, flowers were the subjects most readily available. My Uncle Edouard Nicolle, Seigneur of Anneville, is a keen gardener and renowned as a plantsman."

"You're French?"

"I spent my entire life, save the past five years, on Jersey," she clarified. "Mr. Pinnock came to the island one summer at my uncle's invitation. I painted the horticultural specimens he collected during his visit."

"And as a result, you were added to his collection." He regarded her in brooding silence before saying, "I am English-born myself, but for many years I lived abroad."

"In Portugal. Your manservant told me."

His tone was guarded when he asked, "Did he reveal anything else about my family?"

"Not that I recall. Is Luis the keeper of your darkest family secrets?"

"He is my valet, Mrs. Pinnock, not my confidant." He glanced again at the drawing and muttered inscrutably, "Just as I suspected, it was your cipher. What does the first initial signify?"

"So-*phie*," she answered, giving the proper inflection. "My husband always called me Sophia."

"Unusual. It's generally the other way round."

She bristled at his designating Tobias as odd; her objection to having her name Anglicized had faded long ago. "You've not descended upon Chiswick at this late hour to discuss botanical illustration," she hazarded, taking back her watercolor. "Why *are* you here?"

"To resume the interview begun several days ago. After you left Bevington, Mr. Moncrieff put in an appearance." He narrowed his eyes. "That surprises you?"

"He neglected to mention it."

"You remain partners?"

"Nânnîn." With a smile, she added, "I'm no longer afflicted by the Scottish curse."

"I see." After a pause, he asked, "Do you keep any port? I rather fancy a glass."

"My servants have retired for the night," she said pointedly. "I'll have to fetch it myself." She lifted the lamp from her table.

Reaching out to take it, he said, "Allow me."

Sophie proceeded to the dining room, and the belatedly chivalrous earl followed close behind with the light. Going to the rosewood cellaret, she knelt down. "Lower, please," she instructed, turning the tasseled key in the lock. She opened the door and felt about for the cut-glass decanter and a glass, then placed them on the sideboard.

Her hand trembled as she withdrew the stopper. His nearness made her feel twitchy—and wary. She trusted this arrogant nobleman even less than she liked him, which was to say not at all. And she regretted discarding her fichu, for her low neckline exposed entirely too much of her chest.

They returned to the parlor. Sophie's visitor took his wineglass to the settee. Too uneasy to sit, she drifted over to the fireplace. Lifting the top of a porcelain potpourri vase on the mantel, she raked her fingers through the dried petals of last summer's roses.

After his first sip Lord Bevington commented, "A quality vintage." Amusement softened his voice—and his expression—when he said, "You wish I'd go away, don't you?"

Bearing in mind that this exasperatingly perceptive man was still a prospective client, she composed a careful reply. "I hope I haven't given that impression, my lord. I'm unaccustomed to receiving evening guests. Certainly not aristocratic ones."

"You needn't assign so much value to my title. I was born a commoner."

His revelation startled her. If any man had been born to command, she thought, it was the one lounging on her settee.

"What's more, my background is mercantile. My mother's relatives owned plantations in the West Indies, and the Carysforts of Bristol were active in the Portuguese wine trade. My sister and I received many painful lessons in class distinctions while being educated at English boarding schools."

He was forcing her to revise her opinion of him. She had difficulty imagining him as a schoolboy, much less one who'd been tormented about his humble origins.

"A few months after I came age," he went on, staring at the twisted stem of the wineglass, "our parents died of a tropical fever. My first independent act was to rescue my sister from her academy in Bath and take her to London. Wealth opened many doors to us, but we were too closely associated with trade to be welcomed into the upper echelons. The lack of invitations to fashionable balls and routs troubled me very little, but Cecelia suffered enormously. Females are more sensitive about their social status. Or lack of it."

Sophie confirmed this with a nod. When she'd arrived in England as the bride of a professional man, she'd learned that merchants and tradesmen were not treated as respectfully as in Jersey. Her Nicolle pride had occasionally been stung by the condescension of a highborn client, or his wife.

"After receiving numerous slights during that unhappy year, my sister and I deserted soggy London for sunny Lisbon. She found herself a husband there, a gentleman from Sintra."

He did not strike her as a confiding sort of man,

and she wondered why he'd chosen to reveal so much of his history. She didn't flatter herself that he wanted her to like him. Perhaps he hoped to allay her antagonism.

"Why," she asked, "did you return to England if neither you nor your sister cares for it?"

"Because I inherited—quite by accident and most unexpectedly—the earldom and the estate entailed upon it. Old Lord Bevington was the last twig from a branch of Carysforts ennobled many centuries ago. The direct male line died with him. An army of lawyers traced the family pedigree all the way back to the sixteen hundreds and determined that I was the rightful heir to his property and title."

"What a stroke of good fortune," Sophie marveled.

His lips curled derisively. "It wasn't till I arrived in Gloucestershire to claim my birthright that I discovered the cruel trick fate had played. My tenants at Bevington graze cattle and make cheese, and the rents are low compared to more productive farming districts. My castle is a drafty ruin. Because my predecessor contributed no money to its upkeep or embellishment, I've spent the better part of a year making it habitable. For my sister's comfort, I was obliged to purchase a town house in Clifton, near Bristol Hotwells. Her physician believes a regular dose of the mineral waters will benefit her."

If only, thought Sophie, the doctors had been able to prescribe a cure for Tobias. But no medicine yet known could strengthen a failing heart.

"Having spent a fortune refurbishing the interior of my castle, I am eager to improve its setting."

At last he'd touched upon the topic that most concerned Sophie. Her pulses raced in anticipation, even as she warned herself not to hope.

"Mrs. Pinnock, the position of landscape gardener remains open. If you still wish to be considered a candidate, you'd better show me those Blue Books of yours."

She crossed to the glass-fronted mahogany bookcase displaying the entire collection. Determined to show the designs she'd produced herself, she gathered up the most recent editions and carried them to the settee.

"Not every client chooses to follow my recommendations," she acknowledged when he opened the first book.

"Sit down beside me, and explain what I'm looking at."

Sophie perched on the edge of the cushion, keeping her back straight to prevent him seeing more of her bosom than her gown already revealed. "That's my plan for Bastwick House in Shropshire. Unlike Bevington, it sits low in a valley. As you can see, it's an ancient dwelling and well suited to the picturesque style. If you turn to the last page but one, you'll see more clearly where the larger oaks were removed to open up the view. The final sketch depicts the vista to the west, framed by the remaining oaks and chestnuts."

"Was this your notion?"

"Yes, my lord."

She'd agonized about sacrificing so many mature trees, until Fingal Moncrieff had reminded her that if she didn't, Repton certainly would—and pocket a sizable fee for doing so.

"There used to be a shrubbery walk to the rear of the house," she continued, "not unlike the one at Bevington, though it wasn't walled and had no canal running through it. I replaced the evergreens with a lawn."

He reached for the next Blue Book. "Alderbury Lodge."

"The owner commissioned a Gothic tower and wanted advice on new plantings. Exotics, mostly."

Evidently unmoved by the Alderbury Lodge plans, he took up another set. "Mainwaring Park. A Palladian mansion. What did you do here?"

"Parterres," she intoned, wishing she could forget them. "Terraces. On the south side of the house. I eliminated them."

The degradations committed at Mainwaring Park would forever haunt her. Those parterres had been exquisite, lovingly tended by generations of Mainwarings. The present baronet, infected with the improving disease, had decreed that they must go, so Sophie had obliged him. And Moncrieff had taken all the credit.

"I've seen enough of these," the earl stated in his unequivocal fashion. "Now let me look at your garden."

"My garden?"

"How else am I to judge your skill? I have no intention of visiting all these places you've shown me."

"But it will soon be midnight," she protested. "And there's snow."

"Not any longer." He climbed to his feet. "If you're too ashamed of your own grounds to let me tour them, I'll be on my way."

"Wait." She couldn't resist his challenge. "I'll get my cloak. And a lantern."

Marveling at her obedience to the persuasions of a madman, she left him to retrieve her scarlet cloak from its peg by the kitchen door. A relic from her girlhood, it was shabby from frequent exposure to foul weather.

During the widow's absence Cass resumed his

study of Tobias Pinnock's portrait. An ordinary man, unremarkable in face and form. Yet he'd succeeded in winning the hand—and presumably the heart—of that hardheaded little Jerseywoman.

Amazingly, this impromptu eleventh-hour visit to Chiswick had stopped him from brooding about his encounter with Sir Michael Tait, and he was no longer tortured by his gnawing suspicion about why Luis had been accosted. Now all the thoughts and questions careening in his mind centered on Sophie Pinnock.

She returned with a lantern, cloaked in a garment that made her look even smaller and more dainty.

"We'll go out this way," she announced, lifting a damask curtain to reveal a set of French doors.

He followed her out to a broad terrace. The cool night air was invigorating, and carried a fresh scent. "Flowers in January?" he asked, pointing to a classical urn. Peeping through the light snow cover was a plant bearing large white blossoms.

"*Helleborus*. Commonly called the Christmas Rose." She held the lantern high as she led him along a stone-paved walkway. "Do you mean to inspect my kitchen garden?" she demanded, her voice as tart as unripe fruit.

"I want to see everything," he replied.

She heaved an impatient sigh before turning down a pathway veering sharply to the right.

"This long border provides flowers for cutting," she said with an expansive gesture that opened her cloak and briefly revealed her compact, lushly rounded figure. "In summer these bricks are scarcely visible behind the foliage, the plants grow so thickly here. My roses are dormant now, but you can see how high they climbed last year. I grow a few modern specimens, but I do love this dear old-fashioned *Rosa mundi* best of all." She held the light up to the brambles to show the ice-glazed hips.

They passed through a gate into a tidy kitchen plot with rows of glass frames protecting the tenderest plants from the winter chill, and a hothouse in the corner where produce could be forced. Espaliered apple and pear trees grew all around the wall, leafless skeletons outlined by the clinging snow.

"Come April they'll be in full bloom. And from summer into autumn I'll have a fine selection of cherries, nectarines, and apricots."

Continuing her tour, she took Cass to a spacious, grassy area sheltered by mature cedars. Life-sized statues, ghostly in their whiteness, formed a graceful semicircle. Yew hedging concealed the pedestal of each, giving the impression that each god or goddess was floating in space. A powdering of snow frosted the neatly clipped evergreens.

"Was this your husband's design?"

The lady laughed softly. Fondly. The first genuine sound of mirth he'd heard from her, and it rang out in the chilled air like music.

"Tobias was too busy making landscapes for other people. What you see here resulted from *my* planning, and the work was done at my direction. From time to time, I even dirtied my own hands. I was the one who went to Mrs. Coade's stoneworks to choose the classical figures. They aren't genuine marble."

Cass surprised himself by being utterly charmed by her grove. Simpler than the plans depicted in the Blue Books and yet more formal, it testified to the versatility of its creator.

She was still smiling reminiscently when she said, "Come, my lord, if you wish to view the willow walk." In her haste she nearly slipped on a patch of ice.

"Careful." The cautionary word slipped out involuntarily—he repeated it so often to Cecelia and the child.

With her rapid progress across the lawn the lantern light grew dimmer, enticing him to a stand of willows with arching, whip-like branches that dipped down to the river's edge.

"My favorite retreat in summer," she confided, indicating a rustic seat perfectly sized for two. "On bright days I come here to sketch the view. Or if I'm feeling idle, to watch the boats drift past. And I often bring bread scraps for the swans nesting on the other side."

As the black waters of the Thames lapped at the reeds along the riverbank, Cass studied the pale oval of her face.

This unworldly little creature fascinated him. First and foremost, because of her singular beauty. But he also appreciated her rare ability to see beyond the lay of the land and search out the possibilities hidden there. Not only did she understand the mysteries of nature, she shaped and molded it at will. She was blessed with taste and talent, and possibly a touch of genius.

The candle stub in her lantern flickered and suddenly died.

"Mrs. Pinnock. I—you—" He was unsure how to phrase his desires.

She looked around, her almond-shaped eyes as dark and fathomless as the river itself. "What is it, Lord Bevington?"

"I want you to recreate the Bevington Castle grounds," he said, more abruptly than he'd intended. "To make all the necessary drawings and provide plant lists. You shall hire the labor and supervise the alterations. From start to finish, however long it may take."

"*Ma fé*, here is a sudden change," she murmured. "At our last meeting you scorned my competence and turned me away from your door."

"An error of judgment which I pray you'll overlook."

"You're choosing me over the illustrious Humphry Repton? And Emes, and Mickle—and the other *gentlemen* you interviewed?"

"A pack of bores. I covet my own copy of your Blue Book, with 'Earl of Bevington' stamped in gold on the cover, exactly as you promised. You've seen what remains of the castle gardens. Surely such decay and neglect inspired you to make a change?"

She shuddered beneath her cloak, as if shaking off a hurtful memory.

From a distance, a bell tolled twelve times. Cass waited for the last chime to fade before saying, "You must turn Bevington into a masterpiece of the modern landscape style. Tear down the crumbling stone walls, rip out that old-fashioned shrubbery walk and all those scraggly roses. The canal can go as well, and that gloomy avenue of trees along the drive."

She shook her head. "You move too fast, my lord. I haven't accepted the position."

"Why so hesitant? A few days ago you were courting my patronage."

Gazing over the water, she said, "You're certain to be a demanding client. I've had them before."

"I'm not concerned with the process, only the result," he assured her. "On my honor, when we lived in Sintra I never once dealt with those who took care of our pleasure grounds. I left that to Cecelia."

"You had a garden in Portugal? What was it like?"

"A miniature Versailles. Endless parterres with fountains, finicky little plots hedged with box. There was an orange grove, too, and more fig trees than you've ever seen in your life."

He had an extraordinary desire to take her there. The warm southern sunshine would melt her cool reserve. She'd have no need for that woollen cloak, she could wear wispy gowns of white muslin that would flatter her coloring. And her curves.

But instead of whisking her away to a sunnier clime, he must lure her to his gloomy castle in Gloucestershire.

"As I said the other day, I'd want you to stay at Bevington. I'll not be there to interfere, I won't take up residence until midsummer, at the earliest. Should you wish to return here on occasion, my traveling carriage would be at your disposal. As for your fee—what say you to a guinea per day, to complete my Blue Book? And double that amount while the alterations are in progress."

"Your lordship is generous. Nonetheless, I need time to consider." Lifting her dark head, she told him serenely, "I cannot think clearly after midnight."

"But—"

"Lord Bevington, I've treated you with greater courtesy than you did me when I traveled across the country at your whim. For the better part of an hour you've had my undivided attention. I served you a glass of vintage port and let you look at my designs. You have explored my gardens. So you will not, I trust, be cross if I leave you and return to the house. The hour is late, and I was quite weary before you arrived."

Dismissed—by a pert young slip of a widow!

"I'll not keep you from your rest a moment longer," he told her coldly. "Good night, madam."

Striding across the snow-frosted lawn, he tried to believe he'd be better off without her. And he failed.

This second, more substantive interview had convinced him beyond any doubt that Sophie Pinnock was brilliantly capable. Her tiny white hand, with deft strokes of the paintbrush, could turn her visions into works of art. She had enhanced the beauty of the surrounding terrain and imposed order upon it. He would not be content until she had done exactly the same at Bevington Castle.

Where'er you tread, the blushing flowers shall rise,
And all things flourish where you turn your eyes.

ALEXANDER POPE

Chapter 3

"**Y**ou must've been thinking t'always snows or rains 'ere at Bevington, ma'am," said the maidservant who shared Sophie's quarters. "But at long last the sun's come out to welcome you." She placed a squat china teapot on the gateleg table.

"This is February, after all." Now that the showers had ended, Sophie could be philosophical about them.

An assurance of fine weather, she thought wryly, had not been included in the earl's lavish offer. She'd been promised only that tempting guinea per day and her room and board. In return, according to the legal document her attorney brother-in-law had drawn up, she must produce "Designs for a Modern Landscape, bound in Blue Leather," and afterwards "Supervise the Labor necessary to implement said Designs." And, taking her employer at his word, she reserved the authority to hire the contractor and workforce she deemed most capable of executing her plans.

Lord Bevington had promptly signed and sealed and returned the papers to her legal representative. At that point, all communication from him had ceased.

Not only had her journey to Gloucestershire been hindered by mud and delays, upon her arrival she received blank stares from his lordship's servants. Fortunately Mr. Andrew Searle had emerged from the book room to support her claim of being the earl's landscape gardener, whereupon she'd been shown to her gatehouse lodging.

By the end of that first trying day at the castle, Sophie's grievances against its master had eclipsed her satisfaction in gaining him as a client. His long silence, rather than assuring her of the autonomy he'd promised her, signaled all too clearly his disinterest in her activities, and her welfare.

Surveying her airy sitting room, she acknowledged that her accommodations gave her no cause for complaint. The surrounding walls were paneled with honeyed oak carved in a linenfold pattern, and plasterwork decorated the low ceiling. The pair of old-fashioned armchairs flanking the stone fireplace were covered in frayed and faded needlepoint, but they were perfectly comfortable.

On opposite sides of the long, narrow room were broad diamond-paned casements. One framed a view of the outer gate and the long, oak-lined drive beyond; the other looked out on the inner courtyard and the many arched doorways to the castle keep and towers. While waiting out the wet spell, Sophie had often curled up on the cushioned window benches to watch the comings and goings of carriers delivering goods and the artisans working feverishly to improve the earl's residence.

"So you'll be going out this morning?" asked Nan Parham, bringing her a plate of food.

Sophie had quickly developed a taste for the sharp, rich cheese produced in the district, usually served to her melted on toast. Eagerly placing her napkin on her lap, she answered, "I want to continue exploring the grounds, and I need to talk with the gardeners."

"Mr. Wilkins tends the kitchen gardens only. With the new earl soon coming to live 'ere, he and his son are busier than ever."

Sophie frowned, recalling her only encounter with the dour kitchen gardener. A simple request that he pot up some auriculas produced the same incomprehension she might have expected had she addressed him in Jèrriais. First he'd muttered that he hadn't been told to take orders from her, then grudgingly admitted he wasn't used to messing about with flowers.

" 'Tweren't always so," Nan continued, wagging her curly golden head. "The old earl had Mr. Jones to look after his grounds. For at least twenty year he lived in that prettified cottage on t'other side of the wood."

Sophie looked up from her plate. "Is he still alive?"

"Aye, and has a little house in the village. Keeps to himself nowadays."

"Did his age prevent him from working? Was he too infirm?"

"Last time I saw him he looked much as he ever did. I'd reckon him to be me da's age." In answer to an inquiring glance, Nan said succinctly, "Forty-odd years."

"I want to meet this Mr. Jones."

"Likely you'll find him by the church. Sexton lets him putter about the burying ground, trimming back the ivy and suchlike."

With twenty years' experience behind him, So-

phie mused, Mr. Jones must be a master of his
trade. Moreover, he'd know exactly which sorts of
roses had been planted in years past. Perhaps he
could even tell her where she'd find the missing
key to the pavilion. These questions, and so many
others, constantly plagued her.

She sorely missed her own well-regulated household and tidy gardens. Refilling her teacup, she
imagined her dear, devoted Mary in the kitchen,
polishing the copper pots until they gleamed, and
Willam in his hothouse, sowing seeds in wooden
trays.

Fighting against homesickness, she reminded
herself of her salary, and the prestige she expected
to gain from this commission. Of how restless she'd
been before coming here. This change of scene was
as necessary to her well-being as having a complex
and consuming project to fill her days. At Bevington she could work independently, without interference from the perfidious Moncrieff.

" 'Ere's your egg, ma'am." Nan set the china cup
down before her.

Sophie's spoon slipped from her grasp and fell
to the floor. "Zut," she grumbled, picking it up.

"Drop a spoon and love will come soon," Nan
quoted merrily on her way out.

The foolish rhyme echoed in Sophie's mind
throughout her solitary meal, and later when she
climbed the stone stair spiraling up to her bedchamber. The joy of loving, in her experience, had
been eclipsed by the pain of losing the beloved one.
She changed her slippers for a pair of sturdy half-
boots, and settled her scarlet cloak upon her shoulders.

Her pensive gaze fell upon the heavy Jacobean
bedstead. Because she'd never shared it with Tobias, she didn't feel his absence as keenly as in their

bed at home. The flower-embroidered counterpane, a wedding gift from her Tante Douce, had never been used and therefore held no tragic associations.

Guided by Nan's directions, she looked for the well-worn path the castle servants used when going to the church or village. Lying just beyond the outer archway, it wound down the slope of a hill to a pair of neatly shaved yews marking a side entrance to the burial ground. A rusty-breasted robin fluttered down to the ground and poked at the damp turf with the point of its beak.

"You must be that female the new earl sent for to improve his grounds."

Sophie looked away from the bird and saw a wiry man pushing a one-wheeled barrow around the side of the church.

"Are you Mr. Jones, who worked in the castle gardens?"

Slowly he nodded. His features were bony, his face all sharp angles, and he had long graying hair pulled severely back in a queue.

"Your services are sorely missed," she told him frankly. "The hedges want clipping. The grassy walks haven't been rolled. As far as I can tell, no one has bothered to propagate annuals for planting out this spring."

" 'Tis the proper time for it," he commented, selecting a hoe.

She reached down to pinch off a leaf from the low bush growing beside a stone marker. "Rosemary in a graveyard?"

"In Wales we use it to mark the graves of older people, for it signifies remembrance." He trilled his *r*s and *l*s, and there was a faint underlying sibilance to his speech. Indicating a smaller stone close by, he said, "Here, where an infant is buried, violets

will bloom. And for the children lying over there,
I planted primroses and daffodils."

"What a charming custom." She studied the
many headstones, some cracked with age and covered in lichen, others starkly new and pristine.
Only one was left unadorned; it occupied a lonely
corner far from the rest.

Curious, she walked over to the gray slab to read
its inscription: *Here lie the bones of Frances Charlotte.
Born a Virgin, died a Harlot.* Looking to Mr. Jones,
she asked, "Who was this lady?"

"The last earl's mother, a notorious adulteress.
Or so claimed her lord, who composed the verses
himself. He refused to have her interred inside the
church with the rest of the Carysforts. Legend says
he murdered her, though 'twas never proved."

"Poor Frances Charlotte," Sophie sympathized.
"You should plant something for her, too. *Rosa
mundi*, with its pale petals stained with red, would
suit a lady of dubious virtue. Whatever her sins,
she doesn't deserve so bare a grave."

"Softhearted," he muttered.

Or had he called her softheaded? She was confused by his odd, unfamiliar accent. "Mr. Jones,
would you consider returning to your former position?"

His sparse brows shifted downwards in a frown.
"Why should you want me to? There'll not be any
gardening work left ere long. Not after you've dug
up all my earl's treasures, and mine, and cast them
onto the rubbish heap."

"*Nânnîn!* Oh, no," she protested, sensitive to the
pain she read in his strange, pale eyes. "I wouldn't
discard them, I couldn't. I'd give the plants away,
to you or anyone who wanted cuttings or divisions.
I've a particular fondness for roses—indeed, I'm
quite desperate to know which ones have been

planted. Before they bloom I shall probably have
to move them."

"You'll find a variety of the damasks and gallicas
and albas."

"Can you make up a list for me?"

"I suppose."

Sophie sensed his reluctance to assist her. She
watched him flex his thin, dirt-caked fingers—his
hands were delicate, almost womanly, with wrists
as slender and fine-boned as her own.

"My work is hampered by more than a lack of
information," she continued. "I'm distracted by the
neglect I see everywhere. I want the herbaceous
borders tidied and the dead leaves cleaned out of
the canal. The flowering shrubs haven't been
pruned. I can't do it all myself—indeed, I shouldn't
make the attempt, that isn't what Lord Bevington
pays me for. If you fail me, Mr. Jones, I must hire
a person who knows even less than I do about
which specimens are worth saving."

"Why must any of them be lost?" he wondered.
He took up a hoe and hacked at the brambles en-
croaching upon Frances Charlotte's gravestone.
"The shrubbery and the canal walk were created a
century ago. The laburnum arch and rose bower
have been maturing these two decades. What manner of man is this new earl, that he sees no beauty
in what already exists?"

"I know not." It was a question she had often
asked herself, about Lord Bevington and many a
previous client.

"I've had but one master, may his soul rest with
God. I want no other."

Clearly he intended their conversation to end
there.

Sophie, wise in the ways of his kind, knew exactly how to phrase her appeal. "There can't be

enough work in this churchyard to keep you busy day in, day out. How much have you to do, after you've planted a rosebush for the Harlot Countess? Yews and box want clipping but once or twice a year, and ivy is easily kept in bounds. Besides that, your talent and experience are wasted here. You're a master gardener, not a groundskeeper."

"Aye," he admitted gruffly. "There's truth in that."

At least he hadn't refused her outright. "If you decide you want to work at the castle again," she told him, "ask for me at the gatehouse."

Before she turned to go he said, "When the village folk began talking of his lordship's lady landscape gardener, I never imagined she'd be a mere lass."

If he ever worked with her, she thought wickedly, he'd quickly discover how strong-minded—and demanding—a mere lass could be.

Bein seux, Emrys Jones wasn't what she'd expected either. He was intelligent and well-spoken, and not a bit deferential. Proud, *aussîn*. Even though he'd been intrigued by her request for help, he hadn't immediately agreed to it. He didn't conceal his disdain for her assigned task, but seemed resigned to the inevitability of change. And he was a dedicated worker, otherwise he wouldn't have taken on the unpaid job of churchyard caretaker.

Trusting that he'd soon give her the answer she hoped for, Sophie spent the remainder of the day neatening the terrace gardens. With a pair of secateurs borrowed from the otherwise unhelpful Wilkins, she clipped away the dead stalks of the perennials. The sun warmed her back as she bent over to trim the lavender borders.

Her fragrant task was so absorbing that until Andrew Searle spoke, she didn't even notice that he'd sat down on one of the stone steps to watch her.

Lord Bevington's tenant seldom emerged from his cottage beyond the chestnut grove, designated "the Wildernesse" on an old estate map. According to the chatty Nan, he was composing a lengthy poem and remained in seclusion for days at a time.

"I beg you to excuse my yawns, Mrs. Pinnock. I was awake all night scribbling, and slept the morning away. You've been more industrious, I see. But shouldn't you be sketching?"

"I can't begin till I've studied more of the illustrated books in his lordship's library. I draw inspiration from prints of buildings similar in style to Bevington."

His green eyes swept across the battlements and looming towers. "In my opinion the castle is sufficiently picturesque as it is. I can't fathom why Cass needs to be rid of those quaint knot gardens and the long arbor and all the rest of it."

Striving to keep her voice neutral, Sophie said, "Those were his instructions." Tenderly she brushed damp leaves away from the budding white crocuses.

"My own preference is for the romantic," the gentleman volunteered in his languid fashion. "Enclosed gardens are so ideally suited to dalliance. One can only wonder how many lovers have sought the privacy of the shrubbery walk, or used the pavilion for their assignations."

Sophie laughed. "You ought to be writing novels, Mr. Searle, not poetry."

He looked capable of neither. In the shabby coat and faded breeches, his hair mussed and his eyes pink from lack of sleep, he resembled an exhausted, overworked farmer.

"But many of my poems do tell a story, they are narratives. Would you like to hear one?"

Without waiting for a reply, he embarked upon a recitation. In a slow and rhythmic cadence, he told the tale of a humble lady whose misplaced love for a nobleman resulted in heartbreak, a curse, death, and revenge. Sophie could clearly envision each character, the windswept moor where the heroine roamed with her false lover, the mossy sepulchre in which she was entombed, the velvet-hung bedchamber she haunted on the baron's wedding night. Searle's carefully modulated voice brought the scenes to vivid life, with such chilling effect that by the poem's conclusion she felt cold and shivery.

"What is the title?" she asked when he finished.

" 'The Blackened Betrothal.' I hope you found it pleasing."

"I've never heard anything like it," she said frankly. "I shouldn't like to read it alone, late at night. However did you think up such a tragedy? Is it based upon a local legend?"

Andrew shook his head, his shaggy, golden brown locks whipping about his face. "I dreamed part of it, the rest I made up. I write such pieces to make young ladies shudder, and receive a pittance for them. I prefer more serious compositions. Lately I published a philosophical essay on the nature of mankind, an examination of our inbred reluctance to embrace a more complete freedom." With a shrug, he added, "My notions are considered radical, and I have difficulty promoting them."

Sophie cultivated a few radical notions of her own, and since coming to Bevington Castle they had flourished.

For the past half century landscape gardeners had professed to study the "genius of the place" before making improvements. A false claim, in Sophie's estimation. Rather, they laid down arbitrary rules and codified their pet principles so they could impose their visions—and occasionally the client's—upon a mature landscape.

Why, she wondered, must so many glorious gardens be altered to conform with a single prevailing style?

The decay of the Bevington pleasure grounds inspired her to repair them, not replace them with an artful—and by definition counterfeit—representation of an Italian painting. This was no proper place for jagged boulders and nonnative conifers strategically positioned around a grotto and a cascade.

These walls and towers dated from the Middle Ages, their crenelations and oriel windows had been added during the Renaissance, and the gardens had taken their present form in the age of the Stuarts. Each era was notable for man's attempts, through architecture and landscaping, to create order in a sadly disordered world.

The result was a beauty well worth preserving.

Intruding upon her reverie, the poet commented, "You look like someone preparing to set out on a holy crusade, or on the verge of fomenting revolution."

"I'm no crusader. Nor a revolutionary." Regretfully she added, "Not by my actions. Only in my head and heart."

"Ah, that's how we all begin," he informed her sagely, before he ambled off.

She must be careful not to speak so frankly. Andrew Searle was a close friend—possibly a confidant—of the earl. She could only hope he was too self-absorbed to ever ask exactly what sort of mutiny she contemplated.

* * *

Fifteen miles separated Summit House, Cassian Carysfort's Clifton residence, and his estate at Bevington. Invariably he covered that distance on horseback, taking a circuitous route through Thornbury, Rockhampton, and Stone—villages whose grim names belied their charms. The weather, remarkably bright and mild for mid-February, had prompted him to travel to the castle and assess the progress of the workers. He was accompanied by his lurcher bitch, valiantly keeping pace with Saladin, his coal-black thoroughbred.

Along the winding, hedge-lined lanes he met more than one farmer's cart bound for the Tuesday market at Berkeley. The respectful cap-tuggings and bows indicated that he was recognized by the people of the district and gave him a welcome sense of belonging.

When he came upon a shepherd whose large flock blocked his way, Cass was forced to go down an unfamiliar track. Narrow and rutted, it turned out to be a more direct route than the one he'd formerly relied on. And every bit as scenic, with splendid vistas of the Welsh hills on the other side of the Severn Estuary.

Nearly a year as lord of Bevington, he mocked himself, and still he was learning his way around the countryside. He regretted having so few opportunities to explore it. In Portugal he'd been free to pursue his own interests, but here in England he dared not drop his guard over his sister. Or the child.

He spent nearly every morning at the New Pump Room, bored but uncomplaining while Cecelia took her daily dose of water from the Hot Wells. He accompanied her to the Clifton shops and purchased whatever trifle she fancied. He made certain that she rested in the afternoon. Their dinner was a long and dismayingly formal meal, a Portuguese habit Cecelia refused to discard. In the evening she took up her needlework and listened to him read aloud from a novel, or entertained him by playing on the pianoforte while he glanced at his Bristol newspaper.

Cecelia's love for Daniel had always been a complex and curious thing. Since coming to England she'd seemed more detached than ever, leaving him to the care of his plump Portuguese nursemaid and Luis Costa. As a result, he was still more fluent in the servants' language than English. A lively, healthy lad, he was less capricious than his parent and had a quicker wit, and would soon be old enough for a tutor. With his ward's future education in mind, Cass had offered the tenancy of the cottage *ornée* to his learned friend Drew Searle.

Wealthy enough to please herself in choosing a husband, at present Cecelia showed no greater interest in matrimony than Cass himself. She held herself aloof from the gentlemen she met, with the possible exception of the poet. Drew visited Bristol regularly to deliver verses to his printer, and each time he called at Summit House. He'd even presented Cecelia with a bound edition of his published essay, greatly to the amusement of her brother. Cass doubted that she understood a word of it. He hadn't bothered to speculate on the significance, if any, of their relationship, but he was confident Drew posed no threat to his sister's fragile peace of mind.

But someone else did. Hands clenching the reins, he considered Sir Michael Tait. Divorced from his wife, mired in scandal, the scarred baronet would be the worst possible match for a female as sensitive to public disapproval as Cecelia. And that was without taking into account the disastrous events that had caused the duel.

He entered the Vale of Bevington, populated by herds of cows and their keepers, and his spirits soared at the sight of his castle looming on the horizon. The sudden surge of possessiveness was as novel as it was startling. High time he felt an attachment to the place—in a few months he would live there. And he trusted that those walls of rose-hued stone were thick and sturdy enough to make his troubled sister feel safe and secure.

Cass handed Saladin over to the young groom raking dung in the stable-yard. As his first order of business, he decided, he'd review the Widow Pinnock's designs for his new landscape. He strolled to the gatehouse, commanding Echo to wait for him under the breezeway, where she was perfectly content to nose out interesting scents.

"Mrs. Pinnock isn't 'ere," an aproned maidservant declared as she admitted him to a sunny parlor. "She spends most fair days out in the gardens, sketching and weeding and chatting with Mr. Searle."

"Oh?" Cass directed his attention to a pair of watercolors hanging on either side of the fireplace. One depicted the Pinnock villa in Chiswick and the other, he assumed, was her uncle's manor house in Jersey. "Does she seem satisfied with her living arrangements?" he asked the bright-haired girl.

"Aye, my lord. She's a quiet, pleasant lady to work for, easy to please and not at all demanding."

None of his Clifton servants would say the same about Cecelia.

"I've a notion Mrs. Pinnock might feel a bit lonesome," she confided, "though she never admits it. If you ask me, Mr. Searle would gladly keep her company. He often stops by of an evening just when she's about to sit down at table, but she always makes me send him away."

That Drew would establish a friendship with Mrs. Pinnock was an outcome Cass hadn't previously considered.

Continuing his explorations, he wandered from the parlor into the small adjoining room, furnished with a table and chair. The tall, south-facing window provided abundant light and overlooked a corner of the terrace walks. A selection of leather-bound volumes occupied the window ledge—he hadn't realized there were so many books devoted to the theory of landscapes. He studied some of their title pages: *Planting and Rural Ornament* by William Marshall, and *The Florist's Directory, or a Treatise on the Culture of Flowers* by James Maddock. Propped on a tiny easel was an oval miniature of Tobias Pinnock painted on ivory, another of the personal belongings that had accompanied the widow to Bevington. Cass recognized the Argand lamp and shagreen-covered paint-box from his visit to her home in Chiswick.

Spying a familiar book, Cass picked up the bound copy of Andrew Searle's essay on the freedoms of man. In a rare display of virtue, he repressed his urge to look inside and see if the author had written a revealing inscription on the flyleaf.

Here was proof of an intimate friendship, he thought with displeasure, possibly of a flirtation. He hoped Drew wasn't distracting the widow from her duties.

With a sense of foreboding, Cass went in search of her. He passed through the long laburnum arch. The appearance of the shrubbery walk, he noted, had improved since his last visit. He peered behind each neatly shorn topiary while the lurcher dashed ahead of him along the broad alley of oddly shaped evergreens.

In the rose garden a gray-haired man perched atop a ladder leaning against one wall, his hands protected by thick leather gauntlets. Deftly he sheared away thorny branches and tossed them down to the ground.

Echo froze. The tawny fur at the back of her neck stood on end as she delivered her most menacing growl.

"Pray keep your dog close," the gardener called out. "The earth in these borders is fresh-tilled for seed, and mustn't be trampled."

"Where might I find Mrs. Pinnock?" Cass asked the proprietary stranger, who had a strong Welsh accent.

"Somewhere hereabouts. In the wilderness, mayhap."

Wilderness? Unwilling to admit his ignorance, Cass retreated toward the shrubbery walk.

"T'other direction, sir," the man corrected him. "There's a gate behind the pavilion."

"Come along, Echo!" Cass called sharply.

Colorful crocus blooms brightened the knot gardens, not as unkempt and shaggy as he remembered, and the canal was no longer fouled by the leaves and twigs that had made it so unsightly. Going to the rear of the ornamental building, he found a gate with intricately wrought iron bars separating the formal gardens from the deer park.

And there was Sophie Pinnock, adrift in a sea of white snowdrops, holding a bouquet of them in the crook of her arm.

Echo gave an impatient yelp. As soon as Cass opened the gate she raced toward the lady, who laughed and twirled about, enticing his dog to dance with her. Echo capered blissfully, bowing and leaping, and when her new friend ended their brief game her long tail drooped.

"Here, you must have one of these." Sophie Pinnock waded up to Cass and inserted a blossom into the lapel of his riding coat. A faint flush tinted her cheeks, and her dark eyes shone with delight. "Have you ever seen a more glorious display?"

Enchanting, Cass agreed, focused on her lovely face. Swayed by pure impulse, he bent his head to kiss her rosy, smiling mouth and found it as smooth and soft as the petals of her flowers.

Letting them fall, she twined her arms around his neck. "*Oh, las,*" she breathed. "*Oui-dgia.*" And then she returned his kiss.

Deeply shocked and supremely flattered by her provocative response, Cass grew bolder. One hand splayed itself across her fluttering rib cage, just below the swell of her breast. The other roved up her arm to her neck, slipping under the woollen gown and pushing the strap of her shift away from her shoulder to caress her heated skin.

She gave a faint gasp, not of alarm but of delight. He continued kissing her, ravenously, wondering how he would ever be able to stop and hoping he would never have to.

Her pliant body suddenly tensed. "*Ma fé,*" she cried, "what have I done?" She ripped herself out of his embrace and sank to the ground.

The dog, sensing a human's need for comfort, stretched out on the grass beside her.

"I cannot imagine what came over me. Or what you must be thinking."

Cass was thinking that the little widow was remarkably adept at love-play, but thought it best not to say so.

He bent to gather up the scattered snowdrops. Lightly, with feigned carelessness, he asked, "Don't you know what day this is? The Feast of St. Valentine, when any man bold enough may kiss a fair maid.''

"You are no ordinary man," she protested. "You're the Earl of Bevington. And I'm not a maid. I cannot excuse what just happened, except to say that I—" She glanced down at the flowers he'd returned to her, long black lashes shielding her eyes. "You see, it has been a very long time since . . ." As her head drooped, a lock of brown hair slipped down to cover one flaming cheek. "So long."

His pulses stilled when he heard that wistful, haunting phrase.

Studying the tiny fingers curled around the bouquet, he saw a gold signet ring. A man's piece, cut down to fit. A keepsake of someone dear to her.

While he'd held her to his heart, passionately kissing her and receiving her kisses, she had been remembering the husband she'd lost. In that moment of comprehension, a bitter and wholly irrational jealousy was born. And with it, a desire so intense that he wondered how long he could bear to let it go unslaked.

Someday he was going to take Sophie Pinnock in his arms again. Next time, he vowed, she would yearn and sigh for him and no one else, living or dead.

His spacious garden made to yield to none,
Was compass'd round with walls of solid stone.

ALEXANDER POPE

Chapter 4

Placing her ringed hand on Echo's head, Sophie Pinnock commented, "She's quite unusual. How did you come by her?"

"Her mother was a poacher's dog," Cass replied, "seized by my gamekeeper Parham, who gave me pick of the litter. Echo is a lurcher—which is to say a combination. A smattering of collie, a soupçon of greyhound. Bred for speed and endurance, and particularly skilled at chasing rabbits."

With an entrancingly lopsided smile, she murmured, "I hope she's discreet, *aussi*, and will say nothing about what she just witnessed."

Her jesting tone and renewed composure made Cass wonder if her senses had been roused as much as he'd believed.

"We must count ourselves fortunate," she continued evenly, "that Mr. Jones wasn't peering over the wall."

"The gray-headed fellow I saw clipping the rosebushes?"

She nodded.

A Welsh name, and a common one. "Not the gardener in my predecessor's time?"

"*Oui-dgia,*" she confirmed, nodding. "Emrys Jones. Do you know him?"

"I've heard of him," he told her curtly. "And I don't want him working here."

Sophie scrambled to her feet. "What do you mean? I almost went down on my knees to him, he was so reluctant to return to Bevington."

"You should have left well enough alone."

She regarded him soberly. "Why, what is the matter?"

"He must be dismissed. At once."

"That's hardly an explanation."

"It must suffice."

With a vigorous toss of her head, she muttered, "*Non, non, non.* You've given me no cause. Your dislike of him seems quite—oh, what is the word? Arbitrary," she finished triumphantly.

"Not at all," Cass insisted, uncertain whether he could—or should—explain his reasons for getting rid of the Welshman. She'd been married and had experienced physical love. But he doubted she was aware that some men lusted after members of their same gender. He didn't care to enlighten her.

With a harshness born of discomfiture, he declared, "My reasons are no concern of yours, Mrs. Pinnock."

"Emrys Jones is a skilled gardener," she shot back. "He might disapprove of the alterations I intend to make, but he's a valuable source of information—and advice." She drew herself up to her full height. "I will not send him away, Lord Bevington."

"Not even at my command?"

"You have no power of command—in this instance. You signed a document granting me the authority to hire whomever I please. What's more, you gave your promise not to interfere."

Cass had no answer to that, for she'd hemmed him in with the truth. Studying her determined expression and the mutinous set of her mouth, he recognized her as the hardheaded little businesswoman. The avid creature he'd held in his arms, who allowed him to kiss her and touch her, had vanished.

She had a habit of defying him, this female whose stubbornness flared at their every encounter. He didn't like it, wasn't accustomed to it. Passive Cecelia seldom questioned his decisions. Daniel, a mere child, was by definition obedient. His servants did his bidding dutifully, either from loyalty or else to obtain promotion and a higher wage.

He couldn't permit this vixen, however pretty and desirable and talented, rule him. "Madam," he raged, "I do *not* tolerate disrespect from an employee."

"And I, Lord Bevington, cannot continue working for someone incapable of keeping his word."

Echo, roused by their angry voices, prowled restlessly between them, her ears flicking back and forth.

Cass feared he'd gone too far. If she resigned . . .

Faced with the prospect of losing her, his fury subsided. He must keep her here at Bevington, even if it meant accepting the temporary employment of Emrys Jones.

But, he reminded himself, Sophie Pinnock's employment was equally temporary.

Preferring not to dwell on that oddly troubling fact, he said quietly, "I pride myself on never breaking a pledge, madam. Jones stays for as long as you have work for him here, but not a minute longer. I assume you have some finished designs for me to look over?"

"Preliminary ones only. And not many."

"I'll see them now."

Sophie barely had time to congratulate herself on her victory before she found herself back in the position of humble laborer. Their relationship had been strained from the outset, and was now adversely affected by his advances—and her reaction.

Oh, las, those kisses.

So long . . . Her own plaintive words lingered in her mind. *Not ever* would have been nearer the truth. No man had kissed her like that. Her susceptibility alarmed her as much as it must have amazed him. Walking back to the house with her silent and glowering employer, she wished she could forget what had happened. But every time she glanced up at his face, her gaze sought the very lips he'd used to such tantalizing effect. His expression was guarded, revealing nothing of his mood.

She had invited those kisses. In all innocence, quite unintentionally, but the harm was done. If she had any sense, she would pack up her things immediately and depart for Chiswick, where she wouldn't be plagued by this new and shameful longing. Her heart raced anew at the memory of being imprisoned by his arms. She'd felt so deliciously overwhelmed, so gloriously alive—so entirely female.

Tobias had been an affectionate man, seldom a passionate one. It was disturbing to find out now, after losing him, that perhaps they hadn't been as well-matched in that respect as she'd always supposed. She'd discovered a new sort of passion in a field of snowdrops, and now was conscious of her dangerous vulnerability.

At least, she consoled herself, she'd managed to overcome the earl's mysterious and unstated objection to Emrys Jones. Her experiences with Fingal Moncrieff had taught her the effectiveness of a logical argument backed by strong feelings. Her case had been helped by Lord Bevington's detachment. The process of garden planning didn't matter to him, he was interested solely in the result. While she couldn't make a habit of wrangling with her client, she fancied she could work her will upon him again, and win future concessions. Over time, perhaps, she might even temper his misplaced enthusiasm for the picturesque style.

Although the terrace steps were broad enough for them to ascend side by side, the earl stepped back so she could walk up before him. Near the top he came to a sudden halt.

"Blast and damn!"

His outraged stare guided Sophie's eye to a carriage standing before the gatehouse. It had just arrived, for the footman was opening the door and unfolding the step. It was a splendid vehicle to have inspired the earl's critical response, varnished to a brilliant sheen and adorned with a painted crest.

Turning to Sophie, he said, "You're about to meet my sister Cecelia—Mrs. Fonseca—and her son Daniel. And here is Luis—you will remember him." He strode forward and greeted them in an over-hearty tone. "What brings you to Bevington so unexpectedly?" he asked the lady.

"The merest whim," she responded softly but audibly. "Need I give you a reason? For that is how you reply when I dare to question your actions, *meu irmão.*"

Seldom had Sophie seen a pair of siblings so much alike—their resemblance was startling. Cecelia Fonseca's features were more delicate and her complexion paler than her brother's, but both had curling black hair and the same brilliantly blue eyes. Her extreme slimness gave her an air of ethereal elegance, and her height made Sophie even more regretful about her own lack of inches. And that modish traveling costume made a plain morning gown of gray kerseymere seem positively frumpish.

Examining the lady's son, Sophie received an instant impression of what her employer must have looked like in childhood. There was no sign of Daniel Fonseca's foreign parentage; in appearance he was entirely a Carysfort.

He gestured at her, chattering to his uncle in Portuguese. Sophie caught the words "*Menina bonita.*"

"Don't point, Daniel, it's rude," chided his mother. "You must make an effort to speak English."

Said the earl, more gently, "The pretty young lady is Mrs. Pinnock. She's staying at the castle."

"*Quanto tempo?*" asked the child.

Sophie couldn't avoid his lordship's enigmatic stare. "For as long as she pleases." Shrugging, he said, "I confess my ignorance of the proper form for introductions. Cecelia, am I supposed to present Mrs. Pinnock to you, or the other way round?"

"Need we stand on ceremony? Mrs. Pinnock, my brother tells me that you shall make the Bevington gardens as fashionable and famous as we wish them to be." After rearranging the folds of her indigo velvet carriage dress, Cecelia tucked her hands back into her fur muff. "I'm eager to see the new furnishings from London, Cass. Shall we go inside?" Before they proceeded to the courtyard, she added to Sophie, "Daniel will not trouble you. Luis has instructions to keep him amused."

The manservant grinned. "To also keep him from tumbling into the canal. I careful of him always, senhora, I leave him alone never."

"I know. *Estou muito contente*, Luis."

Fortunate woman, Sophie thought, admiring Cecelia's graceful progress through the gatehouse arch. Why shouldn't she be content? Beautiful and rich, with a living keepsake of the husband she'd lost.

In the early years of her marriage to Tobias, Sophie had longed to have a child. Initially she'd blamed herself for her failure to conceive, her only sadness until the greater tragedy had befallen her. When her husband's health had failed, his doctor had cautioned that physical exertion would severely damage his heart, an edict which destroyed Sophie's lingering hope that she would become a mother.

She was covetously regarding young Daniel when Andrew Searle came up the terrace steps.

"Sturdy little chap, isn't he?"

For the first time since coming to Bevington, Sophie welcomed the poet's company. The earl's coolness after their heated dispute about Emrys Jones, and his sister's casually dismissive air forced her to seek an ally.

"Have you encountered his mother, the beauteous Cecelia?"

"Just now. A most accurate description."

Shrugging, he said, "A pity she isn't more clever and less dependent upon her brother. Cass spoils her, and I daresay Fonseca did the same. I get the impression he was quite a bit older than she. Daniel, was your papa an elderly gentleman?"

The boy hung back, so Luis answered for him. "He a *bebé* when Senhor Fonseca die, he no remember *nada*." He took his charge's hand.

Sophie smiled and asked, "What sort of games do you like to play, Daniel?"

He gazed up at her solemnly. "*Tio* tosses the ball to me."

"In the Portuguese, *tio* mean uncle," Luis translated.

Sophie asked, "Can you find a ball, Luis?"

"Servant boys are sometimes playing the cricket," he told her cheerfully. "I borrow from them." Off he went, ever eager to please.

Daniel showed concern at being abandoned.

"I have a *tio* of my own," Sophie confided. "Mine also lives in a grand house surrounded by gardens. I was fond of visiting him. Don't you like to come here, to the castle?"

He nodded shyly.

She asked Andrew Searle if he knew any children's tales.

"None that I recall," he admitted. "Shall I invent one?"

"Even better," she approved. "Daniel, when Luis returns I shall teach you a game I played when I was your age. And afterwards we'll go up to my parlor for tea and toast, and Mr. Searle can tell us a story. Would you like that?"

"*Sim*," said Daniel softly. Then, with greater confidence, "Yes."

The dog came up from behind to lick his ear and he began to laugh. Ignoring the adults, he focused his whole attention on Echo.

"You like children," commented Andrew under his breath. "Do you regret not having any?"

Attempting a smile, she answered, "I used to dream, but it wasn't meant to be."

"You're young yet. Many a lonely bachelor seeks a wife."

This conversation was veering too close to the

personal to suit Sophie. "One cannot tell what the future may bring," she said carefully. "But I'm satisfied with my life as it is now." Solitary and quiet and sometimes rather dull, she thought, but much less so here at Bevington.

The servant's return ended their dialogue. Luis had succeeded in locating a ball, and they all went to the flat stretch of turf commonly called the bowling green. Sophie gave instructions for the version of catch-ball she'd played as a child on Jersey.

"The person tossing the ball into the air calls out the name of the player for whom it is intended. If the person called catches the ball before it touches ground, he gains a point and can call and toss to another. But if he fails to catch it, he loses a point. Shall we begin?"

Naming Daniel first, she threw the leather ball in a low arc so he could easily reach it. The little face beneath the thatch of dark curls was solemn no more, and his bright blue eyes sparkled with pleasure.

Their noisy play attracted the notice of Emrys Jones, still tending the roses on the opposite side of the stone wall. Sophie waved when she saw him atop his ladder, spying on their game. Not until he inclined his long head in response did she recall Lord Bevington's violent reaction at hearing his name.

"Senhora," cried Luis, "I call out, but you miss the ball!"

Her preoccupation had cost her a point.

The small drawing room opened onto a balcony from which Cass watched the foursome down on the green. He studied one of the moving figures more intently than the rest.

Thinking back over the times he'd been near Sophie Pinnock, he couldn't picture her at rest. At their first meeting, she'd paced up and down the morning room in a flutter of disappointment over his abrupt refusal to hire her. During his late-night visit to her Chiswick villa she'd led him through her gardens, darting in and out of shadows with her lantern. Earlier today she'd romped with Echo in a wilderness of snowdrops, laughing and skipping about.

But in his arms—ah, there she'd been still, except for the rapid beat of her heart and the heave of her chest as she gasped her pleasure.

His fingers curled tensely on the iron balustrade.

His valet, his close friend, his nephew—also his dog—inspired her smiles. He'd succeeded only in rousing her defiance, and raising the specter of a dead husband.

She ran across the grass to catch the ball Daniel had hurled in her direction, but it flew past her outflung arm and soared over the garden wall.

Cass saw Emrys Jones scramble down his ladder. Moments later he climbed back up, showing the ball. He then tossed it down to Luis, who laughed at whatever comment he'd made.

Luis Costa was a remarkably attractive youth, with considerable personal charm. Even Cass was aware of it, and he had a lively appreciation of— and appetite for—females in general and Sophie Pinnock in particular. He would not let a confirmed pederast prey upon his valet. Or the child.

"Meu irmão?"

His sister's plaintive voice called him back inside. Out of weariness or boredom, she'd settled on one of the yellow damask chairs surrounding a card table. Unlike the energetic Sophie, Cecelia was happiest when lounging.

"The arrangements here please me very well,"

she commented, surveying her surroundings. "This room will always seem hopelessly antiquated to me, but no one could possibly imagine in what disarray we found it a year ago."

"I followed your guidance when selecting the furniture," he reminded her, "so much of the credit goes to you."

"I'm trying desperately to convince myself that living here won't be so bad. Though I confess, I'll miss the shops."

"My dear Cecelia, what can be left for you to purchase? You've single-handedly depleted the entire stock of every milliner, mantua-maker, and modiste in Clifton."

"Unfair!" she cried.

"Take comfort from the likelihood that on Sunday mornings you'll be the grandest lady in Bevington church. Our neighbors and tenants will study your bonnets and gowns as a guide to local fashion."

Cecelia made a face. "With such a fate as that hanging over my head, I may well chose to remain at Summit House. In Clifton I've discovered the delights of anonymity."

He moved to the door. "Continue your tour of the house, if you wish. I must see to a matter of business."

He went back outdoors, down the terrace steps, through the tunnel of laburnums to the green. The shaggy turf beneath his feet belonged to him, yet he felt like an intruder when he joined the lively party. His arrival brought a swift end to their game.

Daniel's cheeks were flushed like ripe apples, dimpled by a broad grin. Luis idly tossed and caught the ball, his dark brow furrowed in concentration. Andrew Searle looked more alert than usual, doubtless because Sophie had gravitated to his side. She hastily smoothed back wisps of dark hair that had slipped from her chignon, unaware that Cass much preferred her in an imperfect state.

"Warm enough, Daniel?" he inquired. "Luis, take him to the kitchen, I'm sure he'd be glad of some food and drink after his exertions."

The lady stepped forward. Her eyes were flinty, no longer molten as they'd been in the aftermath of his fiery kisses. "I invited him to my rooms," she said. "Mr. Searle is going to tell us a story."

Hoping to soften her, and to please her, Cass suggested she order refreshments from his kitchens.

"This is my party," she responded with quiet dignity, "and I won't trouble your lordship's staff. I've taught Nan Parham to make apples wrapped in pastry—bourdélots—as well as a Jerseywoman. And she's certainly capable of brewing tea." Andrew and Daniel and Luis were already making their way to the terrace steps when she added, belatedly, "Does your lordship care to join us?"

His need to protect those in his care warred with his earnest wish to placate Sophie Pinnock. He would have accepted her unenthusiastic invitation if he hadn't desired a private conference with Emrys Jones. "Not today."

Again he'd offended her, this time with his swift refusal of her hospitality. The excessive formality of her curtsy and the rigid set of her shoulders as she followed her guests to the gatehouse told him that he'd erred in refusing her hospitality.

Frustrated, he kicked at a tuft of grass with the toe of his riding boot. Looking around, he found the Welshman peering down from the ladder.

"Come here to me, Jones," he commanded. "I want to speak with you."

The silvered head vanished behind the broken, stone-capped ledge.

Cass waited impatiently until the gardener emerged from the long arbor of laburnums, carrying that deadly-looking pair of shears.

"My lord?"

Cass was uncertain how to begin. Never before had he informed an employee that he would not tolerate the practice of perversions. "You've lived at Bevington a long time, I understand."

"Twenty year."

"Before that you lived in Wales?"

"I was steward to a landowner across the Severn. My master had a need to reduce his staff, and he recommended me to the Earl of Bevington."

Surprised, Cass said, "I thought you came here as a laborer."

"Nay, my lord. I kept the accounts and oversaw all expenditures till his lordship passed away. No one e'er remembers that," he commented bitterly.

"Why, then, did you become a gardener?"

The ghost of a smile flickered across the narrow, pointed face. "Gardening was a pleasure, I ne'er expected it to be my profession. I was impertinent enough to offer advice to his lordship. In time he enlisted me to maintain these grounds."

Cass recalled the portrait hanging in the library. It depicted the late earl, wearing a wig of frothy white curls and a gaudy satin coat, observing a man planting a rose tree—Emrys Jones.

"According to Mr. Prowdie, the solicitor, you inherited a house in the village and receive an annuity. You appear to want nothing. Yet you now work for Mrs. Pinnock."

"We have an understanding," Jones explained. "She misliked the untidiness all round, and needed to know what was planted where. I don't accept wages." He nodded in the direction of the walled gardens. "I set many of yon roses in the ground, and I'll tend them till they're moved. Does your lordship object?"

Those gray eyes pierced like the pointed blades of his shears. "Not unless you do something objectionable," said Cass. "In the weeks before I take up residence, my servant Luis will be spending time at Bevington. He has numerous duties to perform. I would not want him to be—" He searched for a word.

"Distracted?"

"Harassed," he stated firmly. "Do you understand my meaning?"

"I keep to the gardens, my lord. Your young foreigner is a household servant. We aren't likely to meet. Is there anyone else I must not harass?" Hostility hardened the gardener's voice.

Damned Welshman, Cass thought. "I trust I've made my point," he said loftily. "Return to your task."

Emrys Jones retreated down the arbor, his head bowed and his figure shadowed.

Cass congratulated himself on delivering a discreet but unmistakable warning. A carefully chosen euphemism, and the deed was done. Thankfully, he need never discuss the man's sexual inclinations with Sophie Pinnock. As soon as she had converted the formal landscape to a more natural one, the gardener would go away again.

And so would she.

The carriage rocked and swayed, and Cecelia moaned at every jolt.

"Better than traveling across Portugal," Cass commented.

"Hardly," she gasped, holding onto the leather strap.

He peered through the window to assure himself that Saladin behaved, for Luis was in the saddle with Daniel perched in front of him.

"You used to be an entertaining companion during a journey," his sister commented. "Since we left the castle you've barely uttered a word. You haven't even asked my opinion of your lady landscape gardener. Your account of her was very misleading. I imagined her to be a widow of more advanced years, plain and sedate."

"I believe her age is close to yours. But I never said she was plain."

"Andrew Searle is positively smitten."

Cass jerked his head away from the glass pane. "What makes you think so?"

"Feminine intuition," she said on a superior note. "And the way he hovered so attentively." Oblivious to his grim face, she prattled on, "It's no wonder, she's quite lovely. She would be stunning if she were better dressed. Perhaps I should encourage her to order a few new gowns, to enhance her allure. It would be a most suitable match."

"Suitable in what way?"

Cecelia waved a languid hand. "Andrew Searle hasn't any relations, and very few friends. Mrs. Pinnock's husband died, and her family is far away on some island. She has money of her own and a house, and he is virtually penniless. However, now I think on it, there does appear to be an impediment."

Cass lowered his eyes and began studying the stag head carved into his signet ring.

"Aren't you curious to know what threatens to keep this promising couple apart? Or perhaps I should say *who*."

"I can't imagine."

"*Meu irmão*. My oh-so-interested and frightfully jealous brother," she teased. "For he, too, has fallen under the spell of the captivating little widow."

Cass forced a careless laugh, spoiling its effect by saying too emphatically, "Sophie Pinnock can have as many flirts as she wants, marry whomever she pleases. I don't care, as long as she produces a superior landscape plan."

His sister's faint giggle indicated that she didn't credit a word of his assertion. Much to his dismay, Cass hadn't believed it either.

High on a hill with beauteous structures spread
Delightful Clifton rears its rural head,
And looks with pleasure on the vales below,
Where towns are planted and where rivers flow.

WILLIAM HEARD

Chapter 5

Formerly his purest pleasure, composing poetry had become a disheartening form of drudgery to Andrew Searle. For the better part of a month he'd labored over a poem, artfully rephrasing the philosophies of his published essay. After laboriously completing the first section, he found that his words flowed more slowly each day.

Struggling to summon an appropriately poetic vision from the recesses of his fevered brain, he stroked one flushed cheek with the tip of his quill.

Nothing.

His free hand shot out to grip the handle of a tankard. One more swallow—no harm in that. He lifted the vessel to his lips. The wine was faintly bitter, augmented with laudanum.

A sharp rap sounded on the windowpane. He looked over and saw Sophie Pinnock—she smiled and nodded at him, the hood of her red cloak forming a cowl about her face.

A scarlet nun. There might be a poem in that image, thought Andrew, going to open the cottage door.

"You're wandering this wood at an early hour," he greeted her, his spirits rising at the sight of her bright eyes.

"Not so early as you think, sir—it's well past noon. Did you forget to wind your timepiece again?"

Their friendship had prospered, and she was already familiar with his habits and quirks, and even a few of his failings. Admiring the effect of a yellow daffodil pinned to her breast, he observed, "Your flower is a welcome sight on this blustery day."

"Emrys Jones gave it to me, a token of St. David's Day."

"Be glad he didn't give you a smelly leek." Could this really be the first day of March? He'd expected to be finished with his poem by now.

"He's in a rare good mood, because his countrymen vanquished the French invaders. The Welsh are a fierce race indeed! You've heard the exciting news from Fishguard?"

"They talk of little else in the Bevington Arms taproom." Recalling that Sophie had neatened his disordered rooms on a previous occasion, Andrew wasn't about to let her escape. "Will you come in?"

"Not today. I stopped to ask if you wanted to join in my ramble."

"Tempting. But I've set myself the task of finishing six lines of poetry by nightfall."

"Mr. Searle, you do your health no good by sitting hunched over your papers all day. This fresh air will benefit you, I'm sure."

"This *cold* air." He gazed pointedly at the overhanging branches, whipping about in a violent gust.

"On my island we say, 'Quant Mars veint coume un agné, i s'en va coume un touoré.' When March comes in like a lamb, it goes out like a bull. I prefer rough weather early instead of late—when it can harm tender plants."

He struck his chest with his palm. "This tender plant dislikes rough weather at any time of the month."

"You should come along with me," she said coaxingly. "My maid Nan, whose father is gamekeeper here, tells me there's a doe with twin fawns somewhere in this wood. I'd so like to see them, wouldn't you?"

Andrew hadn't the will to decline. If exercise inhibited the effect of the opiate, he could take another dose when he returned. Besides, he wanted as much of Sophie Pinnock's company as she would grant him. The quiet isolation he'd experienced at Bevington was less conducive to writing than he'd imagined, and the solitary hours depressed his spirits. The village blacksmith's daughter, who adequately satisfied his sexual desires, was no companion in any real sense, merely a convenience. Ready enough for a vigorous session of rumpy-pumpy, but out of bed she irritated him with her uncouth accents and slatternly appearance.

Unaccustomed to physical exertion, Andrew quickly grew tired of walking. As they followed the deer track winding through the woodland, he was conscious of his deep, heavy breathing and dampening brow. His scarlet-cloaked companion moved briskly and effortlessly, pausing only to point to the nuthatches trilling to one another atop the lofty trees. With a whispering flash of gray wings, they darted from trunk to trunk in search of food. Sophie soon strayed from the path, and bent down to exclaim over a patch of precocious wood violets.

"I don't know how you can bear to keep indoors all day," she declared when she rejoined him. "With so many gardening tasks, and the endless marvels to discover here in the woods, I've made very little progress with his lordship's designs." Her hood fell back, revealing a pair of flushed cheeks.

"What a child of nature you are," he commented.

"*Oh, las,* you must mean I've leaves caught in my hair. Or has my cloak dragged in the mud again?" She glanced down to check.

"You look splendid to me, Sophie. Do you object to my calling you by your name? I feel as though we're comrades."

"Are we?" She seemed surprised. "But you, sir, are a poet and an author. I must treat you with the same respect I'd show your illustrious friends Mr. Coleridge and Mr. Wordsworth. If I ever met them."

"I can assure you they would be charmed by you—as I am."

She resumed her swift march to the heart of the wood, leaving Andrew to wonder if he'd forced a premature intimacy. He knew next to nothing about female expectations. This one had given the impression of being approachable, but perhaps he'd misinterpreted her warmth of manner and high spirits.

Cass Carysfort, whose amorous career had been a long and spectacular one, could no doubt tell him how to proceed. Even in their schooldays, his best mate had been devoted to the fair sex. Andrew couldn't remember a time when Cass had lacked a sweetheart. He hadn't shared the details of his most recent exploits but undoubtedly there was a mistress somewhere, one whose identity he preferred to keep to himself.

"Senhor Searle!"

Luis Costa was loping after them, hat in hand.

"Where senhora is?"

"Here," Sophie replied, stepping out from behind a broad oak tree. At the sight of her employer's Portuguese valet, she felt a curious mixture of anticipation and dismay. Had the earl returned to Bevington?

"Senhora." The servant's heels came together and he bent low from the waist in a polished bow.

She smiled at the formality, so incongruous in this wilderness setting.

"You return with me."

"To the castle?"

"Where senhorio live—in Clifton. You travel there today. Is his command."

His high and mighty lordship had slyly avoided a confrontation—and a debate—by sending his servant to give the order. *Zut*, but he was a wily *dêmon!* "Can you tell me *why* I've been summoned, or how long I can expect to be away?"

Luis shook his head. "He say to Senhora Fonseca you staying in blue bedchamber. Is very fine." With one of his gleaming smiles, he added, "And he send his carriage. Most comfortable for you."

Said Andrew Searle, "Strong inducements, indeed. It seems I must bid you farewell."

No one cared whether it suited her convenience to go to Clifton. Nettled, Sophie said, "I've no choice, then, if everything is arranged. Mr. Searle, I look forward to resuming our ramble as soon as the earl allows me to return. Whenever that may be," she concluded waspishly.

Living with Tobias Pinnock, working as his assistant, she'd grown accustomed to traveling at short notice. By the time she returned to the gate-house, she'd made a mental selection of clothing she intended to take with her.

Nan Parham's bemused reaction to the abrupt summons reinforced Sophie's annoyance.

"Whatever can the new earl be wanting, so sudden-like?" the girl wondered, voicing the very question that nagged at her mistress. She said darkly, "He may be a lord, and handsome as he can stare, but he hadn't ought to treat you so harsh. Why, you're a proper lady."

Sophie interrupted this show of support by telling Nan which garments she wanted packed into her *baheur*. Then she sat down to write out a list of instructions for Emrys Jones. At her behest he'd potted up a variety of favorite plants—double wallflowers and sweet williams and campanulas—and the seedlings required regular attention. He was ready to sow the hardy annual flowers in the borders, and needed to know about her preference for larkspur, oriental mallow, and nasturtiums. At the bottom of the page she added a pithy reminder that he hadn't yet provided a list of the rosebushes. How cross it would make him!

"Carry this note to Mr. Jones, please," she said, holding it out to Luis. "He's working in the knot gardens."

As he took the paper, his face wore an uncharacteristic frown. "I glad to do anything senhora ask. Only—senhorio, he warn me no go near Senhor Shones."

Sophie was unsure how to answer this puzzling statement, for she had no right to contradict the earl's instructions to his servant. But Luis apparently decided that her wish superseded his master's, and with an aquiescent bow he hurried off to fulfill her request.

By the time he reappeared, she had changed into her green traveling habit and finished her preparations.

"Is what you wear first time you come to Bevington," he commented. "Color of—of *musgo*. Plant covering damp places, like growing velvet."

"Moss," said Sophie as she stood before a mirror, carefully setting her bonnet on her head. "Did you find Mr. Jones?"

He nodded, his countenance quite pensive. "This *jardineiro*, I think he no like me. After he take letter, he turn and walk away fast." After lifting her box to his shoulder, Luis shook his head. "*Ai, ai, ai*, am forgetting! Senhorio, *ele disse-me*—he tell me is something you are needing. Say he want you bring—" He wrinkled his brow. "I cannot remember words. In my language, *matériais de desenhos*."

"Designs?" But of course, she thought, the earl intended to review her drawings. Her sense of impending doom increased tenfold.

Not that she was wholly unprepared. But she'd produced only a few rough sketches, none that could pass for a proper landscape plan. Each time she settled down to work, she invariably made a detailed drawing of the existing scenery. Shoving page after page between the stiff boards of portfolio, she was appalled to see how many studies she'd made of the castle towers—the terrace walks—the pavilion—the canal.

If her unrefined proposal for a new landscape failed to impress her employer, she might well find herself on the very next coach bound for Chiswick. Surprisingly, that distressed her. At first Bevington Castle had seemed as unfriendly as its master. Had she actually become attached to the place?

She tied the broad ribbons of the portfolio and tucked it under her arm. Resigning herself to what-

ever unpleasantness fate held in store, she made
her way down the spiral stairway.

The Portuguese servant's assurances about the
comfort of the earl's carriage had not prepared her
for its luxurious appointments. The seats were upholstered in leather and remarkably well sprung;
the glass windows on either side were equipped
with folding screens that could be lowered to shut
out errant beams of sunlight. Pinned to the interior's silken lining was a flower holder containing
a nosegay of daffodils.

"Is all right to pick for you?" said Luis, climbing
in after her. "Are so many here."

Indeed there were, and she'd miss gazing down
upon their golden glory from her lofty gatehouse
chambers. She regretted having to leave them, and
wished she knew whether it was only for a few
days, or forever.

Sophie spied a milestone at the edge of a hedge-
row, and realized she and her chatty escort were
but five miles out of Bristol. In his broken but com-
prehensible English, Luis had entertained her with
tales of his family and his native village in Portugal.

"How did you become Lord Bevington's valet?"
Sophie wondered.

"Senhor Carys-fort," Luis corrected her. "He no
was senhorio when I meet him. *Aconteceu há seis
anos*—seven year ago it happen. He stop in Colares
one day to let horses rest and drink, and see my
sister Inês by the fountain. Promise he give her
money and clothes, take her away with him to live
at his *palácio* at Sintra. He want her for—because
of her—she have such—" He cupped his hands
over his chest to illustrate breasts.

"Oh."

Sophie's days as a blushing virgin were long past, and she was seldom shocked by any man's behavior. The former Mr. Carysfort was ruled by his desires—that much she already knew. There was absolutely no reason why his servant's revelation should make her feel so wretched.

"Inês agree to be—I do not know the word," he concluded, shaking his head.

Sophie could think of several, but had no desire to expand his vocabulary.

Eh bein, she thought. Luis Costa's bosomy sibling had been Cassian Carysfort's mistress. Hardly surprising—beneath that hard, uncompromising exterior he was a passionate man, as she'd discovered on one unforgettable occasion among the snowdrops. Having experienced the power and persuasiveness of his kisses, she could understand how masterfully he'd overcome the girl's scruples—assuming that she'd had any. Possibly the parents had insisted that she make the most of a good opportunity. Portuguese peasants might have no qualms about handing over an attractive daughter to a man of wealth and power, in the hope of gaining by it.

"One day, when I carry message from *família* to *palácio*, he say do I want to be servant, he offer to pay me well like Inês. I happy to work for him and Senhora Fonseca." Luis exhibited pride rather than shame over his sister's surrender of her virtue, from which he had benefitted greatly. But his smile faded when he said, "I no like leaving Portugal. One day I go back there, see my home again."

"Did Inês not come to England?"

Shaking his head, he replied, "Senhor send her home to Colares long before. Much money he give her. She and *esposo* have two boys now."

The eldest, Sophie gathered, had been sired by

Cassian Carysfort. That was the way these affairs ended, whether in Portugal or in England: the girl, falling pregnant, was paid handsomely enough to attract a husband and returned to her village. Inês was hardly an object of pity—unless her pride or her heart had been bruised by her abductor's brusque dismissal. And even if he'd bestowed a small fortune upon her, still she had suffered the stigma of raising his child where its bastardy would be common knowledge.

This troubling revelation about her employer made Sophie wonder about his other mistresses. Had there been many of them, did he have one now? Her curiosity would have to go unsatisfied— encouraging a servant to gossip about his master was contemptible, and she couldn't take advantage of Luis Costa's confiding nature.

Sooner than she expected the toll road brought them to Clifton, a peaceful hilltop village scattered across furzy downland. Rows of pale stone town houses overlooked busy Bristol and the deep gorge the River Avon had carved into the landscape. Sophie noticed that fully half of one long crescent was merely a facade, its roofless structures pitted with holes where sash windows ought to have been.

"Because of French war," Luis explained, "no money for finishing houses or making more. Builders and carpenters not working now, and must set mantraps to keep away *ladrãos*—thiefs."

They proceeded up a steep incline to a triangular common grazed by sheep. The postilion pulled up his horses in front of a large stone-built residence in the Palladian style.

"Is called Summit House. Senhorio has finest view in Clifton, *é verdade!*"

The house was indeed impressive, Sophie acknowledged grudgingly. Older in style than the plain-fronted terraces stretching along the green, it was partly hidden from the road by a low wall and had a front lawn unrelieved by plantings or ornaments. Half a dozen steps ascended to the entrance, where a pair of slender columns supported a triangular pediment above the front door.

She followed Luis inside, and found herself in a broad hall that extended the entire length of the house, lit by great chandeliers placed at intervals. Standing beneath one of them was her employer. Sophie tensed as he moved forward.

"Mrs. Pinnock, here you are at last. I'm very pleased to see you again."

A greeting more gracious than she'd ever received from him, accompanied by a winning smile. Even so, her nerves remained on edge. "Good day, my lord," she answered coolly. "Am I to learn why you so urgently demanded that I come to you?"

"Not demanded. Requested."

"You should be more careful in the wording of your *requests*. And perhaps you might communicate more clearly your reasons."

When he lunged at her, she almost expected him to box her ears for impertinence.

"Come with me." Gripping her arm, he towed her down the long hall to the door at the far end and led her out onto an elevated landing. There was a plunging double stairway, and he forced her to go down, hurrying her to the bottom.

Sloping away from the house was a wasteland with a few stunted, windswept trees and jutting boulders. Because the property dropped off sharply at a cliff edge, it had an unobstructed view of the rooftops and conical glassworks of Bristol, as well as the woodland on the opposite side of the ragged gorge.

"What is your opinion?" he asked.

She drew a deep breath. "Magnificent."

"Not the distant prospect. I want to know what you think of the nearer landscape."

She regarded him uncertainly. "What do you mean, what 'landscape'?"

"Ah, precisely," he said, with a vigorous nod. "You, Madam, shall tame this wilderness. The man who built this house had no money left over to complete whatever vision he may have had for his grounds, and subsequent owners left it in its natural state. I have no vision whatsoever and am vastly weary of Cecelia's complaints. We depend upon you to perform your magic here."

"What about my work at the castle?"

"For the time being, you must concentrate all your efforts here at Summit House."

Sophie knew she ought to refuse on principle, in protest. The trouble was, she didn't want to. Her fingers already itched, she was desperate for a pencil and sketchpad. This undeveloped terrain, unlike the well-established gardens at Bevington, presented an ideal opportunity to create a picturesque landscape that would complement the elegantly Palladian house.

"You must have some sort of plan in mind." She prayed he wasn't contrary enough to insist upon a formal garden here, where it was least wanted.

"My sister and I will be guided entirely by your judgment, Mrs. Pinnock."

She was so pleased by his response that his warm tone and even warmer smile couldn't discomfit her. Treading the rocky, uneven ground, she said, "But I haven't got the necessary paper, or pencils. No pen or ink, or watercolor paints to mix and work with."

"Whyever not? I instructed you—rather, I *re-*

quested that you bring your drawing materials with you. Did Luis neglect to tell you?"

"I misunderstood. He didn't know the English word, and I had difficulty translating his Portuguese. I thought I you wanted to examine my completed sketches, and those I've brought."

"Never mind. He can go back to the castle for all that you require. I'll order fresh horses put to the carriage."

"*Sécours dé grâce!*" she cried.

Cass stared, wondering what the devil he done to annoy her.

"You can't make him travel so far a second time in a day. It wasn't his fault that I failed to interpret your wishes correctly."

Amazingly, he was starting to like being dictated to by this tart, straightforward little woman, whose brown eyes sparkled so delightfully. "As you wish, madam," he said, feigning meekness. "He can go tomorrow, or even the day after."

Manfully, and with great difficulty, Cass had tried to forget about Sophie Pinnock during the fortnight since their momentous encounter at Bevington. And despite his tendency to dwell upon her lovely face and lively personality, he'd almost been persuaded that it was a ridiculous infatuation and would likely be of short duration. The novelty she represented, he'd told himself, would soon subside. Besides, he reasoned, Drew was also interested and had possibly developed more serious intentions. For the sake of a long friendship, he would stifle his eagerness to embark upon a flirtation.

Life was complicated enough. Not only was he concerned about Cecelia's fragile state of mind and health, there was also the chance that Sir Michael Tait might make a nuisance of himself. Such considerations prevented him from pursuing any female just now, however appealing.

His good intentions had been undermined by his sister, who had immediately detected his burning jealousy of Searle. Even more surprising for a lady so self-absorbed, she had correctly identified the cause. And Cecelia had even suggested a way to separate the poet and the lady landscape designer. Mrs. Pinnock's expertise, she declared, would be extremely valuable here at Summit House. After a token but feeble show of resistance to her scheme, Cass had dispatched his valet to Bevington with orders to bring back the very person he was trying to put out of his mind.

She was pacing well ahead of him now, lines of concentration etched into her white brow. Murmured phrases spilled from her lips—not French, but that similar patois peculiar to the Isle of Jersey.

"Clusters of native conifers *à des bords—excellent*. Cedars could go just here, *p't-être*." Her hands moved constantly, illustrating. "Wild dog roses scrambling down the hillside, ivy made to ramble across these great rocks. And a serpentine path of crushed pale stone, *absolument*, to harmonize with the color of the house."

She was going about this business far too quickly. Cass, determined to keep her near him for as long as he could, broke in upon her flights of fancy. "You needn't decide all at once. After the long drive you'll be wanting tea, and a chance to rest before coming down to dinner."

"Coming down? *Nânnîn*, I prefer a tray in my room."

"Cecelia won't hear of it. She regards you as our guest, the first we've had since coming here. I warn you, she still follows the Portuguese custom of formal dining, and arrays herself in finery even when we are but two at table."

"In that case I beg to be excused. None of my gowns would be suitable."

He smiled. "My dear Mrs. Pinnock, a beautiful lady is a pleasure to behold no matter how simple her attire."

Her expression was disapproving. "Lord Bevington, I would be much obliged if you'd refrain from making personal remarks. Our association must continue to be—to be—"

"Businesslike?" Her flushed cheeks indicated that her thoughts had already strayed from gardenmaking. Very likely she had also remembered their last meeting, and the heated kisses she'd bestowed as well as received.

With a single compliment he had made a breach in that damnably frustrating reserve of hers. This was, he congratulated himself, a promising start to what he trusted would be a protracted and highly stimulating alliance.

She yet more pure, sweet, straight and fair,
Than gardens, woods, meads, meadows, rivers are.

ANDREW MARVELL

Chapter 6

The dining room reeked of money and superior taste. The tall windows were curtained in Nile green damask, and an Aubusson rug with pastel hues covered the floor. Mr. Sheraton's London workshop had produced the long parquet table and its matching chairs, and the elegant mahogany sideboard. A giltwood-framed mirror and a variety of tasteful paintings adorned the walls.

A beautiful room for beautiful people, thought Sophie. Despite the frothy neck ruffle and blue silk bow at her breast, she felt woefully underdressed in her muslin gown. The brother and sister were exquisitely turned out: he in starched neckcloth and black tailcoat, she in bronze silk with a topaz necklace and dangling eardrops.

Sophie lifted a forkful of fish to her mouth, listening to the pair converse in their light, well-bred voices. There was, she perceived, no depth to their exchanges. They talked at each other, and confined themselves to trifles. Did her presence inhibit them, or that of their liveried footmen?

Mrs. Fonseca caroled on about her latest purchases. Lord Bevington alluded to the financial crisis that had struck the country, yet seemed unaffected by it. They were so rich, marveled Sophie, that rampant bank failures and a currency shortage didn't concern them in the least. The lady saw no reason to curtail her daily visits to the Clifton shops. The gentleman had just decreed that his garden designer might order as many plants as she pleased without counting the cost. The recent invasion scare and the French landing in Wales hadn't unsettled the Carysforts' rarified existence.

This meal was dragging on endlessly. Sophie had been warned, yet she was amazed by the number and variety of courses—and with each, another bottle of wine. A bowl of soup and a breast of chicken in the privacy of her room would have suited her far better than the platters of meat and fish spread out before her and the tureens brimming with rich sauces. At home she seldom ate elaborately prepared dishes, and since her husband's death she'd continued eating the simple, healthful fare she had provided during his illness.

The presence of the little boy Daniel would have enlivened the meal, but he'd been tucked into his bed hours ago. With a smile at her hostess, she said, "I was pleased to renew my acquaintance with your son, Mrs. Fonseca."

"If he makes a nuisance of himself, you must be sure to inform his *criada*, Maria."

"I can't imagine he will. He doesn't seem at all naughty to me."

Mrs. Fonseca wore a pained expression. The earl smiled broadly.

"Daniel," he explained, "has a habit of wandering off. We permit him to play on the green only if Luis or Maria accompanies him. But at the castle he'll be able to roam to his heart's content.''

Cecelia looked surprised. "I'm not sure it's wise to grant him too much freedom."

"What harm can befall him at Bevington?"

With a delicate, pale hand, she picked up her fish knife and pushed at the food on her plate. "He might tumble into the canal. Or meet with some accident in the stables. And those dense woods— what if he got lost in them? So many poor, beggarly people live in the countryside, he could be stolen away."

"Be easy, Cecelia. Luis is vigilant enough to prevent such mishaps. The time for mollycoddling the boy is past. Let him get as dirty as he pleases and make mischief. As I did," he added with a grin.

"You were incorrigible, and I can't conceive of a worse example of conduct for my son."

Clearly Daniel's upbringing was a sensitive topic, and Cecelia Fonseca had a highly developed protective instinct—having lost a husband, she was desperate to ensure her little boy's safety. Love and fear, Sophie had discovered during her own marriage, were never very far apart.

The arrival of the fruit and cheese signaled that her ordeal was nearly over. The strain of socializing with a client was new to her, for whenever she and Tobias had been called in for a country house consultation they'd stayed at a nearby inn. No patron, until now, had offered her more than a glass of ratafia and a biscuit. She didn't approve of such intimacy with her employers—far better to maintain a proper distance.

"Step into the drawing room, Mrs. Pinnock," Cecelia invited, effectively preventing Sophie's intended flight back to the blue bedchamber. "I've been trying out a new piece of music, and want to show off my progress. You must join us, *meu ir-*

mão—I'll not have you sitting here alone with your port."

They removed to a chamber across the hall, even more ornately ornamented with a rococo plasterwork ceiling and sculptured marble chimneypiece. The mongrel dog lay stretched out before the hearth. At her master's approach she thumped her long tail in greeting and lifted her head from the carpet.

The earl guided Sophie to the settee, seating her near the fire, and chose for himself an armchair directly across from her. The soothing notes of a sonata and the warmth of burning coals soon coaxed her into a state of relaxation. While studying her surroundings, she studiously avoided the gentleman's gaze. This oppressive luxury did not please her as well as the comforts of her own parlor at Chiswick, or Bevington's antique grandeur. If this were her house, she'd choose this east-facing room for dining and use the west-facing one as a parlor, to take advantage of the afternoon light.

The earl stared at her. She lowered her eyelashes, wondering what he'd think about her brazen rearrangement of his fashionable furniture.

"Well done, Cecelia," he commented when his sister finished her piece.

Widowhood, thought Sophie, was the only trait she shared with her willowy, impeccably dressed, and musical hostess. "I wish I could play so beautifully," she said. "I learned to play when I was a girl, but I liked sketching far better."

"And I can scarcely draw a straight line," Cecelia answered. She leaned forward to blow out the candles in the holders affixed to her instrument. With light and graceful steps, she made her way across the room. "I hope you won't mind, *meu irmão*, if I retire early tonight."

"Are you feeling unwell?"

Cecelia's thin shoulders lifted in a shrug. "Ever so slightly fatigued. Your pardon, Mrs. Pinnock, for deserting you on your first evening. I'm afraid Cass has a habit of hiding behind the *Bristol Gazette* or Mr. Farley's *Journal*. But you're not his sister, so perhaps he will be more attentive." With a vague smile, she glided out of the drawing room.

Sophie hastened to say, "I shan't keep you from your papers, my lord. It is time I went upstairs, *aussîn*."

He prevented her from following his sister with a sharp, "Not yet. Please stay," he added more mildly, "for I really do wish to see your designs for my new landscape at Bevington." Crossing to the door, he stuck his head into the hall. "Edward, fetch Mrs. Pinnock's portfolio from her chamber." He directed a questioning glance at Sophie. "Would you care for tea? Cecelia has a standing order for a tray to be sent in at eleven, but we can have it sooner."

She declined the offer, hoping to escape him as soon as possible. When the footman had delivered her portfolio and promptly vanished, the earl moved a candelabrum from the mantel shelf to a low table.

"I'll spread the drawings out on the floor." His foot gently prodded the dog's flank. "Up you go, my girl, I need that place."

Echo rose and stretched, then leaped onto the settee and curled up next to Sophie.

"I'm afraid," said his lordship, with false gravity, "you've become entangled in a conspiracy. I grant Echo the privilege of lying there after Cecelia goes up to bed. In the morning a parlormaid brushes any fur off the cushion and she turns it over every week. My sister is none the wiser."

Leaving the mongrel in full possession of the settee, Sophie joined him on the floor and opened her portfolio. Bleakly she stared at a detailed watercolor of the terrace walk before sorting through the contents. When she found what she wanted, she said apologetically, "These are preliminary sketches."

The landscape depicted in the black ink and sepia wash designs was rough and wildly picturesque. Thickly planted roses and ivy concealed the retaining walls of the terraces. Italianate statues and classical urns decorated the bowling green. The laburnums were missing and the shrubbery walk as well, with only a few bushy remnants of evergreen left behind to fill the space. She'd removed the wall of the rose bower and had taken away the arbors. The antique knot gardens had vanished, giving way to an unobstructed carpet of grass. A serpentine river meandered past the pavilion—a support for more creeping vines—toward the deer park and a sham ruin.

If Emrys Jones ever saw this plan, thought Sophie, he would never speak to her again.

Lord Bevington examined each drawing closely, and reviewed them yet again before giving his opinion. "A drastic alteration."

"For the most part, I did what you asked," she defended herself. "I tried to."

"I'm not dissatisfied, Soph—Mrs. Pinnock. Quite the opposite."

She was sorry to hear it, because now he would expect her to implement the plan. A major restructuring of the grounds would take at least a year, if not two. And during that time, he would require her to return to Bevington Castle.

"It will be a lengthy process," she warned. "And costly. An engineer will have to redirect the flow of the water. Laborers are needed to take down walls and masons must be hired to construct the ruin from the stones. As for gardeners, it will take an army of them to position all the new plantings."

"Yes, of course," he said absently. He was looking at her study of the golden daffodils and colorful crocuses growing along the upper terrace. "A charming picture. There's a liveliness to this one that the others lack."

His discernment startled her. Painting the castle gardens as they appeared now had inspired her to greater feats of artistry than creating the new plans. "Your designs will look prettier after they are finished in watercolors and bound in your Blue Book," she assured him.

As they both reached for the drawing of the spring bulbs, his fingers brushed against the back of her hand—deliberately, she was certain. He hovered so close that her shoulder was grazing his shirtsleeve—when had he removed his coat? To her dismay, she discovered that her full white skirt had billowed across his long legs.

The candlelight made his black hair glisten. His thick lashes cast dark shadows, like strokes from a charcoal pencil, across his cheekbones. He turned his head. His mouth was only inches away, temptingly close. She felt faint and flushed. She had difficulty breathing—swallowing.

All that wine at dinner—she was tipsy, that's why her mind was so muddled. And he'd been drinking, too. She didn't trust him, and trusted herself even less. *Oh, las,* if he put his arms around her now, she would disgrace herself again. His ardent gaze was already melting her resistence.

"Sophie," he said softly, turning her name into a caress.

Unable or unwilling to save herself, she swayed toward him.

Her hot blood was abruptly chilled by a long, low moan.

She and the earl both jumped. Then they shared a shaky laugh, for the noise had come from Echo, slumbering soundly on her cushion.

"*Ma fé*, it must be late," she said, her voice strangled by shame. Nervously she twisted the ring encircling her finger—Tobias's signet. Her companion saw her doing it, and drew back as though she'd struck out at him.

"Yes," he answered, his tone subdued. "After traveling some fifteen miles and enduring a long evening, you've earned your rest. And you'll need it, for I predict that Cecelia will invite you to accompany her to the New Hot Well tomorrow morning." His hand closed firmly on Sophie's forearm as she gathered up her artwork. "Leave them. Not just the Bevington plans—all your drawings."

An argument would only serve to prolong her agony. "*Oui-dgia*."

"I wish you a good night, Mrs. Pinnock."

Pausing in the doorway, she turned back to say, "*Bouonne niet* to you also, Lord Bevington."

She could not fathom why his return to formality should make her feel so forlorn.

Sifting through a drawer in search of a pen-wiper, Andrew Searle unexpectedly found a silver shilling. Delighted to learn that he wasn't entirely destitute, he decided to visit his friend and fellow poet Samuel Coleridge. This piece of silver, together with his meager collection of copper coins, would adequately fund a journey to Somerset—provided he didn't stop at Bristol and allow himself to be tempted by the booksellers' wares.

High time he took a holiday from writing, he told himself while searching the untidy cottage for his sturdiest shoes. He thrust his shaving gear and some clothes into a battered valise and pocketed his purse. Armed with his trusty and well-traveled walking stick, he set out for Nether Stowey.

He followed the Severn Estuary to the mouth of the Avon, arriving some time after the last ferry had departed. He slept in a hay-barn that night, like a vagabond, and caught the first boat the following morning. During his crossing, he offered the driver of a milk wagon tuppence to carry him as far as an Axbridge inn, where he hired a horse for the rest of the way, intending to return it in two days.

Sam Coleridge occupied a thatched cottage at the farthest end of Lime Street, but the glowing descriptions in his letters didn't prepare Andrew for the muddy lane, or a small and derelict dwelling. The happy couple and their lodger had just sat down to dinner when Andrew knocked at their door. Their greetings were surprised but perfectly cordial and welcoming. Another place was set at the rickety table, and he shared their meal of parsnips and boiled pudding.

"It gladdens my heart to see you," said the poet when Andrew apologized for his unexpected arrival. "Sara and Charles will confirm that I've been feeling rather low."

"Sam is always better for having company," his wife commented.

"He has me," Charles Lloyd declared, apparently slighted by her comment.

Mrs. Coleridge pressed her lips together as if trying to hold back a retort. All eyes returned to their plates, and Andrew sensed a heightened tension in the cramped dining room.

The former Sara Fricker, whom he remembered as quite pretty and amiable, had lost some of her bloom during the year and a half since her marriage. A slight acquaintance with the unpredictable and eccentric poet had resulted in a long and rocky engagement, but apparently they had settled into a cozy partnership—though perhaps not as perfect a one as her idealistic spouse had envisioned. She listened with rare patience to Sam's dreamy oratory, cheered him as best she could during his bouts of depression, and was an attentive mother to their infant son Hartley. She alone was practical and capable enough to deal with the common concerns of life: money, food, clothing.

"If our venture in rural self-sufficiency fails," said Sam morosely, "we needn't go far to seek shelter. This hovel, you see, lies conveniently near the local poorhouse."

The sparsely furnished house was overrun with mice, whose scurryings kept Andrew awake much of the night. Sam, so concerned about the welfare of animals that he ate meat but once a week, couldn't bring himself to kill them.

The establishment's sole servant was a moony girl with a weak chest, ill-suited to hard labor. Sara Coleridge, therefore, was constantly harried and overworked. Her ambitious husband lacked any agricultural experience and was unaccustomed to tending a garden and orchard. Their student lodger was, in Andrew's estimation, no fit companion for a melancholy poet. Even worse, Charles Lloyd suffered from uncontrollable fits of frenzy. But because he also represented the couple's chief source of income, they were reluctant to send him back to his family. And they were in sore need of companionship, for the villagers suspected them of being radicals and Jacobins—rightly so—and they were shunned.

Sam, mired in apathy and dejection, isolated from the familiar bustle of Bristol, resorted to regular doses of laudanum.

"What a favor you did me when you recommended it," he said one afternoon while he struggled together to prepare the ground for a row of cabbages. "I wouldn't have survived my illness last autumn without those twenty-five heavenly drops every four hours."

Always interested in the drug's effect on others, Andrew asked, "What's the most you've taken at once?"

"Upwards of seventy drops. And you?"

"Two or three teaspoons. My teaspoon measures exactly one hundred drops. But my tolerance exceeds yours because I've used the drug far longer."

Seven years, he thought, since Cass Carysfort had educated him in the use of opiates. He'd been slaving away as a journalist in London, writing for the gutter press, and Cass had been caught up in the social whirl. Laudanum had made their very different worlds appear less bleak, it had sustained their confidence and lifted their spirits. Many a night they'd met at Andrew's lodgings and dosed themselves into a transitory sense of cheerfulness. Although his memories of that period in London were hazy, in his diary he'd faithfully recorded their experimentations in the weeks before Cass's inexplicable flight to Portugal. It would be interesting to review it when he returned to Bevington.

Resuming his inquiry, he asked, "Have you done a great deal of writing since coming here to live?"

Shrugging, Sam replied, "I compose very little. I absolutely hate composition. At present I'm editing verses for a new edition of *Poems on Various Sub-*

jects—by myself and others—for Joseph Cottle's press in Bristol. I shall continue using the laudanum, for it alone induces the dream-like state that inspires my best poetry."

"Lately my own muse has slumbered," Andrew admitted. "Every attempt to rouse her has failed. Without the laudanum I'd get nothing written at all. I came here because I hoped a change of scene might refresh me."

"Writing is a hopeless profession," declared Coleridge gloomily. "Friends become carping critics and counsel you to alter your verses to conform with their opinion. Have I told you of Charles Lamb's comments about my *Destiny of Nations*? They don't bear repeating. What's more, he mislikes my choice of refuge. 'Remember,' he says, 'you're not in Arcadia when you are in the West of England.' "

"A Londoner," Andrew muttered. "What does he know?"

"The only encouragement I've received of late comes from that fellow Wordsworth. You met him in Bristol shortly before my marriage." Impatiently, Sam shoved at the dark fringe tumbling over his brow. "Nowadays my penury forces me to write reviews of ridiculous novels. I'm sick to death of reading about castles and dungeons and horrors."

Andrew resolved never to show his friend "The Blackened Betrothal," the story ballad he'd once recited to Sophie Pinnock, or any of his similar efforts.

Sam pursed his full, plummy lips disdainfully. "And yet my latest scribblings make as little sense to me as they did to Lamb. There's a great work swelling in my mind, I'm sure of it. I'm haunted by images of a rolling sea, and sails that refuse to billow in a calm. And a bird—a large, strange bird."

Andrew cast a pitying glance at the wild-eyed, shock-haired fellow wielding the hoe. Then he transferred his gaze to his hostess, seated on a nearby stump with young Hartley balanced on her knee. In a counterpoint to her spouse's anguished recital of woe, Sara was singing like a nightingale as she pinned their son's baby cloth.

Sam paused in his work. "My advice, friend, is to accept the position as tutor to Lord Bevington's nephew. You'll be happier for it, and better compensated than any poet. With the patronage of an earl, you could do very well for yourself. Open a school, mold young minds."

"That's your ambition, not mine." He would continue his writing, whatever else he might decide to do.

Andrew departed Nether Stowey with four fresh poems in his pocket, all devoted to domestic subjects. Despite their tribulations, Sam and Sara had forged a strong marital bond, one that he greatly envied. A solitary existence, he now believed, had stifled his creativity. He needed a woman of his own. He couldn't go on fending for himself, or begging favors from his friend Cass. A wife, monied and efficient, would cater to all his wants. The prospect of sleeping beside a warm female body, eating regular meals, and living in a servant-run household had a strong appeal.

Retracing his route in the direction of Bristol, his thoughts centered on the marriageable females he knew.

That sluttish girl in Bevington village had a flair for bed-sport, but was illiterate, dirty, and hadn't a penny to her name. A female without funds was no use to him.

Cecelia Fonseca, the polar opposite of his low-born mistress, was entirely too rich and beautiful for a humble poet—even one whose work she professed to admire. Seven years ago he'd adored her from afar, and her indifference had been excruciating. In the throes of despair he'd written dozens of sonnets and had sought solace in liquor and opium. But during her long absence from England he'd managed to recover, and she was no longer the exquisite butterfly for whom he'd sighed. Foreign living and marriage and motherhood had matured her, dimming her luster.

His thoughts turned to Sophie Pinnock. Attractive, but not dauntingly so. Sensible and serene. Past the age of romantical fantasies but still of childbearing years. After dandling the infant Hartley on his knee a few times, Andrew rather thought he'd like having sons of his own. As an artist, and an artist's widow, she wouldn't be troubled by his devotion to his work. Most necessary of all, she had both money and property.

Andrew assumed she'd be eager to stop traveling the country in the service of clients. Though he expected her to abandon the design of landscapes as soon as she remarried, he couldn't imagine her leading an idle life. Upon reflection, he decided that she could give drawing lessons, receiving pupils while at the same time producing and rearing his children.

He prided himself on being too rational and experienced to fall prey to a female again, but by the time he reached the city he was quite desperate to see Sophie Pinnock again. Summit House was only a bit out of his way, and in any case Cass was sure to offer him a bed for the night.

Wearily he trudged up the steep streets leading to the heights of Clifton, partly obscured by fog.

His leg muscles rebelled during the ascent of Sion Hill, but he forced himself to keep going. Charming Sophie waited for him at the top. He could see the pale stone house—nearly there.

"Senhor Searle!" the Portuguese servant greeted him at the door. "You have walked from castle?"

"Somerset," Andrew panted. "I need to see—I was hoping—I say, would you tell Mrs. Pinnock I'm here?"

"Senhora gone away. She take Daniel and senhorio's dog to the Durdham Down."

A ramble across the downs—so like her! Exhaustion, unfortunately, prevented him from chasing her down. "Lord Bevington is here, I trust."

"Senhorio go after them an hour ago and no has returned."

Andrew's optimism was rapidly waning, and frustration sharpened his voice. "And Mrs. Fonseca, is she at home to visitors?"

"Resting, as she always do in afternoon. I no allowed to disturb her. But I tell her you stop, senhor."

He'd never much liked Luis, ceaselessly grinning and nattering on in broken English. Now Andrew heartily wished him at the devil, damned foreign upstart that he was. But his own dependence on Carysfort goodwill prevented him from forcing his way in.

He lacked the strength to tramp the fifteen miles of road to Bevington; he would have to hire a horse in the village. Before starting back down the hill, he saw a group of men at work behind the house. Most were armed with shovels, others were raking gravel. Their presence explained the summons that had removed Sophie Pinnock from Bevington.

Cass never ceased to find ways to spend that fortune of his, Andrew observed sourly. Improve this, alter that. Well, he'd best make good use of the lady's services while they were still available to him. It wouldn't be long before she retired from her profession, changed her name from Pinnock to Searle, and began devoting all her time and her whole attention to her new husband.

The morning rose that untouch'd stands
Arm'd with her briers, how sweet she smells!

SIR ROBERT AYTON

Chapter 7

Cass's attempts to improve his foundering relationship with his lady landscape gardener were thwarted not only by her devotion to her work, but also by his sister's incessant demands. For two full weeks Sophie Pinnock was a constant but elusive presence in his household. Her mornings were claimed by Cecelia, pitifully starved for female companionship and conversation, whom she accompanied on routine visits to the Pump Room and the shops that bored Cass. During the remainder of the day she consulted with the contractor and supervised the crew of laborers leveling and reshaping the grounds. In the evening, her attention again turned to Cecelia.

The opportunity he'd waited for came one morning at breakfast, when Sophie asked Cass if his carriage was available to take her to a nurseryman's establishment on Durdham Down. Eager to get her alone, he volunteered to drive her there himself in his smart new phaeton.

"*Nânnîn,*" she protested firmly, "I couldn't impose."

110

"But I'd already planned an outing," he replied.
"A pair of bay horses is being brought round for
me to try, and this excursion of yours will permit
me to study their faults and merits." When she
failed to answer, he added, "You can depend on
me to get you there and back in perfect safety, Mrs.
Pinnock. I'm an experienced driver."

Cecelia readily supported his assertion, saying,
"It's true. When he stayed with our Carysfort cousins in Oporto, he won a gold cup at a competition.
He's just as clever about boats—he even sailed up
the coast of Portugal in his yacht." With a reminis-
cent smile, she said to her brother, "You were so
amazed when you returned from your voyage and
found that Daniel had learned to walk during your
absence."

"And quite cross to have missed those first
steps."

When he assisted Sophie into his phaeton, she
commented, "A sailor, and a charioteer—your
lordship's accomplishments are more numerous
than I supposed. What other talents have you neglected to mention?"

"I daresay they'll reveal themselves in due
course," he responded. "Are you comfortable?"

"*Oui-dgia.*"

The body of his expensive and highly fashionable acquisition was painted bottle green and bore
a thick coat of varnish; the seat, covered in cordo-
van leather, had a graceful curving back. The bay
horses were every bit as handsome as the carriage.
But their habits were unfamiliar, and he had to concentrate on his driving as they neared a treacher-
ously uneven stretch of Gallows Acre Lane.

His pretty passenger spread a broadsheet upon
her lap, a catalogue of plants offered for sale at the
nursery gardens. Now that her sketches for his new

landscape were complete and the workers had shifted earth and rock, her busy little mind was consumed with Latin names and habits of growth and prices.

"I'll be disappointed if Miller and Sweet cannot supply me with Madagascar periwinkle," she said, eyes fixed on the page before her. "The white flowers will look especially fine by moonlight."

"Cecelia is most unlikely to be wandering outdoors after the moon is up."

Smiling, Sophie looked over at him. "I mean to make so splendid a garden that she'll be tempted to use it at all hours."

"If she doesn't, I shall," he vowed. A moonlit garden was the perfect place to carry out the seduction of its fair creator.

"I intend to provide your sister with plants she knew when living at Sintra. Portugal quince, dwarf Portugal laurel, white Portugal broom. If they can be had," she added, returning her attention to her list. "There are other possibilities. This red Roman honeysuckle might provide a welcome note of color. But olives are rather dear at two shillings and sixpence, and so tender. However, if planted in tubs, they could be kept in the hothouse over the winter."

"I didn't know about any plans for a hothouse."

"Eventually one of the laundry rooms will be converted," she said sunnily. "Parts of the lead roof can be replaced with glass to let in more light, and a stove is already in place. Mrs. Fonseca and I were discussing it just last night. Didn't you hear us?"

Cass had been looking rather than listening, imagining how she would look lying in his bed. Pale, bare limbs caressed by firelight, hair streaming across the pillows ...

He sighed.

Her forefinger slid down the page. "Lombardy poplars, six feet tall, fifteen shillings the hundred. I need but twenty-five, which allows for a few failures. I wonder if I can get the lot for three shillings?"

"Will there be roses?" Cass asked, knowing her fondness for them.

Once more he summoned up his favorite image of her. Stripped of her gown and petticoats, her mahogany tresses unbound and disheveled by his foreplay, she reclined on his great four-poster. He showered her with handfuls of wine-red rose petals, an exquisite counterpoint to her alabaster skin, before drawing her tenderly into his arms . . .

Her calm voice called him back from his dream. "*Oui-dgia*, several sorts of roses. I've already ascertained Mrs. Fonseca's color preferences, my lord. I need to know yours as well. If you have any."

"Red ones," he said firmly. "The deepest, darkest red. Like burgundy wine. Isn't there one like that?"

"You must be thinking of the Velvet rose. It has a semi-double and a double form."

"When does it bloom?"

"June. Usually by Midsummer Day."

So long a time to wait. But, Cass consoled himself, anticipation would make the realization of his fantasy all the richer.

"It's quite an ancient rose, listed in Gerard's *Herball*. I'd expect to find it in a garden as old as the one at Bevington. But I won't know if you've actually got one till Emrys Jones completes that inventory I've requested. I'm hoping for my own favorite, *Rosa mundi*. I've a weakness for striped and mottled roses," she confided. "Tobias didn't much care for them."

Cass was quick to assure her, "I consider striped roses quite the most interesting, myself. By all means plant some at Summit House. And at Bevington also, if they are lacking."

She beamed upon him joyfully, cheeks pink and eyes glowing. He felt an ache in his chest as he gazed back at her. So lovely—so unattainable. For if he attempted a simple, harmless kiss, she would turn away from him. And start toying about with that damned ring she wore, the relic of the man whose name she spoke so reverently.

Driven to action by an attack of jealousy, Cass flicked the whip at the glossy rumps of his bays and the phaeton picked up speed. Glancing over at Sophie, he saw no evidence of alarm. One hand secured the broadsheet on her knee, the other gripped the low side of the carriage for support, but she was smiling.

"You don't mind going so swiftly?"

"Pon du tout, my lord. Not at all." On a laugh, she added, "You assured me you were trustworthy, so I've little fear of being tumbled into the hedge!"

"Have done with all these 'my lords'," he pleaded. "Let us be Cass and Sophie, if only for this one day. Is that so much to ask?"

"Oui-dgia, for it would be most improper."

"I don't see why. I was born a commoner. And I haven't a scrap of lordliness about me."

"Nevertheless, you're my employer." Her face brimmed with mischief when she asked, "Would you be satisfied if I simply called you 'Mr. Carysfort' rather than 'Lord Bevington'?"

"No, damn it, I wouldn't!"

"Mind your language. My lord," she added wickedly.

"You, madam, are by far the stubbornest creature I've ever encountered."

"So I've been told, and always by men. My brother, my uncle, my husband." She paused reflectively. "Fingal Moncrieff, too."

"Whatever became of your Scotsman?"

"He wasn't *my* Scotsman," she said direly.

"He wanted to be, didn't he? When he came to Bevington for his interview, he declared his honorable intentions."

"*Vilain*," she spat. "He felt no affection for me, not a jot. He courted me because he was ambitious and meant to rise in the world by using me. I was so very lonely and bereft that he thought I'd want him."

"But you didn't."

"The match was perfectly suitable and quite convenient, *dé vrai*. But our business partnership was so contentious that a marital one had no appeal for me. He's a competent architect," she admitted, "and must have found employment by this time."

Cass slowed his horses for the approach to the toll booth. On the other side, at the edge of Durdham Down, lay the nursery. Miller and Sweet, having outgrown their former premises at St. Michael's Hill, had transferred their flourishing nursery business to a more rural location. Spread across many acres were row upon row of trees and shrubs, and a succession of glass-paned houses where fruit and flowers were forced for the Bristol market.

Sophie, clearly in her element, scrambled down from the carriage unassisted. She rushed towards the offices, halting just long enough to say, "I fear I shall try your patience mightily, my lord—I could spend hours here."

"I don't mind if you do," said Cass generously.

"The bays are in the care of the nurseryman's son, and he offered to walk them for me if we're delayed."

John Sweet, the proprietor's elder son, led them through the grounds. His evident respect for the Pinnock name didn't prevent him from patronizing Sophie, until she began pelting him with questions that were specific and indicative of a comprehensive knowledge of horticulture. Cass enjoyed watching her march down each narrow alley of saplings, tapping her chin in a distracted manner as adorable as it was deceptive.

Consulting the catalogue, she informed Mr. Sweet that she required a selection of forest trees. "Beech, Scotch fir, larch—as mature as possible."

"Beech is priced at eight pence for a ten-foot specimen, madam, and larch are six pence for eight feet. I regret that our Scotch firs are but three feet in height, but you can have them for a mere sixteen shillings the hundred."

"I want only a quarter that many," said Sophie, "for a quarter the cost. Have you weeping ash?"

"Indeed, madam. Right this way."

"And Lombardy poplars, I'll want those as well."

Cass followed behind them, admiring the gentle sway of Sophie's hips as she embarked upon an earnest discussion about cedars of Lebanon. After placing an impressive order for trees, she insisted on seeing the display of ornamental shrubs and subsequently crossed rhododendrons, flowering almonds, and bush laburnums from her list. Surveying the Portugal laurels with satisfaction, she requested a dozen. Her only disappointment was the unavailability of Portugal quince.

With a mournful sigh, she said, "*Tchi pitchi.*"

"You might seek it t'other side of Bristol, madam, at Lauder's nurseries on Lawrence Hill."

Sophie turned to Cass. "Do you know where that is?"

"I'm Bristol born and bred," he reminded her. "I could find my way there wearing a blindfold."

She inquired about the packing procedure for her purchases and settled on a time for their delivery. Her steps were light and bouncing, almost childlike, when at last she and Cass made their way back to the phaeton.

"*Eh bien*," she cried, "the Earl of Bevington is going to have the grandest garden in all the West Country! People will come from afar to admire it." Her tiny gloved hand pawed at his forearm. "You must remember to tell everyone that I made it for you, my lord."

"Perhaps I will, perhaps I won't," he teased. "The odds in your favor would be vastly improved if you'd call me Cass. Or even Cassian."

"*Zut*, but you are persistent. *Têtouongne*, as we say on my island."

Her inflection indicated that it was not a complimentary term. "What does that mean?"

"Pigheaded."

"I was less specific when I called you stubborn." Bending his head close to hers, he said, "Very well, then. I am a Gloucestershire pig. And you're a little Jersey cow, with great brown eyes."

She jerked her hand away as if flames had risen from his sleeve to scorch her. "*Dé vrai*. It is true, so beware my sharp horns!"

During their cross-country drive to Lawrence Hill, and throughout Sophie's consultation with Mr. Lauder, Cass was preoccupied with the problem of convincing her to look on him more kindly. It was imperative that he begin his campaign before she left for Bevington, which she'd do after planting the forest she'd bought for him today.

With a flash of inspiration, he realized what he had to do. If she couldn't see beyond his title, he must show her who he'd been long before becoming Earl of Bevington.

"Do you mind delaying our return to Summit House?" he asked, as his high-stepping horses bore the phaeton away from the nursery gardens.

"What's the time?" she asked, folding up the catalogue Mr. Lauder had presented to her.

"I can't take my hands from the reins to get my timepiece. You'll have to reach into my waistcoat pocket yourself."

A moment later he felt her fingers moving under his coat, searching for the chain. His spine tingled at the contact. When she leaned in closer to study the face of his watch, he breathed in her lavender scent.

"Past two already! Mrs. Fonseca invited me to go with her to the New Hot Well, but she'll have gone by now."

It took all the willpower Cass possessed to keep from taking advantage of her proximity. The strategic placement of one wheel in a rut would send her sprawling across his lap. But he'd set his hopes higher than a furtive cuddle.

He guided the horses into the heart of his city, to the old market cross and the remnants of the ancient wall, and the twisting lanes familiar to him from his earliest youth. He showed Sophie the docks where the Carysfort ships were unloaded, the warehouses in which the barrels of port and sherry were stacked and stored. If this descendant of Seigneurs of Jersey looked askance upon his family's mercantile background, she was considerate enough not to comment.

"Perhaps you'll allow me to make a few pur-

chases of my own," he said. "I warn you, my sort
of shopping may not amuse you as much as buying
plants or helping my sister choose her bonnet trim-
mings. Redcliffe Street, as you see, is populated
with wine and brandy merchants."

He went directly to Merchant Fry's, where he received a respectful greeting from the lad responsible for tending the customers' horses and carriages.
As Cass escorted Sophie into the shop, she re-
marked that he must visit it often.

"Yes, certainly, my lord," said the delighted proprietor, when he announced he needed to stock Bevington Castle's depleted cellars. "It is well that
you make the selections yourself, being so particular in your tastes. Step into my office, for I'm sure
the lady will be more comfortable there."

Cass and Sophie accompanied him to a smaller
room with chairs for his most illustrious clients.
"Can I tempt you to try my wares?" he asked
brightly. "I've an excellent sherry here. Twenty-five
pounds the dozen," he added, beaming at Cass.

After pouring out two samples, he sat down behind his desk to study a ledger. "Let me review
your lordship's account. Beginning with the ports—
you were satisfied with the Old Lisbon?" Cass nodded, and he went on, "I need hardly ask whether
you care to lay in a supply of Carysfort Vintage
Red. Every sip a reminder of the Douro Valley—
the birthplace of port."

To Sophie Cass explained, "A generation ago,
the wines of northern Portugal were deemed harsh
and heavy and undrinkable, for our British palates
inclined towards the lighter clarets from France.
The Portuguese trade suffered greatly until the
makers began following the example of the Abbot
of Lamego, and fortified their product with *aguar-
denta*, a type of brandy. That step interrupted the

fermentation, producing a sweeter, richer wine. There are also tawny ports, mellowed by a longer aging in wood."

"Speaking of wood, my lord, at the Customs House I heard about a shipment of Madeira due to arrive soon. Shall I put you down for several barrels?"

Cass also put himself down for other varieties on offer. "Some Italian wines, of course—the Aliatico. Of the French, I fancy a first-growth claret, a burgundy, some champagne—"

"White or red?"

"White. Also, a quality hock. My sister favors Rhenish wines."

"Very good, my lord. And when will you take delivery?"

He considered before replying, "The middle of May, let us say. Send everything by water, up the Severn to the landing place at Parham Pill." Turning to Sophie, he said, "This sherry is worth having, wouldn't you say?"

"I'm not enough of a connoisseur to venture an opinion of its quality," she answered. "But I like it well."

"Send two dozen bottles round to Summit House," Cass instructed Mr. Fry.

"Excellent, my lord," said the wine merchant, his eyes twinkling his pleasure at Sophie's response and the resulting purchase. "And should you think of anything else you require—rum, or geneva, or cognac—I know my colleague Mr. Ireland will be only too happy to oblige."

"I'll save those for another day," said Cass.

His business concluded, he reclaimed his carriage.

"I must say," said Sophie as they drove down Redcliffe Hill, "I'm amazed at your prices. In Jersey we wouldn't pay more than twenty-five shillings, in our own currency, for a dozen bottles of port. And our wine houses sell thirteen bottles to the dozen. All our goods come duty-free, and thus more cheaply."

"If ever I lose my fortune, I shall go there to live," said Cass. "I believe I could survive quite happily in poverty, as long as I didn't have to give up fine wines."

He crossed over the bridge again, driving Sophie past St. Peter's, where his maternal grandparents had wed, and a nearby hospital his family had supported with generous donations. He showed her the Theatre Royal before cutting over to Queen's Square to point out his Grandfather Carysfort's house.

"My parents exchanged their vows in the front parlor," he explained, "and immediately afterwards set sail for the West Indies. Each brought a fortune to the marriage. Father hoped to return to England one day and purchase a country estate. I'm not certain Mother shared his dream. Whenever she came to this country, she missed her island—the warmth and the sunshine. Neither of them could possibly have imagined their son would one day become a lord and inherit a great castle."

Cass prodded the horses forward with a gentle stroke of the whip. He proceeded around the square and negotiated a sharp turn, exiting to the west. Across the drawbridge spanning the River Froom lay College Green, and beyond it Park Street, where he halted before a building with a brick front and stone dressings.

"My uncle's house. I was born here, in an upstairs bedroom, when my parents were visiting Bristol. They lingered for nearly four years. They were so fearful about taking me to an island plagued by heat and fevers that they left me behind, in damp England and a town rife with consumption. Some years later they returned, and Cecelia was born. Not in this house, for by then my uncle had acquired his country place."

"And your parents sailed away again, without either of their children."

"Exactly. They made two more Atlantic crossings, the last one right after I left university. Then they went back to the island and never returned. There was an outbreak of fever, and both succumbed."

"I'm so sorry."

"I regret not knowing them better. I remember them vividly, so does Cecelia, but almost as strangers. She always regarded our aunt and uncle as her parents. Quite rich, but a generation removed from active participation in trade, so my sister has no real understanding of where money comes from, or its value. A lifetime of being pampered has made her a trifle self-centered, but she has a good heart," he said staunchly.

"What happened to your family's West Indies property? Do you own it still?"

"I did consider going to live on the island, despite my reservations about owning and working slaves. But all accounts of plantation life make it sound like an outer circle of hell—intense heat, unremitting labor, regular crop failures, the threat of hurricanes. That wouldn't have suited Cecelia, so I sold everything to my mother's brother. We went to Portugal instead."

"How did you know you'd like it any better?"

"I can't remember."

"You must have had a reason for going."

"Cecelia's poor health. And we had cousins there."

These questions, which indicated a flattering interest in him and his past, were devilishly inconvenient. He needed to conceal the true motive for the hasty move to Portugal, even from someone as discreet and benign as Sophie.

"You lived abroad long enough for your sister to marry and have a child and lose a husband. And then you brought her back, even though she didn't care to live in England again."

"She told you that?" When she bobbed her head, he said, "It must have been raining. Like our mother, she misses sunshine, and those hot, lazy afternoons we knew in Sintra."

"What do you miss most?"

He looked down at her. "Difficult to say. I can't decide whether it's the Portuguese wines—or the women."

He'd hoped to pique her with his provocative reply, and was disappointed when she calmly resumed her study of the nursery catalogue.

Discontent marred what had been, up to that moment, a most enjoyable outing. Sophie, perverse and unyielding creature, apparently derived more pleasure from her horticultural pursuits than from his company. But he wouldn't let this latest blow to his pride deter his efforts to entice her into a flirtation—if not more.

In their determination to show off their city, the Carysforts insisted on taking Sophie to the original Hotwell House on the Bristol side of the Avon Gorge near St. Vincent's Rock. This was a sacrificial gesture by Cecelia, who preferred the gentility of the newer spa in Clifton, and Sophie was reluctant to refuse so unselfish an invitation. Although she wanted to spend the morning at Summit House, keeping an eye on the men planting the new trees and shrubs, she obediently arrayed herself in her whitest and most fashionable morning gown and took her place in the earl's town carriage.

Cecelia Fonseca was a riddle Sophie despaired of solving. There was no doubt that she dearly loved her little boy, yet she consigned him to the care of servants and was only remotely involved in his daily routine. Her late husband rarely surfaced in her infrequent reminiscences about the years she and her brother had spent abroad. Her impetuous kindnesses were contrasted by intermittent spells of aloofness, and she had a disconcerting habit of retreating upstairs to her rooms whenever Sophie felt there was a chance of their becoming closer.

Her attempts to be a friend to the sister were less successful than the brother's concentrated effort to befriend her.

As a result of living in the earl's house and being toured around the Bristol environs on a daily basis, she felt more comfortable with him. Nonetheless, she couldn't consider their warmer relationship a lasting one. As his employee, she was too vulnerable to let down her guard completely. Her inabilty to forget what had transpired in the field of snow-drops—and the emotions stirred up by the episode—continued to trouble her. The tale Luis had imparted about Inês, the Portuguese mistress, was still fresh enough in her mind to make her wary. Judging from the way Lord Bevington deflected even the most innocent questions about his lengthy residence in Portugal, he was hiding other unsavory secrets.

"You really should drink the water," said Cecelia when they arrived at the Pump Room. "It's warm, with a mild and pleasant flavor, and does me a world of good."

Laughing, the earl said, "Mrs. Pinnock is in splendid health. I vow I've never seen a finer complexion."

His sister went on, "I remember how busy and elegant this place seemed to me when I was a girl. There were musicians playing, and weekly breakfasts and balls in the Long Room."

"The high season won't begin till May, Cecelia. That's why you find it so slow."

She shrugged. "The clientele won't improve. Lords and ladies used to flock here, but now all I see are down-at-heel merchants and hopeless consumptives."

With a playful smile at their escort, Sophie observed, "There's at least one lord here."

"I doubt that even my exalted presence can bring the Hotwell back into vogue," he replied. "For me, the mineral spring is the lesser of its advantages. I prefer strolling along the parade and watching the ships pass up and down the Avon. And the view of the gorge is magnificent. Come, Mrs. Pinnock, you're too lively to remain indoors with a pack of invalids. Allow me to show you these marvels while Cecelia takes her daily dose."

"Yes, do go with him, Sophie. When I'm finished here I shall go directly to the Colonnade, where the shops are. You can meet me there."

Sophie promenaded with her patron up and down the formal tree-lined walk. The scenery was indeed majestic, and she wished her style of drawing was bold enough to capture it.

"*Pèrfection!* Watercolors would never do it justice," she declared, "although black ink and a sepia wash might serve. If only I'd had more practice painting in oils, what a picture I could make! I've often had the same thought at Bevington. I can accurately render the castle's architecture and the unique color of the stone, but lack the dramatic flair necessary for expressing its—its essence."

"Your sketches of the Bevington gardens are exquisite," he told her.

She was silenced by the recollection that soon she must return to his castle to complete her unfinished work. The employment contract stipulated that she produce a picturesque landscape similar to the one she was making at Summit House, but on a far grander scale. The elimination of Bevington's historic garden was a burdensome, soul-destroying assignment.

At times—and this was one—she was tempted to tell the earl about her reluctance to carry out his wishes. But that would anger him, and she couldn't bear the indignity of being sacked by her very first client.

Deep down, she knew that expressing her true feelings to this man would be far easier than confiding in Tobias, whose fragile heart would have been shattered by the confession she hadn't dared make.

Her husband had risen to fame by destroying old gardens to make way for new. Wifely devotion had compelled Sophie to assist his efforts. Throughout their marriage she served him faithfully as partner, carefully concealing her private prejudice against every project they had undertaken. She had let him die believing—falsely—that she shared his philosophies of garden design. The guilt of that necessary deception would forever haunt her.

Her association with her employer might have been refreshingly uncomplicated if he hadn't spoiled it by kissing her. Their every encounter was colored, to some extent, by her expectation that he would try it again. And if she let him, her scruples would dictate her resignation. He would then bring in someone else—most likely Repton—to carry out his alterations.

Oh, las, but he was temptation personified! Vital and strong, a masterpiece of flesh and blood and bone. His physique could be the model for heroic statues, and his handsome face the pattern for pictures of Greek and Roman gods. And if her instinctive and tumultuous awareness of his magnificence was a betrayal of her dead husband, there was nothing she could do about it. But to reveal to him what she'd never even told Tobias—*impossibl'ye!*

"Sophie, is something the matter?"

"*Nânnîn,*" she lied feebly.

"Perhaps we should go back to the Pump Room for a glass of that miraculous water."

Forcing herself to smile, she shook her head. "Might we explore the Colonnade? I've just remembered that I need a length of lace to freshen a gown."

The curving breezeway was connected to the Pump Room and housed ground-level shops with living quarters and lodgings above. Sophie separated from the earl long enough to make her purchase. She exited with her parcel and found him leaning against one of the tall white columns.

"Come here," he said, "and hold out your hand. I bought something for you."

When she did as he commanded, he placed a tiny object in her open palm. A gold ring, set with a single, sparkling gem.

"A souvenir of your visit to the Hotwell. The stone is a crystal, mined locally. We call them Bristol diamonds."

"It looks like a real one," she marveled. "You are most kind, my lord—"

"Cass," he interrupted. "Or even Cassian. No one calls me that, but if you chose to I'd be delighted."

"Cassian," she said gently, as a means of softening her rebuff, "I cannot accept such a gift."

His hand joined with hers, forcing her fingers to close over the ring. "Keep it, Sophie. I don't insist that you wear it."

His diffidence was a facade. In his eyes she read his hope that she would.

Even though their hands were gloved, the contact caused her heart to skip several beats. Why did she always respond to his touch, his smiles—his kisses? And why, she wondered, must he add to the complexities of her situation by making her like him too well?

"I am your employee," she said. Her statement hadn't come out as the firm refusal she'd intended, but a regretful one.

Cass read the confusion in the fine brown eyes turned up to him. "You never fail to point that out. As a justification of your dislike of me in particular, or authority figures in general?"

"*Pon du tout!*" she contradicted. "I don't dislike you. And your authority over me is limited by the contract terms."

Because his need was more than a physical yearning, Cass didn't fully understand it. He shrank from analyzing his emotions, or even acknowledging his uneasy suspicion of the cause. He simply knew that when she was absent, he missed her. If she frowned at him, he longed to make her smile. Her laughter enchanted him, her gravity tore at his heart. Surely ordinary, uncomplicated lust hadn't turned him so moony, and increasingly desperate for assurances that she cared for him, even a little. That she regarded him as something more than the man who was paying her to design landscapes.

Barely containing his frustration, he continued, "You aren't my servant, Sophie. If I wish to converse with you—which I greatly enjoy—or admire your drawings, or even give you a ring, what's the harm?"

"That depends on your motive."

The only way he could ever gain access to that tantalizing body was through her stubborn mind. He must try to reason with her.

"I am a man. Not a saint, but certainly not an ogre. You're a beautiful, intelligent, and highly desirable woman, living in my household. And I do desire you."

He waited for the storm to break, certain that she would rage or run away, or worse.

Her lush lips parted, but she made no sound at all.

"Did you think me lost?" trilled Cecelia.

His sister was coming. Before turning to meet her, he saw Sophie slip the ring into her reticule to hide it.

"I fell into the clutches of a stupid, tiresome female who for some reason thought I was interested in her aches and pains."

"Softly, Cecelia," Cass warned, "else you'll be overheard."

A party of visitors was advancing, two wizened old ladies and a young man with a halting gait. Sophie stepped out of the way but Cecelia stood rooted to the ground, her body rigid and tense as she stared at the threesome. Her immobility forced them to form a single file, for the passage was narrow.

"My pardon, ma'am," said the fellow, as he limped by.

Her hand clutched her throat. She whirled around to stare after him, unaware that her brother had hastened to her side. Murmuring distractedly and gesturing at the passersby, she collapsed against him.

Sophie rushed forward to lend support, placing her arm around the slender waist. Cecelia's body went completely limp. With a hiss of crushed silk and lace, she collapsed on the ground, unconscious.

Few self-supported flowers endure the wind
uninjured . . .

WILLIAM COWPER

Chapter 8

C ass, hovering over his sister's prostrate form, raised her head and shoulders from the paving stones. "Cecelia, Cecelia," he said urgently, desperate to rouse her.

"What shall I do?" asked Sophie, admirably controlled.

"Smelling salts." He slipped the embroidered silk purse from the slack wrist and handed it over. After digging about inside, she passed him the tiny silver-chased vinaigrette. He held it beneath Cecelia's nostrils until they twitched. Her effigy-like figure tensed, then stirred.

Gasping, she rocked her head back and forth to escape the acrid, unpleasant odor. Her eyes opened, and her lips parted for a moan. "I saw him, Cass. He found us!"

"You're mistaken," he soothed her. In her confusion and fear, she was forgetting the necessity of silence. "Can you sit up?"

"Where has he gone?"

"You mustn't worry," he insisted. "A strong resemblance, I grant you, but the man you fear looks very different now. I know, I met him in London."

Cecelia stared at him. "When?"

"Two months ago."

"You should have told me."

"I knew it would alarm you, and for no good purpose. Come now, make an effort to rise—we mustn't attract attention." She let him help her up, and Sophie stepped forward to offer additional support. "Stay with her," said Cass, "while I find the coachman. Cecelia, quiet yourself. Sophie will lead you over to that bench, and you must wait for me there. I'll be but a few minutes."

As he left, he heard his sister say wonderingly, "How odd that he should call you Sophie. He never does."

Cass hastened to the carriageway to explain the situation to his driver, then went into the Hotwell House to purchase a glass of water from the pretty female dispensing it from the pump. He scanned the depressing assembly of the aged and infirm, seeking the man responsible for Cecelia's panic.

Despite his limping gait, he carried himself well. Cass judged the fellow to be in his early twenties, and related to the pair of elderly women. His build was very like Sir Michael Tait's had been seven years ago, and his facial features were remarkably like those of the baronet—before the duel.

Discovering a stranger's name was a simple business. The Master of Ceremonies maintained a subscription book, listing regular customers who paid their twenty-six shillings a month for entrance to the spa.

Cass was grateful for Sophie's placid acceptance of his sister's listless explanation of her dizziness. Her composure, both at the height of the crisis and during the homeward drive, was particularly impressive, and she aided his efforts to distract the brooding Cecelia. But as they vied to engage Cecelia's interest, he was unable to tell how the declaration of his desire had affected her. She appeared unmoved, giving calm, collected answers to his queries about her island.

"What sort of social life did you lead? Are there public assemblies, as we have here and at Bath?"

"Seldom," she answered. "Only one St. Helier hotel has rooms large enough for dancing. Our Jersey roads are so rough that my family seldom troubled to make the journey from Anneville."

"Your uncle, as part of the island aristocracy, must have provided entertainments," Cass prompted.

"Not on the same scale as an English lord. A few of our seigneurs are rather grand, but not Uncle Edouard. He manages his own estate, tills his gardens, and brings in his crop. Any tourist to the island who shares his horticultural interests invariably calls at Anneville Manor. That's how I happened to meet my—how I met Mr. Pinnock."

Cecelia turned her head from the window. "Really?"

Cass had heard quite enough about Sophie's romance with the Englishman. He forestalled another account of their whirlwind courtship by saying, "Your uncle must be responsible for this affinity you have for gardens."

"*Oui-dgia*. He and my aunt were childless, and I was their only niece. I often stayed at their home, and after my father died they persuaded my mother to let me live with them for long intervals. I grew up in two worlds. At the manor house I spoke English or French, and had my drawing lessons and was presented to distinguished men. When I was at the farm with Méthe and my brothers, I spoke common Jèrriais, and kept house and milked the cows.''

"How many brothers?" Cecelia asked.

"Three, all older. And every one of them a *cotchîn*—a rascal. They mocked my airs and graces."

Cass commented, "I'll wager you were the sort of sister who bent them to your will."

"And how they teased me for my managing ways. We had such fun together! They took me to the fairs at Lessay and Guibray, and each Good Friday we had our picnic at the seaside. Our circle of friends was large, and we were related to most of them. As we say on the island, everyone is a cousin."

Once more, Cecelia joined in. "Are your brothers married?"

"Only the eldest. Philippe will succeed Uncle Edouard as Seigneúr of Anneville, so he was regarded as a great catch by the girls from landed familes. But none had a chance after his fancy lighted on a wealthy shipowner's daughter. They have two children now. Brelade engaged himself to a French *emigrée* whose lack of a dowry troubles Méthe. According to Tante Douce, who writes me all the family gossip, Tanmîn is courting a neighbor who promises to make a fine dairywoman. He's ready to settle down to farming himself. The upheaval in France has hampered trade."

"One always hears that Jersey's soil is rich and her climate mild. Farming, I gather, is a common occupation."

"But we have many seafarers as well," Sophie elaborated, "for no one on Jersey lives more than a few miles from the water. The sons of landholders often become sailors or fisherman, or seek a career in the navy. Uncle Edouard offered to purchase commissions for my brothers, but they didn't care to go out of the island."

"And what about you?" Cass asked, curious to know how willingly she'd left her home.

"I always assumed I'd stay at Anneville," she admitted, her gaze alighting on an unfinished crescent of houses they were passing. "Even though I never expected to wed an Englishman, I don't regret coming to live in this country. I was slow to learn English ways—after I lost Tobias, I did fall back into my Jersiaise habits. My family expected me to return, but I couldn't leave my dear house, or my lovely garden. Someday I'll visit them, but I doubt they could convince me to stay. I've changed just enough that I fit in quite comfortably here in England."

Cass thought she'd fit especially well into his particular corner of England. If they hadn't been interrupted, would she have accepted him as her lover?

"Cass," said his sister upon entering Summit House, "may I have a word with you before my nap?"

Torn between his duty to poor Cecelia and his eagerness to resume his highly charged conversation with Sophie, he accompanied them up the staircase. On the middle landing he detained Sophie by taking her hand.

He removed her snug kid glove. She blushed and tried to stop him—he might have been stripping off her gown, she looked so shocked. He kissed each of her tiny fingers, then pulled her gently forward so he could savor those plummy lips.

She shrank from him, backing up against the wall. "Go to your sister, my lord. She needs you now."

She rushed up the remaining steps and he followed. Before she could withdraw to her blue bed-chamber, he asked in a low voice, "And when shall I come to you?"

"Nou-fait," she whispered. "Never." Tears glittered among her thick, black eyelashes.

She slipped inside the room and closed the door in his face, shutting off his protest.

He had been completely honest and open with her, no concealment of his true feelings. If only he'd been able to kiss her, he thought as he continued down the corridor to Cecelia's suite. She liked being kissed. Time to abandon the reasonable approach for a physical one, for her initial reluctance stemmed from surprise rather than unwillingness, he was sure of it.

His sister had already collapsed on a French rococo chaise longue. The instant he closed the door behind him, she wailed, "I knew no good would come of visiting Hotwell House! Why did I let you persaude me? That man—the very image of—of—" She paused.

"Of Sir Michael Tait," he said, completing her unspoken identification.

"And while I'm recovering from *that* shock, you tell me you actually met him when you were last in London!"

"It's no wonder you're distressed," he said quietly. "I've more unpleasant news for you. According to the Master of Ceremonies, the young man we saw was Captain Roderick Tait. The younger brother."

"Roddy? Impossible, I'm sure he's only a schoolboy."

"Seven years is long enough for him to grow into a soldier. Apparently he was wounded in France and received his discharge. The old aunts took him in and are caring for him during his recuperation."

"His resemblance to his brother is astonishing."

"You wouldn't think so if you'd seen the baronet lately," he told her reluctantly. "His appearance is greatly altered." He chose not to describe the scarred face, lest he arouse any misguided sympathy for their hated enemy.

"Is it possible Sir Michael is also in Bristol? Or Clifton?"

"Every week I scan the list of new subscribers published in the paper. His name hasn't appeared."

"You missed the captain's."

"Only because it hasn't yet been printed."

Cecelia's trembling fingers mangled her handkerchief. "Oh, what shall we do? He could also come here."

"He might," Cass conceded, "if he learned our whereabouts. When our paths crossed in London, it was not by chance. He insisted that I deliver a letter to you. I destroyed it, so I've no idea what he wanted to say."

Climbing to her feet, she said, "I won't see him."

"You don't have to. I promised to keep you safe, didn't I?"

She clasped her arms around his neck. "You must be so weary of my clinging. I'd be lost without you."

Gently he patted her back. "I'm here, Cecelia. And will be for as long as you have need of me."

She sighed. "I'm not so selfish—or blind—that I don't realize your dilemma."

"Which one?" he muttered.

"I'll wager my best taffeta bonnet that you hate being burdened with me and all my troubles. I may be dense, but I've noticed how entranced you are by that pretty, love-starved Mrs. Pinnock. Every night you sit by her on the parlor sofa, pretending to admire her sketches while you peer down the front of her gown. You've driven her to every nursery garden in and out of Bristol. Just today I saw you holding her hand in the Colonnade. And," she concluded triumphantly, "I heard you call her Sophie."

"Your powers of observation," he said in a wry voice, "are exceptional indeed."

"And yet you keep silent about her. I'm hurt, I confess, by your failure to admit that your interest in Sophie Pinnock is not wholly due to her artistry. We've always shared our dreams and sorrows. How else could we have survived so much?"

"I couldn't tell you, not until I'd spoken with her. I'd just begun when you came upon us in the Colonnade."

"I can't imagine you needed to speak at all, you give yourself away whenever she's near. Unworldly she may be, but she must have known you meant to have her for your mistress. I guessed it, and I'm not half as clever as she is."

"You don't mean to talk me out of it, I hope."

Cecelia smiled. "*Meu irmão*, I know your history with women. Your little widow won't be your first conquest, and I'll be much surprised if she turns out to be your last. If I must accept her into our household, so be it. In fact, I'll do everything in my power to help you win her. One of us deserves a taste of happiness." Frowning, she wandered over to her window. "But there's one thing you mustn't expect of me. I will not—cannot—no, *dare* not make her my confidante."

"We can trust her. I'd stake my life on it."

"That may be. But no good can come of opening up our past to Sophie Pinnock," she declared. "If she knew our secrets, she would despise us both.

You'd lose your *amante*, and I a pleasant companion."

Cass hated to think his sister might be right.

Seven years ago, he'd lived recklessly, stupidly, seeking out the prettiest whores in London and consuming far too much liquor and laudanum. Maddened by his anger at another and hatred of himself, he'd committed a crime. Afterwards, he'd done other terrible, unspeakable deeds.

From the day he'd returned to England, he had tried to be a better man. He was beginning to believe that Sophie, a priceless gift bestowed by the most generous of fates, was a reward for his reformation.

Her love still belonged to her husband. Knowing his unworthiness, he would not attempt to win her heart. But he needed her companionship, and was desperate for the release of his pent-up passions. He was unattached. Sophie's status as widow made her conveniently free of society's stricter rules about sexual conduct. There was no reason they couldn't be together, and be happy. Provided he kept quiet about his past.

"Each time she questions me about Portugal," Cecelia went on, "or seems curious about how I met Fonseca, I'm so uncomfortable I can't give sensible replies. Luis is danger enough to my peace of mind, he gabbles on and on without thinking."

"I've warned him repeatedly to be careful in what he says. As far as I know, he has been."

"And now these Taits have suddenly appeared in Bristol," she concluded morosely. "My poor nerves will never be the same."

Cass sat down on one of her cushiony armchairs. "There is a remedy: a swift and strategic retreat before the enemy advances farther into our territory. It's time we left Clifton and removed to Bevington."

"So soon? Before the summer?"

"Immediately."

She considered his plan. "I suppose we've no other choice. But I'll need several days to make ready."

"No matter. As long as you remain here at Summit House, you needn't worry about running into Captain Roddy or his aunts. I'll hasten to the castle this afternoon and forewarn the staff. Luis will go with me, he knows how to organize everything to your liking. And I'll take Daniel. In a few days I'll be back to fetch you. Sophie also—her work here is nearly done."

The neatness of the arrangement pleased him.

In a few days he would collect his mistress-to-be and sweep her off to his castle, and they could begin their affair in a romantically secluded and pastoral setting.

He felt certain that his courtship would swiftly reach its desired conclusion. Despite an apparent setback, he had cause to congratulate himself. At long last Sophie had addressed him by name. When he'd stated his intentions, she hadn't slapped him or fallen into a faint. And, he thought jubilantly, she still possessed the ring he'd given her.

"Para que é isso, senhora?" Daniel Fonseca pointed at the small wooden object in Sophie's hand.

"Inglês," Luis chided him from the bottom step of the stone stairway. *"Repita, menino."*

"What is that for, Missus Pinnock?"

"This is a dibber," she explained, permitting him to examine her instrument. "It makes holes in the ground for planting. Would you like to try?" When he knelt down at her side, she showed him how to use it. "Take these seeds and place one in each of the holes. Yes, that's right. Cover them with some dirt—*pèrfection!* What a talented assistant he is," she told Luis.

"*Claro,*" he replied with a nod, running his hand across Echo's rib cage. "He like to be—how to say? Opposite of clean. Maria always scolding about it, but I say he only is little boy and need to play. In *palácio* at Sintra, even when he very little, we often catch him climbing in fountain. Once he hide in stable loft for three hours. *Ai,* but senhora was distressed!"

"I can well believe it," said Sophie. Cecelia Fonseca regularly demonstrated her tendency to succumb to emotion.

Delegating her duties to Daniel, Sophie studied the landscape. The near-completion of her assignment gave her an uplifting sense of accomplishment.

More than half of the trees and shrubs were already in place, arranged in artful groups. Tobias had taught her the technique of making a fresh planting appear natural, and she believed the result would have pleased him. The canes of wild dog roses obtained from the downs now dangled over the cliff edge as she had envisioned. Strategically positioned clumps of upright cedars framed the view of the gorge, and those elusive Portugal laurels bordered the new path of crushed stone.

"More seeds, *por favor,*" pleaded Daniel, tugging at her skirts with a grubby hand.

Smiling at his eagerness, she offered him the entire packet marked *mirabilis jalapa: Marvel of Peru.*

The door opened above on the landing and the earl stepped outside. He'd changed his town clothes for riding dress, Sophie noted. She was relieved that he was going away, for she wished she never had to face him again.

He leaned over the balustrade to call down to his servant, "Luis, I'm off to Bevington, so you must pack my gear—yours, too. If we leave within the hour, we can make the castle before sundown."

"*Sim*, senhorio. I come at once."

Daniel dropped the seed packet and dashed up the steps after Luis. "Take me, Tio, take me!" he cried, flinging himself at his uncle.

The earl lifted him high in the air. Much to Sophie's amazement, he said indulgently, "Tell Maria to get out your trunk and start filling it with clothes. And not the best ones, either."

"Is Echo coming with us?"

"Not today," Cass replied. "We'll leave her here to guard your mother and Mrs. Pinnock." After Luis and the boy went into the house, he made his way down the stone steps.

Sophie was glad of her menial garb. Her long pinafore of brown Holland cloth was plain and unalluring, and at the moment she preferred to be both. "Will Mrs. Fonseca let Daniel go away with you?" she asked coolly.

"He'll be out of her sight for only a few days, and during that time Luis and Maria will keep him out of harm's way."

"As they did when you lived in Sintra, and he hid himself in the stable?"

His dark brows slanted downward, forming a vertical crease. "Luis told you about that?" Accepting her silence as affirmation, he said firmly, "Nothing of the kind will happen while Daniel is in my care. Keep Cecelia cheerful, should she pine for us. She has learned to look on you as a friend—and she needs one."

"How long must you be away?"

"Oh, you'll see me again before the week is out. Will your work be finished by then?"

"I expect so, since you won't be around to dist—" She interrupted herself.

"Distract you? Is that what I've been doing?" He sounded vastly pleased with himself.

"The longer I stay in Gloucestershire," she continued, "the greater the expense for you. I receive a guinea each day, and that's no small sum. I should think you'd be impatient for a return on your investment."

"Indeed I am. More impatient than you seem to realize."

With a fond smile and a few words, he'd revived her shame about what had passed between them at the Hot Wells. And afterwards on the staircase, when he'd kissed her. And outside her room, where he'd made it quite plain that he intended to lie with her.

All those lingering glances . . . the occasional brush of his hand against hers . . . the light in his eyes when he greeted her at breakfast . . . his habit of sitting so close to her in the evenings when he reviewed her sketches . . . These were the techniques of a practiced seducer.

He had a talent for shrewdly assessing his victims and using their vulnerabilities to his advantage. By promising money to Inês, the Portuguese peasant, he'd lured her to his bed. Obviously experience had taught him how vulnerable a lonely widow was to a barrage of soft looks, kind words, fleeting caresses—and heated kisses.

She watched him survey his grounds, but his satisfied smile failed to lighten her resentment.

"When you resume your work at Bevington, you'll have to bear with my distracting presence. I'm taking up residence at the castle earlier than I'd originally planned. The purpose of today's journey is to make the final household arrangements on my sister's behalf. You and I, in future, will spend a great deal of time together. I hope you're as glad of that as I am."

So there would be no escape after all—not from his attentions, or from the hateful task he expected her to perform. Her misgivings about altering the landscape at Bevington had strengthened over time. Here was her chance to state her objections and save herself from the turmoil and heartache that lay ahead.

"Sophie," he said, with excruciating tenderness, "don't look so dismayed. I promise not to rush you. If I did, neither of us would be satisfied."

She wanted to believe he referred to the changes she must make to his gardens, but it was useless.

"Don't be afraid of me. All I've done is tell you how much I want you."

"And what you want to make me," she said angrily. "Your *contchubinne*. Did you seriously believe I would accept such a proposition?"

"Why shouldn't you? Think how wonderful it will be when you and I are—"

"*Nânnîn*," she broke in. "There will never be such a time. A more intimate relationship is not possible. Do not, I beg you, mention it again."

He came closer. "You've no cause to feel insulted."

"If you think that, you have no understanding of a woman's feelings."

"I never claimed to. But I do understand this."

He framed her face with his hands and began kissing her. And she hated him for it, because her body's instantaneous, heated response proved his assertion. Her heart leaped about in her breast as though it had never been bruised. Her mind, entirely prejudiced against him, proved most unreliable when he pressed his hips against hers suggestively, and she had trouble remembering why she should make him stop.

Her struggle to detach herself made him hold her even more tightly. He looked down at her with vivid blue eyes. "Say you will be mine."

"I cannot." She was unable to continue, he'd kissed her into a state of breathlessness.

"I refuse to acknowledge that as an answer. While I'm gone, Sophie, you will have time to accept the inevitable. You belong with me, in every possible way. And we will find great joy together—I swear it."

His fingers traced her cheekbone in silent farewell. Slowly he turned and climbed the stairway, pausing once to look back at her before entering his house.

Desperate to relieve her agitation, Sophie trod the meandering path of her making, which ended at the cliff. *Non, non, non*, she wouldn't be swayed by the gallantries of the handsome, insistent, and breathtakingly desirable Earl of Bevington. Capitulation could only lead to *d'sastre*. Becoming his mistress—*impossibl'ye!*

A virile lover he would undoubtedly be. But any pleasure she might derive from the liaison would be overshadowed by the loss of her reputation. His passion had proved short-lived in the past, as Luis Costa's sister could attest. He was too volatile, unlikely to remain faithful to any woman for very long before moving on to the next. She would be discarded, paid off, sent back to Chiswick and an existence that would seem more solitary and less fulfilling than ever before.

More chilling than any of these considerations, the one that strengthened her resolve to guard herself, was an overpowering reluctance to dishonor her dead husband. She'd been faithful to Tobias while he lived and so she would continue to be, even though he was lying in St. Nicolas's churchyard in Chiswick. The marriage vow that she'd made in the distant past, when life had been so simple, would ordain her behavior now, in this complicated present.

Sometimes occasion brings to light
Our friend's defect long hid from sight.

WILLIAM COWPER

Chapter 9

With Luis riding Saladin, Maria sitting outside on the coachman's box, and Daniel quietly gazing at the scenery, Cass was free to concentrate on Sophie Pinnock. His conscience had stirred after a long sleep, and was gnawing at him.

In the early stages of their acquaintance he'd shared a few basic facts about himself, when they seemed most likely to encourage a change in her attitude. Lately, in an effort to make her like him, he'd discussed his family background and his upbringing. Today, eager to advance her seduction, he had revealed his desire.

His connection to her was growing stronger every day. Now he wanted to tell her everything, and couldn't.

He considered the events that had occurred from the time he'd liberated Cecelia from her ladies' academy and taken her to live with him in London. Not even Drew Searle, Cecelia's admirer and Cass's companion in excess, had been privy to their many sufferings. The brief yet crucial foray into society—

the hysterics and quarrels, public snubs and private humiliations—had ended with a duel, drastically altering the direction of their lives.

"Prepare to die," he said as he took the remaining weapon from the case his second held out to him. Tait, the challenged party, had chosen first.

"Are you here to avenge your honor, Carysfort, or to commit a murder?" the baronet asked.

"To make certain that justice is done." Cass welcomed the heavy, deadly feel of his loaded pistol. It gave him the power to redress all wrongs.

He was no true gentleman. Ostensibly he was here to defend his honor, but what had really brought him to this desolate heath was a searing and most ungentlemanly desire for revenge. If all went as Cass intended, the services of that surgeon waiting in the carriage would not be wanted.

Regardless of the outcome, his plans were unalterable. Whether or not he killed the baronet, he and Cecelia were sailing off to Lisbon today. If he was killed, she would go alone.

"Gentlemen," said Tait's second, *"you are certain that there's no possibility of reconciliation?"*

"Let us get on with it," Tait muttered.

Cass and his adversary marched their ten paces, turned, and waited for the signal to fire.

One of their seconds released the white handkerchief, weighted by a pebble. Two successive pistol shots shattered the silence of the dawn.

Both duellists survived, but each had been permanently damaged. Tait's scar was the more visible. Outwardly Cass appeared unscathed; his wounds were well concealed, hidden in his mind and heart and soul.

Opium and Michael Tait had been his downfall.

He accepted full responsibility for everything that had preceded and followed his early-morning exchange of fire with the baronet. And for the remainder of his time on earth, he would strive to make amends to Cecelia.

Resting his head against the seat-back, he returned to the problem of Sophie, that pattern-card of frankness.

Judging by the evidence, her husband had been a good sort, honest and trustworthy and everything else that was admirable. Cass had no hope of ravishing the paragon's devoted widow if he confessed to a period of debauchery and inebriation that had culminated in a murderous encounter on Hounslow Heath. For once he was willing to be guided by Cecelia, and would keep quiet about their past.

He craved Sophie's respect no less than he prized her lovely face, but he also lusted for her sweet body. His mind dwelled upon all those tantalizing curves—her gently rounded cheek and chin, the swelling breasts and flaring hips. Her hidden parts must be similarly delectable. He dreamed constantly of the day—no, the night—when she would let him peel away her clothes and examine her thighs and calves and ankles.

"Tio Cass?"

He opened his eyes.

"Will we be there soon?" For the first time Daniel showed signs of restlessness, drumming his heels against the bench.

"Fairly soon. Come sit here," he invited.

The child scrambled down from his place and climbed up beside him. Out of habit he curled his arm around Daniel's shoulder, pulling him close.

"Tio?"

"Mmm."

"Why doesn't Mama ever hold me? You do. And Maria and Luis. Even Senhora—*Missus* Pinnock hugs me sometimes. But not my mother."

At a loss, Cass struggled to find an answer. Much to his sorrow, his sister's obsessive devotion to the boy and constant concern for his safety rarely translated themselves into motherly behavior. He couldn't possibly clarify Cecelia's inability to express her affection, for Daniel was far too young to make sense of the explanation.

"I remember to speak *inglês* always now, except with Luis and Maria, just as Mama wishes. But still she doesn't love me."

The pensive declaration prompted Cass to say, "You're mistaken, Daniel. She loves you very much, more than anyone or anything in all the world. Late at night, after you've fallen asleep, she slips into your room and watches over you."

"*Realmente?*"

"I've seen her," he confirmed. "If you kept awake long enough, so would you."

"*Padre* watches me," announced Daniel. "From up in heaven. He pushes away the clouds and looks down. Once I caught him doing it."

Cass supposed that Maria, her head stuffed with Catholic superstitions, had encouraged this belief. "And what does your father look like?"

"Like a man."

Amused by the comprehensive simplicity of this reply, Cass said, "Well, if you catch him spying on you again, be sure to point him out. I'd like to see him myself."

The boy did resemble his sire—beneath the youthful roundness of his face Cass could trace the familiar lines of nose and jaw—but fortunately for everyone he was even more like Cecelia. As a child her complexion had been just as pink and healthy, her mouth had curled upward instead of down, and her blue eyes had shone in innocent joy.

Daniel's stomach rumbled loudly. Giggling, he placed his hand over his belly.

"Hungry, are you?"

"*Sim.*" The child nodded vigorously. "And thirsty. Are we almost there?"

"Not quite. This is Alveston village. If you like, we can stop at the Ship. I'd be glad of a tankard myself."

Situated on the busy Bristol-Gloucester route, the inn was a flurry of activity on this bright spring day. After Luis had refresehd himself, Cass ordered him to ride on to the castle ahead of the carriage.

The weather was warm and mild, so Cass chose to drink his ale outdoors. Daniel, seated on an inn yard bench with Maria, tucked into a meat pie and a slice of currant cake. The yard was bustling: hostlers and grooms harnessed horses to departing vehicles and watered the animals whose masters dined within.

"Ho there, Nib!" shouted an aproned waiter, hanging out of an upper window. "Dr. Jenner is leaving. Make haste to fetch his horse!"

Within minutes a soberly dressed gentleman briskly exited the inn. In his late forties, he had a broad forehead, a masterful nose, and a smiling mouth.

Cass rose. "Dr. Edward Jenner?"

The man paused and turned. "I am he. Lord Bevington, isn't it? Forgive my failure to notice you. My mind was still running on Medical Society affairs—we just concluded a lively discussion of *angina pectoris*. Our meetings last for many hours— after presenting scholarly or scientific papers, we share a formal dinner. But with my dear wife expecting to lie in at any time now, I must forgo our evening festivities and ride home to Berkeley."

"I'll not detain you longer than a moment or two. A timely and convenient encounter."

"Your lordship isn't ill?"

"Thankfully, no. It's my sister, Mrs. Fonseca. Presently she's in the care of a Clifton doctor, but I need to know we can rely on someone in the neighborhood of Bevington."

"I should be delighted to wait upon you both. I'm honored to name other members of the local nobility among my clients—Lord Berkeley and his lady, and Lord Ducie's family at Tortworth Court. I travel in all weathers and my fees are reasonable."

Cass was impressed by such confidence, exactly what one sought in a physician.

Dr. Jenner showed an interest in his sister's symptoms. "Is she troubled with palpitations in the chest?"

"No."

"That rules out a heart complaint. Are her cheeks flushed, and does she often appear short of breath?"

"I haven't noticed it."

"Not consumption, then. Appetite good?"

Cass shrugged. "No worse or better than usual. She's never been a hearty eater."

"Tremors in her limbs or extremities?"

He shook his head emphatically.

"Sleeplessness?"

"Yes, I believe so. When she's dejected, or overly excited."

The doctor's graying brows were naturally set high, and they rose still higher. "Interesting. Her disposition is a nervous one?"

"Decidedly so."

"Ah. Well, I'm more than willing to attend her,

my lord Bevington, but I must warn you that I haven't any cure for a bad set of nerves. In such cases I can only advise fresh country air, plenty of exercise, and wholesome food." With a glance at Daniel, he asked, "Your son looks to be a sturdy lad."

"Nephew—my sister's child. His health, unlike hers, is excellent."

"Six or seven years old, I'm guessing. Last summer I successfully inoculated a lad of his age against the smallpox using a new method I've developed. I'm eager to repeat the trial. But if Mrs. Fonseca is the anxious sort, she won't favor a procedure that can only be considered experimental, despite its great promise."

"Is it a dangerous operation?" asked Cass.

"Not at all. I would infect him with cowpox. It's a mild strain that apparently makes our local dairymaids immune to the more virulent forms of pox. At most your nephew would suffer a slight fever for a day or two, and during that time I'd keep him under close observation. The recovery is swifter than with the old variolation treatment, which I underwent as a child."

"I, too," said Cass. "Daniel was born in Portugal, and hasn't been inoculated yet. I'll raise the issue with my sister, if you think it wants doing."

"Trouble is, we haven't any cowpox cases in the district now, so I've no means of extracting lymph from an infected person. But I or my nephew Henry, who assists in my practice, can variolate young Daniel in the usual way, should that be his mother's preference. Ah, here's my horse, saddled and ready." Dr. Jenner took the hand Cass extended and shook it firmly. "A pleasure, my lord. You should know, our countryside buzzes about

your lady landscape gardener, and all the changes
to be made at Bevington Castle."

The reference to Sophie made Cass smile.

"I happen to be a keen gardener myself, and take
a most particular interest in her progress. I've de-
vised a secluded little grotto of my own behind my
house in Berkeley, where I vaccinated young Jamie
Phipps last summer."

With a cheery smile, he climbed upon his horse.

Daniel, his appetite satisfied, was content to play
simple games with Cass during the rest of the journey to Bevington. He counted black sheep on either
side of the road, and before the novelty wore off
the carriage turned into the drive. It passed beneath
the outer arch and swung around to the stone-
paved stable-yard.

Cass climbed out first and helped the child
negotiate the folding steps. "From this day on-
ward, Daniel, the castle is your home."

"Forever and ever?" asked the child.

"Until you become a man," said Cass. "Remember how you picked out your own little room in
the tower many months ago? Luis will have a fire
going, to make it bright and cozy."

Maria held out her hand to the boy, and he took
it, murmuring excitedly in Portuguese as she led
him away.

For the rest of that day and part of the next, Cass
roamed his vast domain, working his way from top
to bottom. In the many corridors, colorful strips of
carpet covered the ancient stones or wooden floorboards. The thousands of diamond-shaped windowpanes were at long last cleared of dust and
grime. In the picture gallery, a coat of light paint
provided a contrasting background for a collection
of dark landscape paintings. A glittering chandelier
of Waterford crystal hung over the new mahogany

dining table. The tapestry hangings in the morning room, great hall, and small drawing room had been cleaned. Floral wallpaper freshened Cecelia's chosen bedchamber, decorated to her taste with chintz draperies and furniture upholstered in petit point.

While touring his refurbished rooms, Cass didn't picture his sister in them. No, Sophie was the person he imagined seated on the elegant giltwood sofa in the long drawing room, and studying the portraits in the great hall, and poring over the books in the library. In the morning room, he could see her standing at the tall casements, looking down upon the gardens—exactly as she'd been doing the first time he laid eyes upon her.

He wanted to share his castle with her. Sophie, he was sure, could learn to love its oddities and beauties in a way Cecelia never would.

A whim carried him to her quaint, old-fashioned parlor in the gatehouse. Giving in to his desire to see the room in which she'd slept—and would again after her return—he climbed the spiral stairway. Her oak bedstead was a plainer version of his, and the other furnishings appeared to be well-made, if a trifle ordinary. She should have better ones, he reflected.

He was intrigued by a wood-paneled door set into an arch in the wall. There was no handle, so he was unable to discover where it led.

Mentally he reviewed the layout of the castle. Very likely this uppermost room of the gatehouse adjoined his own suite. And if he could obtain the key—

Before he'd completed the thought, he was hurrying out of Sophie's bedchamber, down the steps, into the courtyard.

He located his housekeeper in her sitting room and told her he'd found a door that wouldn't open.

"D'you mean that low wooden one at the back of your lordship's dressing room?"

"The very one. Have you got the key?"

Mrs. Harvey waddled over to an array of hooks protruding from the wall, each holding a key ring. "Let me take a look. Upper floor, the master's chambers—'twill be with this set. All of 'em brass, save this gurt iron one. That's surely the one you need."

Thanking her, he slipped the key off the ring and carried it away with him.

Nothing could be more perfect. A door connecting his rooms and Sophie's. His exultation knew no bounds.

His Jacobean bedstead, with carved posts as thick as tree trunks, looked a great deal more inviting now that it had a goose-down mattress and plump pillows. As for those needlework hangings—he wasn't sure he liked them, but at least they were nicer than the old moth-eaten ones.

He passed into the narrow, closet-like space fitted up with a shaving mirror and a bureau and a wardrobe. The arched door was at the far end, its wood whitewashed to blend in with the pale stone of the wall. He slipped the iron key into the crude metal locking mechanism and turned it.

A feminine shriek put an end to his explorations.

A blonde girl in mobcap and apron clutched a rag to her bosom. "Lord Bevington!" she cried.

At a loss, he stared back at her.

"I'm Nan—Parham. Mrs. Pinnock's waiting woman," she explained, bobbing a curtsy.

Now he remembered—he'd met her once before. "Right. Of course."

"Your lordship's valet told me she was coming back 'ere soon, so I come up to do a bit of dusting," she told him, her eyes wide with alarm.

"Carry on," he said, embarrassed to be caught intruding. "I needed to know where this passage led. Now that I do, I shall leave you to finish your work."

Retreating to his dressing room, he shut the door and leaned against it.

Would the housemaid tell Sophie what he'd done? He preferred to inform her about his discovery himself. Examining the key, he wondered what he should do with it. Best to keep it close, he thought, and hid it in the uppermost drawer of the chest.

With a dreamy smile, Andrew Searle looked away from the brilliant blue kingfisher fluttering up from the woodland stream. "And how," he drawled, "is the estimable Mrs. Pinnock getting on?"

"She has improved the grounds of Summit House," Cass reported. "My sister is most pleased."

"Her lively presence is much missed here at Bevington. I trust you'll send her back."

Cass eyed his friend with suspicion as they strolled towards the cottage ornée. Why should Drew miss Sophie? "When she does return, she'll be busy with the task I hired her to perform," he warned. "She won't be at leisure to amuse you."

"Poor girl, you work her so hard that she must regard you as a slave driver." After a pause, Andrew said, "Sorry for that slip—I know you dislike reminders of your plantation origins. Step inside, old fellow, there's a matter we need to discuss."

The cottage looked as though a tempest had struck it. Heaps of clothing and piles of books and stacks of filthy dishes covered every surface. Andrew collapsed onto a chair by the table where he ate and worked, judging from the bread crumbs and papers everywhere.

"Do sit. I can't converse sensibly with you looming over me." When Cass complied, he continued, "I've been thinking about the tutorial position you offered when I first came to Bevington."

"Oh," said Cass in relief. He'd prepared himself for an awkward and one-sided discussion, with Drew rhapsodizing about Sophie. "Then you've finally decided to accept?"

"Regretfully, I must decline to take on your nephew as pupil. I've formed an alternate plan for my future."

"Tell me about it."

The poet shook his shaggy head. "I cannot be more specific, not yet. But my planned endeavor requires me to settle nearer London. My mind has been dulled by rural living."

Cass gave him a sharp, suspicious glance. Rural living, he wondered, or too much laudanum?

"It's possible I'll be begging for assistance—a temporary loan."

"You won't have to beg," Cass said. He'd pay any price if it meant ensuring Drew's departure prior to Sophie's return. "When are you giving up the cottage?"

"Not immediately. I'll notify you as soon as my arrangements are finalized. If I hadn't drunk up the last of my wine, we could raise a glass to toast my prospects. I'm afraid this is the best I can offer."

Cass recoiled when his friend brandished a blue glass vial.

"Come now, there's no harm in it. Quite the opposite, it will smooth away the worries denting your brow and put a smile on your face. That's what you used to tell me—remember?"

Laudanum. Cass remembered the despair that

had driven him to use the drug, but the agonies he'd suffered in freeing himself of its grip had been far worse. "It doesn't agree with me," he insisted.

With an air of superiority, Drew commented, "What a stodgy chap you've become."

"I'm more careful now," he said grimly. "I take fewer risks." Because seven years ago his insobriety had cost him dearly, and nowadays he had so much to lose.

"One day," his friend declared blithely, "I shall write a treatise on the blessed powers of opium. It will be my first composition after I've won my heart's desire."

"You ought to give it up altogether," responded Cass. "Every dose steals more of your energy, and drains you of ambition. Trust me, I know."

Andrew took a defiant sip from his bottle. "My friend Sam Coleridge would laugh to hear you talk so. In his experience—and mine—the drug inspires greater things. If I showed you my most recent verses, you'd see how very wrong you are. I'll make clean copies, bring them to the castle tonight."

"Not tonight," Cass protested. "I've rent books and tenant lists to study before I leave for Clifton in the morning."

The poet accompanied him to the door. "You aren't miffed?"

Cass placed a hand on his friend's thin shoulder and said soberly, "I've looked out for you since we were schoolboys together, and I can't shake myself of so old a habit."

Making his way through the deer park, he reflected on Drew's persistent interest in Sophie. Nothing she'd ever said or done indicated that it was reciprocated. His only real rival, it seemed, was the late Tobias Pinnock.

He tried to think of some service he could perform that would please her. She wanted a rose list from Emrys Jones, he recalled. By getting it, he might obtain a rich reward.

He located the Welshman in the rose garden, kneeling in the dirt and pulling up weeds along the edge of the wall. Two bright spots of color appeared on his pale cheeks when he learned that Cass expected him to produce the desired item on the spot.

"I'm aware of Mrs. Pinnock's request," he said impatiently. "She'll have her list."

"She's asked you for it repeatedly. What prevents your compliance?" Cass received no answer. "You may be here at her invitation, but the gardens are mine. If you expect to stay on, you'd best summon up more respect than you've shown heretofore."

"I've told your lordship, Mrs. Pinnock is the only one who can dismiss me. I receive no pay," the man reminded him, "so I'm beholden to no one."

As obdurate as the lady he worked for, thought Cass, and every bit as impertinent.

"Have you any other message for me, my lord?"

He did not, although he had a personal need of information. "I want to know if there is a particular specimen with petals the color of wine growing here. A Velvet rose, Mrs. Pinnock called it."

"Aye, and many. The plants sucker freely, they spread themselves about."

"Show me."

Jones led him around the enclosure, pointing out each of the tall, twiggy shrubs growing against the wall and a few others that clung to the arbors. Young leaves were springing up along the canes.

"If left undisturbed, you'll have flowers afore

July. But if they're moved, they mightn't bloom at all this year."

"Leave them where they are," Cass commanded. He had to preserve them, so he could scatter their wine-red petals over Sophie's naked white body.

"Isn't that for Mrs. Pinnock to say?"

"Neither you nor she will do anything here that hasn't been sanctioned by me. Is that clear?"

"Perfectly, my lord," said the Welshman, glaring into the distance.

Cass turned his head and saw Luis Costa picking the variegated tulips growing in the border.

Holding up his bouquet, he called out, "Beautiful flowers, so many colors! You teach me names, Senhor Shones?"

"He's far too busy to bother with you," Cass rebuked him. "And you have much to do yourself. Come away now."

The youth's shoulders slumped, but he answered obediently, "*Sim*, senhorio."

"Have I not warned you," said Cass furiously, as they crossed the springy turf, "to keep away from that man? I brought you here to prepare the house for Senhora Fonseca, she depends on you to arrange things for her. But I cannot leave you behind if you're going to defy me."

"I no defy," Luis promised.

Not only was Cass cross with Luis. The stubborn Welshman had annoyed him. Drew's use of opium frustrated him. He was plagued by his own failings, past and present. And he feared that if Sophie Pinnock ever discovered the bitter truth, he'd have no use for those velvety rose petals.

All these pent-up feelings exploded in the direction of his valet, whom he bullied into a state of distress.

"I so sorry for making senhorio angry. I keep away from Senhor Shones."

"See that you do. And for the love of God, Luis, keep quiet about Portugal. You could do great harm by talking too much."

"*Sim, sim.* I no want to hurt Senhora Fonseca and Daniel."

"Then be careful in what you say, and to whom you say it."

Luis lifted his dark head, and eyes that were dark pools of conviction. "I have sweared it, on souls of my ancestors. And I wish to die, senhorio, before ever I break my vow to you."

Improvement, the idol of the age,
Is fed with many a victim. Lo! he comes,
The omnipotent magician . . .

WILLIAM COWPER

Chapter 10

Sophie pressed a hand into the small of her back and rubbed at the ache. She'd been sticking brown and shriveled anemone corms in the ground, a late planting to extend the summer display. By the time they bloomed, in a rainbow of colors, the Carysforts would be permanently settled at Bevington, miles away from their lovely town house and its improved setting. But she was a gardener, she must consider the future—not only this year but all the ones to follow.

She dropped her well-used dibber into the large pocket of her brown pinafore, where it joined bits of string, empty seed packets, and a round white pebble she'd found. Then she lowered her weary body onto the bottom step where Luis Costa and young Daniel had often sat to watch her work. Over the past two days she had missed their interested questions as she'd gone about her tasks.

Echo's inquisitive nose discovered the freshly tilled soil, prompting Sophie to call out, *"Nânnîn!*

163

If you *dare* dig up those anemones—" She didn't state what the punishment would be, for her sharp cry had been enough of a deterrent.

The culprit cocked her head, and her ears lifted. With a piercing yelp, she raced around the side of the house. She soon pranced back into view bounding beside her master.

His face lit up when he saw Sophie, his smile sent her spirits soaring to the skies. Until she recalled why she should distrust it.

"Here you are, exactly as I left you. No, don't take off your pinny, it makes you look so industrious."

Sophie forgot to welcome him, she was so dismayed by the dark splotches all over his breeches. *"Ma fé,* what have you been doing? You have dirt on your—" Her astonished gaze fell upon his firm thighs and calves. "On your clothes."

"Yes, I know."

He held out his hands and she took them. She breathed in the mingled scents of sandalwood shaving soap and leather saddlery.

"I bring you good tidings. Yesterday I talked to that man Jones, and again this morning—"

"You brought my rose list?" she asked eagerly.

"I haven't. But I did manage to discover some names, and committed them to memory. *Rosa mundi* is there just as you hoped, he says it has striped petals of carmine and white, or palest pink."

"Yes, I know—it's my favorite." Delighted by his new enthusiasm, she made no attempt to unclasp their hands. "What else?"

"Alba semi plena," he enunciated carefully.

"The fabled White Rose of York," she interrupted. He stood so close that the buttons of his riding coat pressed against her breasts. "Go on."

"And Velvet roses. I saw them myself—leaf buds have begun sprouting. I told Jones he couldn't move them until after they've bloomed."

A strong gust of wind whipped her pinafore like a sail, and trifled with his hair. Impatiently he plowed his fingers through the black curls in an effort to restore order, disarranging them far more than the breeze had done.

"I found a florilegium in the castle library. The Velvet rose is a form of *Rosa gallica*, with masses of petals, the deepest red imaginable."

Why he should be so intensely interested in that particular variety, Sophie couldn't imagine. His conversion from indifferent client to fellow rose-fancier was as endearing as it was perplexing.

She asked, "Did you dirty yourself grubbing about in the rose beds with Mr. Jones?"

"Daniel insisted on one last game of rough-and-tumble before I left Bevington. As you see, my compliance cost me dearly. I'll have to discard these breeches, unless you think they can be salvaged."

"My servant Mary cleans her husband's dirty leathers with soft soap and a flannel," Sophie recalled. "Doesn't your valet have a trick of his own?"

His mouth compressed into a taut, flat line. "I expect so."

The blue eyes had narrowed until they were slits, and he was glowering as he hadn't done for quite a long time. Sophie wondered how Luis had displeased him. Seeking to restore his good mood, she told him that his sister had recovered from her indisposition.

"But she hasn't yet left the house, not even to visit the Pump Room. She isn't idle, though. She has sorted through her gowns and set aside the other possessions she wants transferred to the castle. Her trunks are stacked in the upper corridor."

"Not for long. The carrier fetches them tomorrow, and we'll depart the following morning. I trust you'll also be ready to travel?"

"At a moment's notice," she responded promptly.

"Excellent."

After he went up the stairs and into the house, she realized that he hadn't alluded to the shameful proposition he'd made on the day of his departure.

The earl's return put an end to the increasingly frantic scurryings of the harassed servants. Unlike his sister, an impetuous and disorganized manager, he issued commands calmly and clearly. Cherished ornaments were stripped from the tabletops and mantel shelves, wrapped in brown paper, and placed in sturdy packing crates, each identified with a letter inscribed in black chalk. The furnishings disappeared beneath the Holland cloths that would guard them from the ravages of dust and sunlight. Tradesmen's bills arrived hourly, and were settled on the spot.

The next morning, Lord Bevington spent an hour closeted in his study with a pair of lawyers, one old and one young. In his absence, his sister fluttered about the house distractedly, dodging the footmen and maids and brushing off Sophie's attempts to calm her. With the arrival of the carrier's wagon, chaos reigned once more. Echo signified her disapproval of the proceedings with flattened ears and drooping tail. Lying down in the middle of the entrance hall, she ignored all attempts to shift her.

As the solicitors passed her on their way out she growled at them ferociously, until silenced by her master and ordered outside.

Marching over to Cecelia, the earl said, "You're wearing yourself out, for no good reason as far as I can see. Did the footboy fetch your daily dose of well-water from the Pump Room?"

"I suppose so," she said absentmindedly. "I haven't drunk it yet."

"Do so now, otherwise you'll forget. And please, let these good people go about their business undisturbed. Go to your room and read your novel, or lie down for a nap."

"But the carrier has just come, and I must—" Her head swiveled to follow the progess of a manservant. "Treat that box with especial care, Edward."

"Yes, madam."

"You're supposed to call him Bitton," Cass reminded her, "we've promoted him from footman to butler."

"I know," she said wearily, "but my mind is all a muddle. You're right, *meu irmão*, I do need rest." She drifted up the staircase, supporting herself with the handrail.

Next he suggested to Sophie that they also make themselves scarce while the staff loaded the trunks and boxes onto the wagon. "Take refuge in my study—but mind you don't trip over the stacks of books."

Sophie stepped carefully around the obstacles as she entered his private retreat. The room had already lost much of its character, for the glass-fronted cabinets no longer held his collection of mementos from other lands, and the usual array of wine and brandy decanters was missing.

He cleared away the news-sheets cluttering an armchair and encouraged her to sit.

"Can't I help you sort through your books?"

"If you don't mind, I'd be grateful. This lot is ready to be wrapped and crated."

They worked together in companionable silence. He roamed from bookcase to bookcase, selecting volumes and dusting each leather cover with a rag before he surrendered it to Sophie. By studying the title pages she educated herself about his primary interests—agriculture, foreign travel—and discovered that he read French as well as Portuguese. He preferred plays to poetry, and the absence of any classical texts told her that he'd given up on the Greeks and Romans when he finished his schooling. Many of his books were antiquated, printed in old-fashioned type on rough, thick paper. Others were so new that their pages hadn't even been cut.

"Here's one you'll like," he said, presenting her with an octavo edition. "*Bacon's Essays*. Didn't he write one about gardening?"

She nodded. "I haven't read it for a long while, but I remember the opening sentence. 'God almighty first planted a garden—and indeed, it is the purest of human pleasures.'"

When she reached for a sheet of newspaper to wrap around it, he told her to keep it separate from the rest. "It's yours now."

"What if you should need it?"

"I can probably find another copy in the castle library. Perhaps you'll value this little book more than the ring I gave you."

The ring.

Sophie's first impulse had been to return it to him, lest she be compromised by keeping it. But sufficient time had passed that she could regard it as harmless, and she hated to give up her only souvenir of her visit to the Hot Wells. Examining the book of essays, Sophie remembered that Andrew

Searle had presented her with a copy of his philosophical treatise, a far more personal gift than this. But he hadn't expected her to become his mistress, either.

Their cozy comradeship ended abruptly when Edward Bitton announced the arrival of two gentlemen callers.

"Waiting on the doorstep, my lord—no room for them in the hall." He handed over a pair of cards.

Cass's brows darted upward as he read the inscription aloud. *"H. Repton, Landscape Gardener. Hare Street, near Romford, Essex."*

Sophie glanced up from Bacon's gardening essay. *"Sapresti!"*

When he surrendered the card, Sophie glared at the familiar scene, a landscape of woodland and water. Two male figures—the great man and an assistant—posed before a surveying instrument, observing a party of laborers wielding axes and pushing wheelbarrows.

"And this," he said, handing over the second card, "belongs to your former associate."

"Fingal Moncrieff? *Bouôn Dgieu,* why would either of them come here?"

"By all means let's find out," said Cass, nodding at his servant.

The most famous garden-maker in the land strode confidently into the library and removed his round-brimmed hat, bowing low. His hairline receded almost to the middle of his skull; the powdered locks were cropped short at the sides and pulled tightly back in a queue.

"Lord Bevington, my apologies for intruding at this inconvenient time. And Mrs. Pinnock is here as well!" He nodded in Sophie's direction. "Madam, as always it is a pleasure to meet you."

"The pleasure is mutual, sir." Jumped-up haberdasher, she fumed while bestowing a false smile upon him.

Her husband had been amused by her disdain for his professional rival. Tobias had regarded Repton as a clever practitioner, working hard to fill the void created by the death of the great Capability Brown. But in Sophie's opinion he was no great artist, nor a master of horticulture.

"We stopped at Bevington Castle yesterday," he was telling the earl, "and your groundskeeper said we'd find you at Clifton. By happy coincidence I was on my way to Blaise to call upon my client Mr. Scandrett, who is altering a hillside cottage on his property in accordance with my Red Book recommendation. Moncrieff, my architectural assistant, is just the man for the job."

"Mr. Moncrieff and I have already met," said Cass thinly.

The Scotsman insinuated himself into the conversation by commenting, "That was before Mr. Repton invited me to join his practice."

"Quite so," Cass agreed. "At that time you were trying to impress me by claiming another artist's designs as your own. I hope you gained your present position more honestly."

"Mr. Repton," said Sophie hastily, "is fortunate to have such a talented associate." Moncrieff's flashing eyes and ruddy cheeks warned her that he was losing his fragile control over his temper.

A vindictive man, he might well retaliate with a fatal dose of the truth. She shrank from acknowledging their past conspiracies, and couldn't bear for her employer—or his—to learn that she'd engaged in dishonest practices. Too many patrons had received Blue Books attributed to Tobias Pinnock but which had actually been Sophie's creations. And she wouldn't let her former partner wreck her chances of establishing a respectable trade under her own name. Or worse, impeach Tobias Pinnock's lasting reputation for integrity in the presence of his most illustrious and influential competitor.

Smiling at Repton, she added, "Had you solicited my recommendation, sir, I would have given it wholeheartedly. Mr. Moncrieff is entirely worthy of your trust."

The architect's flush receded, but his manner was stiff when he said, "I thank you, madam. How astonished I was when that fellow Jones informed us that you alone will be responsible for improving the landscape at Bevington."

Impossible to improve upon perfection, she thought.

"Mrs. Pinnock has already done great things here at Summit House," said the earl. "I am vastly pleased with all that she has accomplished, and invite you both to tour my fine new landscape."

His compliment failed to gladden Sophie. She was horrified by the prospect of hearing Humphry Repton pass judgment on her handiwork. But there was no evading the ordeal, Lord Bevington was determined to show off his grounds.

The splendid view across the Avon was the first thing to excite Repton's admiration. "The drama of the gorge is sublime," he enthused. "And in the distance, hanging woods and outcroppings of rock—magnificent!"

Fingal Moncrieff bobbed his carroty head, but added nothing to the great man's raptures.

"The arrangement of boulders and trees in the foreground is most appropriate," Repton continued. "I, too, would have planted conifers, their vertical lines provide a most desirable contrast to the rectilinear shape of the house, with its classically

Palladian structure." Rather than addressing Sophie, he directed his remarks to her employer. "The positioning of these pines and cedars, and their maturity, gives the impression that they've grown here for many years. Yet they must have been planted quite recently."

"Within the past fortnight," Cass confirmed.

"Astonishing." Deigning at last to notice Sophie, Repton said, "I am curious to know, Mrs. Pinnock, how you managed to achieve such naturalness."

Did he seriously expect her to impart her secret? It was a simple but effective one: she'd selected the largest available specimens and planted them closer than the recommended distance so the branches would touch one another, as in a forest. Then she'd covered the bare ground underneath with mosses and ferns, knowing they would thrive in the damp shade. She wanted to do more than imitate natural scenery—by directly copying nature, she'd succeeded in recreating it.

"It's a trick I learned from my husband," she said, but offered no details.

"He instructed you to use so many evergreens?"

"That is my own choice. Conifers provide foliage in winter months, when deciduous trees are bare."

"You have included a great many flowering shrubs, I see."

"Not even the most modern landscape can do without color and fragrance."

Said Fingal Moncrieff dourly, " 'Twould not be a Pinnock design without floral displays."

Sophie glared at him. A great debate had raged during their uneasy partnership, and she knew he disapproved of her methods. "Flowers are lovely to look upon. They lift the spirits. They perfume the air. They can be cut and taken indoors. They can be dried for potpourri or distilled to make fragrant water. I'm far too practical a gardener not to consider the utility of the plants I choose."

Focusing his round eyes upon her, Humphry Repton said ponderously, "Madam, you should consider the primary rule of landscape gardening— to impress upon the viewer the importance of the landowner. Our clients come to us because they want to be in the forefront of fashion."

"And you, sir, care too little for the function of pleasure grounds. They are meant to be used, and lived in, and enjoyed."

Clearly nettled by her criticism, he answered quickly, "Yes, yes, that is also important. Certainly it is."

Having won this concession from him, she was emboldened to point out, "Yet your parks, like those of Capability Brown, are dominated by extensive grassland—vast green fields with a few clumps of trees. You both have replaced far too many gardens of old-fashioned, highly scented flowers that delight our senses of sight and smell. As for the ornamental water features you recommend—*ma fé*, I cannot understand why you chose a winding serpentine river over a canal."

"Straight lines are not natural," he decreed.

"Nature must rule," Moncrieff added. "Artifice should never intrude."

"Oh? What is more instrusive than felling a formal alley of trees that has stood for a century? Or replacing native varieties with exotics? Consider Mr. Beckford of Fonthill—he planted one hundred thousand specimens last year, few of them English. For some unfathomable reason he's determined to create an Alpine forest on the chalky hills of Wiltshire. There is nothing natural about that! Or desirable," she concluded pithily.

"Sophia," Moncrieff intoned, "remember to whom you are speaking."

Disregarding the Scotsman, she resumed her attack upon Repton. "You wreak havoc everywhere you go, sir. You advise your fashion-conscious patrons to knock down their garden walls and ancient woodlands. But unless they live on for fifty years or more they won't see their magnificent new landscape reach its peak of perfection. By then you'll have gone out of fashion yourself. How does it feel to know that future designers will regard your style as antiquated, and be called upon to 'improve' your undulating parks and remove your stylistic embellishments?"

"Madam, you have followed the tenets of modern landscaping here at Summit House."

"I destroyed nothing," she defended herself. "Have you never once regretted sacrificing so many historic Tudor and Jacobean gardens in your effort to satisfy your patrons' desire to be fashionable?"

"I admire beauty in any form," Repton acknowledged. "The human mind has an inborn appreciation of order and symmetry, it is true. In your case, Mrs. Pinnock, it seems to be overly developed."

"Why must we always reduce existing gardens to something inferior, why can we not preserve what is already there?" She studied the faces of her listeners. Repton was skeptical, Moncrieff frowned, and the earl was—

The earl!

He'd kept silent so long that she had forgotten about him. All this time she'd spoken her mind freely, never realizing that she was repudiating all the high-flown theories she had tossed about when showing him her Bevington sketches. She'd made it clear—in front of witnesses—that she harbored a distaste for the task he was paying her a fortune to perform. *Bêtasse*, she mocked herself. Oh, what a great fool she was! Such recklessness would be rewarded with dismissal.

Her two male rivals coveted her Bevington project. They were transparent in their desire to steal her noble client. And she'd made it so very easy for them.

"My lord," said Repton silkily, "I am amazed that you would consult a reactionary—indeed, a revolutionary. Perhaps this explains why your planned alterations at Bevington Castle are proceeding so slowly."

"You are mistaken," said Cass, coming forward to stand beside Sophie. "I insisted that Mrs. Pinnock leave her work there in order to supervise the changes my sister and I wanted here. I assure you, she has produced a splendid set of plans for the castle grounds."

Sophie's mortification intensified at his steadfast defense.

The castle's flowery borders and shaded shrubbery walks and overgrown rose bower meant more to her now than the prestige she'd sought two months ago. And she couldn't even save them by resigning. Repton and Moncrieff would fall all over themselves to take her place, and gleefully tear down walls and uproot the plants they considered uninteresting.

While Lord Bevington was seeing his visitors off the premises, Sophie wandered to the edge of the cliff. Drearily she stared out over the view that had so excited Repton.

Everything had gone wrong. If she didn't extricate herself from this impossible and hopeless situation, it would only worsen. She had to consider her reputation, her private one and her professional one, and the dangers to both.

For a long time she stood there, meditating on her mistakes and pondering methods of repairing the damage.

When the earl returned, she held her position. She was reluctant to face him, fearing that he could sabotage her newly formed decision with a single smile.

"I believed I knew you rather well, Sophie," he said, in that deep, rich voice. "But when you attacked Repton, you managed to surprise me."

She stared at the rugged vista without seeing it, saying dully, "I should have known better. Two against one—I stood no chance against them."

A firm, insistent hand on her shoulder compelled her to turn around. His blue eyes shone down at her from a great height. "My brave Sophie."

The impact of his kiss caught her off guard. Her emotions were running high, her resistance was at low ebb. She tried to swim against the rising tide of desire, but it washed over her, choking her. It dragged her down to the depths, then relentlessly pitched her onto an unfamiliar shore.

She clutched at him like a drowning victim, parting her lips for his life-giving breath. Was he her salvation? Or had he called forth this tempest in order to destroy her?

"*Nânnîn*. No, you cannot." Again his lips claimed her, interrupting her protest. "Do this. Not now."

He rubbed his cheek against hers. "Is it so terrible?"

"Intolerable," she managed to say and took a backward step. "Lord Bevington, I am resigning my position."

Her announcement had a profound effect. His

black head jerked up and his eyebrows swept downward in his fiercest frown. "You're bound by a contract—at your insistence, not mine."

"I'm asking to be released. Don't make this more difficult than it need be."

"Damn it, Sophie, what a vexing creature you are!"

"I'm giving up my career as a landscape gardener altogether."

"To do what? I can't imagine you as a lady of leisure."

She put a greater distance between them. "I shall seek employment as a botanical artist."

"By all means, if that's what you prefer. You'll find a multitude of plants at Bevington to inspire you, I have enough growing there to fill whole volumes of illustrations."

"I'm returning to Chiswick," she insisted. "To be near Mr. Curtis, the printer—he purchases my pictures, and often pays me to color the finished engravings. He has a display garden himself, in the Fulham Road. The subscription fee is two guineas, but he grants me free entry." Aware that she was rambling, she concluded, "Besides, I have my own garden—and I've neglected it far too long."

"And what about mine?"

"Naturally I shall finish your plans. After that, any contractor can carry out the work. I'll be happy to suggest some names."

"I don't want anyone else. I've always intended for you to supervise the alterations yourself. Your contract stipulates it." He shook his head at her. "One encounter with Repton, and you decide to give up. This isn't like you."

"I'm not giving up, *pon du tout*. I view this as retirement." Lifting her chin, she explained, "In my own mind, I've attained the pinnacle of success. For just under an hour the most highly respected of all landscape gardeners regarded me as a successful rival—and accused me of being a threat to our profession. What was it he called me? A reactionary. A revolutionary.''

"His opinion be damned, and to hell with him.''

"I've labored in his shadow just long enough to know it doesn't suit me,'' Sophie declared. "I was terribly unhappy in my partnership with Fingal Moncrieff. When he stole my portfolio I retaliated in the only way I could, by setting up as a competitor—to him, and to Repton and Mickle and Emes and the rest of their kind. I'm satisfied with my achievements, insignificant though they may seem to others. I've completed the project here at Summit House, and you declare yourself satisfied. Rest assured, the final watercolors and planting recommendations for Bevington will be presented to you in a blue leather binding as agreed.''

He regarded her silently for some time before saying, "You want me to believe Humphry Repton's visit is the reason for your resignation. I suspect it has more to do with what passed between us before I left for Bevington.''

She forced herself to meet his piercing stare. "Yes, that also contributed to my decision. Stop smiling at me like that,'' she chided. "It will do you no good.''

"You always smile back so prettily, I never guessed it was distasteful to you.''

"It is. I hate being preyed upon. And if I continue plying my trade, it won't be long before I must fend off some other aristocratic patron.''

"Is that all I am to you, a *patron*? After ogling you and touching you and stealing kisses at every opportunity?''

"That's all you can ever be,'' she answered. "I

have been a wife, Cassian, I am a widow now. I do not aspire to be anything more."

"You are also the woman I want. I need you, Sophie."

"Stop, please," she begged him. "I feel torn up inside when you say such things. This is a sad end to our association—but end it must."

He had to keep her at Bevington. His great house needed a mistress. So did he.

There would be no permanence to their relationship, he reminded himself. He was falling in love with a woman whose prior experience of love made her incapable of reciprocating. A grand passion could not be one-sided. She'd leave him eventually.

The prospect was like a slash across his heart.

Coveting this enigma that only one other man had possessed, he reevaluated his strategy—not objectively, but from her unique perspective. Sophie came from a good family, her uncle was Seigneur of Anneville. She'd been wed to a man both respectable and respected. Taking these facts into consideration, Cass could see why she was so affronted by sexual overtures from a libidinous earl. She knew her own worth. And he was rapidly discovering it.

What would her answer be, he wondered, if he suggested a more honorable alliance?

Marriage had never been an option in his previous entanglements with Englishwomen. Those who had shared his bed had belonged to an unsuitable class, and his encounters with them had been brief. In Portugal, his most enduring liaison had been with a married noblewoman, and its chief purpose had been to alleviate boredom.

Don't even think of it, he warned himself. Sophie would never commit herself wholeheartedly to another man—unless he possessed all the excellent qualities of Tobias Pinnock and perhaps not even then. Better to take whatever he could get, and be satisfied.

He advanced purposefully, trapping her between two large boulders and the cliff edge. "I won't let you go, Sophie."

"You have no power to stop me," she said defiantly.

Each gazed fiercely back at the other.

Their long, intent regard was broken by a frantic voice calling, "Lord Bevington! Missus Pinnock!"

A young woman hurtled toward them, her feet scattering the fresh-laid gravel.

"Isn't she one of the castle servants?"

"Nan Parham," said Sophie, alarmed by her maid's reddened eyes and blotched cheeks.

His voice was taut with dread as he asked, "What's the matter, girl? Has Daniel suffered an accident?"

"Nay, he's hearty enough, but so downcast because of what's happened. 'Tis your lordship's valet, the foreigner. He's gone missing. No one's seen him for two days." Nan paused to fill her lungs with air. "That Portugee woman, Maria, come to me this morning. I could 'ardly understand her—she was weeping into her shawl, and every other word was gibberish or else a groan. She kept making a cross over herself, the way the papists do."

"Why?" Cass prompted.

"She says he's dead." Her eyes welled with tears.

Alarm inched down Sophie's spine. "*Nânnîn.* Such a thing isn't possible."

"She took me to his room, I saw his bed myself— 'tweren't mussed, or slept on. His clothes were in the wardrobe, folded up so neat-like. We even found his valise," she added sorrowfully, bowing her head.

"That's not sufficient proof that Maria's fears are true," said Cass. "She's a good woman, but far from clever—or rational. She builds up every minor catastrophe into a crisis of major proportions."

"Did you come so far on foot, Nan?"

"Nay, ma'am, I rode 'ere on the stagecoach. Maria said his lordship needed to know, and she paid the fare. 'Tweren't no inside places, so I sat 'igh up on the roof."

"*Ch'est damage*," Sophie sympathized. "I can imagine how uncomfortable that must have been. I'll take you to a quiet place where you can sit down and drink some tea."

"Wait," said Cass.

Sophie, already leading the travel-weary Nan towards the house, looked back at him.

"Here's a chance to prove your famous boast that you can be ready to leave at a moment's notice. We depart for the castle immediately—you and Cecelia and me. Nan, you're coming with us, but this time you shall sit inside the carriage."

The girl mumbled her thanks for his generosity.

"There must be a logical explanation," he added. "Luis wouldn't run away, certainly not when I've saddled him with so many household responsibilities."

"It seems unlikely," Sophie acknowledged. "He would not dare to risk angering you."

"Are you implying that he's afraid of me?"

The question startled her. "*Nânnîn-dgia*. His devotion to you and Mrs. Fonseca is remarkable. And he's so fond of Daniel." She'd tried to quell his obvious concerns, yet his face was more somber than before.

"I shouldn't be at all surprised to find that he

has returned, safe and sound, by the time we reach Bevington.''

If only he'd smiled at her, Sophie might have been comforted by his hopeful prophecy.

And of all love's joyful flame
I the bud and blossom am.

GILES FLETCHER

Chapter 11

Springtime was the season most closely associated with poetry. So why, wondered Andrew Searle, was composition as unsatisfying now as it had been in the dark depths of winter? Seated on the stump of a felled oak, surrounded by nature, he struggled to recapture his lost enthusiasm for his art.

Looking to love for inspiration, he came up empty. The awkward and thus far woefully ineffective courtship he'd begun should inspire fine and touching verses. But he simply wasn't able to create anything worthwhile.

Sophie Pinnock's impending departure from Bevington was a severe blow to his dream of making her his wife. If he attempted a passionate appeal, flinging his arms around her and declaring his undying devotion, she would surely think he'd lost his wits. Abandoned gestures of that sort were for men more heroic than he. He preferred a more reasonable approach, and required time to organize his disordered thoughts into coherent persuasions.

He was studying the diary he'd kept seven years ago in London, when he'd been a poorly paid journalist. During the height of his infatuation with Cecelia Carysfort, he'd written a number of sonnets detailing her beauty and charms. They were simple and effective, and if he made a few minor deletions and amendments—altering references to hair and eye color—he could present them to Sophie.

He thumbed through the entries. Page after page detailed his wild exploits with Cass. Together they had frequented brothels and bagnios in the Covent Garden district. They had visited the roughest and most dangerous taverns of Seven Dials, drinking and exchanging rude jests with the regulars. As dawn broke over the vast city, they had slunk back to their very different worlds—Cass to a grand terrace house in Marylebone, Andrew to his dismal one-room lodging near Blackfriars Bridge.

Arriving at a familiar and significant passage, he read every word.

Last night Cass produced a vial of Bristol glass, assuring me that its contents would soothe my pangs and heart-burnings. (Knowing not that his sister is the cause.) Laudanum, he declared, is the remedy for his sufferings. What they might be I cannot guess, blessed as he is with his handsome phiz—a quick mind—the roguish charm that endears him to the fair sex—abundant wealth—rich and influential friends.

At his urging, I swallowed the dose. Laudanum's power over my mind is not easily described. Vapors of calmness suffused my hitherto busy brain, a sense of lassitude stole over my corpus. A wondrous sensation indeed. Alas, my funds are too limited to allow frequent indulgence. But Cass is a generous friend, he offers to supply the miraculous substance whenever I may require it.

Reviewing this account of his introduction to the drug, he realized how that fateful vial had altered the direction of his life. He continued turning the leaves of his journal, each filled with enthusiastic and rapturous descriptions of the dreams and visions induced by the opiate. Andrew alternately smiled and frowned over his writings. Unaided, his recollections of that period were vague.

At first he'd been conservative in his use of the drug, while Cass had consumed it lavishly and recklessly, desperate to escape a gnawing problem that he refused to discuss. But eventually he'd ceased taking it altogether, swearing never again to seek solace from what he referred to as a wickedly intoxicating fluid.

"For God's sake, man, come back to earth."

Andrew looked up from his book.

His friend stood before him—vigorous, healthy, liberated from their shared vice.

"I hope I'm not interrupting your work."

Shaking his head, Andrew answered, "I was reliving our London adventures."

"Are you still as fervent a diarist as you were back then?"

"It is a habit, I could not stop if I wanted to."

"Another day has passed, and still no news of Luis," said Cass heavily. "Three full days. I'm beginning to believe he may have deserted me after all."

"Is it such a loss? I never have understood your fondness for that boy."

"A discreet and reliable servant is hard to come by. Were you conscious of anything unusual in his behavior before he vanished? Did you ever observe him with a stranger?"

"No strangers hereabouts, to my knowledge. Twice on the same day I saw him with that Welsh gardener. At midday and again at dusk."

"Do you remember where?"

"The first time, they were under the laburnums. Jones was attaching the vines to the frame, and Luis stood by chattering at him. Later I noticed them strolling together among the roses. It was nearly dark."

"And you're certain he was with Jones that night?"

Shrugging, Andrew replied, "I assumed so. But no, I'm not positive. You should ask the man."

"I don't think he would admit to it. When I wanted to know what he was doing at the time Luis disappeared, he claimed he was drawing up the list of rose specimens for Sophie Pinnock. Not that she wants it any longer." Cass kicked at the decaying leaves with the toe of his boot. "She plans to leave the castle as soon as she's made a copy of my landcape design for herself."

"How long will that take?"

"Judging from her diligence, I'd say she means to finish as quickly as she can. Am I such an ogre, is that why everyone is abandoning me? You'd rather live near London. Luis took off without a word. Now Sophie is going back to Chiswick. I wish—" Again he jabbed the ground with his foot. "I don't know what I wish."

Andrew mulled over this ambiguous remark, disliking its implications. Cass had the look of a man struggling to unburden himself.

He couldn't possibly be seriously involved with Sophie Pinnock. Oh, he might lust for her, but that wouldn't last—the instant the object of his desire removed herself from his orbit, his fancy would light upon another. He could have any woman in the world, he need but produce that devilish smile and crook his finger. Sophie was a simple, honorable woman, nothing like the flashy trollops Cass had consorted with in London.

"I've fallen in love with her, Drew."

He summoned a laugh, but there was no life in it. "You, Cass, in love?"

"My heart has spoken. Hers, it seems, lies buried in her husband's grave."

Andrew also assumed this to be the case, and wasn't troubled in the least. Having nothing more than affection to give her, he demanded nothing more in return. A hopeless passion was not for him, as he'd learned when he'd been dazzled by the rich and beautiful Cecelia Carysfort. She had stirred his muse and fired his emotions—but he hadn't really known her. Sophie, such a steadying, calming influence, had become a true friend. She was a source of support and companionship—she would cure his wretched aimlessness. With that busy little lady at his side, he could lead a better and more productive life.

He was relieved by his rival's evident distress. If the widow hadn't tumbled to Cass, with his good looks and title and great wealth, then there was still a chance he could win her for himself.

"This is a most inconvenient time to embark upon romance," Cass continued. "Cecelia is down with one of her nervous attacks, and I'm struggling to manage the estate. I don't relish the prospect of traveling back and forth to Chiswick to see Sophie. But I cannot hold her here against her will, like a villain from one of your wild gothic poems."

Andrew narrowed his eyes. Was he being mocked?

"It seems the only way I can keep her respect—assuming that I've got it—is by setting her free."

"You're agitated, you aren't making any sense," he declared. "You ought to have a glass of wine. Or," he added, thinking of his own needs, "a calming dram."

"No," said Cass emphatically. "Whatever frustrations lie ahead, I shall meet them. Never again will I disintegrate into that numb, ineffectual being I became under the influence of the drug you imbibe so freely. It destroyed my life, and Cecelia's, and—" He broke off. "What a damned fool I was. If Sophie ever learned of my weakness, how she would despise me."

Weak, indeed, thought Andrew disdainfully. Cass had dabbled but a few months only, he couldn't possibly comprehend the true power and effectiveness of opium and its extract.

His hand curled on the journal lying on his lap, a detailed record of the foul history Cass meant to conceal from his ladylove. A powerful weapon. Rather, he amended, it might have been if it hadn't also revealed every flaw in his own character.

"Go to London," Cecelia pleaded. "It's our only hope of proving Sir Michael abducted Luis."

"Is that what you believe?"

"Don't you?"

Cass studied his sister. Worry had taken its toll on her slender frame, and her cheek was as white as the damask pillowcase on which it rested.

"I'm not sure. I've made inquiries, but none of the servants ever saw Tait here, and there's no report of his stopping in the village. This is such a quiet hamlet, the presence of an unfamiliar gentleman in town garb would be noticed and commented on."

"He might have sent someone else to do his dirty work. That would be more like him," she declared bitterly.

Cass recalled his encounter with the scarred baronet, whose brawny footman had raised a cudgel against Luis. Tait had already demonstrated his capacity for violence.

"Will you go?"

Cass nodded. "I've no other choice. With each passing day there's less likelihood that Luis will reappear as magically as he vanished. But you must promise to behave sensibly while I'm away. No more lying in bed all day, or refusing your meals."

She managed a listless nod.

"And you must take more exercise, as Dr. Jenner recommends. Walk in the gardens, they are truly a sight to behold. Devote yourself to Daniel. He's so withdrawn, not himself at all. He clings to Maria, and won't go to bed unless Echo is allowed to sleep beside him. He wants comforting, Cecelia."

"What can I do?"

"Read to him. Teach him to play the pianoforte."

"He's too young to learn."

"You began your lessons at the same age," Cass reminded her.

"So I did." She heaved a plaintive sigh. "My aunt instructed me."

"The boy is lonely without Luis. He's attached to Sophie as well, and now she's preparing to leave."

"*Meu irmão*, you aren't letting your pretty little widow slip away?"

Her question startled him. He'd supposed she was too worried about Luis and too fearful of Tait to consider his affairs. "She has resigned. All that remains to be settled between us is her fee for services rendered."

"That is *not* all," she declared with more vigor than she had displayed in days. "I thought you were going to offer her your protection."

"I did. And it was refused, in no uncertain terms."

"You might have told me!"

"My pride was wounded. But not, I think, as much as hers."

"I must say, I'm surprised," she told him.

"She's not just another one of my fancy women, as you seem to think. I was slow to accept the truth of it myself. Trouble is, I've made such a muddle that now I don't know what to do."

"Don't be a simpleton, Cass. Let her know you care, perhaps you'll discover she cares for you."

Heartened by this comment, he asked hopefully, "Has she said something to you?"

"No."

"That's encouraging," he said with heavy sarcasm. "She doesn't talk about me. She doesn't talk *to* me. We've scarce exchanged a dozen words since our journey from Clifton. She avoids me."

"That could be a good sign. If she were indifferent, she wouldn't be at such pains to keep away from you."

"Cold comfort."

He valued Sophie's companionship, he appreciated her wit, he was dazzled by her face and form. She was as intoxicating as opium, and even more addictive, for each small dose of her gave him a stronger craving.

But this stubbornly virtuous female, who would not have him as a lover, had given him no chance to reveal his new aspiration to be something more.

Her husband.

It was possible—though far from certain—that he might, over time and after exhaustive persuasions, entice her to his bed. But he was not fool enough to suppose that she would love him for stealing her precious honor. Only by offering matrimony could he hope to rise in her esteem. He needed to demonstrate that he wasn't merely a selfish, opportunistic cad, wanting only to pounce on her and paw at her, that his feelings were as strong and true as Tobias Pinnock's had been.

His latest and most secret ambition was not to be shared with anyone, not even his sister.

Making his way to the chamber door, he told her, "I'm off to the cellars. No," he said, in response to her raised eyebrows, "not to drown my sorrows, but to determine how many additional wine racks are needed. The shipment from Fry's is due to arrive in a few weeks' time."

He spent an agreeable half hour in the musty, dark vault. Stripped of coat and vest, he helped his butler shift a number of smaller casks from one side of the room to the other to make room for his recent acquisitions.

Nobleman he might be, but he wanted no majordomo in his household. He liked this young Bristolian. Not only was Edward Bitton undaunted by the size of the establishment over which he presided, he had an aptitude for selecting wines.

"Your palate is remarkably acute," Cass praised him as they worked together.

" 'Tis no great wonder, my lord," the young man replied. "You might say my grandmother was in the wine trade. She worked as a cork cutter."

Wiping his hand on his breeches, Cass surveyed a set of wooden shelves. "The estate carpenter does a commendable job. It's time I had him come take measurements for the new racks."

Said the butler, reviewing the notations in his cellar book, "There's great deal of wine here that wants drinking, my lord. The last earl laid down a quantity of the eighty-eight. And some of the cognacs have been sitting here since the War in the Americas." He rapped his knuckles lightly against one of the casks.

"No time like the present," Cass asserted. He ran his eye over the ledger. "My predecessor was partial to Bristol milk—my uncle's name for Spanish sherry. We were weaned on it, my sister and I. Pour out a glass for Mrs. Fonseca and carry it up to her bedchamber—and bring another to me. I'll be in the library."

"Yes, my lord."

Cass picked up his coat from a stool and flung it over his shoulder. "You can spend the rest of the day drawing off samples and rating them. Drink as freely as you please, you'll not be waiting at table tonight. I daresay I shall be the only one dining downstairs, and a footman can serve me."

Smiling broadly, Bitton said, "Thank you, my lord."

Cass wandered upstairs to his book-lined refuge, intending to select a guide to estate management to take on the journey to town. He found Sophie standing behind the broad leather-topped desk, sorting and stacking papers—with Drew assisting her.

For once, his friend's hair was neatly combed and he wore the least shabby of his jackets. This was perhaps the only time in their long acquaintance, Cass realized in dismay, that his attire compared unfavorably with Drew's. Unfortunately, there was no way to repair his loosened cravat and rumpled shirt.

Sophie glanced up briefly, commenting, "A few

days ago you were covered in dirt, my lord, and now—sawdust? You and Daniel have been playing rough again."

He might have known his sharp-eyed Sophie would notice. Carelessly he replied, "Country living has a detrimental effect on my appearance." He laid his coat across the back of his chair. "Were you waiting for me?"

Said his friend, "Mrs. Pinnock is putting your designs in the proper order for the printer. I've recommended Cottle of Bristol, who serves Coleridge and me so well."

"There," said Sophie, placing a title page on the top of the stack. "All is ready. I'm including detailed instructions about the materials and fonts I want used, and a sketch of the Bevington coat of arms for the cover. However, if your lordship prefers that I use the same firm responsible for all the other Pinnock Blue Books, I can carry them to London."

Favoring the option that would detain her the longer, Cass said curtly, "My own book should be produced in Bristol. We ought to discuss financial arrangements—a subject that can be of no interest to you, Drew," he told his friend pointedly. No tactic was too foul if it earned him a few precious minutes alone with Sophie. Love, lust, longing—the potent combination was unbearable.

He gritted his teeth when he saw how warmly she shook hands with the poet and thanked him for his advice about the printer. As he exited, Andrew narrowly avoided a collision with Bitton, arriving with the requested glass of sherry.

"Shall I fetch another for madam?" the butler inquired.

Cass looked to Sophie, but she shook her head. After dismissing the butler, he sat behind the desk.

"Do you mind if I look?" he asked, indicating the papers she'd arranged so carefully.

"They belong to you."

He made a cursory study of the written descriptions, plant lists, and annotations to the printer about typesetting. Then he examined the accompanying artwork. Each scene was meticulously drawn in pen and ink, finished with a watercolor wash. Despite his admiration of the artist's technique, Cass had an uneasy suspicion that she'd derived scant pleasure from her labors, that the joy of creation had been dimmed by regret. Because someone else would be responsible for bringing her visions to life?

She hovered nearby, anxiously awaiting his opinion.

"You have certainly earned your fee," he told her.

"I hope so." She reached for her own copy and placed it in her portfolio.

He studied the gentle contours of her profile. Her milky skin seemed paler than usual, or was it merely in contrast to the dark arching brows and incredibly thick lashes veiling her eyes?

Impetuously he reached for her hand. It was cool and smooth, like marble. "Sophie, I'm leaving for London tomorrow. To investigate Luis Costa's disappearance."

"The situation must be serious to take you so far," she responded gravely.

"I fear it may be."

How he wished he could share his and Cecelia's suspicion that Luis had been spirited away, that their enemy could be privy to the full history of their long residence in Portugal. No matter how discreet and trustworthy the valet might be in the abstract, if treated brutally—by Sir Michael Tait or another person—he was unlikely to hold his tongue.

But by telling her the truth now, he would lose all hope of achieving the greatest desire of his heart.

"Luis often seemed homesick," Sophie said meditatively. "Whenever he talked of Sintra and Colares, he stopped himself. I think it distressed him to speak of the places that were dear to him. Perhaps he decided to go back to Portugal, and didn't say so because he didn't want to disappoint you."

"Not only would I have permitted him to return, if he wished it, I'd have paid him his back wages and covered the costs of the voyage."

"Vessels bound for Lisbon sail from Bristol, don't they? You should make inquiries among the shipping agents there, before going all the way to London."

"I dare not delay my journey any longer." He bounded up from the chair.

After chewing her lip uncertainly, she asked, "Then we are to say our farewells now?"

"Unnecessary. You will stay at Bevington until I return."

"I'm sorry to disoblige you, my lord, but—"

"Just listen to me, Sophie. I don't speak as your patron, or as the Earl of Bevington. I stand here before you, an ordinary man with a most extraordinary affection for you."

"I will not stay. *Nânnîn-dgia!* How can I, when my work here is done? It isn't proper."

"Propriety be damned. I'm begging you. I have my reasons."

"I know them well," she retorted. "You mean to make me your *contchubinne,* and that I will never, ever be. I'm no ignorant Portuguese peasant, like

Luis Costa's sister. I can't be bought, or swept off my feet by—"

"What in bloody hell are you talking about?"

"You know." She chopped the air with her hand. "Inês. Luis told me how you lured his sister away from their village with an offer of money. She had large—she lived in your palace and was your— your—" A fiery flush stained her cheekbones. "He used the Portuguese word, he didn't know the English one," she concluded lamely.

"In English, the word is wet-nurse. I paid Inês to suckle Daniel. Cecelia wasn't able to."

"*Oh, las.*"

There was no mistaking the relief in that gusty sigh. "Why, Sophie, were you jealous?" His fingers followed the line of her jaw, then probed the fullness of her lower lip.

"*Pas eune mie.*" She shoved his hand away. "Not a bit."

"Liar," he said, turning the word into a caress. "And I thought you honest and true, a very marvel of virtue."

"My virtue," she said breathlessly, "is what you want to destroy."

"You jumped to the wrong conclusion. And not only about my association with Inês. My behavior has been crass at times, I admit, but my intentions are no longer so dishonorable as you believe."

Her head tipped back and she stared up at him. Her dark eyes were entirely blank.

He hadn't planned to make his declaration in his shirtsleeves. But he couldn't hold it back any longer, he needed to show her that he wasn't the villain whose motive she mistrusted. If he parted from her without expressing his deepest desire, she would go back to her Chiswick house, a shrine to her late, lamented husband. He must not let her, he could not bear to lose her.

Despite his great longing to hold her in his arms and whisper the words whirling in his brain, he stood stiffly. One hand balled itself into a fist, and he flattened the other on the desktop. He needed support, he was quaking from head to foot.

When he could no longer bear the tense silence, he broke it by speaking from his heart.

"I want you to stay, Sophie, but not as my mistress. If you are willing, I prefer to have you for my wife."

*The rule is certaine, that Plants for want of
Culture, degenerate to be baser in the same
Kinde; and sometimes so far, as to change into
another Kinde.*

FRANCIS BACON

Chapter 12

The slanting rays of an afternoon sun showered gold over the gardens. The most pleasant and peaceful time of day, thought Sophie as her
artist's eye feasted on the exquisite effect of sunlight shimmering on the canal. With her tasks complete, she could revel in solitude and idleness,
leisurely contemplating the scene before her.

This was her birthday, although no one was
aware of it. A new year, a fresh beginning—and
the proper time to consider her future.

I prefer to have you for my wife.

Twenty-one today, and she'd received three offers of marriage from three men. First Tobias, when
she was brimming with the optimism of extreme
youth. Next, the annoying Fingal Moncrieff, as
soon as her second year of mourning ended. And
now the insistent, compelling, and utterly bewil-
dering Earl of Bevington.

From the instant she first saw the man, she'd been acutely aware of his handsome face and splendid physique, although his arrogance had swiftly obliterated her favorable impressions. At the beginning of their association she hadn't guessed that her titled and wealthy employer would jolt her dormant emotions back to life, much less that she would be so moved by his kisses and embraces. The belief that his advances were a calculated attack upon her honor had strengthened her resistance.

The proposal changed everything.

Sophie bent over to gather a selection of wallflowers springing up along the terrace walk—white for moonlight, yellow for sunshine. Heartsease spilled out of the border and onto the path, and she was careful not to tread on the tiny tricolored blossoms.

The loss of a husband had harrowed her soul. The deep wound had eventually healed, just enough that she'd perceived the emptiness of her quiet life at Chiswick. Craving activity and an occupation, she'd accepted an offer of employment from a persuasive nobleman, never guessing that he would awaken her desire for so much more.

She snapped the stems of the gaudy, variegated tulips, adding them to her haphazard bouquet. The petals were fringed and boldly striped: crimson on white, yellow on blue, violet on pink.

Her flesh tingled at his touch, his warm glances heated her blood. In his arms, she melted. But that volatile earl did not, she fretted, inspire the same sweet tenderness she'd felt for her staid, dependable Tobias. Even so, her attraction to him was a powerful and disturbing one. She was torn, fearful that these turbulent new emotions might nullify her abiding affection for her departed spouse. He wanted to rush her into matrimony, without giving her sufficient time to discover for herself whether she cared for him enough to wed him. And he was so impatient—he would demand an answer the moment he returned from London.

She paused beneath the arching laburnums to study the racemes hanging from each branch. In a few weeks they would burst into golden bloom. Would she be there to see?

Entering the topiary garden, she asked herself whether the castle had enchanted her, or its master. Both, she decided, for the man and the place were so closely intertwined that neither her heart nor her mind could separate them.

If she married him, she must remain at Bevington—no great hardship, she felt so much at home. Yet she was aware of a faint, lingering nostalgia for her Chiswick villa, and an unbroken attachment to the garden she had made there.

She emerged from a cluster of clipped yews and came to a sudden stop. *"Ma fé!"* she gasped, as a figure in ghostly white glided toward her.

"Forgive me for startling you," Cecelia apologized. "After so many indoor days, I finally grew restless. I've worn myself out, and there's no bench to be found. What glorious flowers!"

Sophie handed over her bouquet. "Take them. They'll brighten your chamber."

"But you've chosen them for yourself."

Smiling, she said, "I can gather more. *Dé vrai*, they belong to your brother and I'm sure he'd want you to have them."

Cradling the bouquet in the crook of her arm, Cecelia fell into step with Sophie. Their conversations were less laborious than in the earliest stages of their acquaintance. But their experiences had been quite different, apart from being wed and

widowed, so they had never really confided in each
other.

Now Sophie couldn't even raise the one subject
that interested them equally—Cassian. She'd
promised she would maintain a circumspect silence
until after she had given him her decision, and the
strain of keeping the secret from his sister made
her uncomfortable.

Horticulture, she concluded, was the safest topic.
"Do you still miss your garden in Sintra?" she
asked.

The lovely face brightened. "Oh, yes."

"It must have been quite splendid. According to
his lordship, it was formal in style."

"Grander than this, yes, and more open, with
nicer walks—they were patterned on the Trianon
gardens at Versailles. Our grounds were delightfully sunny."

"Perhaps they only seem so in retrospect," said
Sophie.

"Oh, but I had to carry a parasol whenever I
went for a stroll," Cecelia insisted.

"And did the palace belong to your brother, or
your husband?"

"Cass purchased it outright from the Fonsecas,
impoverished Portuguese nobility, before the marriage. They couldn't afford its upkeep."

Cecelia seldom mentioned Senhor Fonseca,
whenever she did her decided neutrality gave no
clue about her feelings for him. Nevertheless, Sophie had always assumed their match had been one
of love, not of convenience. Now she wondered if
the gentleman had chosen the rich Miss Carysfort
in order to maintain his familial connection to the
property.

As they stepped into the rose garden, she asked,
"Do you imagine you'll marry again?"

"I'm quite certain that I shan't."

"Not even for your son's sake?"

"He has an attentive and careful guardian in my brother, he needs no stepfather."

"But you might fall in love," she persisted.

Cecelia gave a mirthless laugh. "One mistake is enough for a lifetime."

She must be exceedingly tired, thought Sophie. Never before had she revealed so much, so succinctly.

"You, I gather, had a happy marriage. Fortunate creature."

"I was fortunate," she agreed. "When I met Tobias Pinnock I was young, and dazzled by his fame. He never betrayed my trust, or made me regret our hasty marriage."

"Some couples are more blessed than others." Cecelia's chest rose and fell with her sigh.

"My devotion to him may have been the sort that comes but once in a lifetime," Sophie said. "I wonder if it would be fair to encourage a marriage-minded suitor. If I should ever have one," she hastened to add, belatedly recalling the need for concealment.

"At least you've encountered true affection, you'll know when it finds you again. I was led astray by foolish dreams and false promises, and paid a very high price. I want no more of love and passion and all the nonsense we dreamed of as giddy young girls."

This summation of her romantic past surprised Sophie. Never had she known such a passionless female.

"All I crave nowadays is perfect peace and seclusion."

"*Ah, ça,*" she cried, "I can think of no more peaceful or secluded existence than yours!"

Cecelia shook her head until her dark curls danced. "I cannot be easy in my mind, not even here. Not when I'm so constantly plagued by worry. I want Daniel always to be safe and well. I am so afraid that Luis has come to harm—I wish he would return."

"He will."

Sophie had tried not to give in to the dread shared by the Carysforts. She couldn't understand their pessimism about their servant's disappearance—unless they possessed some crucial piece of information that they were keeping from her.

"And my brother—I am concerned for him as well." Cecelia cast a sidelong glance at Sophie before speaking again. "He behaves so oddly. We used to share every thought and feeling, but not lately. Of course, I've been secretive myself. I'm tempted to tell you my plan for the future, Sophie, for I could use an ally."

"I dislike conspiracies," Sophie told her frankly.

"Cass, you see, regards the castle as his rightful home. I accept that he must live at Bevington, and we've agreed that Daniel will benefit from a country upbringing. But I would rather have remained at Summit House. When my son is old enough to go away to school, I shall return to Clifton."

"Do you think the earl would try to prevent you?"

"He might, he's so protective. But if he took a wife—" There was a pregnant pause before Cecelia continued, "I do wish he'd marry, for then he might not oppose my wish to live on my own."

Sophie struggled with the concept of an independent Cecelia.

"I'm certain I could be more active—and useful—if I parted from Cass. He indulges me, too much, and dictates to me." Smiling, Cecelia went on, "My lack of resistance doubtless contributes to his expectation of ruling others. The woman he marries will have to be very firm with him if she wants to correct this fault.''

Sophie bit down hard on her lip to hold back her enthusiastic agreement with this observation. How much did Cecelia know, or guess, about her brother's marital prospects?

Soberly, Cecelia went on, ''I am ready to do as Cass has done, and reform myself, to follow the example of the aunt who raised us. She was a good and generous woman, who allotted much of her time and our uncle's money to any number of charities—schools and foundations and relief societies. I'll always regret that I was too flighty to heed her teachings. I should have done. But I turned my back on stodgy, middle-class Bristol and ran off to London with Cass to live among the lords and ladies.''

Sophie was pleased to find an unperceived depth to Cecelia's character. She'd unjustly catalogued the earl's sister as a spoiled, self-concerned female, condemned to boredom by an excess of leisure and money.

''Wouldn't this be an ideal spot for a garden seat,'' observed Cecelia, indicating the broad niche halfway along the wall.

''Emrys Jones believes it was a hutch for fowls. Peacocks, most likely.''

''It would be delightful to sit here and admire the rose arbors and the canal.''

''*Oui-dgia*. But they are going to be removed,'' Sophie reminded her. ''Tomorrow a contractor comes from Gloucester to give me an estimate for labor costs.''

''You've been more busy than ever since Cass went away. I feel his absence keenly—he may be a

managing sort of brother, but he knows exactly
how to amuse me. Dine with me tonight, Sophie. I
must take advantage of your companionship while
it's still available to me. How you shall be missed
when you leave Bevington!"

Flattered, Sophie accepted her invitation.

Her suspicion that Cecelia would spend the evening talking about her brother turned out to be
well-founded. Throughout dinner she listened to
timely and illuminating reminiscences about his
youth and education and his favorite pursuits.
While Cecelia was occupied with her needlework
and Sophie drew a charcoal sketch of her, she was
entertained with even more of his lordship's exploits. By the time she retired to her chamber, she
no longer doubted that the earl's sister was promoting a match.

Lying in her bed, she resumed her examination
of Cassian Carysfort. When she sifted through the
complexities of his character, she found much to
admire.

He displayed a remarkable devotion to his sister
and her child. His wife could expect similarly kind
treatment.

Few wealthy gentlemen bothered to take on the
management of a large estate personally, or
showed so great an interest in local affairs. He paid
his servants well and treated them humanely.

He was intelligent, his mind broadened by travel
and books.

His dog adored him.

Oh, las, but he could be so disagreeable—how he
tried her patience! Making demands, imposing his
will. Even his sister was affected by it. Cecelia na-
ively believed that the right woman could reform
him. Sophie, possessing many more brothers and
an uncle, had learned early that a man's general

temperament could not be altered to suit. At best, his bad habits could be amended.

He had a most distressing appreciation for modern landscape gardens.

And despite his occasional bursts of candor, he harbored secrets—probably unwholesome ones, to be so closely guarded—and Cecelia had let slip something about his efforts to reform himself. But she resolved to judge him as the man she knew in the present, not be swayed by speculations about what he'd done in the past.

The next morning she received a message from the contractor, regretfully informing her that he must survey a site for another client and had to postpone their meeting until later in the week. Sophie only wished the interview could be delayed indefinitely. It signaled the next step in the improvement process, the dismantling of the gardens she'd valued at first glance and now dearly loved.

Her gatehouse rooms were littered with the various materials she'd used for the creation of the new design: maps, books, folios of engravings. With the help of her maidservant, she gathered them up and carried them back to the library.

"Do you s'pose his lordship will ever read all the books 'ere?" Nan wondered, scanning the tall mahogany cases.

Laughing, Sophie replied, "I trust he's too wise to make the attempt. It would take a lifetime."

As soon as she dismissed the maid, she replaced each volume where she'd found it. Most belonged on a single shelf, a treasure trove of castle lore—financial records compiled by the various Bevington stewards, a family history comissioned by a previous holder of the title, and other ephemera. She crammed a folded estate map between two unmarked folios. Reconsidering, she tried to dislodge it and found that she had to remove one of the folios first.

The one she took out was heavier than she'd expected. As she struggled to hold it, a paper fluttered to the carpet. Retrieving it, her attention was caught by even lines of flowing script.

Bevington, November ye 16th, 1765. Rec'd from Jas. Wheeler of Gloucester, via Ebbersley's wagon and pack'd in matting:
1 Le Roche Courbon dwarf Plum, 1s. 6d.
3 Black Old Newington nectarine, ditto.
Lilacs/syringa vulgaris (2 purple and 2 white), 6s.

Sophie knew those lilacs. They marked the four corners of the rose garden. Until they bloomed she could only guess which were purple and which were white, but they were tall and vigorous, covered in green, satiny leaves.

She abandoned her original task and carried both folios to the desk. There were more papers inside the covers. A complete set of architectural drawings for the pavilion. A collection of receipts from nurserymen in Gloucester and Bristol, with purchases itemized. She found a variety of letters, some addressed to the earl and some to Emrys Jones. One was penned by Lord Mountstuart, describing at length the improvements Capability Brown had made at Cardiff Castle for his father, Lord Bute. But despite the glowing recommendation, Lord Bevington had been disinclined to consult the great man, or had been unable to afford him. Otherwise, there would be no gardens now, merely an open park with Brown's signature clumps of trees.

The second folio contained the oldest records. The most fascinating were stiff parchments covered with small, precise, and very ancient characters. Frowning with the effort, she tried to decipher the continuation of a letter whose first page was missing.

and in situ for the visite of his majestye the kynge, postes and rayles for the pleasaunce, also to be paynted green and white as seen at Nonsuch. Madam Bullen has shown her favour for peaches, may they be forward this season and in all readinesse. Bevington.

Henry the Eighth had visited the castle—and he'd brought Anne Boleyn! Sophie hoped the peaches had been ripe in time for the royal visit. Too impatient to read through the many letters, she laid them aside—then noticed one written in an ornate but legible hand.

Dearest wyffe,

Our Queen, all goodnesse and beauty, doth make good her promise to stop at Bevington during her progresse through the West Country with her favourite, Leicester. Before comynge to this Court I did order the carver to make two beestes in freestone, staggs collared with rose garlands. I desire each to be mounted upon a base and sett at the approach to ye bowlynge greene. And I charge you also to order from the clockmaker one bronzed sundyal, likewise to be sett upon a stone base among ye knottes of clipped rosemarie. Command for me the gardener neatly to tie up the woodbine and train young trees of appel and pere and chery. I do eagerly await the time when I may kysse you again, dear wyffe, more fayre to me than roses, violettes, and all other sweete flowers.

Not only Henry and Anne had come to Bevington, but their daughter Elizabeth as well. Sophie longed to tell Cassian that the Virgin Queen had paused beneath his ancestral roof. She smiled as she reread the lord's endearments to his lady, an indication that they had been a fond couple. Whatever had happened to their pair of stone stags, she wondered, and that bronze sundial?

She gazed upon the array of papers she had stumbled upon, aware that the full history of the gardens was laid out before her. All plans for their improvement, major and minor, were documented, along with every plant purchase, and each gardener's name and wage.

As absorbing as this record was, the information was of no real use to her, or anyone else. These fragile pages represented centuries of effort and expense and labor, resulting in a magnificent and venerable creation—destined to be destroyed.

Regretfully, she accepted that the folios were a curiosity, nothing more, and returned them to their shelf.

Three days, and still Cass had not located Sir Michael Tait. Three days of scouring London's streets in a relentless, driving rain and returning nightly to his comfortable but impersonal suite in Nerot's Hotel.

He meant to find his enemy, and soon, because he needed to go home. He missed Sophie's fresh face and bright smiles, his sister's music, and Daniel's piping questions.

Seven years ago, during his brief stint as Tait's crony, Cass had learned the man's habits and haunts. The baronet and his scandalous lady, prior to their divorce, had lived in a grand house in St. James's Square. While it remained Sir Michael's property, it was presently leased to a family from Hampshire whose country-bred servants had no knowledge of the owner's whereabouts.

Cass attended a midweek performance at the Royal Opera House, taking a seat in Fop's Alley that afforded him an excellent view of baronet's private box. To his regret, it was occupied by a party of overdressed strangers—like Tait's residence, his theatre seats were rented out to strangers.

While the ladies and gentlemen on the stage warbled their arias and duets, Cass thought about Sophie. Did she care for this sort of entertainment? He tried to imagine her in this setting, swathed in satin with plumes rising up from her dark hair, and couldn't. When he thought of her, she never wore opera dress and elbow-length kid gloves, she was always aproned in brown Holland cloth, her little hands protected by gauntlets of thick leather.

He visited a gentlemen's club formerly frequented by Sir Michael. Vaguely he remembered yearning to belong to a select society in St. James's Street, where he might rub shoulders with dukes and ministers of state and wealthy bankers. Tait had often tantalized him with political gossip and other tales that circulated in White's exclusive gaming salon. Apparently the baronet continued to pay his annual fees, but he no longer asserted his membership rights, for the club steward couldn't remember the last time he'd come by.

Cass was learning that Tait's interests, like his own, had altered over time.

Keeping a private opera box no longer appealed to him. Mingling with other aristocrats, or government officials, as his title permitted him to do, didn't interest him in the slightest. As an earl and the owner of a great estate, he could probably join any of the great clubs, but his desire to become a clubman had waned.

London was no use to him at all. Every dream for the future centered on his Gloucestershire castle, and the flower-loving lady waiting for him there.

Out of desperation he broadened his search, even though he knew instinctively that Sir Michael, if still in town, would not stray far from St. James's. One afternoon, bored with his endless trudging about in the rain, he stepped into Hatchards bookshop in Piccadilly to read the newspapers.

A clerk was receiving a set of music books from a printer's boy. Cecelia, thought Cass, would be glad to have the current popular tunes. Her appetite for new pieces was insatiable.

He consulted with the clerk, who told him apologetically, "None of this music is for the pianoforte. The selection we presently have available is for stringed instruments."

The man he sought was a violinist. Or used to be.

"I've a friend who might be interested to know it." This description of the baronet burned his tongue; Cass hadn't regarded him in that light for a very long time. "But perhaps you already supply music to Sir Michael Tait?"

The clerk replied, "Possibly. I can look at my ledger." He turned back several pages, his finger sliding slowly down each column. "Why, yes, his name does appear—twice in the past six months. On one occasion we supplied him with a German songbook, and we also dispatched some Italian music to his house."

"You've got his direction there?"

The young man showed him the book, pointing to a house number in Cleveland Row, St. James's.

When he'd purchased a ballad-sheet for his sister, Cass left the shop. He stopped at the nearest hackney stand as an available vehicle pulled up. Urging its driver to make haste, he climbed inside.

The brick row house was narrow and small, squeezed between larger, more impressive ones. The door lacked a knocker, so Cass struck it with his ivory-handled sword-stick. When no one came he opened it himself. The building was divided into separate flats. Which one was Tait's?

He went from door to door, studying the engraved cards nailed to each, when his answer cascaded down in a series of notes from a violin. He climbed the staircase, following the music to its source—an upper room at the back of the house.

The door was ajar. Peering through the gap, he saw an empty chair with mahogany ball and claw feet and curved armrests, and on the floor the fringed corner of a carpet.

The musician played on.

Cass stepped into the room.

Sir Michael Tait stood before a wooden music stand positioned near the window. His bow stilled in mid-stroke.

"Surprised to see me?" asked Cass.

Tait lowered his instrument. "Beyond description."

"You must have expected me, sooner or later." His gaze lingered on the disfiguring scar. "I've come to rescue my valet."

The baronet's lips curled. "I don't know what you're talking about. Stop storming about, Carysfort—sorry, Bevington—and tell me why you're here. In terms that I can understand."

"Where's that henchman of yours? I expect he'll tell me what I need to know, provided I offer a large enough reward."

"If you refer to my footman James, he's at Oakes Court—my country property near Guildford." Carefully Tait laid his violin in its case. Reaching for a decanter of amber liquid, he asked, "A glass of cognac?"

Cass had no intention of accepting any hospitality from his enemy. "Don't even try to ingratiate yourself, this is not a formal call. I came to find out what the bloody hell you've done with Luis Costa."

"The foreign youth? I've not laid eyes on him since I last saw you, whenever that was." The baronet stroked his cheek—the intact one—and said mildly, "I'm not sorry you've come, even though a false errand brings you. I've long wondered why I never had an answer to the letter I sent to your sister."

"I prefer to leave her out of this discussion."

Tait sipped from his glass. "I've been thinking about her. I always do when I play that piece, it's my part from the duet we used to perform together. Our last time was at that party my wife gave in St. James's Square. Seven years ago."

"The night sticks in my mind for quite a different reason. That's when I issued my challenge to you."

Tait winced. "Did Cecelia keep up her music? She was enormously talented—one of the few points my wife and I could agree upon. She's in England, isn't she?"

"Your wife? How should I know?"

"Your sister. I did manage to find proof of that."

Cass stiffened. "What do you mean, proof?" He regretted his words; it was a mistake to react.

"For a long time I assumed you'd left her behind in Portugal. But then I discovered that the pair of you returned to this country in February of last

year, in the company of someone called Daniel
Fonseca."

Careful, careful, Cass warned himself. Say nothing, show no alarm.

"She married, you said. But you led me to believe she was a grieving widow. Her name *is* Fonseca, is it not?"

"That's no business of yours," Cass stated firmly,
searching for a way to discover the informant's
identity without being too obvious. "Did this report come from your brother? I understand he has
returned from the wars."

"Who told you that?"

He shrugged. "My source, like yours, must remain anonymous."

The baronet strode forward, face taut with fury.
"Damn your arrogance—and your mysteries! Get
out, Lord Bevington, and don't return unless you
want a bullet through that cold, black heart of
yours. I had my chance, seven years ago—and
aimed my pistol at the sky and fired in the air. In
doing so, I acknowledged my fault. Your honor
was preserved, you didn't have to wound me."

"What do you know about honor? If you had
any understanding of the concept, you'd realize
that while you live and breathe I'll never have complete satisfaction."

Cass reached into the open instrument case and
lifted the violin from its velvet nest. His hand
swept across its gleaming varnish, his fingertips
plucked the strings. "I remember this well. Its associations are not the happiest for me." He raised
it high above his head.

"Careful!" cried Tait. "For God's sake, man—it
came from the Guarneri workshop!"

"Who talked to you about my sister? Tell me!"

"Not until you've told me exactly where she is."

His anger and frustration erupted with the sound of splintering wood. Repeatedly he slammed the violin against the jutting shelf of the mantelpiece until the severed body was held together only by the strings. Then he let it fall to the floor.

Tait stared down at his broken treasure. "You bastard."

Cass congratulated himself that his cruel act of vandalism had been more effective than any words or threats.

Outside, the rain still streamed from the leaden skies. This time he didn't hail a hackney, he walked back to his hotel. A drenching couldn't possibly make him feel worse.

Tait had found out about Daniel, most likely from Luis Costa. He'd sent his burly footman to Oakes Court—was the hostage being held there? He'd made a false connection between Daniel and Cecelia, but through sheer persistence he might uncover part of the truth—and could be vindictive enough to make his discoveries public.

It was time, Cass decided, to expand his investigation. He hated to put off his journey back to the castle but felt compelled to travel to Surrey instead.

Conjuring his sweet Sophie's image, he hoped she missed him, was thinking about him. His abrupt marriage proposal had confused her, that he knew. But had it pleased her?

She didn't love him, and wishing wouldn't make it so. But he prayed that she cared just enough to stay with him. He needed her so very much—in his house, and in his bed, and yes, even in his gardens.

He intended to court her, tenderly and with great care. Eventually he would win her away from that sainted husband of hers. When she had married that most fortunate of men, she'd bestowed her body and her life upon him, vowing to be faithful through good and ill, until death came to part them.

Cass would be satisfied with nothing less.

A flower was offered to me,
Such a flower as May never bore . . .

WILLIAM BLAKE

Chapter 13

"Isn't this a Scotch rose?"

Emrys Jones made a cursory examination of the prickly cane Sophie held. "Aye. A pink one. And 'twill be among the first to bloom."

She scrawled the species name on her sketchpad and moved on to the next bush. "And this one, *de Meaux*, is a Provence rose?"

"The last to be planted here," the gardener informed her, "and mayhap the prettiest. At the height of bloom it's covered with miniature pink blossoms."

"I long to see it!" Tapping her chin with the pencil, she studied her notes. "My inventory is nearly complete. As for the half-dozen you're unable to identify, I'll need to consult the purchase records. From their size and the thickness of the canes, I should think they're the oldest of all."

"This one has leaves in the gallica shape, but if it has a proper name, I ne'er knew it. It might've been here as long as your *Rosa mundi*—hundreds of years, belike."

Sophie touched a bract of tender new foliage, a living connection to ancient history. She wanted to paint the plants exactly as they looked now, green with promise as they rambled along the stone wall and climbed up the arbors.

"Now you'll have no more thought for roses," muttered the Welshman, tying an errant branch to the trellis.

"Whyever not?"

"Here comes his lordship."

Sophie whirled around. Seven long days of missing him, of wondering whether or not she could become his countess. Self-consciously she smoothed her chignon, vaguely aware that Emrys Jones had slung his hoe over one bony shoulder and was rapidly exiting the garden. She had eyes only for the tall, broad-shouldered figure crossing the lawn.

How weary he looked, and so pale. The deep lines etched into his brow told of failure and disappointment.

"You couldn't find Luis."

With a doleful shake of his head, he answered, "It appears to be a lost cause."

Terribly concerned by his appearance, Sophie asked if he was ill.

"I've a headache. And I feel like my body has been stretched on a rack and flailed with a stick. Those blasted rains cut deep furrows into the roads, and for the better part of two days I've been bumping over them. Just beyond Guildford my carriage met with a mishap, and I had to wait for a repair to the coach-wheel."

"Guildford? We thought you'd been in London all this time."

He gazed silently down at her for a moment, his face grave. "I came up empty in both places. It is difficult, but I'm trying to accept that I may never learn exactly what happened to Luis. I pray you're right, that he did board a ship bound for Portugal."

"Wherever he may be, he's safe and well. I expect you'll receive a letter from him soon, explaining everything."

"My optimistic Sophie," he said softly, gratefully. "Tell me, are you truly mine now?"

She used her sketchbook to shield her uncertain heart. "I've considered all that you said to me before you went away."

"And?"

She hesitated, still tottering on the brink of certainty and not quite prepared for the plunge.

"May I know my fate?" he asked gently.

"*Dé vrai*, it would be a most unequal match. I never aspired to wed a man of rank, or great fortune. Or to be a countess."

"Yes, I was born into a wealthy family," he said, "but I entered this world a commoner, exactly as you did. The title came to me in recent years and through an accident of genealogy. I rarely encounter other aristocrats, in town or locally. I expect to cultivate a neighborly relationship with such people as the Ducies and the Berkeleys, but nothing more."

"But what will they think if you wed a woman who has been your employee?"

"They'll never share their thoughts with us, so why worry? Your pedigree is far superior to Lady Berkeley's, that much is certain. Her father was a Wotton butcher, and she lived with the earl as his mistress for many a year. Of the five children she's borne, only the youngest is legitimate." With a twisted smile, he continued, "As for inequality— I'm all too aware that the niece of the Seigneur of Anneville is quite above my touch."

"Oua don!" she protested. "That's nonsense."

"My sister values your companionship. I'm confident that you'll be an affectionate to aunt to my nephew Daniel. And you're the ideal chatelaine for Bevington Castle, for you already know my servants well and you have their respect."

Sophie bowed her head, humbled by his homage.

"Does that signify acceptance? You might as well have me. If you tried escaping to Chiswick, I'd simply chase after you and implore you until you give in."

He took her hand. Instead of kissing it as she expected him to, he studied her bare fingers. She'd recently removed her husband's signet, and the pale imprint had vanished from her skin after several days of garden work.

"You used to wear a gold ring," he said softly. "I hope its absence means you feel ready to accept one of my bestowing."

Forgive me, Tobias, Sophie pleaded. I do not want to be alone forever. This man doesn't demand too much, only that I join his family and share his home. I do believe my life with him will be a pleasant one.

"My lord," she began, "you do me great honor. I am willing to become your wife."

Cass was wounded by her lack of enthusiasm—she seemed perfectly composed, apparently resigned to the inevitable. Her still face and subdued manner proved that he hadn't won her love, merely her acceptance of his name and title and worldly possessions. Had his persuasions somehow worked against him? The marriage he'd described was one of mutual convenience. To her, he realized with a pang of regret, it probably would be. For him it was so much more.

Determined to endear himself to her, he said, "You shall have whatever you want for a bride-gift, Sophie. Anything you desire is yours for the asking."

"How could I possibly ask for more?" she wondered. "As Lady Bevington I will have so very much." Her gaze shifted from his face to the castle ramparts, then moved to the surrounding arbors, and her thoughtful expression was replaced by one of longing. "But yes," she murmured. "I do have a request. There is something I should like—and it's important to me."

"Then you shall have it," he promised rashly. He didn't expect her to demand jewels, or a financial settlement, for she wasn't acquisitive. Her lack of regard for material things was part of her charm. What could she possibly desire?

"These gardens. They must not be altered. I'm not merely asking your permission to preserve them—I want to restore them. I know exactly how to do it. *Janmais d'ma vie*, never in my life was I so amazed, for in your library I found a whole collection of letters and purchase accounts and even some sketches—a complete history. The original pleasaunce was set within the castle keep. The terraces were built later. A pair of stags carved out of stone once stood at the entrance to the bowling green, I know their dimensions and how many men were required to set them in place. The canal and the pavilion were added a century ago. Topiaries were nearly always here, and knot gardens. Roses, too."

"But what about that fashionable modern landscape you designed?"

"I never cared for it as much as you did, *dé vrai*. If you just consider how long the castle has stood here, you'll understand that formality is more appropriate than—"

"I understand that this means a great deal to you, Sophie. That's the only consideration that weighs with me."

Her eyes sparkled, and the corners of her delectable mouth curved upward. "No arguments? No debate?"

"None," he replied, enchanted by her teasing smile. "From this moment these grounds are yours. Do whatever you please to them."

"Chièr Cassian, mèrcie bein des fais!"

She flung herself at him, pressing her full lips against his in a hasty kiss, far too brief to suit him. But she'd given it freely, and joyously. She'd called him by his name!

"I'll find Emrys Jones and tell him."

"Right now? But we haven't chosen the day for our wedding." He was impatient to settle the matter, but already she was dancing across the grass, the sketchpad tucked under her arm.

She'd pledged to be his wife, he reminded himself. He would take comfort where he could, and disregard the abrupt desertion that marred the luster of this most shining victory of his life.

Cass lowered the wick of the oil lamp on the mantel to reduce the size of the flame. After shrugging out of his coat, he unwound the constricting cravat from his neck.

It had been a long and momentous day.

That damnably uncomfortable inn at Newbury where he'd breakfasted on cold ham and scalding tea, and his tedious journey along rain-slicked roads were dim memories now. He'd won the hand of his ladylove. Only, he hadn't actually laid eyes on her since she'd left him in the rose garden.

While dining with his sister, he'd given her a concise, severely edited account of his meeting with Sir Michael Tait. His failure to find Luis in Cleveland Row or at Oakes Court was a disappointment to Cecelia.

To cheer her, he'd revealed his marriage plans. As she dried her tears for Luis, she'd pelted him with eager questions. Did he and his future countess prefer a private license to banns? Which rooms would Sophie occupy after their marriage? He didn't admit it to her, but he doubted his bride-to-be had spent a single moment considering such things as banns and bedrooms.

Going into his dressing room, he slipped the studs from his shirtsleeves and placed them in their box. Tonight he greatly missed his valet's ministrations and distracting chatter. But he dared not think about Luis, poor fellow, or that cruel devil Tait, or he'd be awake till sunrise. Off came his shoes and stockings and breeches.

He could hear female voices coming from the adjacent chamber—Sophie and her waiting woman—then metal grating against metal as one of them stirred the fire. Then there was a long silence.

Was she in her bed? Did she lie there dreaming of him, or of rosebushes and statues of stags and crumbling walls?

The creak of a floorboard told him she was still up. He moved to the connecting door and flattened his palm against the whitened wood. "Sophie?"

He waited, heart hammering, for acknowledgement. Light was leaking through the gap between the bottom plank and the low, uneven threshhold.

"Is it you, Cassian?" she called back. "Where are you?"

His fingers crept toward the iron ring. Twisting it, he swung the door open.

She wore a nightgown, long and white and edged with lace. Waves of unbound hair fell almost to her waist. One hand was clamped to her throat in a gesture of surprise, and the flame from her chamber-stick shone upon a ring with a large, clear, glittering stone.

A Bristol diamond.

His pent-up breath eased in a sigh of satisfaction.

"Why are you here?" she asked.

"This is my dressing room."

"*Ma fé,*" said Sophie, peering at his chest of drawers with shaving mirror on top, and the wardrobe. "And all this time you were so near."

Taking her elbow, he led her through the narrow passage to his bedchamber. "Here is the room we'll share."

Up came her chin. "But I like the convenience of my own entrance and stairway. I don't want to give up my parlor and my little study where I've been keeping my books and papers and paints."

Was she implying that she preferred separate accommodations? "You need only give up the room you've been sleeping in." He trailed her to the casement. Through the sheer fabric of the gown he could see slender legs, the graceful curve of her hips.

"Your windows must look out on the gardens."

"They do," he confirmed. "In the mornings when you wake, they'll be first thing you see—after me." He covered her shoulder with his hand, and felt her warm flesh beneath the filmy muslin. His heart shuddered at the contact.

"How soon shall we be wed?" she wondered, looking up at him.

"Marriage by license is swift but might appear unusual—if not furtive—in our little hamlet. I feel a certain duty as lord of the castle to follow the rites proscribed by the church, even though we'd have to wait for the vicar to cry the banns on three consecutive Sundays."

"I don't mind. For that way I'd have time to write my family at Anneville beforehand."

"Will any of them come, do you think?"

"If I asked it," she told him. "But I won't. It's a long journey, at a time when no one can be spared from farm and orchard work."

"Patience is not a virtue I can claim," Cass confessed. "Any delay will be hard to bear. When you are near me, and we are together like this, I can think only of—" Light-headed, he drew a sustaining breath. "Of being your husband."

Sophie, increasingly aware of her nakedness beneath her gown, caught the meaning of those husky, wistful words. And she noticed that his gaping shirt revealed a powerful chest shadowed with dark hairs, rising and falling as though from exertion.

"There's a flame inside you, Sophie, it has touched me every time I've kissed you. I long to discover exactly where it lies." The heat of his desire for her showed in the blue fire of his eyes.

Her own craving for physical intimacy was impossible to withstand. Before his marriage proposal, she'd often, albeit blushingly, imagined becoming his mistress. Now she was three weeks away from being his wife.

He'd aroused a passion that was overwhelming in its intensity, tempting her to test its power—and if she did, there could be no turning back. Giving herself to him would be an irrevocable act of commitment.

And a form of renunciation.

Her lingering feelings for Tobias remained pure

and uncomplicated, but she received nothing in return. It was too easy to love a ghost.

She'd made a promise to this man standing beside her, who lusted for her and tormented and teased her. She was grateful to him for bringing her deadened heart back to life. Perhaps by sharing her body with him and giving him the pleasure he craved, she could break free of the clinging specter of her lost husband.

"I am willing to lie with you, Cassian." Fixing her gaze on the pulse that fluttered on his neck, she added, "Tonight." Had she been too bold? "If you want me to."

"If I *want* you to? Dear God, you need to ask? You know how much I—" Suddenly he swallowed. "But—you're sure?"

Oui. Oui-dgia. But the words wouldn't come, panic had closed her throat. So she reached up to frame his startled face with her hands, and drew him down to receive her answering kiss.

He gave her no outward sign of encouragement. His mouth was firm and still, his massive body unyielding. Why didn't he respond? She pressed closer, until her breasts brushed against him—how full they felt, so deliciously sensitive. She wished he would touch them.

He made a sound, it began deep in his chest and emerged as a low moan. Unleashing some powerful force that he'd held in check, he came alive in her arms.

He returned her kisses with a fervor that frightened and thrilled her. His fingers gripped the neck of her gown, crushing the cloth and lace as if they were enemies. She heard the fabric tear, and his palms cupped her flesh, his fingertips grazed her nipples. He exposed her shoulders, then her breasts, lowering his dark head to worship each one with his lips.

Now she was the passive one, unable to move while he took away what remained of her garment. His hands slowly trailed down her bare waist, then swept across the curve of her bottom. He knelt to draw off her stockings, and she felt his hands caressing her thighs, her knees, her ankles. He'd managed to touch every inch of her body—except the secret, hidden place where her fever ran so high, aching for his attention.

He peeled away his shirt and smalls. When he took her in his arms again, she could feel his sex straining toward her, firm and insistent. His heightened state of arousal increased her own desire until she was so weak and helpless with it she didn't know what to do next.

"Bed," he muttered, forcing her backward while at the same time holding her against him. They edged awkwardly across the floor, out of the lamplight and into the darker side of the room. He swept aside the embroidered hangings, and together they tumbled onto the mattress.

Again Sophie felt those urgent hands upon her, sweeping her long hair aside and stroking her nipples. His kiss was an act of possession, his probing tongue mated with hers. She arched her back, ground her hips against him, seeking relief.

His hand rested briefly upon her mound, then his fingers moved down to part the moist and heated folds of her skin. Her yearning manifested itself in soft whimpers.

"Yes, now," he whispered roughly, impaling her with his swollen length.

She gasped at the penetration. There was no pain, only a burning pressure and the sensation of being filled and stretched. Gripping his forearms, she felt tensed muscles as hard as stone. He was so large, so strong, and never had she seemed so small and indefensible.

He drove himself into her, not at all gently but with a wildness that took her breath away. His body rose and fell, again and again, and she felt his rigid flesh deep within her. Thoroughly unprepared for this assault upon her senses, she trembled, she burned.

"Ah," he cried with each stroke. "Ah."

She opened her eyes to find him staring down at her, watching her. Did he realize his power over her, or know that she reveled in all that he did? Was he even aware of her, or was he lost in his own delight?

"Sophie." He drew back, then heaved forward. "Ah, Sophie."

Her sense of self faded as the fire at her core consumed her. She was a writhing mass of sensation. She could no longer think, or see, she could only feel, and what she felt was so strange and yet so exquisite that it couldn't be real. She was cold and hot at once, she was trembling from the inside out—and suddenly she heard her voice cry out as a shattering force rocked her entire being.

He was still there, still part of her. His motions grew more frantic. He made a guttural noise. She felt another pulsing inside her, this time it came from him. His sweat-slick body fell forward, his damp brow rested against her collarbone.

She lay beneath him, stunned by the intensity of his loving. A merging not only of bodies, but of souls.

Cass touched her cheek. "You sing out," he said. "I made you sing." He couldn't mask his relief. "I dared not hope for that so soon—the very first time. But I might have known it could be like this with you." He wished he could see her face better, his curtained bed was darker than a cave. His fingers felt for her mouth, to find out whether she smiled.

This woman, he marveled, had been fashioned for his delight, and he for hers. At last he had experienced the full force of her inner fire. With this shared passion as a foundation, their marriage would surely succeed. Whatever her reasons for accepting him as her husband, she had to acknowledge this bond between them. And time would strengthen it, that was certain.

Unless he lost her goodwill.

He rolled onto his back as the ugly events of seven years ago hurled themselves at him. His brief but harmful experimentation with laudanum. His sister's sorrows. The violent rift with Tait. Their duel on Hounslow Heath. Spilled blood and shattered lives.

How would Sophie react if she found out that he'd wanted to kill a man—had very nearly done it?

He ought to tell her everything. But she lay beside him so sweetly, so trustingly, her soft cheek resting against his shoulder. This was not the time to speak of the terrible things that burdened his conscience, of the grief and blind rage that had driven him many years ago. And he dared not provoke unfavorable comparisons with the worthy Tobias by reciting a sordid tale of vengeance and scandal.

But if he didn't tell her, he cautioned himself, he might endanger her. Tait was cruel and vicious, he was capable of great evil—heaven alone knew what he had done to Luis Costa. If those foul hands ever touched his unsuspecting Sophie . . .

She stirred against him.

"I should go," she told him softly.

"Not yet." But before he could prevent her, she left the bed.

He also rose and covered himself with his shirt. The fire had died down but the lamp glowed weakly—he could see the pale outline of her body as she searched for her nightgown. She slipped it over her head and held the deep tear in the front together with one hand.

"Ruined, is it?"

"Not past mending," she answered.

"I was desperate. If I admitted how long it's been since I had a woman," he said ruefully, "you probably wouldn't believe me."

She had the delicacy not to question him, but her shadowed face gave away her curiosity.

"I hardly remember—most definitely not since I met you. Perhaps I was saving myself for marriage. And then I let my guard down for a moment, and a pretty rogue seduced me."

He accompanied her to her bedroom. After he pulled back the flowery crewelwork coverlet, he asked, "May I stay? I'll leave before daybreak."

"It wouldn't be wise," she murmued, "to—to be together again until after the marriage." Her restraint was a marked contrast to her earlier boldness. "Suppose I presented you with a babe only eight months after the wedding?"

Cass hadn't considered that, and he had to respect her concerns. He only hoped she wasn't regretting what they'd done. "I shall curb my amorous impulses as best I can," he told her, "but these three weeks will be the longest I have ever known. I'll be speaking with the vicar first thing tomorrow."

He returned to his chamber to sort out the tangled sheets. He felt sated, yet ever so slightly cheated, for she'd shared her body but without offering him her love. Not so long ago, he reminded himself, he'd despaired of winning either. So even if this wasn't the total triumph he dreamed of, it was hardly a defeat. Because he'd made her sing.

And many idle phantasies,
Traverse my indolent and passive brain.

SAMUEL TAYLOR COLERIDGE

Chapter 14

The practice of religion, Andrew Searle believed, was for superstitious and gullible folk.
It wasn't piety that lured him to the parish church
on a breezy Easter morn, but the expectation of
meeting Sophie there.

Gathered beneath St. Mary's ancient vaulted roof
were people from the village and castle, the men
clad in Sunday suits and the women wearing their
most festive finery. Andrew didn't bother opening
a hymnal or joining in the celebratory anthem, he
was far too interested in the cozy tableau in the box
pew decorated with the earl's coat of arms.

Cass looked like a nobleman born in his dark
coat and starched white neckcloth, his black hair
brushed into perfect waves. His madonna-like sister was trying to quiet her son, who was bouncing
up and down excitedly. Sophie Pinnock sat with
them. While the congregation chanted responses,
Cass addressed a few whispered words to her
which left her looking pleased and uncomfortable
all at once.

Envy pierced Andrew as Sophie smiled up at the handsome libertine seated next to her.

He concentrated on the vicar's singsong voice, soaring and falling with overly dramatic effect. It struck him as a comical performance, but not enough to enliven the communion rite. Andrew rose with the congregation to recite the creed, then sat again for the announcement of holy days and fasts.

The vicar settled his spectacles on his nose. Pitching his voice still higher, he read from a paper, "I publish the banns of marriage between Cassian Moreton Carysfort of St. Mary's parish, Bevington, and Sophie Elise Nicolle Pinnock of St. Nicolas parish, Chiswick."

He paused, waiting for the mild furor to subside.

"If any of you know cause or just impediment why these two persons should not be joined together in holy matrimony, ye are to declare it. This is the first time of asking."

Andrew's prayer book slipped from his hands and struck the stone floor. No one noticed. All attention was focused on the earl and his lady landscape gardener. The parishioners murmured and bobbed their heads, ignoring the vicar as he launched into the Offertory. Miserably trapped, Andrew sank down on the pew, storm clouds breaking in his head.

Cass. Sophie. An engagement.

But she was destined to be his own wife, the mother of his sons. His salvation.

Cass fancied her, he'd been quite frank about it. Still, Andrew hadn't imagined he would ever offer marriage—not to a commoner, the widow of a professional man. He was an earl and should select an aristocratic and socially prominent damsel like the ones he'd danced with and been spurned by in

London all those years ago. He was an eligible catch now, he had a title as well as a fortune.

As for Sophie, she couldn't possibly be in love. Andrew had believed her far too attached to her Chiswick home to exchange it for a castle. What could be her reason for agreeing to this preposterous match?

Yet again he'd been rejected even before he'd had a chance to propose. Cecelia Carysfort had always been beyond his reach, towering above him on her pedestal. But Sophie had tidied his cottage and rambled the wood with him. He sat with her while she painted; he showed her his poems. At night they met in his dreams.

He sat numbly throughout the general confession and the absolution, uncomforted by the assurances of divine redemption. He didn't want to think about sin, and refused to believe that the loss of Sophie could be a judgment upon him.

Later, when the parishioners filed to the front of the church to receive the sacrament, Andrew climbed to his feet and slipped out through the nearest door. He found himself in the churchyard, surrounded by headstones. The scent of moss and evergreens was stifling, redolent of death.

He searched his pockets for the blue glass bottle, a sure method of keeping his demons at bay. It wasn't there—he must have left it at the cottage.

Plunging through a gap between the tall yews, he took the hillside path winding up to the castle. By the time he reached the gate to the deer park, his lungs burned and his legs ached. Sweat dampened his face, his fatigue all the greater because of his unanswered craving for the drug. He lurched through the woods, desperate to reach his cottage.

He was thrown into confusion by the sight of a

blurred figure sitting on his favorite tree-stump. "Friend!" the man greeted him.

Andrew blinked to clear his vision. "Sam!" he replied with false joviality. "What brings you to Bevington?"

"You, of course."

After submitting to a hearty embrace, Andrew took his fellow poet inside. As he hastily rearranged furniture and cleared away books and papers, he carried out a surreptitious search for his bottle. Where the devil had he left it?

Sam accepted a glass of wine and claimed the better of the two chairs. "I've been at Bristol, where I conferred with Cottle about the new edition of my poems. He mentioned he'd had no news of you lately, and I realized I hadn't either, not since you stopped with us at Nether Stowey. Too busy scribbling, eh?"

"Constantly," lied Andrew.

"I'm glad to hear you've found your muse again. You'll be surprised by my current venture—making plays. I've more time for composition now that Charles Lloyd has gone to Dr. Erasmus Darwin's sanitarium. Mightily expensive, that place, but the poor fellow's mind is well worth saving."

Andrew opened a cupboard. No bottle.

"But I've not been lonely, for Wordsworth called on me a fortnight past. What a profoundly insightful man he is! We stayed up till the candles guttered, talking of our plays and whether we should attempt to have them produced in London. Mine is a Spanish tragedy in blank verse, which I've titled *Osorio*."

Sam Coleridge was never merely content to discuss his own projects, he had a habit of encouraging the confessions and confidences of his friends. As the visit wore on, he scented a crisis, Andrew could tell from his questions. To stave off an inquiry, he handed over a selection of his story ballads and encouraged Sam to read them.

He was reluctant to admit the evil of his situation to his hero, the most gifted of all his poet friends. If he did, his woes would be related to any number of others: Charles Lamb, William Wordsworth, Robert Southey. Andrew desired their admiration, not their pity. He would not be mourned over like that madman Charles Lloyd, and described by all as a poor fellow.

Failing to locate his laudanum, he made up a fresh mixture. With trembling hands, he scraped away at a cake of crude opium with a knife edge to loosen the grainy powder, and added it to a glass of water. Speedily he consumed four teaspoonfuls of the tincture.

He offered to share with his visitor, who readily accepted. "I hadn't intended to remain above a few hours," said Sam. "But you know how it is with the elixir—in a very little while I shall find it beyond my powers to rise from this chair."

"Stay the night," Andrew invited him. "You can take my bed, and I'll sleep by the fire."

They talked and drank together for the rest of that day and into the night. Under the drug's influence, Sam grew less voluble. He sat silently, mouth open, for minutes at a time. When he did speak, he acknowledged his struggles with the forthcoming edition of his poetry and expressed a flattering desire to collaborate with Andrew in future.

"However, that must wait till after my visit to Wordsworth and his sister. In the meantime, what will you be doing? Tutoring your Lord Bevington's nephew?"

"I declined the post," Andrew replied. "And in

a most decided fashion, so I doubt his lordship will renew the offer. I'd intended to set up an establishment nearer to London—oh, Sam, the hopes I had! All dashed to bits, by a woman's weakness, and the selfishness of a man I regarded as a friend."

"A blighted romance?"

Regretting his bitter outburst, he muttered, "I hope not—it's not certain yet. I've nowhere to go now, having already informed the earl that I would leave this place. I'm so damned feeble—with any exertion, I feel as though a heavy weight is pressing down on my chest. Perhaps I'll turn out to be comsumptive, like my mother." He drew a long, labored breath.

"You can make everything right again," was Sam's languid response. "Tell the earl you'll dedicate your next poem to him, then you'll regain his favor."

Darkness fell. After many hours the waking dream-state produced by the laudanum gave way to drowsiness. Sam sought the bed in the corner, and Andrew settled down on a nest of blankets before the hearth.

He slept deeply throughout the night. At dawn he woke, feverish and agitated, his body damp with perspiration. Unwrapping his sheet, which had wound itself around him like a shroud, he stumbled to the table and grasped a quill, eager to put his visions down on paper. He wrote in haste, finishing his journal entry long before Sam began to stir.

Their breakfast consisted of a stale cottage loaf and fresh butter, with a pot of weak tea.

"I want to hear about this curious dream you had," Sam said.

"No dream," Andrew replied, "a most vivid nightmare. Although it didn't seem so at the beginning, because I was at a wedding feast. The bride was bright as an angel, the groom handsomer than the devil."

"Were these people known to you, did you recognize them?"

He nodded. "But I didn't share in their happiness. Sorrow rose inside me, I could not stay. Suddenly—magically—I was transported to a great ship with huge white sails, in a becalmed sea. All the passengers on board, and the crew, were dead."

"Dead?" Sam echoed in fascination.

"Skeletons, their bones visible beneath pale, transparent flesh. Except for one," he amended. "A dark youth. At first I thought he was a corpse, but he wasn't. He cursed me. Said I had done a hellish thing." His shaking hand gripped his teacup, and he drained it in a gulp.

"What then?"

"I heard a roaring wind. Thick black clouds filled the sky. To escape the gale, I leapt into the water. My limbs felt numb, I thought I was drowning. And yet I could not die. I *wanted* to die."

"Why?"

Despair, thought Andrew, and guilt. Sophie was forever lost to him. Cass, his friend, had stolen her from him. Envy burned in his heart, wrath flowed through his veins. And murderous visions rose in his mind.

"The waves cast me onto the shore," he went on. "I struggled to my feet and walked deep into a forest. It was this one, and I came to this very cottage. On the table I found pen and paper—as you see before you. I sat down and wrote out some words—*the Hermit in the Wood*. At that moment I awakened."

Sam was staring at him, lips parted. "You describe it so vividly. You should make a poem of it."

Andrew reached for his journal and ripped out the pages. Crumpling them in his fist, he let them fall. "I don't like remembering."

His friend rescued the papers and placed them on the table, flattening out the creases with his palm. "A wedding. The skeleton ship. A curse. And a hermit in a wood." He pressed his knuckles against his prominent teeth. "These elements in combination with my vision of the great seabird, might make an epic ballad."

"If you say so."

"May I keep your notes? They might be useful."

Andrew nodded absently. A liberal dose, he told himself, was certain to wash the ghoulish images from his mind. Leaving Sam to pore over the written account of his fearsome dream, he went searching for his bottle of liquid delight.

"Marriage settlements," Cass explained to the portly young man seated with him in the library. "When I first returned to England I consulted you about the provisions I wanted to make for my sister and the child. I'm planning to be wed in a fortnight, and must ensure the financial welfare of my wife."

"With all respect, your lordship would be better served by my senior partner."

"Over the past year, Mardyke, you've handled my affairs with admirable precision."

A flush stained Mr. Mardyke's dumpling cheeks. "My lord, I'm most gratified by your good opinion."

"The castle and its lands will naturally descend to my firstborn son, who will hold the courtesy title Baron de Somery in my lifetime. My Carysfort inheritance will provide for the countess and our younger sons and any daughters. I've written down the amount I wish to settle upon each."

Mardyke took the paper and studied it. "And what does Mrs. Pinnock bring to the marriage in the way of income or real estate?"

"You need not consider that. Her property remains her own, for her sole and separate use, as ordained by her late husband's will." Moving away from his desk, Cass instructed, "You will travel to London, at my expense, to collect some documents from her brother-in-law, also an attorney. To him you must deliver this letter from Mrs. Pinnock, informing that family of the engagement."

"Yes, my lord."

"While in town, I want you to call upon Mr. Balthasar Prowdie in Arundel Street. Due to ill health and advancing age, he's retiring from practice and must surrender all deeds and documents relative to the Bevington estate. Henceforth they will be your responsibility."

His visitor's eyes popped. "My lord!" He swallowed, then said, "I will do my best for you."

"I've no doubt," Cass told him. "Prowdie will explain the rent structures and incomes—prepare for some long sessions, for he's slow of speech, and meticulous. He offers to house you, but I expect you'll be more comfortable at Nerot's Hotel. If you give my name there, the staff will take especial care of you."

The dazed expression had left Mardyke's face, and his voice was calm when he replied, "I shall do whatever your lordship thinks best."

"Lastly, I come to the most important of your tasks. A week from Sunday, the third reading of the banns will occur at St. Nicolas church in Chiswick. After the service, you'll receive a signed certificate from the cleric. Bring it to me, posthaste, for I mean to be wed the following morning—the first of May."

"You may depend upon me, my lord." A spark of humor flashed in the gray eyes.

"Good man."

Before he could say anything more, Sophie surged into the room, Echo prancing in after her.

"You're here—I thought you might be," she cried breathlessly. When the attorney rose from his chair, she added, "*Pardon*, my lord. I've interrupted you."

"This is Mr. Mardyke, my man at law from Bristol. He is staying the night."

The young man bowed. "My felicitations, madam, on your approaching nuptials. Is there anything else, my lord?"

Cass shook his head absently. With Sophie so near, he could only think of her. He couldn't recall ever seeing her so deliciously disheveled—there was a smudge of dirt on her chin, loose strands tumbled from the dark coil of hair at her nape. And on her gown—could that be hay clinging to the fabric?

"Then I shall excuse myself to review these papers, and make ready for the journey to London. And Chiswick," Mardyke concluded, with a smile.

As the door closed behind him, Sophie asked, "Did you give him my letter to the Pinnocks?"

"I did." Cass pinched her cheek. "What have you been doing, mucking out my horse boxes?"

"Very nearly. Cassian, I've made the most wonderful discovery! I found a stag."

"It was bound to happen. The deer park is teeming with them."

"*Nânnîn*—in your stables. A stone stag—I told you a pair of them was made at the time of Queen

Elizabeth's visit to the castle. It was covered with a horse blanket, with an old saddle on top. But the head and antlers are missing," she added forlornly.

He struggled to contain his amusement. "My sweet Sophie, I shall commission a dozen stags, if you want them. Carved from purest marble."

"*Ma fé*, how you spoil me."

How I love you, he thought, wishing her face would light up for him and not merely for his promise to adorn her gardens.

Joy and good fortune had finally found him. Like the hero of a fairy tale he would dwell here in his castle, a beauteous countess at his side. For her sake he would forget the haunting betrayals of his past, and concentrate on a happier future.

The dog nuzzled Sophie's knee, seeking her attention. Stroking the long nose, she said, "If only I could find the other stag. I mean to keep up my search."

"Have you any Jersey-bound letters? Mardyke can post them for you."

"*Oh, mais*, I've been so busy I've not yet written my family." Gently tugging on Echo's ears, she said, "I shall do it tonight."

"Be sure to tell them how charming I am," he advised her. "But you should probably refrain from mentioning how eagerly I await our wedding night."

"*Démon!*" she cried, flouncing away from him. "Is that all you think about?"

At least he had his priorities straight, he thought, vexed about taking second place to a headless stag.

Sophie read her letter twice before folding and sealing it. Her sudden engagement to her aristocratic employer, an acquaintance of fewer than four months, would perplex the people who loved her most. She tried to allay any concern they might feel.

Although she hadn't pretended to be madly in love, she'd characterized the earl as generous-hearted, affectionate, a devoted brother and uncle, and a man of excellent reputation. Scattered throughout the lengthy epistle were the words "respect" and "admiration," which failed to depict his vibrant personality and gave no hint of the pent-up passions he'd released.

She'd felt all fluttery inside when Cassian had alluded to his desire for her and showed his impatience to have her in his bed again. She remembered the weight of his body against hers, the way he'd mumured her name at the moment of ecstasy, and a quiver of anticipation surged through her.

This intensity of feeling, this giddiness, couldn't possibly last, she warned herself. It was spring. She'd endured a long period of celibacy. She was about to be wed. But she wasn't sixteen this time, she was twenty-one, and well aware that marriage was a serious commitment with serious consequences.

The evening silence was shattered as a shower of tiny hailstones struck the windowpanes. Sophie, fearing damage to her flowers, hurried to the casement. There was no sign of a storm, the sky was clear enough that she could see stars. She drew back again in alarm when bits of gravel rattled against the glass—a signal from someone below? She could just make make out a male figure on upper step of the terrace. Cassian? Her pulse quickened at the prospect of moonlight dalliance with her intended.

Without hesitation she reached for a shawl and rushed down her spiral stair. The breezeway was cold, and she shivered. "Where are you?" she called softly.

"Over here."

It wasn't his voice.

"Didn't mean to alarm you," Andrew Searle told her, "but I had to see you. Don't want Cass to know," he mumbled. "Something I need, you must ask him for me."

"Yes, of course," she agreed. "What is it?"

"Perhaps he told you I declined to tutor the little boy. Meant to go to away—but my great plan came to nothing. My health is poor, I may not be able to find employment elsewhere. I'd like to stay on at the cottage, for the time being. Until I'm better."

He did look dreadful, continually licking his cracked lips and rubbing his eyes. Sophie assured him that he needn't fear being cast out. "But if you're ill, Dr. Jenner should see you."

"I need no doctor." He swept up her hand and squeezed it tightly. "Only you," he rasped. "Your kindness, your friendship."

She tried to free her hand of his convulsive grip, but he wouldn't release her. "*Oui-dgia*, I am your friend. And so is the earl."

"You are contented with your engagement?" he asked.

"Mine is no blackened betrothal, Mr. Searle." Her attempt at a jest failed to raise a smile.

"I've known Cass most of our lives," he told her gravely. "A man of many faces, many moods. In my youth I loved him as a brother. But in later years, his cruelties and callous selfishness almost made me hate him."

She stared. "You use strong language, sir."

"He means to have you, Sophie. Always he gets what he wants. You couldn't escape this marriage even if you wished it."

"But I don't," she stated firmly—truthfully.

"He'll use you. Hurt you. And lie to you, so sweetly that you believe in him and everything he says." Lowering his voice to a near-whisper, he said, "I speak from bitter experience, Sophie, when I warn you not to make the mistake of giving your heart to a Carysfort. For if you do, assuredly it will be broken."

Every thing doth pass away;
There is danger in delay:
Come, come gather then the rose,
Gather it, or it you lose!

GILES FLETCHER

Chapter 15

"**D**aniel, have pity on your aged uncle!" Cass chased the wayward ball as it rolled across the green.

Sophie, seated at her easel, laughingly reminded him that he'd suggested the game.

"To my regret," he panted, stooping to capture the ball. "Young rascal, he doesn't understand why I must conserve my strength."

"Nor more do I."

With a wickedly suggestive grin, he confided, "I shall need all my stamina for the wedding night. I can't risk disappointing my bride."

"*Scélérat!*" A fiery blush spread across her face. "You scoundrel!"

"Tio Cass," called Daniel, "toss the ball!"

The third reading of the banns had taken place that morning. On the morrow they would be wed— provided Mr. Mardyke returned with the necessary certificate from Sophie's parish priest in Chiswick.

Preparations were going forward as though the ceremony would proceed. All the tenantry, villagers, and farm laborers had been summoned to the castle for a lavish wedding feast at midday. Under Bitton's supervision, the footmen had arranged long wooden tables and benches in the forecourt. Emrys Jones was already cutting flowers for decorative May garlands.

And the lord of the castle continued to jest about the wedding night to come.

Many faces, many moods. Andrew Searle's warning words haunted Sophie on this day of nervous anticipation.

During the previous four months, her future husband had displayed every one of his faults. He had a temper, *vraîment*. He could be imperious, *sans doute*. But because he'd never given her cause to doubt his word, or his integrity, she had nothing to fear. Poor Mr. Searle's illness had brought about his strange fancies and inexplicable mistrust of Cassian.

She swept her paintbrush across the paper, adding a violet wash to her watercolor of the irises springing up in front of the ivied wall. Carefully she fanned the tip over each petal, deepening the purple tints.

"Sophie, have a care!"

She looked up as the ball soared past her head and vanished in the tangled foliage.

"I'll find it," she promised, abandoning her camp stool.

She felt behind the clumps of irises, where she imagined it to be. Her searching hands parted the thick curtain of greenery growing up the wall, and instead of coming in contact with stonework they met no resistance.

She had uncovered an opening. Eager to explore, she crept inside.

"Sophie," Cassian called to her. Distance and the barrier of ivy made his voice indistinct.

The cavern smelled of dampness and mold. She moved warily through the darkness, one step at a time. Her foot struck the ball and she crouched down to pick it up. It was wedged against a solid object of cold stone.

"What's become of you?" Cass lifted the vines to peer inside, admitting enough light for Sophie to make out a large, pale shape.

"*Sécours dé grâce*," she whispered. "The other stag." Then, louder, so he could hear, she said, "Ask Emrys Jones to cut back the vines so I can see."

With eager hands she traced the animal's back, then slid them up the neck, feeling for the collar of roses. She studied the head—ears and antlers were intact.

"How long have you been hiding here?" she wondered aloud, her voice echoing in the dank gloom.

Later, after Emrys Jones hacked away the ivy, the cave's vaulted shape was revealed.

"If I fitted it with a door," he commented to Sophie, "I might stow shovels and rakes and such inside."

Daniel tugged at his uncle's sleeve. "Don't let him have it, Tio," he pleaded. "I want to play here."

Cassian looked to Sophie for guidance. "An ideal play place for a child," she acknowledged. "Mr. Jones, you can use the space at the back of the pavilion for your tools, as we discussed the other day."

"Aye, ma'am. Day after tomorrow I'll get a party of strong men to shift yon statue."

"You'll do it tomorrow." When she saw the gardener's raised brows and Cassian's black frown, she realized her error. *"Oh, las, les neuches!"* In her excitement at finding the long-lost stag, her approaching marriage had flown from her mind.

Cassian turned away from her and marched across the greensward, fists tensely curled at his side.

Many faces, many moods. The words echoed as she trailed after him. Now he was angry, offended by her forgetfulness.

"Où est qu'on vos en allez?" she cried, once again lapsing into Jèrriais.

He did not stop. She quickened her pace and caught up with him. His jaw was clenched, his nostrils flared. Desperate to appease him, she could only repeat, "Where are you going?"

"You don't need me hanging about, getting in your way. Go back to that creature Jones, and your wretched stag, and all those damned bloody flowers."

"I'm sorry if I seemed distracted. But you agreed that I could restore these gardens. *Your* gardens."

"Mine? When were they ever? They belong to you and that Welshman."

"You're being absurd," she said in exasperation. "Why do you dislike Emrys Jones?" Her question had struck a nerve, she could tell. Suddenly he looked more uncomfortable than wrathful.

"Fool that I am, I gave you leave to employ whomever you pleased. I must abide by my word." He continued his interrupted progress towards the house.

Sophie picked up her skirts and hurried after him. "A brief time ago you teased me about our wedding night, and now you flee me as though I'm an enemy." Trying for a lighter note, she smiled. "With this demonstration of how disagreeable you can be, I'm tempted to cry off."

That stopped him in his tracks. "You can't. Not after letting me—not after we—not after that night. I'm honor-bound to give you my name."

"*Pon du tout*," she contradicted. "I was no trembling virgin, no victim of seduction. I acted of my own free will, and gave myself because I chose to. Yes, we were bound by a pledge. But should either or us, or both of us, want to be released from it—"

"Is that what you want? To break our engagement on the eve of the wedding?"

"*Ma fé*, I was simply stating the facts."

"You don't have to snap at me," he said petulantly.

"I can't help it. We've a saying at home, '*Qui épouse ou Jèrriaise, janmais vira à son aise.*' If you want to live in peace, don't wed a Jerseywoman."

"I thank you for the warning, madam." He moved swiftly to the terrace steps and vaulted up them two at a time.

His annoyance had not subsided by the time she saw him again, at dinner. He twirled the stem of his wineglass in an endless rotation. He drank a great deal but seldom touched his food. He rarely turned his face in her direction, and when he did it was bleak. No smiles, no laughter—he resembled a man doomed to attend his own funeral on the morrow rather than his wedding.

If there was to be a wedding. For the solicitor hadn't returned with the essential document; the ceremony couldn't take place without it.

And then insight came to her in a flash. His ill temper earlier in the day, and now, grew out of his fear that their marriage would have to be postponed. He felt powerless, thwarted. Like his sister, he was unskilled at controlling his emotions; frayed nerves and dread of delay made him testy.

Hoping that the arrival of Bitton with a choice port would smooth the creases in his brow, she accompanied Cecelia to the drawing room. But when he joined them there, he looked no more cheerful.

He listened to their discussion about the preparations for the feast—the baking of cakes and the roasting of meats—for a few minutes. Then he said, "So much effort, for an event that may not even take place."

"If not tomorrow morning," Cecelia answered brightly, "then the next. The food and drink will keep for one more day."

"What the devil has detained Mardyke? Something must've gone wrong. He met with an accident on the road. Or else that clergyman at Chiswick fell ill and failed to call the banns."

The clatter of carriage wheels broke in upon his gloomy predictions and he crossed to the window. "A chaise and four is coming along the avenue," he announced.

Sophie went over to look. The vehicle's glowing lamps marked its progress up the incline, and the horses hung their heads in fatigue, mouths foaming.

"Mardyke," Cassian told her on a triumphant note. "And that certificate." The taut muscles of his face relaxed. "Jerseywoman though you may be, pert and argumentative, I shall marry you tomorrow." He kissed her hard on the mouth.

Another transformation, thought Sophie, and it came so abuptly that it made her head spin.

He placed her hand on his arm and led her out of the room, down the staircase to the great hall, where Bitton was relieving the attorney of his valise. All smiles and good humor, Cassian welcomed him.

"Mrs. Pinnock," Mardyke greeted her respectfully. "I bring a letter from your brother-in-law."

It was two pages, uncrossed, and contained few surprises. Writing on behalf of the family, Mr. Pinnock stated the general disapproval of her haste in contracting a marriage to the Earl of Bevington. And in the final paragraph he hoped that she wouldn't forget their goodness to her at the time of Tobias's death, and her duty to preserve his property for his eldest nephew—and rightful successor.

When she folded up the letter, Cassian asked, "Do the Pinnocks object?"

"I thought they might break the connection, out of pique. But apparently they have a selfish motive for maintaining it. They must make sure young Toby gets what he deserves." After a brief consideration, she said, "If he shows an interest in landscape design, and an aptitude for it, he shall have my husband's books and instruments. And after he completes his apprenticeship, I'll provide a sum of money to help him set up in business."

"Generous," he commented.

"It's what Tobias would have done himself," Sophie asserted. "Is the certificate in order?"

"Most certainly," the attorney replied. "I had it from the cleric this morning after early communion. I made wondrous good time from Chiswick, and halted only long enough to change horses. I felt like a heathen traveling on Sunday, there were so few carriages on the road, but it allowed for a swifter journey."

"You must be exhausted," she said sympathetically. "I've never heard of anyone covering such a

distance in a day and a night. Let Bitton take you
to the room you occupied the last time you were
with us." She felt quite comfortable asserting the
rights of chatelaine, even though they wouldn't be
hers for a few more hours.

Cassian regarded her with transparent affection.
"Yes, Mardyke, by all means go upstairs. Tell Bitton what you require in the way of refreshment."

"Your lordship is most kind. But I cannot retire
until I've turned this over to you." He indicated
the small leather-covered case on the trestle table.
"Mr. Prowdie had forgotten to give it to you. Shall
I open it?" At the earl's nod, he inserted the miniature key in the lock and raised the lid, revealing
a jumble of jewelry.

"*Grand Doue!*" cried Sophie.

"I'd no idea the Bevington collection was so impressive," said Cassian.

"There are even some diamonds," Mardyke informed them. "In the document box is an inventory
detailing the provenance of significant items. Most
of what you see here is a century old, or more. The
earl before the last one was at odds with his countess and gave her no more than a marriage ring, and
your lordship's predecessor never had a lady to
adorn."

Sophie picked up a brooch of cabochon emeralds
and dangling freshwater pearls set in heavy gold.
"How quaint."

"That piece dates from Tudor times."

Sophie wondered if it had been worn by the
Lady Bevington who had welcomed Queen Elizabeth to the castle, whose husband had commissioned the stone stags.

Cassian's long fingers sifted through the heap of
bracelets, pendants, rings, and collars. Passing the

chest to Sophie, he told her, "You should keep these. Wear them, if you choose."

She studied his face, seeking clues to his state of mind. The blue eyes were unclouded, the mouth soft and smiling. Looking at him now, she could hardly believe this was the same tempestuous man who had berated her in the afternoon and avoided her eye throughout dinner. Now he was bestowing his ancestral jewels upon her.

In future she would try to keep her own temper in check and learn to be patient with him. They were both stubborn, equally determined to prevail in any dispute. This marriage, unlike her last, would be far from peaceful.

And yet, she reminded herself with a secret smile, it was certain to be exciting!

A lark's song broke the silence of the morning, waking Sophie from a warm, deep slumber. She lay very still, staring at the flat wooden canopy overhead, and wished the butterflies tumbling in her chest would be still.

Her wedding day.

What a youthful bride she'd been five years ago, standing at Tobias Pinnock's side in St. Martin's church. Eager and shy, pleased to be a wife but desolate about leaving her close-knit family and island home for England.

The sun shone brightly today, as it had then. A good omen.

Last night before going to bed, she'd removed her late husband's miniature from her workroom. She'd placed it with his signet ring, inside the little box of valuables on her dressing table.

When Tobias had once predicted her remarriage, she'd tearfully begged him to be silent. Now she could be a little comforted by the knowledge that he'd expected this day to come—but he'd never imagined she would one day become a countess.

Nan appeared at her usual time, carrying a fistful of lilies of the valley. "You might carry these, ma'am, or wear them in your hair."

"That's very thoughtful, Nan," she replied, touched by the gesture.

Cheeks ruddy with excitement, the maidservant tied the fastenings of Sophie's cream silk bodice. The gown divided in front to reveal a coral-colored underskirt edged with a lacy flounce.

Cecelia soon arrived on the scene, arrayed in lemon taffeta. "Oh, you are so charming!"

Sophie extended each of her arms in turn so Nan could button the long, tight sleeves. "I haven't the proper gloves," she mourned. "My only white ones are long, and I need short."

"Wear mine. Nan, go and look in the topmost drawer of the chest in my dressing room. Make haste, now, for his lordship has already gone down to the church."

Sophie swallowed and found one of those butterflies stuck in her throat.

"Let me arrange your hair," Cecelia offered. She wielded the brush and comb, then expertly wound Sophie's dark mane into curls and secured them to her head with gold pins. "You needn't make do with the gamekeeper's daughter as your abigail now, you know. One of the Bristol employment agencies can provide you with a good Frenchwoman."

"I'm not fashionable enough to warrant a Frenchwoman, and I prefer to keep Nan Parham. She's clean and cheerful and has proved her competence. I can ask no more than that."

"Cass might decide to cut a dash in London. Wouldn't you like that?"

"*Pon du tout!*"

Tucking in a few white flowers at the back of Sophie's coiffure, Cecelia said, "There, now. You look utterly lovely, and smell divine. What about jewelry?"

"My pearl earrings."

When Nan delivered the gloves, Sophie remembered that she needed to keep her hands bare for the duration of the service. She gave them to Cecelia. "Keep these for me, till afterwards." She gathered up the remaining flowers in an informal bouquet, drew a deep, steadying breath, and announced that she was ready to proceed to the church. She made her way carefully down the spiral stair, with Nan helping to carry her skirts.

"Follow along with us," she said to her misty-eyed maid, "and mind I don't drag my hem along the grass. You may sit at the back of the church during the ceremony, if you wish." She knew that this would raise Nan's status within the household hierarchy, for no other servant would be present.

The girl curtsied. "An honor to me, ma'am."

"You will continue waiting on me, as you've always done. But with my own rise in the world it's only right that I increase your wages."

Nan shook her golden curls as if dazed. "Dear me." Immediately proving her worthiness, she bent down to keep Sophie's trailing skirt from dragging across the stone-paved courtyard.

The three women followed the hillside path to the church, entering by an ancient Norman portal that never failed to remind Sophie of the similar style of architecture that prevailed on Jersey. Although the interior was chilly and poorly lit, the morning sun enriched the colored panes in the east-facing altar window. Nan smoothed Sophie's overskirt once more and fussed with the lace on her sleeves before slipping into a pew at the rear.

Sophie followed Cecelia up the broad center aisle. Cassian, pacing back and forth in front of the choir stalls, came to a sudden stop. Sophie gave him a smile and received one in return. She moved forward, but came to a sudden stop when Andrew Searle stepped out from behind a marble tomb of a recumbent Bevington in armor. His face looked as white as that of the carving.

The vicar observed, in his squeaky voice, "A bride, a groom, two witnesses. My lord, shall we begin?" Glancing down at his prayer book, he warbled, "Dearly beloved, we are gathered together here in the sight of God . . ."

Sophie recited her vows calmly, in contrast to Cassian's swift, brusque responses. She sensed his impatience to get through the ceremony. Clasping his right hand, she promised to love and cherish him—but she stumbled over the word *obey*. A taunting gleam flickered in his blue eyes, and she wondered how soon he would make her rue that particular clause. And for the first time, she realized, she'd mentioned love in his presence.

He took her left hand and slid a ring over the fourth finger, a wide band of gold with a single table-cut diamond. She had no time to examine it before they knelt. The vicar prayed over them, then bestowed her hand on Cassian and declared, "Those whom God hath joined together, let no man put asunder."

A blessing followed, then a psalm, followed by any number of prayers and exhortations. When the service ended, the clergyman led the newlyweds and their witnesses over to the marriage register, and everyone signed it.

Cecelia, tears sliding down her alabaster cheeks, hugged her brother and kissed her new sister-in-law.

Andrew Searle hovered silently. Sophie tried not to think about the cryptic warning he'd voiced the other night. He was mistaken, her heart would not be broken. Whatever his grievance against Cassian, it hadn't spoiled their friendship—otherwise he would not be groomsman.

The entire wedding party proceeded down the aisle toward the door. Cecelia returned the gloves. "Wait, let me see your ring first," she said, before Sophie could put them on. "How grand it is!"

"One of the Bevington jewels?" Sophie asked her husband.

He nodded. "I removed it from the box when you weren't looking. God knows how old it may be."

Emrys Jones waited in the churchyard. His long gray hair was unbound, hanging loose about his shoulders, and he held a flowery garland. "All happiness to your ladyship," he said. His rare smile vanished and he snatched the bouquet from her grasp. "Nay, nay," he scolded, "these bring bad luck. The flower heads hang downward, bowed in sorrow."

"Your Welsh superstitions have no meaning for me. I'm a Jerseywoman."

"Carry this instead," he insisted, pressing the garland upon her.

Bound up with white and pink ribbons, it contained an array of blossoms to match: blackthorn flowers, crab apple, snowy wood anemones, pale pink lady's-smock. She thanked him, and as Cassian drew her along the stone-flagged walk, her shoes crushed the ill-fated lilies of the valley.

Daniel raced across the castle courtyard to meet

the newlyweds. In his arms he carried a wriggling puppy whose pointy nose and floppy ears matched Echo's.

"Whose is it?" Sophie asked.

"Mine!" he declared blissfully. "Tio Cass gave her to me this morning. Her name is Rosa—that means 'rose' in Portuguese."

"Parham's lurcher bitch whelped again," Cassian explained. "Cecelia and I felt it was time for Daniel to have a pet of his own." Fingering the pink satin ribbon encircling Echo's slim neck, he asked, "Where did this come from?"

"I dressed her up so she could come to your party." Glancing up at Sophie, the child asked, "What am I to call you? Tia Sofia?"

"Tante Sophie," she told him. "Let me kiss you, it's my privilege now you're my nephew."

A cheer went up from the country folk as their lord and lady passed by long tables, and mugs of ale were lifted in toasts. Sophie smiled and nodded as Cassian presented individual farm tenants and villagers to her, greeting each by name.

A tall, fair-haired lady approached her, smiling broadly. "I'm sister to Matthew Parham, m'lord's gamekeeper. Our family have a dairy, and I make the cheeses."

"I used to make them myself," Sophie told her, "when I lived in Jersey. Now I know where to go when I miss my cows."

"Oh, m'lady, I'd be pleased to welcome you anytime," Miss Parham declared.

Cass, overhearing this exchange, marveled at his bride's ability to endear herself to others. He hoped she could show him how to make himself popular with his people. He didn't want to loom above them in his hilltop fortress, descending once a week to attend church and only addressing them in a prepared speech at the twice-yearly agricultural fair. He wanted to know them all, from the most prosperous shopkeeper to the lowliest laborer in the field.

His marriage, he believed, would add some much-needed shine to the thickly tarnished reputation of the Earls of Bevington. The two men who had held his title earlier in the century had never been well beloved. One was typically described as brutal and cruel, and figured in local legend as a wife-murderer. His son had been a reputed sodomite.

When they took their seats at the head table, more toasts were drunk and the platters of food began to circulate. Determined to perform his duty as lord of the castle, he prepared himself for a long day of feasting and receiving felicitations. He partook of the dishes in front of him and sipped the vintage wine Bitton poured into his glass.

This was, he realized, his first family party.

He'd always been at school when his aunt and uncle had feted Cecelia on her birthdays. At his coming of age, shortly after he left university, he'd still been mourning his parents and there had been no celebration. His sister's Portuguese marriage—a nasty business, a necessary evil—had been finalized in secrecy.

He looked down the table at Daniel, covertly feeding pieces of bread to his pup. A splendid boy, lively and bright. Growing like a weed, too. With the excitement of the wedding, he'd stopped brooding about—

Cass felt that dreadful, insistent tug of pain and loss and guilt. He couldn't help but think of Luis, even on this happiest of days.

As the afternoon wore on, he grew more and more eager for the delights the evening held in store. He longed to escape with his bride to the privacy of his bedchamber. To remove that pretty gown and caress the soft body beneath. To bury himself deep inside her where he could find sweet relief from all his cares and fears.

Sophie was his solace, his treasure, his dearest wife. And if only he could hold her trust and earn her love, he would have every happiness a man— or an earl—could wish for.

On me love's fiercer flames for ever prey
By night he scorches, as he burns by day.

ALEXANDER POPE

Chapter 16

C ass led his bride along the shadowy corridor, lighting their way with a flickering candelabrum. Echo, still sporting her festive pink ribbon, trotted after them as if assured of her welcome. In the bedchamber they found a fire in the grate, and on a table a bottle of claret with two glasses and a plate of fruit.

"No more," Sophie said, when Cass asked if she cared for any food or drink. "My head still spins from all the champagne we had with dinner." Her gaze veered away as she told him, "Nan won't be coming up to wait on me. You'll have to help me undress."

"I can think of nothing I'd like better. Well, one thing," he amended, following her into the dressing room, "but we'll come to that."

His very first husbandly task was unfastening the back of her gown. She stepped out of the dress and hung it on a peg, then tugged at the front lacings of her boned corset. "Why do you wear it?" he wondered. "Your waist is so slender."

"To make the dress fit better. It's one of my few concessions to fashion." She sat down on a low wooden chest to remove her stockings, and as she leaned forward her bosom swelled over the top of her shift. She glanced up and caught him ogling her. "Wicked man."

"I'm allowed. Weren't you listening to all those prayers the vicar read this morning? Suggestive stuff. All about carnal lusts and appetites, and fornication. Man and woman becoming one flesh. There was that bit about honoring one's wife as a vessel—implying that she needs to be filled. And the part about worshiping thee with my body."

She trembled. From cold, or anticipation?

"Take this." He passed her a banyan, a rich burgundy color, and chose another for himself to wear. "We can sit before the fire, that will warm you."

They removed a pair of cushions from the window seat and arranged them on the floor. No sooner had they settled down at the fireside than Echo joined them.

"Where does she sleep?" Sophie asked.

"Lately with Daniel, only her place with him has now been usurped by her sister Rosa. I daresay she expects me to take her back into my bed again. If you disapprove, I shall train her to lie elsewhere."

She smiled down at the brown muzzle resting against his knee. "I think you'd have an easier time training me to go away."

He shook his head emphatically. "I want you beside me, Sophie. All night, every night. You've sworn to obey, remember?"

"I wondered how long it would be before you pointed that out to me." She shoved at him lightly, playfully.

Capturing her wrists, he pressed her back against

the pillow. As her mouth parted in surprise, he kissed it, using his tongue.

"Enough," he said, pausing for air. "I must pace myself. I've never made love to a countess, and I suspect an extraordinary performance is in order. We'll have but one wedding night, it should be memorable."

He left her long enough to pour out a glass of wine. Returning to the nest of cushions, he asked if she had enjoyed their wedding day.

"*Bein seux.* And your tenants and servants were all so glad to share in the celebrations."

"Many of them expressed pride in having so fair a Lady Bevington. You've lived here many more weeks than I, and have already settled into the rhythm of castle and village life. I still feel an outsider here," he acknowledged.

She reached for his hand and curled her fingers around it. "I confess, I didn't like Bevington the first time I saw it. I remember that day so well—the rain and the fog. The rooms seemed so vast and gloomy. And you frowned at me."

"Did I? Foolish of me. To be sure, I thought you very pert—and excessively pretty for a landscape gardener. I watched you from the library window while you strolled my grounds and fell in love with them."

Said Sophie, shaking her head, "*Nânnîn*, I tried not to care at all. My livelihood depended on making the alterations you wanted. All the same, I wasn't sorry to be dismissed. When I left Bevington I believed it was forever, and that I'd never see you again."

"I doubt you would've done, if that Moncrieff fellow hadn't come here right after you. The drawings he showed me were obviously your handiwork—that's when I began to regret sending you away. I couldn't put you out of my mind. So I went to Chiswick. At the time, of course, my only motive was to hire you to make improvements here. But even then, I was conscious of your many charms."

"*Tchi niolîn*," she sputtered, "what nonsense! You glared at me."

"Frowning. Glaring. You sketch a most sinister character, lady wife."

"You were extremely disagreeable. It wasn't till later, when I was gathering snowdrops, that you demonstrated your amorous nature."

"And what of yours?" he retorted fondly.

She stared into the flames. "There is a wantonness in me, I do not deny it." Firelight added ruddy tints to the dark coils of hair and made her eyes glow. The wine-red garment enhanced her exotic allure.

"We are well matched, Sophie."

Looking him in the face, she said fervently, "I do hope so."

"I shall prove it to you—now." He cupped her cheek in his palm, then slid his hand down the slope of her neck to rest on her shoulder. "As fetching as you are in my banyan, the moment has come to remove it."

He took great delight in exposing every inch of creamy skin and all the luscious curves. Then he began plucking the gold pins from her hair and let the rippling waves cloak her glorious nudity.

He swept his tiny bride into his arms and laid her on his bed. Her eager embrace fired his blood. Fleeting caresses sent chills along his spine. The child-like fingers brushed against the mat of hair on his chest, then slid across his shoulder blades. This creature he'd once regarded as so prim and proper, who had refused to be his mistress, was a wondrously uninhibited bedmate.

His mouth found her breasts, firm and full, and his tongue teased each nipple, urging it to bud for him. Her head rocked from side to side, and her chest rose and fell more rapidly. He studied her reactions, committed them to memory so he would know how best to please her.

He treated her more gently than he had during their first mating, when he'd ravished her and she had reveled in it. Now he cherished her, and was rewarded not merely with her cooperation, but her active participation. She held him and reached for him, and at his murmured encouragement, she stroked his thickened flesh.

He placed his hands along the insides of her thighs, drawing them apart. Her maidenhair felt like silk. She liked being touched there, her gasps told him so. Slipping his fingers into her crevice, moist with readiness, he found the source of her pleasure. How many times, he wondered, could he make her sing tonight?

By the time he entered her, she was already crying out, and his swollen length was sensitive to the pressure of her inner contractions. "Ah, Sophie," he murmured. They fit together perfectly, man and woman made one.

Sophie welcomed his invasion. His strokes came slowly at first, in a mesmerizing tempo, then his body surged into hers with greater force. She marveled at his hunger for her, and hers for him. It crested high, then broke in a wave of physical release, and she caroled to him at the moment of her submersion. And she felt him heave against her as though he, too, had been cast upon the shore by the strongest of currents.

In his arms, in this bed, she felt wholehearted and healed. Was it gratitude that brought tears to her eyes, or a kind of love, or simple relief that fate had offered her this second chance at happiness?

A low, keening sound came from the other side of the bed curtain.

"Echo," said her husband. "I forgot about her." He pulled back the hangings to look out. The dog took this as an invitation and bounded onto the mattress, tucking herself into a ball.

"It doesn't matter," said Sophie.

"If she makes a nuisance of herself, I'll order her off the bed."

She reached over to smooth the damp curls tumbling over his brow—an intimate and wifely gesture. "And if I turn out to be a nuisance, will you do the same?"

Laughing, he kissed her nose. "Never."

They shared a glass of wine, cuddling together among the sheets and pillows. Long silences were interspersed with conversation. Their dialogues centered on their very different perceptions of the prolonged and rocky courtship that had brought them to this state of mutual bliss.

"You were arrogant," she insisted.

"And you stubborn," he maintained.

But if he hadn't been arrogant, she acknowledged, she wouldn't have been so intrigued. "Besides, there was—still is—an air of mystery about you."

Giving her no chance to explain, he pressed featherlight kisses on her lips, her bosom, her belly. She giggled and writhed, and he grew more daring. The dog was speedily and ruthlessly evicted.

Again Sophie experienced that delicious loss of self as he turned her into a wild, desperate being. She opened her body to her mate, she shuddered and sang out, and afterwards slept soundly, cradled in his arms.

* * *

A fortnight into her marriage, Sophie was constantly on the watch for signs that her second foray into matrimony might turn out as well as the first.

She and her husband seldom enjoyed a state of perfect harmony, yet their clashing wills had not made life intolerable. Debates and battles and teases occurred frequently, but more often than not they ended in laughter. Even though their personalities were so different—or too similar—they were fond of one another. And whenever he reached for her hand, and kissed her, and made love to her, she was certain that marrying him had been the right and best choice.

As wife, countess, and castle chatelaine, her responsibilities differed very little from those she'd known at Chiswick. Each morning she met with Mrs. Harvey and Bitton, familiarizing herself with the management of an establishment far larger than the one she'd previously presided over. She laid down rules for the conduct and duties of the staff, relying upon the upper servants to uphold them. She instigated a weekly payment of bills, reviewing all accounts herself—and was astonished by the quantities of candles and flour and sugar required. But otherwise she found no cause for interference.

Emrys Jones visited the house daily to give a report on the progress of the restoration effort. The stone stag, cleaned of grime and cobwebs, now stood at the entrance to the bowling green. Knots of herbs were being laid out within the castle keep to recreate the pleasaunce of earlier times. Sophie had given him leave to hire an apprentice, for she wasn't sure he'd be content to continue in his unpaid post indefinitely. He had also taken on a trio of under-gardeners, members of the prolific Parham family, with fair hair and brawny arms and tanned faces. Sophie had outfitted them with green woollen aprons. The luxury of having so many minions to carry out her wishes could not, however, console her for the gardening time her marriage had taken away.

Husband, sister-in-law, and nephew vied for her attention, and her perusal of the garden archives suffered many an interruption. Cecelia often sought her out to learn her opinion of a fashion plate or a music selection. Daniel begged her to play with him and help him teach the puppy new tricks. And Cassian expected her to be available to him at all hours. He presented her with a small horse and elegant sidesaddle so she could ride with him. He toured her through the countryside in his phaeton. He took her on long, aimless rambles through the deer park.

"I've rarely seen my brother so content," Cecelia told her one day as they sat together sewing. "Or so calm. I don't think he's been cross since the day of your wedding."

"He has—*bein seux*." Sophie had witnessed several outbursts in the past two weeks, and she seemed to be the sole target of his dissatisfaction. She returned her attention to the piece of linen she was embroidering, using a pattern of striped roses she'd designed and drawn herself. It would look well, she thought, covering the chaise longue she'd discovered in an unused tower chamber.

The earl charged into the morning room. "Our horses are waiting," he announced. "Change into your habit, quick as you can, so we may be off."

"Are we going somewhere?" she responded calmly.

"Didn't I tell you? I had a message from Merchant Fry of Bristol. My shipment of wine and port is due at Parham Pill today. I'm riding over to meet the wherry and watch the unloading of the barrels."

Said Cecelia, "It sounds terribly dull for Sophie. Must she go?"

"She was with me when I placed the order, and I thought—" His enthusiasm dimmed. "Forget it," he said with a shrug. "If you don't care to come along, I'll not insist."

Sophie had planned to copy some notations from the old account books. But this was still their honey-month, and she felt obliged to comply with her husband's wish. "I'll meet you in the stable yard," she told him, sticking her needle into the material stretched out on the frame before her.

"Cass, don't encourage her to go dashing about the countryside on horseback," said Cecelia. "She's a countess now, and must keep up appearances. Take her in the carriage, or your phaeton."

With a smile, Sophie retorted, "What good is being a countess if I can't do as I please? Eccentricity is perfectly acceptable in aristocrats. By choosing to wear country clothes and gallop about on my horse, and weed my own flower beds, I show that I'm far too grand to concern myself with convention and propriety!"

Her husband, she noticed, was pleased by her bold declaration. The thunderclouds lifted from his brow and the sun broke out in his smile. Without a thought for the garden research she'd hoped to accomplish, she hastened to her rooms to put on the crimson broadcloth jacket and matching skirt she wore for riding.

Her cream-colored horse, slightly larger than a Welsh pony, was named Cloud. Sophie, translating it into Jèrriais, called him Nouage. Before mounting she fed him a fistful of oats, and his velvety lips tickled her palm as he nibbled.

"Does Echo join us?" she asked, for the lurcher was capering about the stable court expectantly.

"Not today. I want you all to myself," Cassian answered. Advising the groom to shut the dog into a box-stall until the horses were out of view, he climbed onto Saladin's back.

Along their route to the Severn they passed hayfields where men mowed and women raked, and pastures where milk cows feasted on tender spring grasses. Cassian pointed out the various farms, naming the tenant of each one.

"Before much longer, I expect to be as knowledgeable about dairy farming as anyone in Bevington Vale," he boasted. "I started out at quite a disadvantage, for I've lived only in cities, or abroad."

"Dairying is a way of life on Jersey," commented Sophie. "We did the milking ourselves, Méthe and I, with the help of the servant girls. And when I lived at Anneville Manor, I'd go out to the fields early in the morning to visit Uncle Edouard's herd. All those years at Chiswick, I missed having cows."

"Shall I buy some for you?"

"Have a care," she warned, "I might just say yes."

"I'm perfectly serious. You could keep them at the home farm, and let them graze that overgrown field abutting the gardens. The old moat would keep them in place, just like a ha-ha."

She waved her riding crop at some grazing animals. "I don't want these dark brown ones. Mine would have to be Jerseys," she said loyally.

"Next Gloucester market day, I'll make inquiries. Or you can come with me—and demonstrate another of your eccentricities to the local populace by assembling the herd yourself."

The road led them away from the gentle hills and

escarpments forming the vale and into the flatter terrain regularly flooded by the Severn estuary. The constant surges of water cut ditches into the loamy soil, but the lands that had been drained were fertile enough to support a rich carpet of grass.

At Parham Pill a single farmhouse nestled between the pastures and the sandy flats along the broad waterway. Its occupant operated an occasional passenger ferry across the Severn, weather conditions permitting, and provided lodging and refreshments to travelers. The tide was partly out, and the trow that had transported the wine and port from Bristol lay anchored at a distance from the landing. The boatmen had to carry the liquor casks the rest of the way, across soggy sands and shallow pools, to the waiting wagons.

When her husband fell into conversation with one of the drivers, the farmer invited Sophie into his taproom to wait. "There's no one about at this hour," he assured her. "I'll send in the wife to wait upon you."

"If you don't mind, I'd like to look about," she told him. "Have you a dairy?"

"Aye, we've cows enough to keep us in milk and cheese. The wife raises her hens as well, fattening them for market and selling the eggs."

The farmer's lady was unprepared for the Countess of Bevington's tour of her poultry yard. Enclosed by palings, it was spacious enough to accommodate a multitude of fowls, and contained both a pond for her geese and a running stream. At first she was tongue-tied, answering Sophie's questions with nods and shakes of her head. But soon she was volunteering information, boasting about the profits of her enterprise.

"I feed my hens on curds from the dairy, and

steamed potatoes," she explained. "They also get boiled wheat and a small quantity of corn each day. I let my geese graze, and they thrive on't, but they do favor lettuces and cabbages when I have 'em. Each has given me an 'undred eggs a year."

This yield impressed Sophie. "And have you a dovecot also?"

"I'm having one builded, soon's I've laid by the funds for't."

"*Ma fé*, you've got white peacocks! How lovely they are."

"My man made me a present of 'em, thinking to put me in a good humor. A more useless pair I've never known—prancing and strutting." Placing her hands upon her ample hips, the woman glared at the offending birds. "Showy, yes, and rare, but they aren't fit for table or laying. I need fowls what can earn their keep." With a gleam in her eye, she turned on Sophie. "Grand enough for a castle, they are. Will your ladyship have 'em?"

"I couldn't possibly—they were your husband's present to you."

"Nay, nay," the woman answered quickly, "he'll not gainsay me."

"I'll make an offer you can't refuse, he'll have to respect that."

"My lady, I'd pay *you* to take 'em away, I'm that wishful to be rid of 'em. We'll do like the gentlemen when they talk business," said the farmer's wife, "and discuss it over drink. Let me pour out two glasses of my elderberry wine."

Matters were arranged to their mutual satisfaction by the time the earl's barrels had all been stacked on the carrier wagons.

"I hope there's room for a wicker cage," Sophie told Cassian blithely. "I've just purchased a pair of peafowl for the sum of twenty shillings. Pure white, and very beautiful."

"I might have guessed that you're too busy a creature to sit idly by," he commented. "Like a proper countess." When the farmer brought the crate over for his inspection, he acknowledged that the birds were certainly unusual. "The dogs will almost certainly plague them to death," he warned.

"I told her ladyship, they be used to 'em," interjected the farmer's wife, determined to send the fowls away. "Cats, too."

The crate was tied to the back of a wagon. Cassian handed the woman a gold guinea, telling her the extra shilling was to cover the cost of bread and cheese and a bottle of cider. "I thought we might have a picnic," he told Sophie.

"Shouldn't you travel ahead of the carriers?" she asked when they rode away from the farm.

"It's too fine a day to spend in a cellar, and I trust Bitton to see that the wines are properly stowed. Look about for the best place to take our meal. You've the choice of high ground or low."

"High," she decided. "The views down the vale are so pretty."

They found a suitable hillside and left their horses to crop the grass while they enjoyed their own simple repast.

When she had eaten her fill, Sophie lay on her back to study the ever-changing patterns of the clouds that scudded across the blue sky. Her sense of well-being was complete.

Glancing at her husband, she asked, "What makes you smile?"

"My bewitching countess. Is there such a thing as a Jersey witch?"

"*Oui-dgia*," she said lazily. "Mine is a magical island, with many legends and mysteries. We have the Cat of Carrefour, which can shrink in size until it vanishes into thin air. And there's a White Lady who follows people about but cannot be touched. I myself have seen *le Tchan du Bouolé.*"

"What is that?"

"The Dog of Bouley." In a low, sepulchral voice, she said, "A large black hound with enormous eyes, who chases humans by night."

"And you survived the encounter?"

Laughing, she said, "There's no harm in him, a visitation merely foretells bad weather. I know sorcerers who can cure warts, and others who will locate a spring with a willow wand. Farmers and fisherfolk tell many a story of black magic, to explain why the cider goes sour or storms rise at sea. Cows are most commonly afflicted by charms—they cease to give milk, or the cream doesn't turn, or the butter won't come. Anyone can visit a white witch—or wizard—to find out how to undo the spell."

"You're my white witch." He held the bottle to his lips for a drink. "I wish you'd put a charm on my sister, and make her agree to have Daniel inoculated against the smallpox. I've tried to reason with her, and both Dr. Jenners recommend it. But she pays no heed to anything we say."

"Is it so important?"

"The disease can maim—or kill. Young children are especially vulnerable. This new procedure has proved effective for preventing it altogether, and I trust the doctors. Cecelia refuses to."

"But she worries over her son, you know how very protective she is. It's not surprising she's wary of a medical experiment. You may be forward-thinking, Cassian, but your sister is not."

"I am the boy's guardian," he said implacably. "I must take all necessary steps to ensure his good health and welfare. I'd hoped that you could help me persuade her, but if you mean to take her side against me—"

"I've done no such thing," she protested. "I will not take sides at all, or involve myself in this dispute. I'm saving my energies against the day we argue over our own children."

"Will you flout my authority where they are concerned?"

She regarded him intently. "I hope I won't have to. *Dé vrai*, each of us will have strong feelings and opinions, so when we're at odds we must compromise. Shall I share my notions of child-rearing?"

"By all means."

"Our daughters' education," she began, "will be every bit as important as that of our sons. We don't want them growing up to be idle, useless young ladies."

"How could they be," he murmured, "with such a mother?"

"And we shall value our younger boys just as much as the heir. I dislike your English system of primogentiture, with the eldest son being treated as a god and the rest left to fend for themselves in the world. The Jersey laws of inheritance are more fair, with all children, male and female, inheriting a substantial portion of their family's property."

"That's why there are so few great fortunes on your island," he responded, "or intact estates. Every generation subdivides them into smaller holdings." After a brief pause, he said, "You seem pleased by the propsect of bearing my children."

She looked away, towards the slate-colored waters of the Severn and the rolling green hills beyond. "You require an heir, that I know. But I long to become a mother for my own sake as well. My first marriage was barren, and that was a great sorrow to me."

To cover her discomfiture, she began plucking wildflowers to make a chain. She couldn't let him know that abstinence was the cause of her failure to become a mother. Cassian, so vigorous and virile, might think the less of her late husband for his inability to engage in marital relations in his last years.

He tried to help her, inexpertly tugging entire plants out of the ground.

"Take only the part with blossoms," she said, showing him how by pulling some buttercups.

"What's this one?" he asked, handing her a stalk of blue flowers.

"*Tèrrêtre*—speedwell."

"Here's clover, and a moon daisy. These I know. What do you call them on Jersey?"

"*P'tit trêflye*, and *mèrgot*." She crawled across the grass to pick some yellow cowslips. Feeling a sharp tug on her habit, she looked over her shoulder. He held up a pink bloom. "It's a lady's-smock—*Pentecôte*."

She failed to reach the cowslips, for he placed his hands on her waist and turned her around to receive his kiss. His mouth tasted of apples, from the cider he'd drunk, and she supposed hers did also.

"Even in the midst of a meadow, you manage to find an occupation." Taking her flowers away, he laid them on the grass. "Allow me to provide you with another."

"Cassian," she murmured against his neck as he raised her red skirt and black petticoat, "someone might see us from the road."

"They'll assume we're a pair of randy haymakers. Or," he added, his hands creeping up to caress her thigh, "eccentric aristocrats."

* * *

As the weeks passed and Cass saw no outward proof that his love for his bride was reciprocated in part or in full, he grew despondent.

He'd given her his name and a title. He lavished jewels upon her. He had sanctioned her plan to preserve his gardens. He'd bought her a horse to ride and was negotiating the purchase of several Jersey heifers. He had agreed to the construction of a *colombier* so she could keep doves as she had in her girlhood. He gratified her every whim. He indulged her. He adored her.

He did these things to give her pleasure, and not for any personal reward. But he could no longer pretend to himself that she cared for him as deeply and powerfully as he cared for her. While waiting for the longed-for miracle, he tried to convince himself that half a marriage was better than none at all.

What troubled him most of all was the knowledge of how undeserving he was of the love he craved.

His life up to now was littered with mistakes and failures and lies and at least one crime. If Sophie learned about them—from himself or anyone else— their tentative relationship would suffer irreparable damage.

He studied the stately progress of the white peacock as it marched through the rose garden. Behind tall lily spikes topped with bell-shaped blooms, the hen was seeking materials for the nest she'd begun to make in the sheltered niche in the wall. Greatly to Sophie's dismay, she would have to wait until the birds had laid their eggs and hatched their brood before placing her bench there.

Cass strolled through the shrubbery walk to the laburnum arch. The vines were fully leafed out, and pendulous yellow clusters covered the length of the arbor. He approved his wife's foresight in saving it from destruction. Reaching up, he broke off a flower.

The lady he'd won, whose love was so elusive, never sought his company. She was always wandering to one of her many projects—none of which involved him directly.

Altering his tactics, he'd become a less demonstrative and more restrained lover, constantly fighting to rein in his passions. He worried that if he got her with child so soon, he would lose his small share of her attention. Siring an heir was not as important a consideration as she believed; he hadn't been born into an aristocratic family and as yet felt no dynastic compulsion to procreate.

"Rosa, Echo, come back!" Daniel shouted. "Tio, stop them!"

The dogs raced along the tunnel, twin flashes of brown.

"I'm s'posed to keep them out of the garden," said their pursuer, face flushed and black curls in disarray. "They'll chase the peacocks."

"Echo—to me!" Cass commanded.

The lurcher came to an immediate halt and trotted to his side. She lifted her pointed muzzle worshipfully, her brown eyes begging absolution for her misdeed. A pity that his wife couldn't be controlled with such ease, he thought wryly, stroking Echo's ears.

"Have you seen your Tante Sophie?"

"She's in the library," Daniel reported, struggling to lift his pup. "With Mr. Searle."

Cass shared Sophie's concern about his friend's decline, but he also believed it revived memories of her invalid husband. She'd arranged for a manservant to wait upon Drew at the cottage, and required Dr. Jenner to call there weekly.

He wondered whether he could touch her heart by feigning illness himself. If he were sick, he thought, she could not ignore him.

Tossing the yellow cluster aside in frustration, he made his way to the stables. Today he would be riding alone.

Love and harmony combine
And around our souls intwine,
While thy branches mix with mine
And our roots together join.

WILLIAM BLAKE

Chapter 17

The honey-month concluded with a blaze of sunshine and blossoms. Sophie, studying the gardens from the pavilion's broad window, felt a frisson of dejection in spite of the pleasing expanse of stone walls and flowering borders and velvety, well-tended lawns.

Her practical, efficient self had been over-shadowed by a nervous, restless being whose heart fluttered at every encounter with her husband. Her appetite suffered. She spent her nights lying sleeplessly beside him. He rarely initiated lovemaking now, and her own boldness had deserted her. She wanted to reach out and draw him close but never did.

How could it be possible that the fever of his passion had abated after only a few weeks of wedlock? His emotional withdrawal, after the intense and thrilling early days of their marriage, was deeply wounding.

Believing that he'd loved her, she'd foolishly taken his devotion for granted. Now, recognizing its value, she discovered that she'd lost it.

Her restoration scheme was no source of comfort. She had difficulty concentrating on her reference books and plant lists. Nothing could salve the wound that smarted whenever she reflected on the troubling change in Cassian. The terraces and borders and knots overflowed with bright and colorful blooms, yet they seemed paler when he was not at her side to admire them.

Turning from the window, she studied the airy, light-filled room. Ideal for a studio—quiet and secluded, with ample space for a chair and drawing table, bookcases and a desk. She could gaze out over her gardens, or paint them, or learn more about their history from the treasured folios.

Would her husband let her transform this promising chamber into something more useful? Not so long ago she could have counted on his acquiescence, after a lively and short-lived argument. This time, she decided, she wouldn't force the issue.

Making her way down the stone steps she heard his low, measured tones echo in the bathing chamber below.

She peered through the door and saw two black heads bobbing above the water, one large and one small. At the edge of the sunken bath lay two piles of clothes—Cassian's and Daniel's.

Said the boy, "But mine is so much littler than yours, Tio." He looked down and asked worriedly, "Will it ever grow?"

His uncle's booming laugh reverberated off the stone walls. "Have no fear. By the time you reach manhood, you'll have no cause to consider yourself ill-equipped."

Sophie, unintentionally eavesdropping upon this

masculine conversation, put her hand to her mouth to stifle a laugh. As a girl she'd often overheard her brothers comparing their *pinnes* and knew that size was a matter of concern—at any age.

Cassian hoisted the child's naked body high in the air. Daniel wriggled like a fish, squealing in delight. His uncle tossed him higher still, then released him, and he fell into the water with a splash.

"Again, Tio, do it again!" he begged as soon as his head broke the surface.

Observing their play, Sophie felt her heart expand until she feared it might burst. Her eyes grew moist, not from sadness but from an overflowing fount of joy.

And love.

For she was in love, she realized, and positively giddy with it. Love was the reason she couldn't focus her thoughts and energies on anything apart from her husband, and why his recent neglect made her so forlorn.

He was looking straight at her now. Ashamed to be caught spying, she turned and ran back up the steps.

"Sophie!"

She wasn't ready to face him. This newly discovered emotion was too tender and precious, she must guard it as zealously as any seedling. One bitter blast of disdain, or the chill of misinterpretation, might shrivel it.

He burst into the room, a bathing sheet wrapped around the lower half of his body. Drops of water beaded the fine hairs of his chest, and his wet black curls stuck to his forehead.

"I'm sorry—I didn't meant to intrude on your bath," she faltered.

"What have you been doing up here?"

"Admiring the view—thinking what a pleasant

studio this could be. There's so much light."

He studied her for several seconds. "You want to set up your easel here."

"And bring my books and papers over, and a few pieces of furniture. You wouldn't mind?" Her fingers plucked nervously at the lavender ribbons crisscrossing her bodice.

"No." He was staring at her intently. "I don't recall seeing that gown before."

"And I've never seen you wearing only a sheet. Rather undignified," she couldn't resist adding. "For an earl."

"Jersey witch, do you mock me?" He grinned down at her. "Have a care, I might decide to dispense with my covering."

"Go ahead," she dared him.

He was actually beginning to unwrap himself when the barking started—a series of frantic yaps that gave way to keening howls.

"*Oh, las,*" cried Sophie. "The dogs have got into the gardens. Emrys Jones will wring their necks—and mine!"

She darted for the stairway and Cass followed, still clutching his drapery. The animals' cries drew them to the rose bower, and a scene of chaos and destruction.

Daniel, clad only in his shirt, was bouncing up and down on bare legs, while Echo and Rosa raced back and forth along the wall. The white peafowls had retreated to their niche, the hen clucking agitatedly as she and her mate surveyed the remains of the nest. Scattered through the debris were broken eggshells.

"*Tchi pitchi,*" mourned Sophie. "Who did this?"

"Echo," reported Daniel. "She was trying to get at the weasel. See, there he goes!"

Sophie caught sight of a slender, rust-brown

creature scrambling in and out of gaps in the stone-work. Echo yowled even louder in frustration, and stood upright on her hind legs to scrabble at the wall with her paws.

Sophie knelt to examine the eggs, hoping some had survived. With a sorrowful shake of her head, she said, "Nothing left but shells—the weasel made a feast of them. How do we get rid of it?"

"I think we can safely leave that to Echo," Cass replied. "She seems determined to do it in. The power of instinct—she was bred for coursing and seldom gets to use her skills. We'll have to take her rabbiting, you and I."

Sophie was heartened by her inclusion.

Her husband stood before her naked, but for the sheet. He was hers, every splendid inch of him. She longed for night to come so she could run her hands across those rippling muscles and powerful limbs.

"Better find my clothes."

Sophie smiled. Her scrutiny made him self-conscious about his undressed state.

"There it is!" yelped Daniel. "The weasel—running along the top of the wall." He joined Echo and Rosa in the chase, and helped them herd the rodent out of the garden.

"A good thing Cecelia can't see him racing about without his smalls or breeches," said Sophie.

"I'm a bad influence," said Cass.

"On all of us," she retorted.

"Have a care, Lady Bevington. Your sauciness may provoke retaliation. I might just toss you into the canal, pretty gown and all."

"*Bah*, an empty threat. I'm not afraid of you."

"No?" He stalked towards her.

"You'll never do it," she said confidently. "You

can't possibly catch me, pick me up, and dispose of me without uncovering yourself."

"There's logic enough in that elegant head of your to baffle lawyers," he declared. "My university debating society could've used your talents."

"Most men dislike cunning females."

"Stupid men, perhaps."

A sign, she exulted, that he wasn't indifferent. Her fear that he'd ceased to care for her dropped away away as easily as the pink petals drifting down from the flowering almond.

"What are you doing this afternoon?" he asked.

"Going to Gloucester to order a pair of garden seats from the stonemason."

"Is it absolutely necessary?"

"If I do it now," she told him, "I can do other things tomorrow. We've not gone riding together for many days."

"I haven't asked because I thought you so busy with all this." He flung out an arm, gesturing at the arbors of arching roses, heavy with buds.

She wished she knew how to make him cherish these gardens as she did. He was unreasonable, he was possessive—but she'd fallen in love with him despite those flaws.

"I am never too busy, Cassian, when you want me. Come with me to Gloucester, if you would not be too bored."

"I am never bored, Sophie, when you are near."

"It's raining," observed Cass, flinging back the curtains.

"Is that so bad?"

She was glad for the gardens, he knew, but he was concerned about the farms. "It would be if the hay weren't already cut, stacked, and covered, and the turnips for winter fodder hadn't been sown. I'd hoped the rapeseed could be planted this week at the home farm, but that must wait till this wet weather ends." He looked over at his wife. She was sitting in bed drinking a cup of tea, her back propped against the wooden headboard and Echo curled up at her side. "How will you spend this indoor day?"

"Must I decide that now?" she asked lazily.

"Idle wench. You think to remain exactly where you are."

"I would, and gladly, if you kept me company."

He shook his head at her. "Don't tempt me. I'm expecting Mardyke to come from Bristol, so I can prepare the new deeds for enclosure. I'm encouraging some of my green farm tenants to turn portions of grassland into arable land, in exchange for a reduced rent on that acreage. In the long term, it will increase the worth of the land."

"What if the tenants refuse?"

"They aren't likely to oppose me. I own the properties, I pay the land tax. I'm not promoting any radical changes," he assured her. "It's cheaper to grow corn than to buy. With a French war and fewer available markets, prices will be volatile for some time to come. I want my people to be more self-reliant."

"Your tenants are fortunate to have such an interested landlord," she commented.

"I benefit also, for I'm learning a great deal from them. I've a legal obligation to examine their houses and buildings, and instigate any necessary repairs. They maintain the hedges and stiles and fences, and keep all waterways clear. At present these Bevington leases are made at will, for an unspecified length of time. I'd prefer the term to last a minimum of seven years—or even fourteen. But I can't make such a drastic change all at once."

He liked conversing with her about agricultural affairs, it helped him to clarify his thoughts and form his plans. He valued her opinions—as she regularly pointed out to him, she was the daughter of a farmer and sister to several.

Sighing deeply, she said, "I do wish I could convince your people of the superiority of *la vaque Jèrriaise*—the Jersey cow."

"You can't expect the locals to give up their Gloucestershires, despite the success you've achieved with your little herd."

Sophie chewed her lower lip. "I really must visit a dairy house. Nan's aunt, Miss Parham, invited me to have a look at hers."

"You'll be impressed. She's the most respected dairywoman in the vale. Speaking of reputations..." Moving to the bed, he sat down and placed his hand over her knee. "Sophie," he said gravely, "I've some distressing news to relate."

Setting down her cup, she leaned forward. "*Oh, las*, what is it?"

"My efforts to restore the good name of the Earls of Bevington have already failed. Your husband, I regret to say, has lost his good name altogether."

"How?"

"By making a spectacle of himself. With a female. In the meadow on the road to Parham Pill."

She sat up rigidly, an expression of horror on her face. "You cannot be serious."

"Evidently his flagrant act of disloyalty to his countess was witnessed by a regular at the Bevington Arms. He has been talking rather freely, under the influence of strong ale, telling all and sundry of his contempt for such faithlessness. According to his account, the sportive female wasn't even a local trollop, but a stray gypsy lass dressed all in red."

Gripping his shoulder, she gave him a shake. "Cassian, are you teasing me? Oh, how dreadful!"

"But amusing, don't you think?"

"Do you see me laughing? I can't bear to be regarded as the victim of an infidelity—after but five weeks of matrimony!"

"You're missing the joke. Don't you think it comical that no one suspects I was seducing my own wife in that field?"

Sophie bounded out of the bed. "We have to do something to scotch the rumors. But what?"

Cass thought for a moment. "I daresay the fellow noticed our horses. If we ride by his house, me on Saladin and you on Nouage—wearing that red riding habit—perhaps he'll realize his mistake."

"*Chièr* Cassian, you are *ingénieux!*"

"You flatter me."

He was making his way to the dressing room, when she called after him, "You haven't forgotten that Dr. and Mrs. Jenner dine with us tonight?"

"Of course not, I'm the one who asked them." Studying her face, he said, "Why so troubled?"

"Because it's my first time receiving guests formally, as your countess. And I don't know what to wear."

"You look quite fetching in that nightshift, with your hair hanging down your back."

Laughing, she dipped down in a playful curtsy. "Appearing as I am will not improve your reputation, *pon du tout*. Or impress these Jenners."

"They're the ones who should strive to make the good impression," he pointed out. "The doctor is most genial, as you already know, and his wife is a pleasant lady. She was delivered of a child some weeks ago and is beginning to go out again. I wanted you to become acquainted before Jenner conveys her and their brood to Cheltenham, where they spend the summers."

"And is Mrs. Jenner an advocate of her husband's new method of inoculation against the smallpox?"

He gave her a sly smile. "I certainly hope so."

"*Dêmon*. You asked them to dine because you mean to badger your poor sister about that medical procedure."

"It's in Daniel's best interest."

Her guess was correct, he did expect the good doctor and his wife to help him convince Cecelia of the merit of his position. He had to accept Sophie's oft-stated reluctance to involve herself in the dispute. This was his crusade, and he was determined to prevail.

His meeting with Mr. Mardyke took place at midday and lasted well into the afternoon. They discussed the new leases, drafted the deeds, made some revisions, and drank a goodly amount of Old Lisbon.

Before he knew it, he was dressing for dinner. He had to remind Bitton that he needed gloves, and had to ask him to smooth out any creases at the back of his tight-fitting black tailcoat. The young man performed admirably as a butler but was less than adequate as a valet. Cass was accustomed to Luis Costa's fastidiousness, and his great delight in preparing his senhorio for dress occasions.

What the devil had become of that lad?

Although Cass was beginning to accept that he might never know the answer, he hadn't relinquished hope Luis would turn up at Bevington. Complications would inevitably arise if he had revealed everything he knew, but they could be overcome—somehow. Luis was a part of his family, one of his chief responsibilites. His continued absence gnawed at Cass, and even in his lightest moods he was conscious of that inexplicable loss.

If Sir Michael Tait was truly responsible for the servant's disappearance, he'd concealed his involvement with remarkable shrewdness.

Cass joined his ladies in the larger of the two reception rooms, which was decorated in shades of gold and white. Tall mirrors surmounted with the Bevington coat of arms adorned the stone walls, and all the giltwood chairs were covered in ivory damask. Cecelia, wearing a pale, diaphanous silk, blended in with her surroundings. Sophie, gowned in indigo, shone like a jewel in a rich setting.

The Jenners arrived at the expected hour. The doctor presented his wife, a quiet, composed lady with a serious face, whose black mourning honored her recently deceased brother-in-law. Learning that Cecelia had a son close in age to her own firstborn, she thawed visibly.

"Two sons and a daughter," said Sophie. "They must keep you constantly occupied."

Catherine Jenner smiled. "My Robert is but an infant, no trouble at all. But I do keep busy teaching good manners and religious principles to our two older ones." In a softer voice, she continued, "I am relieved to know there's another child in the neighborhood for our Edward to associate with. Lady Berkeley invites him to play with her boys, but I cannot bring myself to let him go."

"Are they so boisterous?" asked Cecelia.

"I'm sure I cannot say, for I've never met them. They are—not legitimate, born when their mother was still Mary Cole. Although at Lord Berkeley's whim she called herself Miss Tudor when she began living under his protection. We heard he meant to be rid of her, when all of a sudden he took her off to London. They didn't bother to announce the marriage till several months afterwards, when the fifth son was born. I gather the earl was desperate for a lawful heir to his title and estate. Poor woman, she'll never live down her past."

"Nonetheless, I should like to meet her," said Sophie.

"The doctor has helped her through many a confinement and inoculates all her children," Mrs. Jenner declared.

From across the room, Cass saw his sister frown. He stepped forward to say, "Do, please, explain to Cecelia that there's nothing to fear from having Daniel treated against smallpox."

"It's a simple business," the lady said earnestly. "Our Edward was treated before he was a year old."

"That was a swine-pox inoculation," her husband interjected. "I waited several years more before performing a variolation using smallpox lymph—with no ill effect. Perhaps it would be helpful, madam, if I gave you a copy of my treatise, *An Inquiry Concerning the History of the Cow Pox, Principally with a View to Supersede and Extinguish the Small Pox*."

"It will have no effect on my opinion, sir," Cecelia replied.

She cast an imploring glance at Sophie, who rose and said with an inviting smile, "Shall we go to the dining room?"

The controversial subject was allowed to rest during dinner. The doctor entertained his host and hostess with recitations from a composition he'd written when younger, an essay on marriage.

"The most prevailing passions in the human breast," he declaimed, "are love and ambition. Marriage is undoubtedly the ultimate tribute of love—though it entails an abridgement of freedom for both parties. The choice of a wife may be dictated by affection or ambition or avarice. Some men seek a bride distinguished by high birth and good family. But we are all equal in the eyes of the divine Being who shaped us, and should follow our own hearts in this most important concern of life."

Cass held up his wineglass, acknowledging that he'd done exactly that in choosing the lady seated at the opposite end of the long table.

His Sophie was not his equal, he reflected, but his superior. He might possess greater wealth, but her bloodline was more distinguished, and she was by far a finer countess than he was an earl. She treated her guests warmly and graciously, with a natural dignity that was more ennobling than her title. But even as he gazed upon her now, so elegant and mannerly, he saw the same Sophie he'd tumbled in a meadow and sported with in their well-used bed.

His pride in her appearance and her deportment spawned a desire to take her to London and show her off to the aristocratic world, but his fierce possessiveness swiftly killed it. She was his to enjoy in private, he would not place her on public view. His reasons for retreating to this stone-ringed fortress were as strong as ever, and they were both safer here at Bevington.

After the ladies withdrew to a sitting room, Cass and the doctor imbibed a sweet, rich, ruby port. He confided, as delicately as possible, the episode at Parham Pill and the gossip making the rounds of the village and farmsteads. Jenner, he learned, had suspected the truth.

"I'll do what I can to convince my patients—and anyone else I may meet—that your lordship is a faithful husband. Though I can't conceive of anyone being foolish enough to doubt it."

"And while defending me against slander, you might also ask if anyone is willing to relieve me of the noisiest, most troublesome pair of peafowl in the kingdom. Their shrieking is certain to start rumors that the castle is haunted. I'd have them slain and plucked and served up on a platter, in the manner of my ancestors, but Lady Bevington would never permit it. The best I can hope for is to pawn them off on someone as gullible as she was when she bought them."

The doctor nodded his balding head, as if well acquainted with feminine foibles. "One day you must bring her ladyship to my house in Berkeley, so I can consult her about my little grotto garden."

"She'd be delighted," answered Cass, pleased that his Sophie's advice was sought by one of the most eminent of medical practitioners. "Do you grow any striped roses?"

"No, my lord."

"Be forewarned, sir. Lady Bevington will undoubtedly prevail upon you to plant them," he predicted.

How oft in pleasant tasks we wear the day,
While summer suns roll unperceiv'd away.

ALEXANDER POPE

Chapter 18

❧

Andrew Searle, reviewing the cyclical life span of the poppy, imagined distant countries with vast crimson fields of nodding flowers. The precious seed heads were harvested and pierced, the flowing juice was captured, molded, and dried, and divided into individual cakes. These were exported to England to be used and sold by apothecaries and chemists. The purchaser then sliced off tiny grains, mixed them with sugar water and alcohol to make laudanum—reconstituting the opium into juice.

Ever since Dr. Jenner had diagnosed him as consumptive, Andrew had taken greater quantities of the drug. No longer bothering to measure out his doses, he'd ceased to rely on his teaspoon. He sipped laudanum directly from his bottle.

The kinder weather of summer, he believed, was improving his health and his state of mind. June had brought long days and warm evenings and late sunsets.

At dusk he sometimes saw Cass and Sophie

walking in the wood, the lurcher chasing after them.

The seemingly devoted bridegroom's assignations with a gypsy mistress figured prominently in local gossip. Eventually he would range farther to assuage his passions—to Bristol or Gloucester, or perhaps even London. Andrew awaited the day when a heartbroken, disillusioned Sophie would turn to him for consolation.

He opened the iron gate leading to the gardens. Her habits were familiar to him, he always knew where to find her.

"Mr. Searle!"

Today she surprised him. He stopped short when he saw her in the shade of the pavilion's columned porch, her arm crooked around several books and the butler at her side. With a smile, she asked if he was willing to make himself useful.

"At your service."

"Take this footstool from Bitton and carry it to the upper chamber, if you please. I'll join you presently."

Andrew had never been inside the pavilion. His steps echoed on the stone floor as he skirted the deep bathing pool. The velvet-covered stool was heavy, and by the time he reached the top of the steep stairway his lungs were laboring hard.

He entered a light and lofty room with pale walls and a high ceiling. In the center stood a carved oak trunk, a table and some haphazardly arranged chairs. Andrew put down the stool and rested on a narrow daybed with a seat of woven cane.

He was mopping his brow with his sleeve when Sophie arrived. Her green bodice, which complemented the ivy leaves block-printed on her muslin gown, accentuated the swelling bosom and womanly hips.

Depositing her armload of books on the table, she said, "Such a beautiful day! God's weather, as we say on Jersey: *du temps du Bouôn Dgieu*. You're wondering why these things are here—this is to be my studio. A place to sketch and paint, and study the letters and receipts I'm using to restore the gardens."

"Can't Cass hire someone else for that? As mistress of Bevington you must have other duties that take up your time and attention."

Her cheeks had turned bright pink. By God, she was blushing!

"Su-supervising your staff," he stammered, trying to banish his image of the newlyweds engaged in their nocturnal activities. "Receiving the local gentry. That sort of thing."

"I prefer to spend my time outdoors. Not that I've abdicated my responsibilities—*naturellement*, I continue to meet with the housekeeper and butler. I approve menus and decide which chambers want airing. It's not so tedious, for my sister-in-law has a talent for hiring efficient servants." Her chin lifted as she said, "But I've made it plain to his lordship what is most important to me."

Andrew's spirits rose at this sign of defiance. So, he thought with satisfaction, the understanding between the lord and his lady was not perfect after all. "And what does Cass say?"

She forced back her shoulders in a determined gesture. "He is learning to accept what I cannot change about myself."

"He never fails to get his way, you know. That is something you must accept—or else be miserable. I did warn you."

Shaking her head, she said, "You mistook my meaning. I am content, I have no regrets. *Ah, ça*, I have known such happiness, Mr. Searle."

Why, he wondered, could she not call him by his name? In his dreams she always did.

"I've heard a terrible tale about your husband," he told her, "and another woman."

"A false report, *bein seux*. Not a word of it is accurate." She actually laughed, poor deluded creature.

"Cass is denying what others have seen?"

"Ask him about it yourself," she said airily. "There's an explanation but not one I can give myself—certainly not to a man. I must go now. We're having a strawberry party in the gardens today—Daniel picked all the fruit himself. Will you join us?"

Andrew hesitated. He didn't particularly care to watch Cass dote on her. On the other hand, it was imperative that he assess the vulnerabilities of their marriage.

He accompanied her to the rose bower, where Cass and Cecelia and the boy were seated on cushions around a low table. All the accoutrements and utensils were gleaming silver: tea urn, sugar bowl, creamer, basins heaped with ripe berries. There were three silver goblets, which Cass was filling with Rhenish wine.

"Sophie and I can share one," he said. "You've been keeping to yourself a great deal, Drew. Can we expect a new volume of poetry or another philosophical treatise in the near future?"

Mockery, and from one who had been his closest, dearest friend. It would be paid back, he vowed, and by deed rather than with words. Coolly he replied, "I contemplate a very different project for the summer."

Seducing the bride you were so quick to betray, he thought savagely.

"Take care not to overtax your strength, Mr.

Searle," Cecelia cautioned him. "Dr. Jenner warned it could have fatal consequences."

"Fear not," Cass interjected. "Drew isn't reckless."

Andrew smiled thinly. "Unlike you." The ladies were amused, but he hadn't been jesting.

"Tante Sophie," said Daniel, "see how 'normous these berries are." He passed her the bowl.

She selected one and sank her white teeth into the succulent flesh. "*Pèrfection*," she declared.

It was, Andrew realized, the same exultant tone he heard in his recurrent dream.

"Tio, can Luis see us from up in heaven?"

The child's piping question brought a grave expression to his uncle's face. "Luis isn't dead, Daniel."

"Maria says so."

"She is mistaken," Sophie assured him. "He will soon be back at Bevington. Your *tio* has sent a letter to Colares and placed an advertisement in the newspapers in Lisbon and London, so he'll know how much we miss him."

"I wish he would hurry home." After this wistful comment, the boy declared that he was full. Under severe questioning, he admitted with a mischievous twinkle that he'd eaten a portion of the strawberry crop while picking it. Calling to his gangly pup, he departed for the bowling green, and the cave in the wall.

Sophie continued to sample the fruit. Andrew watched her, sipping his wine, while the Carysforts engaged in a private dialogue that rapidly disintegrated into a quarrel.

"I resent that charge, Cecelia," Cass blustered. "I'm always careful when it comes to Daniel, you know it well. In this instance, you're the one who's being careless."

"Don't cast blame on me!" his sister shot back. "There's too much uncertainty about this procedure."

Sophie murmured to Andrew, "They disagree about having Daniel inoculated against the smallpox."

"It may be dangerous," Cecelia persisted, looking to the others for support.

"It isn't," her brother declared. "At worst he'll feel unwell for a few days. If he catches the disease, he could be scarred for life, or perhaps die. To me, that seems the greater danger by far. Think on, Cecelia—do you really believe that I, of all people, would allow any harm to befall that child?"

His quiet question blocked the protest on her lips. Twisting one long black ringlet around her finger, she shook her head. "You would not."

"Well, then," he said. "If I fear nothing, why should you?"

Her inward struggle was apparent. "I live with fear night and day. This is little better than an experiment."

"One that has succeeded in the past," he reminded her.

"Perhaps." She chewed her lip. "You'll never grant me any peace till I agree, and my nerves cannot take this constant arguing. Tell Dr. Jenner he may come, but I want to be present while he performs the inoculation."

"We'll both be there. Sophie, too."

Another victory for Cassian, thought Sophie. The force of his will was so strong that he'd overruled the boy's own mother.

He edged closer to her and murmured, "I was studying the roses before you came. My wine-colored one will bloom soon, I think."

Sophie tipped her head to one side. "It is a great

mystery, *vraîment*, your interest in the Velvet rose."

"I shall explain all at the proper time." His blue eyes shone back at her. "I have a plan."

How cruel of him to tease her with soft looks and softer words when they could be observed by others. As a punishment, she jumped up and held out her hand to the poet. "Mr. Searle, let me show you the pink Scotch rose—the buds are already unfurling. If you have your penknife, you can cut some to take back to the cottage."

Andrew Searle was quick to accept her invitation, scrambling up from the ground. She laid her fingers on his arm and together they walked across the grass. Glancing back, she saw that brother and sister had resumed their private conversation. From the way their glossy black heads rose and fell, she assumed that a truce had finally been established.

"They're heavy things, those benches," Emrys Jones grumbled to Sophie. "Nothing for it but to shift them by cart. The turf will be spoiled with hoof and wheel marks."

She ran her hand up and down the pony's nose. "The ruts can be filled in."

"May I ride him?" asked Daniel, tugging at the gardener's green work apron.

At a nod from Sophie, he lifted the child onto the pony's broad back.

The proper siting of her new garden ornaments was of paramount importance to Sophie. Surveying the wall, she said, "Mrs. Fonseca and I want the benches to go on either side of this garden, in the niches. Have you measured to see if they'll fit?"

"Aye, my lady, there's space enough."

"Then instruct the men to carry on."

The Welshman's long head moved from side to

side. "Can't put a bench over here, my lady."

"Whyever not? The peafowls have roosted elsewhere."

"Soft earth. Too soft."

"But we've not had rain in days, and this spot is so sheltered." Disappointed, she pressed her forehead against the pony's cheek. "I wanted to surprise the earl—he'll be back from Lord Ducie's by midday." She considered for a minute, then said, "Tell the Parham boys to fetch shovels and a barrow of crushed stone. They can level the ground and fill it in to support the weight." His reluctance to endorse her command increased her impatience. "Go," she urged him. "We haven't much time—and two seats to set in place."

"My lady, if you but wait, we can make a firmer foundation with flat stones. That would be better by far."

Her nature, as Cassian so often pointed out, was a stubborn one, and he'd given her many a lesson in willfulness. She marched over to the workers and gave the orders herself, explaining exactly what she wanted done. They scattered to obtain the necessary materials.

After they left, Emrys Jones continued his attempt to dissuade her.

"You'll regret it," he told her, holding a basket while she clipped vibrantly pink Portland roses.

The men came back and began to dig, jesting and laughing as they worked.

Sensing a shift in the breeze, Sophie scanned the skies and saw dark clouds blowing in from the Severn—a sure sign of showers. Cassian would get wet, but he'd insisted on riding instead of taking the carriage. Exasperating man!

"Daniel," she called to her nephew, "best go inside. You can't take a chill so soon after the inoculation. And your mother says she'd like to give you another music lesson today."

The child climbed down from the pony's back unassisted. "When are you going to tell me the story of Geoffrey's Leap?" he asked.

"Not till you're able to play a piece for me on the pianoforte."

That inducement sent him hurrying away.

"What does his lordship think of the music lessons?" asked Emrys Jones.

"He suggested them. That surprises you?"

"He seems the sort to toughen yon lad with manly occupations," he said bitterly. "Teach him shooting and fencing instead of letting him practice keyboard tunes and run about the flower beds all day."

Sophie was saved the trouble of answering his strange remark by a shout from the workers.

"Ho there, Mr. Jones!"

"M'lady! Come and see!"

The gardener, his jaw clenched, marched across the grass. Sophie, mindful of her dignity, held herself back to a slower pace.

"Something's buried here," the eldest told them. "Ground's been dug afore, that's why 'twas so soft."

"P'raps it's treasure," said the youngest, who was Nan's brother.

"Makes no difference to you," his cousin retorted. "You'll have no share in't."

The third Parham, who had continued working diligently, suddenly dropped his shovel and backed away. "Hair," he said in a strangled voice, "human hair. Dark." He turned a horrified face upon Sophie. "Your ladyship won't want to stay. I'll swear 'tis a body layin' there."

Giving no outward show of alarm, Emrys Jones

knelt down and thrust his bare hands into the loosened soil. Then he rose, removing his round hat and hanging his silvered head.

Sophie's blood ran cold. "Who can it be?" As she spoke, the memory of a swarthy face and winning smile flashed in her mind.

Non, non, non. Impossibl'ye.

He was in Portugal, where it was always warm and sunny. Not buried in the cold, damp soil of Gloucestershire.

One day I go back there, see my home again . . .

She began to weep, silently, praying that it was not so.

Emrys Jones told the Parham lads to bring more tools for digging—horse blankets—a pail of water. He turned to Sophie, saying gently, "You shouldn't be here, my lady. There are things you must do—a doctor should be sent for, to certify the death."

"Whose death?" she wondered, eyes streaming.

"We'll not be sure till they raise the body."

"If what I fear is true, how shall I tell the earl?"

But she didn't have to.

Her husband heard about the grim discovery as soon as he rode into the stable yard. By then the excavation was complete and the identity of the corpse was no longer a matter of speculation.

When he entered the rose garden, Sophie ran to meet him. He caught her in his arms and held her close while she sobbed into his chest. "I know," he said. "I know."

"Emrys Jones recognized his clothes—and more. I couldn't look. They wrapped him in a blanket and laid him in the cart."

He stroked her hair. She knew it was her place to comfort him, but she felt entirely helpless. This tragedy, unlike the loss of Tobias, had come upon her unexpectedly, without warning. It was an abrupt and horrible end to the idyll she'd been enjoying, and all her hopes for a happy future now seemed as empty as Luis Costa's shallow grave.

All nature mourns, the skies relent in show'rs,
Hush'd are the birds, and clos'd
the drooping flow'rs.

ALEXANDER POPE

Chapter 19

The sorrow that descended upon the lord of Bevington Castle affected his entire household.

To Sophie's astonishment, Cecelia swiftly recovered from a brief spell of hysteria and turned positively stoic. Together they gave Daniel the unhappy news, answering his tearful questions as best they could, assuring him the valet's mysterious death had been accidental.

The Portuguese nurse Maria, who had prophesied Luis Costa's tragic end, was the most vocal of his mourners. She lit candles in her personal shrine to the Holy Virgin and begged senhorio to arrange for the Catholic priest in Bristol to say a mass for her *pobre* Luis.

The rain fell incessantly and ominously the next day. Sophie sought the peace of her pavilion workroom and tried to immerse herself in the history of the gardens. But she couldn't stop thinking about the dark youth who had admired them so much.

Or the long-neglected body, removed to the Bevington Arms for the coroner's inquest.

Nor could she dismiss the multitude of questions raised that morning by the local justice of the peace, who was investigating the apparent murder. She'd been present when her husband had given an account of his castle visit prior to his servant's disappearance, and a description of his futile inquiries in the neighborhood. But his reserve struck Sophie as extremely odd, and she noticed that he said nothing about his trip to London. When Mr. Lott asked whether Luis had been the target of any threats, Cassian had shrugged and professed ignorance.

Footsteps on the stair caught her attention. Andrew Searle, rumpled and glum, materialized in the doorway.

"I'm hiding," he told her sheepishly, "from that Lott fellow. I refuse to speak about what I know, much less all that I suspect."

"You have suspicions?" asked Sophie, laying down her pen. "Even if there was no mark on the body to indicate violence, I fear it is a case of murder," she said sadly.

"Undoubtedly." His lids drooped, hooding his eyes.

"But who would do such a thing? And why? Luis was so friendly, so engaging. I can't imagine anyone wishing him harm."

"Did you never hear Cass upbraid him? All of his dependents have suffered the effects of his hasty temper at some time or other, but he bullied the Portuguese boy more than most."

Sophie's temper surged at the charge against her husband. *"Impossibl'ye!"* she burst out angrily. "He is very good to his employees—I was one of them. You are no friend to him if you can go about saying

such things, accusing him of brutality. And implying he might have committed a—a crime!"

"I've known him far longer than you have," he
pointed out soberly. "Have you forgotten my
warning to you, after you became engaged?"

"It was nonsense."

"Think that if you prefer—if it comforts you."

Her fury was overtaken by fear. "Cassian," she
whispered. "*Nânnîn*—that is madness. He relied on
Luis, he was fond of him. He regarded him as a
trusted and faithful servant. He tried so desperately to find him." Driven by her chaotic thoughts,
Sophie crossed from her desk to the daybed.

Dirt all over his clothes. Why she should suddenly recall that stray detail, Sophie did not know.
"From playing with Daniel," she reminded herself.

"Sorry?"

"Nothing," she said, refusing to let her mind
wander further down that treacherous road.

"Luis was working for the Carysforts at the time
of Daniel's birth. All those years in Portugal, he
lived with them." After a pause, Andrew went on,
"I've often noticed that my friend's affection for his
nephew is more paternal than avuncular. Whereas
Cecelia Fonseca is the least maternal female I've
ever observed. Recollect the way Cass persuaded
her to have Daniel inoculated: 'Do you really believe that I, of all people, would allow any harm to
befall that child?'"

She stared at him.

"His argument made me wonder. But even before then it occurred to me that the boy is his instead of hers. If Cass is Daniel's sire," he mused,
"Luis would have known it. He might have threat-
ened to tell."

"A weak motive for a murder," Sophie declared
shakily. "What difference would the truth make?"

"To a prospective wife—a great difference. Would you have been so quick to accept Cass had you known that another female had borne him a son?"

"*N' m'en pâlez pon!*" she cried. "Do not talk of this, I won't allow it! Yes, my husband has many moods, his temper is uneven. He might have kept a Portuguese mistress, and Daniel might even be his child. But I refuse to accept that Cassian is capable of taking a life. If he were such a *vilain*, I would feel it—I know I would. He is not, Mr. Searle."

Her evident distress pleased Andrew. His plan had not been as effective as he'd hoped, but he'd planted a seed of doubt. She sat before him, stunned and despondent, on the daybed that figured in his most deeply erotic dream of her.

Just last night he'd sported with a lewd and playful Sophie—spreading her creamy thighs to receive him, sighing his name as he poured his seed into her. "You, only you," she had crooned, "will give this castle its next lord."

His vision was prophetic. The next earl would spring from his loins and issue from her womb. Exactly when this conception would occur, he didn't know. Sophie wouldn't turn to him until she lost faith in Cass. But, observing her despair, he didn't think he would have to wait much longer. He had other means of increasing her mistrust of her husband. Cass had many filthy secrets that could be used to blacken him in his wife's eyes.

While Sophie's head was bowed he dug into his coat pocket and removed a small box of hammered tin. With thumb and forefinger he took a pinch of the grainy substance it held and laid it on his tongue—the bittersweet cure for his pangs. Pure opium, mixed with dark West Indies sugar. When she glanced up, he pretended to brush at his nose.

"Have you started taking snuff?" she asked in surprise.

"I began years ago," he replied, "when I lived in London. I picked up the habit from Cass. I could enlighten you about his whole history."

"Whatever I wish to know, I shall ask him myself."

"My dear Sophie," said Andrew wryly, "you would be a fool to believe anything he tells you. Only by lying can he stave off disaster."

The inquest jurors returned a verdict of murder, "by person or persons unknown." Suspicion immediately fell upon a specific person. Rumor drifted outward from the castle like thick black smoke, to the village houses and shops, and all the farms scattered along the vale. The Earl of Bevington had slain his Portuguese servant in a wild rage and buried the body in the garden.

Sophie refused to accept that her husband was responsible for the most heinous crime in Bevington since the unproven murder of Frances Charlotte, the Harlot Countess. Her devotion to him was more powerful and all-encompassing than she'd imagined possible, it went beyond wifely loyalty. She had tumbled into love, and therefore couldn't bear to see him suffering. And even though he never confided the agony he felt at the accusation, she was very much aware of it.

Several days after the inquest the rain clouds lifted. From a desperate need to keep active, she made her long overdue inspection of the Parham dairy, the largest and most productive in the district.

The dairywoman first introduced her to the herd of red-brown Gloucestershire cows. Despite their small horned heads and elegant long necks, Sophie did not judge them as pretty as her Jerseys, but she knew the quality of the cheese they produced.

"I know all my girls by name," boasted Miss Parham before they left the pasture. "There's our Marigold, a nesh little creature. The gurt cow nearest her is Willow, one of our best milkers. We milk them in the field, after dawn and before dusk."

"A task familiar to me, *bein seux*."

The dairywoman reminded Sophie of her own aunt, even though she was tall and strapping, with fading blonde hair tucked under her ribboned mobcap, and Tante Douce Nicolle was small and round and dark-haired. Both ladies were spinsters, yet lived full and busy lives.

"I'm lucky that I've been able to keep my maids and men," Miss Parham said. "As you know, the slightest change—a new pair of hands, for instance—affects the creatures. And their milk."

"I understand you manage the entire dairy yourself."

"Aye, m'lady, with my eldest niece assisting me. You must look over our deyhouse." She led Sophie through an enclosure with benches, where the dairymaids washed the utensils of their trade: tin skimming dishes, butter prints, cheese knives, and milking pails. One scrubbed the inside of a barrel churn with a bristle brush. Another pegged the damp cloths and aprons to a drying line.

The dairy house was airy and well-lit, with a stone floor still damp from a recent mopping and wooden tables displaying neat rows of cream jars. Miss Parham guided Sophie to a spacious room with four large cheese presses.

"We produce double and single cheeses," she explained. "At this season we make both, although we concentrate on our Double Bevington. Come

July we cease making it, for cheeses don't firm up proper in summer."

"How many pounds do you produce?" asked Sophie.

"Near seventy pounds per day, I reckon, over the seven months my cows are in milk." Going to a wooden shelf of cloth-covered cheeses, she lifted the gauzy material to show off the product. "Here are some pressed ones, ready for first salting. We do add color, to oblige the factor and his customers, though 'twas a time when such alteration was frowned on. The cheeses are turned once a day, and when they're firm enough we begin the monthly washing. If they sink down in the water, they're judged good. Those that float are 'hove'— hollow at the center—and sold cheap. If we go up to the cheese chamber, you can see where they dry and ripen."

They climbed a wooden stair to a lofty area filled with long shelves, all lined with cheeses.

"I thought they'd be darker," Sophie commented.

"With aging, the Gloucestershire turns ruddy at the surface. Dairywomen are expected to paint over the outside rind to add more color, which I confess I much dislike. Lord Bevington has given me leave to abandon that false practice. But because yellowy Gloucester cheeses are in such demand nowadays, we dare not leave off the internal coloring. These will be sorted 'cording to dryness, and wiped with a cloth once a fortnight until sold."

"And who takes them off your hands, those that you don't dispose of locally?"

"I deal with a factor from Berkeley, Mr. Hicks. In this dairy we also make whey butter for sale, and that goes out to Dursley market. I've packed

some of my freshest milk butter for your ladyship
to take back to the castle."

When they went downstairs, she presented Sophie with a wooden basket with a lid. Inside were
half a dozen prints of firm butter, each covered
with a broad green leaf.

"Butter leaves, we call 'em," said the dairywoman, "taken from the orach plant. Look underneath."

Sophie removed the covering and found that the
butter was embossed with the head of a stag in a
rose collar, identifying it as a product of Bevington
Vale.

" 'Tis the least I can do, with all the unpleasantness you've known lately. We Parhams have made
it plain that none may accuse our earl of murder
without getting his head broke for it," Miss Parham
said fiercely. "His lordship may count on us to defend him against this foul gossip."

Sophie sighed. "It causes a great deal of harm."

"The more fools they who do the gossiping. We
may ne'er discover what happened to that poor
foreign lad, and 'tis useless to prate on about what
we can never know."

This sensible view was not, Sophie suspected,
shared by many of the locals.

"Our lads ofttimes pass their evening in the village alehouse. They've heard one other person
named as culprit."

Her grip on the basket handle tightened. "Who?"

"That fey Welshman with the longish hair. 'Tis
common knowledge hereabouts that he fancies
men. The old earl coddled him and kept him close,
then left him money and a house. So long as he
troubled no one else and kept to himself, naught
was said 'gainst him—though no parents would
send their sons to work in the castle gardens. If that

poor boy from Portugal was pretty as they say . . .
Well," concluded Miss Parham, shaking her head,
"here I am telling tales myself, after criticizing others for't."

During her ride back to the castle, Sophie considered the account she'd heard from the otherwise
scrupulous Miss Parham. Emrys Jones, decidedly
effeminate in appearance and manner, had fallen
under suspicion. Was there any foundation for it,
apart from his oddity?

Thinking back, she remembered how intrigued
Luis had been by Jones.

Senhorio, he warn me no go near Senhor Shones.

This jardineiro, I think he no like me.

Perhaps, she mused, Emrys Jones had liked Luis
entirely too well.

The gardener had strongly advised against setting the bench in the place where the valet's body
had been buried. To prevent the discovery of his
crime?

As soon as she'd delivered the butter basket to
the castle kitchen, Sophie made her way to her gardens. The Welshman was pulling weeds among the
snapdragons in the lower terrace border.

"Nearly done," he said, looking up.

She wished she could avoid this confrontation,
but she would venture anything to save Cassian.
"I have to ask you about Luis Costa, Mr. Jones.
And—and you."

His lips pressed together.

"I give you my word that I'll hold whatever you
say in confidence. No one else need ever know, so
you can be entirely truthful in your answers."

"I be an honest man, my lady. What cause have
you to doubt it?"

"Did you ever seek him out, or make advances

towards him?" She could hardly believe she'd voiced the shameful question.

Resentment thinned his voice. "Aren't you really asking whether I killed him, and buried his body?"

"I've heard that sodomy is a hanging offense. You wouldn't want to be found out—perhaps you were afraid he'd tell someone. Is that how it happened? I won't deliver you up to the authorities," she promised. "I'll even help you escape. Across the Channel to Jersey, or wherever you care to go. But I must know the truth." She placed a clenched fist upon her breast. "In my heart I believe my husband is innocent."

"But in your head you are not certain." His look was pitying. "I wish I could dispel your doubt, my lady, but I can't. I only took his body out of the ground, and 'tis hard enough living with that memory. I committed no murder. And I'll not remain in a place where I be suspected of it."

"*Bouôn Dgieu*, I don't know what to believe. Do you mean that you are not a—" A what? A lover of men? She was unsure of the suitable term. "That you don't—" She gave up, and regarded him in doubtful silence.

"What the villagers say behind my back, there be truth in it—but not the entire truth. I ne'er loved but one man, God rest him. I'm not one as chases after young boys, howe'er engaging, and Luis was safe from me. I tried to keep my distance, as his lordship warned me to do."

"Warned you? When was that?"

"Soon after you persuaded me to be gardener again. And once more, when he came to Bevington with his servant and the little boy. Followed me like a pup, Luis did, and what could I do to stop it? He was lonely. He liked flowers. We were enough alike that I allowed myself to warm to him a little. A mistake—no one would e'er believe my feelings might be fatherly. After he disappeared, the earl came back and asked me questions. I kept silent about the friendliness between his valet and me, lest it be misconstrued."

That she could understand. Tortured though she was by her personal pain, she couldn't help but be moved by his.

"My lady, much as I want to help you restore and maintain these gardens, I cannot. Nor will you want me to. Not any longer."

"Mr. Jones—Emrys, I didn't mean to insult you. I spoke out of fear, and confusion. Surely you know that I cannot manage without you." This strange and prickly specimen had become more than an associate and fellow gardener—he was very nearly a friend.

"You say that, knowing what kind of man I am?"

"I say it *because* I know. I respect your skills. And your candor." She let that sink in, then added, "As a man who once loved deeply, you must understand my need to protect the one I love."

His gray head bowed. "My lady, I pray your earl is worthy of your trust."

He made no attempt to conceal his doubt. Sophie would have mounted a staunch defense had she not been distracted by the woman waving at her from the upper terrace.

Her mind was playing tricks. What was Tante Douce Nicolle doing here at Bevington? *"Sâbre dé bouais!"* Trouble at Anneville, she thought fearfully, flying up the steps.

But her aunt was smiling broadly and holding out her plump little arms. *"Mé v'chîn!"* she cried. "Here I am, sent by the family to meet this earl you married so suddenly. And to see your home—*ah*, ça, it's grander than the castle at Gorey! His lordship has shown me every room, and even let me have a peek at the kitchen and cellar.''

"Miss Nicolle arrived while you were out," Cass explained to Sophie.

"Tante Douce to you, my lord," the visitor reprimanded him, her cheeks dimpling in a smile. "He thought I needed to sit down, but I had to see everything."

"I might have guessed," he acknowledged. "Having wed a Nicolle female, I know they are rarely restful."

"Give me all the home news," begged Sophie. "Is Méthe well, and Philippe's family, and Brelade and his *emigrée* bride? Will Tanmîn wed his sweetheart?"

"*Oui-dgia* to everything."

"Come up to my sitting room," Sophie invited, "and my maid will bring some tea. You will excuse us, Cassian?"

"*Oui-dgia*—as you and your Tante Douce say."

When the two ladies were comfortably seated in the tapestry armchairs, the elder confessed, "When your letter informed us of this match you were making, we thought it a curious thing. Now that I've seen the pair of you together, I can most sincerely wish you perfect happiness."

"I thought I'd found it," Sophie confided. "In the beginning there were difficulties. Then, for a brief time, I was the most contented creature on earth. Did Cassian tell you of his servant's murder?"

Her aunt nodded.

"I worry that more trouble lies ahead. I shall be glad to have you near me. When Tobias lay dying, I longed for you—even more than for Méthe or my brothers."

"Sophie, things cannot be so bad here. *Tch'est qu'i'y'a?*"

Twisting her hands in her lap, she answered, "Everything is the matter. We hide our secrets too well, Cassian and I. His may be darker than mine, and more dangerous."

"What are you keeping from your husband, *p'tite?*"

"The heartaches of my first marriage, how shadowed it was by deceptions and self-sacrifice. He assumes Tobias and I were constantly happy."

"Then you should explain to him how it was."

"And betray Tobias? *Nou-fait!* He must always be remembered as the great landscape gardener he was. And a good husband to me—for he was that, *aussîn.*" Rising from her chair, she paced the room. "And yet, somehow I must convince Cassian that I care for him."

"You love him."

Sophie, exhausted from emotion, sank down on the window seat. "More than he knows. I waited too long for the proper moment to tell him. The body was discovered, now cruel rumors are circulating—the people here believe he killed Luis. And even his friend Mr. Searle, who has known him many years, is suspicious. That frightens me most of all. Even though it cannot be so."

The enfolding arms could not relieve her mind of care, but she was encouraged by the arrival of so firm and fond an ally.

Releasing Sophie, Tante Douce went to the gate-leg table and opened a small leather-bound trunk studded with brass nails. "Here is your bride-gift," she said, exhibiting several lengths of intricately patterned lace. "It belonged to my French grandmother, for whom you were named."

"Where did it come from? You gave me all your antique lace when I wed Tobias."

"So I believed," her aunt replied. "But long after you left Jersey, I came upon this *baheur* in the attic. I'm so thankful to have another heirloom to present on your second marriage. *Le Bouôn Dgieu* works in mysterious ways, *non?*"

"*Ch'la est vrai,*" Sophie agreed, trying very hard to smile.

Read in these roses the sad story
Of my hard fate and your own glory.

THOMAS CAREW

Chapter 20

Sophie snipped a thorny stem with her secateurs and added a pale pink alba rose to her
overflowing basket. Nymph's Thigh, the French
called it, but the prim English had rechristened it
Maiden's Blush. She moved on to the exquisitely
scented damask Celsiana, with loose petals like
crumpled shell-pink silk, and selected several of
the choicest blooms. From *Rosa centifolia* she
claimed blossoms that looked like large teacups
stuffed with petals, the inspiration for so many
Dutch flower paintings. The miniature form, dainty
de Meaux, provided small pink pompoms, tiny
enough to make a doll's bouquet. For the sake of
variety she searched out some white specimens—a
moss rose and the York rose.

How splendid they would look, she thought, filling the Chinese porcelain bowl in the guest bedchamber.

Cecelia, who had been so fond of her own aunt,
was exerting herself to entertain Sophie's. The pair
of them were probably still in the drawing room,

studying a French fashion book Tante Douce had acquired from a Jersey smuggler. Sophie, uninterested in the latest style of gowns, had retreated to the rose garden to ponder a weightier matter—her husband's amorous past.

Cassian's entanglements prior to their marriage had suddenly become a matter of anxiety. She now wondered if he'd lied when denying that Inês Costa had been his mistress, to cover up the fact that the girl who had suckled Daniel had also been his mother. She couldn't decide which was worse, his unwillingness to acknowledge his own son, or requiring Cecelia to pretend Daniel was hers.

Reconsidering the Carysfort-Fonseca-Costa triangle, she found Andrew Searle's observation credible. Cassian behaved like a father to the boy, and the detached Cecelia like an aunt. What's more, Luis had displayed the fondness and devotion of an uncle.

She stared at the bare ground marking the place where the body had lain, perpetually haunted by her memory of Cassian's dirty garments near the time Luis had vanished. But as she'd told Emrys Jones, she could not accept that her husband was capable of murder.

The Welshman's failure to come to work today was another worry. By voicing her suspicions and probing his privacy with her questions, she had apparently damaged their relationship beyond repair.

Echo, sunning herself on the lawn, lifted her elegant head, attentive to a human presence. Looking around, Sophie saw Andrew Searle pass through the arched opening in the garden wall. She wouldn't listen to more of his groundless accusations against her husband. Trying to look busy, she severed another rose stem.

"I want you to have this." The object he held out

was flat and square, wrapped in tattered cloth fastened with a rusty pin.

"Mr. Searle, I beg you to excuse me. My aunt from Jersey is here, these roses must go into water at once, and—"

"Please." He pressed his offering upon her.

Through the material Sophie could feel a slim volume with soft covers. "A new book of poetry?"

He shook his head. "Read it now, alone. Take it to your chamber in the pavilion. I shall wait down here. You can signal me from the window when you've finished, and I'll come up. You may have questions, which I shall answer as best I can."

He looked so ill and unhappy that she hadn't the heart to refuse. She put down her basket.

Carrying the parcel to her workroom, she sat down on the chaise longue to examine it. Under the cloth she found an ordinary memorandum book with an inscription on the cover: *Extracts from the diary of A. S. 1790, 1797.*

She read the first entry.

15th April, '90. Last night Cass produced a vial of Bristol glass, assuring me that its contents would soothe my pains... Laudanum, he declared, relieves his sufferings—what they might be I cannot guess. At his urging, I swallowed the dose. Its power over my mind is not easily described. Vapors of calmness suffused my hitherto busy brain, a sense of lassitude stole over my corpus. A wondrous sensation indeed. Alas, my funds are too limited to allow frequent indulgence. But Cass is a generous fellow, and has offered to supply me with the miraculous substance whenever I may require it.

2nd May, '90. Never have I seen my friend in such a state. Went in search of two w——s and brought them to my lodging, where they entertained us well. Partook of laudanum. C. imbibed more freely than I. Under its influence he grows calm. Without it—alarming wildness and unpredictability. He has abandoned sobriety and is entirely dependent upon the opiate.

15th May, '90. C. comes often, to sit and talk in his dreamy fashion. He no longer seeks polite society but prefers his solitary pleasures. Produced a cake of opium, mixed the laudanum himself.

10th June, '90. The Carysforts will leave the country, sailing for Lisbon tomorrow. I pray C. can find his peace, and break his fatal reliance upon that most dangerous dram.

Desperate to know more, Sophie continued reading.

Recent entries were repetitions of earlier ones. The poet offered no direct proof, but clearly he believed her husband had been taking laudanum regularly and in great quantities—ever since his return to England.

The record of his erratic behavior was supported by her own experience, and she could have embellished these accounts of his changeable moods from her cache of memories. One minute he was all laughter and smiles, outgoing and energetic. The next he would be gruff and curt, holding everyone at a distance.

His trips to London—two since the first of the year—were documented. Andrew speculated about their purpose and Cassian's activities, con-

cluding that he went there to purchase the drug
and consort with other opium eaters.

Thinking back to his January visit to her house
at Chiswick, she recalled how he'd marched about
her sitting room—tense, abrupt, menacing. But he
had thawed, as if by magic, and when attempting
to lure her to Bevington, he'd plied his charm. *Non,
non,* she protested, he hadn't taken any drug; she'd
been with him all the time. Except, she recalled,
when she'd left the parlor to fetch her cloak. Afterwards he had seemed so much calmer.

He'd traveled to London to search for Luis but
had admitted visting Guildford as well, giving no
explanation. He'd returned to Bevington wan and
fatigued, blaming his condition on the state of the
roads. But when making love to her that night, for
the first time, he'd seemed perfectly well. Had laudanum been responsible for his rapid recovery?

She forced herself to study the journal's final paragraph.

*30th April, '97. Tomorrow they marry. Was I
mistaken to keep silent so long? By telling everything I know, and what I fear may be revealed in
time, I could save her from disaster. If C. is the
boy's natural father, she should know. But can I
convince her, on the eve of the wedding, that C.
murdered Luis Costa in a frenzy brought on by
the pernicious drug? He cannot hide his sickness
forever, and I grieve for his unsuspecting bride.
For I am sure the poor servant is dead, and he
probably lost his life because of what he knew.*

There, starkly written in Mr. Searle's legible
script, was the horror he'd already voiced. And this
time he'd not only presented a motive, he'd documented a long history of instability.

Chièr Cassian, she mourned, why did you not confess these things to me? They are terrible, *vraîment*. But I would not have deserted you.

And she could not desert him now, knowing all.

She returned to the rose bower. Andrew Searle paced the bridge spanning the canal, hands folded behind his back.

"Here is your book. I do not wish to keep it."

"I'm so sorry, Sophie."

She waved away his apology—his pity. *"Non, non."*

"I wouldn't have hurt you for the world, but you needed to know. I hope I didn't wait too long."

"Please go. I cannot make sense of anything just now."

"No, of course not. You are shocked. Your husband is not the man you believed him to be. He married you under false pretenses."

None of what he said had any meaning for her. Putting a hand to her head, she said wearily, "I must think. And pray," she choked, as tears filled her eyes.

She managed to ascend the terrace steps without breaking her neck, but failed to make it all the way up the winding stair to her bedchamber. Collapsing halfway, she wept as she had not done since the day of Tobias Pinnock's funeral.

The sorrow she carried in her heart was akin to what she'd felt then. She had a living husband now, but he was not the man she'd known and loved. Addict, father, teller of lies, keeper of secrets. Murderer?

She faced a repetition of the pain and lies that had plagued her last years with Tobias. Once more she felt duty-bound to safeguard her loved one's health, while at the same time salvaging his reputation. The task ahead seemed even more formidable this time.

Even after shedding all her tears she sat there, slumped over in agony. Her entire body felt leaden and numb, she simply could not move.

A soft exclamation from the bottom of the stairwell roused her from her stupor. "My lady!" Nan Parham regarded her worriedly. "Did you slip and fall?"

"I am not seriously hurt," she lied. "I believe I left a basket of roses beneath one of the arbors. Would you fetch it for me, please, and put them in water?"

When the servant went away, she retreated to her room to bathe her face. Braving the ungenerous mirror, she applied a dusting of powder to her cheeks and nose to cover the redness.

"Sophie, *es-tu toute seule?*"

That was her aunt, calling up to her. "*Oui,*" she answered. With a doubtful glance at her reflection, she hurried down to her sitting room.

"I've had the most pleasant time with your sister-in-law while you were *au gardin*. Such a lovely creature, and such music she makes on the keyboard!" The stream of cheerful words suddenly broke off. "Sophie, *p'tite*, what is the matter?"

"My husband—*oh, las*, he is so very ill, and needs my help. All my strength as well."

When her aunt had led her over to the window seat, she sat down to give a brief account of Andrew Searle's diary and its revelations. She held on tightly to Tante Douce's tiny, plump fingers as she talked of her dreadful discovery.

"Luis Costa's death was an accident. Cassian would never have harmed him—in his right mind."

"And he has a child," her relative said softly. "Do you believe it?"

"I love Daniel dearly, whether Cassian is his father or not, but he is the least of my problems now. I care only about saving my husband from himself."

"How can you?"

Sophie rose. "By persuading him to go away, as he did before. I know his habit of taking laudanum can be broken. If he gave it up when he lived in Portugal, as I think he did, he can do it again." With a flash of inspiration, she said, "We could go to Jersey—home to Anneville. I'll tell him I want to introduce him to the rest of the family. You can support me, saying how very much they want to meet him. I'll not reveal my real reason till we're safely across the Channel."

Nodding her dark head, the other lady said, "Our island in summer would cure any disorder—the healthful sea breezes, the warm sunshine. Brother Edouard would be happy to have you at the manor house again."

"Or we could take a cottage of our own."

"If the earl is so unpredictable, would it be wise to be alone with him?"

"I'm in no danger," Sophie said confidently. "He loves me. And he needs me, now more than ever. I cannot fail him. I will not."

"But he might fail you, *p'tite*. There are men who become so addicted to strong drink that they can never give it up. What if laudanum has too powerful a hold upon him?"

Sophie refused to give in to pessimism. "There was so little I could do for Tobias, my helplessness was unbearable. For Cassian there is a remedy. I have to believe that."

For his sake she would salve over her pain as best she could. She wouldn't think about that empty grave among the roses, or the fresh one in the churchyard where Luis was lying now. Or worry about a little boy unaware that his adored uncle was his father. Or pity the tortured friend who had come forward with so many terrible truths. Nothing was as important to her as Cassian.

During dinner she struggled to maintain her composure. Covertly she studied the handsome figure seated at the opposite end of the long table, and prayed those fine blue eyes wouldn't pierce her protective armor of bravado.

Eventually they retired to their suite of rooms, and her masquerade of unconcern was even more difficult to sustain. Her monthly indisposition had recently subsided—Cassian had counted the days with her. After the weeklong respite he assumed she was as eager for marital relations as he.

She was seated before the dressing table in her chamber, undecided about whether to spend the night in her bed or his, when he came to her.

"Leave your hair loose tonight," he said huskily, undoing her half-finished braid. "For me."

"*Bein seux*, if you prefer."

"Come with me—now." His need was a powerful tide surging at her, breaking through her defenses.

She did not protest, but accompanied him to the room where she'd passed so many blissful nights. Dozens of glowing candles covered every surface— the mantel shelf, the mahogany chest, the window seat.

"Close your eyes," he commanded.

She searched his face for signs of intoxication, or insensibility.

"Don't look so fearful. You can trust me."

His smile was irresistible. She forced her eyelids shut, then flinched at his touch. Slowly he removed her shift, leaving her vulnerable to the cool air, and when she shivered his arm circled her waist.

"I'll lead you to the bed." Slowly he guided her across the floor. "You can lie down now. But no peeking."

Her bare back pressed against the soft coolness of the sheet.

"I'll be back," he whispered.

She heard him moving about, and guessed that he was shedding his clothes. Then she sensed his approach.

"I hope you can find it in your heart to forgive my crime."

Her eyes flew open. He stood naked before her, holding a silver basin overflowing with red. She recoiled, seeing blood. Then he delved deep inside and brought up a handful of—

"Rose petals," she gasped in relief.

They drifted down upon her from above like a crimson snowfall.

As he covered her with his fragrant offering, she said, "This is what you planned to do with the Velvet roses."

"Even before we were wed," he declared, lying down with her. "I used to dream about showering you in wine-colored roses, for I knew how glorious they would look against your skin. The reality is even more provocative than the picture in my mind." His lips grazed hers.

The romantic gesture would have delighted her, if not for her fearsome new knowledge of him. He was still the husband she loved, whose love she yearned to keep. He was also an opium addict and a murder suspect, and even as she returned his passionate kisses she could not forget it. Apparently she had never really known him. The mutual understanding and intimacy they had almost achieved was merely a delusion.

She had always trusted him implicity. Now a large measure of that trust was gone—and with it, her pleasure in the supreme act of adoration. His playful fingers could still make her sing. The muscled body joined to hers provided the joyous release she craved. Her inward tremors and breathless, ecstatic sighs were the same, but at her core she felt hollow and empty and dead. Her physical connection to him remained, but was it no longer enhanced by one of the mind. Afterwards he gently peeled away the crushed petals sticking to her breasts and abdomen and thighs. Then he plucked the ones that nestled in her maidenhair.

"Did I do wrong," he asked, "to destroy your precious flowers, all for a few fleeting moments of pleasure?"

"Not fleeting," she managed to say. "It is a shared memory."

If he expressed such regret about shredding her roses, his guilt at killing a servant so dear to him must be powerful indeed. When she considered the state of his conscience, pity rose inside her, choking her.

"I should have asked before stripping the flowers from the bushes—they belong to you. To obtain them you gave yourself to a selfish, pigheaded, impatient fellow. Do you think your roses worth the heavy price you paid?"

She placed her hand upon his heaving chest, in the place she supposed his heart to be. "I would rather belong to you, flawed as you are, than live without love."

"Without being loved?" he probed. "Or without loving?"

"Both," she answered honestly, compassionately. She wanted to give him one clear and shining hope to brighten his dark despair.

That time is past
And all its aching joys are now no more,
And all its dizzy raptures.

WILLIAM WORDSWORTH

Chapter 21

Daniel cowered outside the morning room, leaning against the closed door. At Sophie's approach he lifted his head to reveal streaming eyes and a tear-streaked face.

"What is the matter?" she asked gently, bending down to him.

"You won't let the bad man hurt me, will you?"

"What bad man?" Sophie could hear Cassian's raised voice, followed by his sister's hysterical tones.

"I was sitting with Tio Cass," Daniel said, snuggling into her embrace. "Bitton brought a letter for Mama. She read it and started to cry. She said, 'We're found out, he's asking about Daniel.' Tio snatched it away from her. He was so angry he said 'damn' and 'bloody hell' and threw the teapot against the wall. My mother cried even harder and then she sent me away."

Sophie tightened her hold on him. The Carysforts shouldn't terrify him with their impetuous outbursts. She didn't care whose son he might be, she only knew he was lonely and fearful and needed comfort. "Daniel, would you like to hear the tale of Geoffrey's Leap?"

"Today?"

"This very minute. My Tante Douce is having tea in the pavilion. She knows the story far better than I."

"Does she?" Sniffing, he wiped his eyes—so brightly blue, exactly like Cassian's.

"She's the one who told it to me. And I'm sure she'd tell you, if you asked her."

The brows jutted down in a frown that strengthened the resemblance. "My mother might need me."

"I'll go to her," Sophie promised him.

He scrambled to his feet. After letting her tuck in his shirt and smooth his tumbled curls, he started down the staircase. The moment he was out of view, she stormed into the morning room.

Her sister-in-law was saying, "But we must keep him away from here. He might try—oh, here's Sophie."

She noticed the scrape in the plastered wall and the fragments of floral-patterned china scattered on the floorboards. Glaring at her husband, she demanded, "What happened, to make you forget yourself in front of a child?"

He had the grace to look ashamed. "I lost my temper."

"You should control it better, you know how sensitive Daniel is."

"Cass is leaving for London," Cecelia announced.

"Personal business," he added curtly. "I shall make my apologies to your aunt."

He would not escape her vigilance so easily. Andrew Searle's writings indicated that Cassian's consumption of laudanum was dangerously excessive. She had to stop him from hurting himself.

"I'm traveling with you." Bravely she met his outraged stare. "We'll stay at my house in Chiswick. It's perfectly comfortable, and William and Mary are there to wait upon us."

"I don't think you should come. Not this time."

What foul, unmentionable errand was taking him away? Better not to ask, she thought, unless she wanted to hear more evasions—or outright lies.

"I've neglected my household for many months, *dé vrai*. And this is a chance to see my roses at the peak of bloom. Never fear, I shall be packed and ready to depart in no time at all—before you are, I daresay." Satisfied that she had scored a point, she turned and left the room.

Her abrupt exit was followed by the sound of shattering porcelain. A teacup had suffered the same dire fate as the pot.

His unruliness was disturbing, but it didn't deter her. She must get him away from the castle, from his clinging, needy sister and impressionable nephew—or son.

At Chiswick she could refine her strategy to take him even farther, all the way to Jersey. And when they were safely settled on her island, she would confront him about his dependence on opium. By encouraging him to talk about his valet's death, she could relieve him of the burden of his guilt. She was strong, she'd been tested before, and she intended to help him battle all his demons.

Her aunt supported her decision, offering to keep Cecelia company and amuse Daniel. "Your place," she insisted, "is with the earl. Stay close by, and give him what comfort you can."

Sophie hadn't been out of Gloucestershire since

taking up residence at Bevington in the midst of winter. Now the hills and meadows along the road to London were mantled with green, leaves covered the trees and the tall, lacy heads of cow parsley bloomed profusely in the roadside verges. During the long hours in the carriage, she alternately studied the view and dozed against her husband's shoulder.

Where the highway was smooth enough to permit reading, he studied a treatise on modern agricultural techniques. Whenever they passed over rough terrain, he closed his book and commented on the promising advances that would, he hoped, improve the yield of his tenants' farmstead. At Littleworth they broke their journey, passing an uneventful night at an inn.

During the final stages of their drive Sophie noticed that Cassian had become tense and preoccupied, and increasingly uncommunicative.

They arrived at her villa in the afternoon. Fresh gravel had been laid in the drive. The front lawn was neatly scythed, and the heady scent of cut grass was her first welcome. The servants, caught by surprise, greeted her with smiles and tears. Unaccustomed to her elevated status, they failed to address her properly and she laughed off their apologies.

Her pleasure in this homecoming faded when her husband announced he wanted to stretch his legs after the long hours in the carriage. Watching him stroll off down the lane leading to the village, she prayed he wouldn't head straight for the apothecary's shop.

"All the bedding has been recently aired, ma'am," Mary assured her. "M'lady, I should've said. The parlor furniture is wrapped in Holland cloth, which I'll remove at once. Ah, but it does my heart good to have you back, ma'am—m'lady. A countess now—though you look exactly as you've always done, not a jot of difference that I can see."

Sophie's lips twitched. "You didn't expect me to return wearing a coronet and velvet robes?"

"Nay, but I didn't think you'd still be wearing that same green traveling habit neither," the housekeeper told her with all the frankness of a longtime employee.

While Mary whisked covers off the parlor chairs, Sophie stepped out onto the terrace. Her planters contained brightly hued perlargoniums; a passionflower vine twined up a trellis, filtering out some of the afternoon sun.

She took her favorite stroll down to the river, pausing in the shade of the willows to watch the swans glide upon the water. The scene she loved and had often painted was unchanged. In contradiction to Mary's observation, she was entirely different. Outwardly she might look the same, but inwardly she bore no resemblance to the forlorn widow who had trod this Thameside path last summer.

Her statue garden, with its smooth lawn and shaved hedges, was as appealing as she remembered, carefully maintained by William and the under-gardener. The flowering border along the outside of the kitchen garden was a jumble of roses, delphiniums, columbines, and poppies, exactly as she'd described it to Cassian in January. She found William pruning the espaliers and nailing the branches to the brick wall to support the fruits that were forming. He showed her the progress of his second sowings of carrots and broccoli and lettuce. Complaining much of snails, he demonstrated the various methods he used to combat the pernicious creatures.

During her brief circuit through the grounds, her housekeeper had restored the parlor to its usual state and thoughtfully placed a vase of roses on a table. Tobias smiled mildly down from his frame on the wall. Sophie's fond gaze moved from the portrait of the prominent man she'd loved dearly and faithfully, to the tall bookcase filled with blue leather volumes.

The last of their kind. She would make no more Blue Books.

When Mary came in to consult her about dinner arrangements, Sophie suggested a simple meal of fish and garden vegetables, to be served on the terrace.

"I've a summery pudding," said the housekeeper. "And I could manage a gooseberry fool, for a choice."

"That will suit us very well. A plain china will do—the Wedgwood creamware."

"Yes, m'lady."

Sophie went to her former bedchamber to sort through the garments she'd left behind in her wardrobe. She found a round gown of white linen printed with multicolored floral sprays, the first she'd ordered from the dressmaker on setting aside her mourning attire. She plaited some cherry-colored ribbons into her thick braid before coiling it at the back of her head in a chignon. Pleased with the effect, she went to the parlor to wait for Cassian.

She sat down with a botanical magazine, which failed to divert her. He'd been away for quite a long time. Had he become lost, or was he wandering the countryside in a drugged stupor?

Tchi niolîn, she chided herself. Nothing so dreadful could happen here in peaceful Chiswick.

She hid the extent of her relief when Cassian returned to the house. He looked unusually rustic. A trace of sunburn bloomed along his high cheekbones, and wisps of straw clung to his black hair.

"What were you doing all this while?" she wondered.

"Exploring. I visited the shops in the high street, and ordered up a pint at a tavern. I made the acquaintance of several sheep—neither friendly nor good conversationalists. When my legs gave out, I sat down to rest against a hayrick."

"You must be exhausted, and hungry." There was strangeness about him, and she couldn't quite define it. "We'll be dining *al fresco*, on the terrace."

"Something you and Mr. Pinnock used to do?"

"Occasionally," she answered, "when the weather was this warm. If you'd rather not—"

"It sounds entirely delightful," he responded, but his smile never quite reached his eyes.

As it turned out, there was nothing particularly delightful about their meal. Cassian was meticulously civil, but his quietude made Sophie wary and nervous. He approved the fish and its accompaniments, complimented her choice of wine, and sampled both the summer pudding and the gooseberry fool. But apart from that, he said very little.

The air was heavy, the scent of flowers wafted up from the border. The evening could have been so romantic, Sophie mourned, yet it wasn't. He was in the sourest of moods, and she was developing a headache.

Rubbing her temples, she asked him whether he carried any laudanum in his traveling case.

"Get some from your woman," he advised her.

"*Bein seux*," she murmured, trying to decide if her question had made him self-conscious.

They removed to the candlelit parlor. Cassian hid his face behind the *Times*. Sophie took up her magazine and resumed her reading. Turning a page, she said, "*Ma fé*, here's a surprise! Mr. Curtis printed an engraving of my hyacinth illustration. Do you remember, I'd just finished it when you visited me here—how long ago it seems."

"Over six months," he said, regarding her over the top of his newspaper. "A great deal has happened to us since that night. I persuaded you to come to Gloucestershire. You created a garden at Summit House. Cecelia and Daniel and I moved from Clifton to Bevington. You and I became engaged and were wed."

He'd left out Luis Costa's unsolved murder. Sophie could think of only one reason for the omission, and it made her feel utterly wretched.

"How long have we been married?" he mused. "Nine weeks, ten? It was selfish of me to propose— in my defense, I never guessed wedlock would be such a hell for you."

She couldn't think what she'd said or done to provoke that bitter remark. "Cassian, what makes you so strange?"

He cast his paper aside impatiently. "I've too much on my mind as it is, without venturing upon the unpleasant subject of our mutual disappointment."

Hurt by the implication that their marriage was failing, she tried not to show it. "Then tell me what business brought you here."

"I can't talk about that, either."

"Now? Or never?"

"I'm not sure." He left the sofa to march about the room, keeping just within the bounds of her Persian rug.

"I'm your wife. Let me help you."

He paused in front of the framed portrait. "You're more his wife than mine. You still love him—and his house, where you are so much at home."

"I lived and gardened here for five years," she defended herself. "Of course I like being back. But it's merely a visit, I don't intend to stay. Nor do I wish it."

"Why not? You'd be happier here with your precious flowers and your fawning servants. And these bloody Blue Books." He flung open the glass doors of the bookcase and began removing leather-bound volumes by the armful. He flung them onto the floor.

"*Nânnîn!*" she shrieked.

He paid no heed, but reached for more, stripping the shelves.

This act of violence was personal, and his choice of weapon was calculated to deliver the most incisive wound. Her pain would have been much less had he knocked over the vase of roses or broken the porcelain potpourri dish on the mantel or thrown his glass of port onto the rug.

"You must listen, Cassian. You've no cause to be jealous. I cannot pluck the past out of my heart, but I don't dwell upon it. Neither should you. If I met Tobias now, I mightn't feel what I did for him at sixteen. And if I'd met you then, I couldn't possibly have cared for you in the way I do now."

"You didn't marry me because you loved me."

She couldn't honestly deny the charge. "You rushed me, I had no time to fall in love—beforehand."

"You found those musty old account books and kept quiet about them while you formed your secret scheme. Your acceptance of my proposal was conditional—you wanted to preserve the Bevington gardens."

"They played no part in my decision—*pon du tout!* Cassian, I am not so heartless!"

"You seemed eager to share my bed, and I rejoiced that it was so. But in this house, Sophie, the bed is yours. And *his*. I cannot forget that."

His tirade had come full circle, back around to Tobias again.

His bizarre behavior had nothing to do with laudanum or guilt about Luis Costa. It was an outgrowth of his resentment of her first husband, and for that malady she had no cure. Her marriage was disintegrating before her eyes, and she didn't know how to hold it together.

"I'm going upstairs to the guest chamber, which your servant so thoughtfully prepared for me."

"For both of us," she insisted, as he stalked out of the room. She'd made the arrangement on his behalf, out of regard for his sensibilities, and much good it had done.

She picked up the scattered Blue Books and replaced them, not bothering to put them in the proper chronological order. She extinguished all the candles save one, and used it to light her way up the staircase.

Evidently her husband intended to sleep alone tonight. By shutting himself away, he'd also cut off her access to her *baheur* and its contents. Going to the other bedchamber, she searched the drawers for an old nightgown. After she had removed her flowery dress, she went to the mirror to unplait her hair. The cherry ribbons had not enchanted Cassian after all. Another wasted effort.

Looking at the bed, she rebelled at the thought of occupying it again. Her unreasonable husband would not, she vowed, consign her to an unwelcome, undesired solitude. She did not deserve it. But how could she possibly soften him?

Inspiration came, and she was quick to act upon it. Taking her chamber-stick, she slipped out of the room.

Cass stretched out on the unfamiliar tented bed, an oil lamp glowing on the nightstand. He wasn't in the mood to read his agricultural book, and despite his emotional and physical exhaustion, he didn't care to sleep.

He ought to be reviewing his plan for tomorrow. But his quarrel with his wife crowded out all thoughts about his strategy for bringing about a meeting with Sir Michael Tait.

What a fool he'd been to lose control, blustering at Sophie and mistreating her books. She'd offered him a semblance of the love he'd sought for so long—why hadn't he accepted it humbly and gratefully? If not for his reckless outburst of frustration, and his jealousy of a dead man, she would lie trembling beneath him this very minute, singing out her pleasure.

The night was uncomfortably warm and still. He climbed down from the bed and went to raise the sash window higher, tying back the curtains to let in a breeze.

A faint knock on the door told him that his Sophie had come to make peace. He didn't deserve her, and never would.

She stood in the unlit corridor, her nightshift hitched up with clenched fists. In the bowl of her skirt she carried rose petals, and when she stepped into the room he saw they were vividly striped, red upon white.

"These are for you." Moving to the bed, she tossed them onto the sheets and pillows.

As she let the final fistful of petals drop, he spied

red scratches all over her hands and wrists. "You've hurt yourself."

"It's dark outside, and the bushes are thorny," she said matter-of-factly.

Cass seized a linen towel and moistened it with water from the washbasin. Wiping her wounds, he said gently, "I'm not worthy of a single rose from your favorite bush, or a drop of your precious blood, Sophie. Soon, I fear, you'll have more substantial proof of my villainy than I've given you tonight."

When he placed his hand upon her shoulders, he saw fear flash in her eyes. Releasing her at once, he raked his fingers through his hair. A damnable mess he'd made of this marriage!

He was ready to make his confession, to tell her about his long-ago duel with Tait and all that had occurred afterwards. But he wanted at least one night of tranquility before chaos descended upon them.

When they crawled wearily into bed, Sophie faced outward, away from him. Cass missed her warmth, he was accustomed to falling asleep with that dark head pressed against his shoulder.

He was alone when he awakened the next morning.

After washing and dressing, he went downstairs to the dining room. Sophie was seated at the circular pedestal table, filling her cup from a silver tea urn, her face pale and her manner reserved.

"Why didn't you rouse me?" he asked.

"I didn't want to disturb you," she answered quietly.

"Sophie—" He hardly knew how to begin his apology. "Last night—"

"You're going in to London today?" she broke in. "Let William know at what hour you want your carriage. Shall I ring for coffee? You prefer it to tea."

The perfect hostess—treating him like a guest. It wouldn't be long before she tossed him out of her house. "I must deliver a message, an invitation to a gentleman living near St. James's. I expect him to visit me later. Before he does, I'll make everything clear to you. I swear it."

"Do it now," she suggested.

He shook his head. "There's no time. The tale I shall tell you is lengthy, and involved. Be patient, just a little while longer."

The look she gave him was the most sorrowful he'd ever received from her. The great brown eyes spoke eloquently of pain. "Very well. And you must be careful."

In too great a hurry for a leisurely breakfast, Cass downed his coffee and set out immediately for the city.

It took him half an hour to reach the gates of St. James's Palace. When a crossing sweep came up to assist him, he held out a silver coin. "I need you to perform a different service than your usual one."

"Aye, sir, anythin' fer a shillin'."

Cass showed the letter he carried. His composition, but Cecelia had penned it. "Take this to Sir Michael Tait's lodging—he lives in Cleveland Row. I'll point out his house to you."

"Aisy enough," the youth replied eagerly.

For the duration of his six-mile journey back to the villa, Cass steeled himself for the ordeal ahead. There was no avoiding it now, he had to prepare Sophie for what promised to be a volatile confrontation with the baronet. Before the day was out she would see the scarred face of his enemy and learn the worst details of his past.

He rushed into the house, startling the house-keeper.

"Returned already, m'lord? You've missed her ladyship, she's just gone."

"Gone?" he repeated. "Where to?"

"She bade me give you her note—I have it here." She withdrew a folded square of paper from her apron pocket.

He took it to the parlor and broke the seal beneath Tobias Pinnock's painted stare.

My lord, she had writtten, *I have taken a post coach to Bevington, where I truly belong. I cannot stay where I am not wanted—or needed. Your devoted—and loving—wife, Sophie Carysfort.* The surname was underlined, several times, for emphasis.

With an oath, he balled the paper in his fist.

"Mary!" he shouted.

Promptly she appeared in the doorway. "M'lord?"

"The nearest posting house, where is it?"

"Turnham Green, m'lord, the Old Pack Horse. 'Fore my mistress went off, she said as how your lordship would have company later. Ought I to prepare any special dishes?"

"I doubt the gentleman will care to dine with me. But a bottle of your late master's excellent port wouldn't go amiss."

"Very good, m'lord." She bobbed a curtsy. "If 'tis not too bold of me to say it, my William and I wish your lordship and our Mrs. Pin—and her ladyship," she corrected herself, "all happiness."

"Thank you, Mary. My thanks to William, also."

"Now we've 'customed ourselves to the change, we feel 'tis a good thing. Eh, but she was a sad little mite 'fore she went off to live in Gloucestershire, so lonesome-like in this empty house."

To prevent Sophie's fond retainers from detecting the strife between them, Cass concealed his dismay over her desertion. He didn't have time to chase her down, not with Tait due to arrive at any moment. Cecelia's letter was sure to have a profound and immedate effect.

He saw that the Blue Books had been returned to their shelves. On the wall beside the bookcase hung a small picture in a frame, Sophie's profile drawn in charcoal. He'd never noticed it before.

With a few simple but effective strokes, the artist had captured the sitter's strength of character as well as her almond eyes and perfect nose and sloping cheek. Clearly the portrait had been made by a man who loved her dearly—by a husband.

Unable to study it any longer, Cass went outside.

Wandering the grounds, he could trace his wife's influence everywhere he looked—the statuary, the clipped evergreens, the profusely colorful borders. Coming upon her willow grove, he sat on the bench to watch the swans, and mulled over what the housekeeper had said to him. He thought long and hard about Tobias Pinnock, and Sophie, and himself.

His reverie was broken by the sound of an approaching carriage. Heart thudding, he hurried across the lawn.

Descending from the vehicle, the baronet inspected his surroundings. When Cass approached, the muscles of his scarred face contracted in a frown. "Bevington! You're also here?"

"This house belongs to my wife. I was recently married."

"I saw the notice in the paper—that's how I learned about Bevington Castle. I'm thankful my letter found Cecelia. I entrusted one to you, many months ago, but I daresay you never delivered it. Take me to her."

"She isn't able to receive you today."

"But I had a message, written in her hand. She begged me to meet her, said she wanted to—" Tait's shoulders sagged. "One of your tricks, was it? I should have guessed. Will you never stop torturing me? Seven years ago you struck me in public, at a social gathering. You issued a challenge and shot me in cold blood, leaving me with this broken face. You've been hiding Cecelia from me. You destroyed a valuable and irreplaceable violin."

"And you killed Luis Costa—or had him killed. You discarded his carcass and left it to rot, practically under my nose."

"You *are* a demented bastard. I hadn't heard about his death, and I'm not responsible for it."

"You deny that he was your spy?"

"I do. How many times must I tell you?"

Cass, a master of prevarication, was impressed by Tait's false sincerity. "From whom, then, did you obtain information about Daniel Fonseca?"

"Not from any informant placed in your household, as you seem to believe. I visited nearly every shipowner in London, and I studied the passenger lists of all vessels sailing from Lisbon in recent years." Tait paused, then plunged on. "You brought Cecelia back from Portugal with you when you came to claim your title and estate. Daniel Fonseca traveled with you. I'm still trying to discover who he might be, but I have my suspicions."

"Keep them to yourself," Cass retorted. "I'm more concerned with solving a murder." He turned his back on the baronet dismissively, and headed for the waterway.

Tait followed him. "Your Luis Costa knew all about the mysterious Daniel. Is he a man? Or a boy?"

"I cannot answer."

"You'll regret it if you don't."

"Are you threatening me, Tait?"

"What good would that do? I haven't your taste for violence, or your talent for fisticuffs. I daresay you mean to rough me up and toss me into the river to drown. Well, get on with it, if you must. I have nothing to live for."

Cass gave a harsh laugh. "God knows how you can make yourself out to be the tragic hero, when we both know you're the villain of this sordid piece. For lack of evidence I'm forced to acquit you of murder. But you were an adulterer. And you seduced my sister."

"I fell in love. So did she."

"That's no justification for what you did. You were married, and she was very young."

"My wife was flagrantly unfaithful, you knew that. Virtually a whore—you must've been the only man in London who never bedded her. I considered seeking a divorce, but it wasn't worth all the bother and expense and scandal. Until I met Cecelia."

"Spare me," Cass muttered. "I've heard all this before."

"I love her still. And now I'm free. She is widowed—a grieving widow. Or so you've said."

Cass clenched his jaw.

"I used to marvel at your honesty—your integrity. In the political and social realm, those qualities are rare indeed. Are you still so honorable, Cass? Do you deal in truth, or falsehood?"

"I don't deal with you at all," he growled. "Neither will Cecelia."

"You challenged me to a duel. No one knew the true cause but ourselves. I was wounded, but not fatally, therefore you weren't compelled to flee the law. You had avenged your honor, and your sister's. Yet you both chose to exile yourselves in a distant country for many years. I'm also perplexed by Cecelia's marriage to the conveniently dead Senhor Fonseca. Was it a fiction, concocted out of necessity?"

Cass maintained his silence. He stared impassively down at his interrogator, dreading the questions to come.

"But what could be the motive for such a deception? I can think of only one. Which would solve the riddle of Daniel." Narrowing his eyes, the baronet said, "You call me adulterer and seducer, and rightly so. But there's one thing you are most reluctant to name me."

"And what might that be?"

"Father to your sister's child."

Then rose the Seed of Chaos...

WILLIAM BLAKE

Chapter 22

⟨————⟩

Sipping tea in the parlor of the Crown Inn at Faringdon, Sophie could scarcely believe what she'd done. To prove she loved Cassian above all, she'd turned her back upon her former home and all the symbols of her past life. She had also left him behind, and if he did anything to harm himself while they were apart, she would be responsible.

During the wakeful hours she had lain beside her sleeping husband, she'd faced the bitter truth that she could not save him by herself. Until he acknowledged his troubles and turned to her for help and comfort, her interference would be a source of contention. Experience had taught her the futility of imposing her will upon a man so willful. And she loved him too much to make him hate her.

The agony of separating herself from him was like reaching deep into her body and ripping out her heart. Could she learn to live with this constant ache of longing and worry, and the hollowness deep in her breast?

At least she wouldn't be alone while she waited

for her husband to complete the mysterious business he'd alluded to but refused to reveal. Cecelia and Daniel, Emrys Jones and Andrew Searle waited for her at the castle. And Tante Douce was there, a sturdy prop and a fount of Jersiaise wisdom.

A serving maid brought food. She'd never felt less like eating but made an effort, even though this cheese could not compare to Double Bevington. She smiled at her partisanship. *Oui-dgia*, she did belong in Gloucestershire.

A gentleman traveler with a valise and portfolio intruded on her privacy, seating himself at a corner table. He ignored her, bowing his rusty head over the bill of fare.

"Fingal Moncrieff," she cried in belated recognition.

He glanced over at her. "Sophia Pinnock? Forgive me—Lady Bevington. What are you doing here?"

"Awaiting a change of horses. I've been at Chiswick and am making my way home—back to the castle. And you?"

"I came from Corsham Court, where I was called in by John Nash—my employer. We met through his association with Repton. I journeyed here to deliver a set of plans to a Mr. Hadlett at Faringdon House."

"Do join me," she invited him. "We can't converse easily from such a distance."

Her cordiality evidently caught him off guard, but he transferred his belongings to her table and took the chair across from hers. "And have you heard about my rift with Repton?"

"Not a thing. What was the cause?"

"A difference of opinion. 'Twas your fault, you infected him with your ridiculous theories about formal garden styles. I don't mean to say that he's completely rejected the naturalistic landscape. But he is displaying a new reluctance to knock down balustraded terraces and garden walls. He even says there may be a place for arbors and statuary—in certain instances."

Sophie was more flattered than angry to hear that her former professional rival had appropriated her philosophies. In fact, she'd be delighted to have Repton actively promoting and popularizing them.

"I think it's an absurdity," he went on. "But as you pointed out that day at Clifton, fashion is fickle. Who's to say these notions won't catch on? He and Nash are both enamored of gothic embellishment, all the rage now. For the planned extension to the north facade of Corsham, they've concocted the most elaborate mix of turrets and battlements and oriels. It puts your Bevington Castle to shame. Here, have a look."

He opened his portfolio and showed her the architectural renderings.

When she failed to make any comment, he said, "You may be perfectly frank, it's not my design. Have you ever seen such a pastiche?"

"So many elements vying for attention," she responded. "Will this stylized house require a stylized garden?"

"That's for Repton to decree." He tucked away the Corsham plans, and removed the ones he'd produced for Faringdon House. "A simple structual alteration. The house isn't yet two decades old, not important enough to warrant the attention of Nash, my illustrious employer."

His interaction with more prominent architects had actually taught him humility, and Sophie liked him the better for it. She felt an inexplicable sense of comradeship, considering that they had never been close friends in the past. But they had worked together, exchanging ideas and arguing over concepts, and he was a link with Tobias.

The servant came to tell her the post chaise was ready.

She rose, gathering up her reticule. "I should be on my way, if I mean to make Cirencester by nightfall."

"The Royal Oak?" he quizzed her, and she nodded. "It was there we had our parting of the ways. I heartily wish your ladyship Godspeed. And should you ever require a garden folly, or something similar, do keep me in mind."

"I shall," she said, and meant it.

She climbed into her conveyance feeling refreshed and far more optimistic than when she'd arrived at the inn. She even allowed herself to hope that Cassian might already be following her.

Her night at Cirencester was peaceful. In the morning she went to a toyshop to purchase a present for Daniel, then continued her journey deep into Gloucestershire. She caught her first glimpse of the castle from many miles away, its distant towers highlighted by a blazing midday sun.

Her coach missed the turn from the road into the long avenue of oaks, and drove straight into the village. The driver's mistake made Sophie wonder whether an entrance lodge was needed to mark the avenue. Each earl had left his stamp on the property, why shouldn't Cassian? His immediate predecessor had added the cottage *ornée* in the wood—picturesque, but not the healthiest dwelling for a consumptive. Andrew Searle would be far more comfortable as tenant of the smart new lodge she envisioned. Fingal Moncrieff could draw up the plans—it should be built of Bevington stone, with crenellations on top and arched gothic windows to mimic the castle.

After paying her coachman and postboys, she deposited her *baheur* under the gatehouse arch and proceeded across the courtyard. Her sister-in-law, she suspected, would be at her pianoforte.

But she found Cecelia seated at the long trestle table in the great hall, waving away Mrs. Harvey and a steaming cup of tea. She struggled to her feet, crying, "Sophie—thank goodness, I never needed you more! Where is my brother?"

"He stayed behind." She might have expected such a frantic greeting—Cecelia was a magnet for crisis. With calm deliberation, she untied the ribbons of her bonnet and took it off. "What's amisss?"

"Daniel has gone missing. We've looked everywhere—in the cellars and the garrets, the keep tower. Even the dungeon. Your aunt is wonderful, she—"

"When did you see him last?"

"At breakfast," Cecelia replied. "At least three hours ago."

"My lady," the housekeeper interjected, "perhaps you would like this tea?"

"Not now, Mrs. Harvey. You may leave us," Sophie told her, reasserting her habit of command.

After the woman retreated, Cecelia continued, "The grooms and gardeners have scoured the grounds, to no avail. Sophie, what if he was abducted?"

She couldn't help but laugh, it was the most absurd of all possibilities. "By whom?"

"His father."

Her head jerked up. Surely Cecelia didn't mean Cassian. "I don't understand. He has no father."

Cecelia sank down on a wooden bench and

gripped the edge of the trestle table. "How we have deceived you, Cass and I. He always wanted to tell you the whole truth, but I wouldn't allow it. I was too afraid to trust you, confide in you. Now that you are such a sister to me, I wish I had."

"So do I," said Sophie. "Who is Daniel's father?"

"The man Cass is meeting in London. His name is Michael. He is a baronet, and used to be our great friend. We began as social acquaintances, then we became lovers. Shameful, I know—and he had a wife. When I realized there was going to be a child, I told my brother. You can imagine his reaction."

Fury and outrage, thought Sophie. And he must have been terribly concerned about his sister's reputation, and her state of mind.

"There was a duel. The very next day we sailed for Portugal."

When Cecelia paused, Sophie said, "And there you created the myth of Senhor Fonseca."

"We didn't have to, we really knew him. He sold his *palácio* to Cass so he could emigrate to Brazil and live off the proceeds. Halfway across the ocean, his ship went down. It was my brother's idea to claim we'd been wed, which would conceal my child's illegitimacy if ever we returned to England. I was sick, heartbroken—I agreed to everything."

"*Naturellement*," said Sophie.

"It was a difficult birth. I thought I was dying, and my son was so tiny I didn't expect him to live. We had him christened right away, and recorded his surname as Fonseca. The wet nurse and Luis Costa were witnesses. That was in February of ninety-one."

"Luis knew your marriage was a falsehood?"

Cecelia nodded. "That's why he was murdered—

either by Sir Michael Tait, or a paid assassin. We aren't sure how the baronet learned about Daniel's existence, or exactly what he knows."

"You mean to say the visitor Cassian was expecting yesterday is a murderer, who tried to kill him in a duel? *Sécours dé grâce*, I was mad to leave him." Sophie put her fist to her mouth, and gnawed at the skin stretched taut over her knuckles. "His temper—he's such a hot-head. *Oh, las,* I cannot let myself think such a thing. I won't."

Somehow she had to keep fearful thoughts at bay. "I'll look for Daniel," she decided. "He wandered off, there's no doubt of it. Did anyone search the deer park? This terrible man you accuse of abducting him is far away in London."

With Cassian.

"He could send someone here," Cecelia pointed out. "Probably the same person who killed Luis. Oh, Sophie, what shall I do?"

She gripped the weeping woman's hunched shoulders. "Don't give in to despair, you'll make yourself ill. Go to the pianoforte and choose which piece of music you'll teach him next. Tell the cook to make up a batch of scones—you know how hungry he'll be after his long ramble."

"You're right." Cecelia blotted her watery blue eyes with a lace handkerchief. "Someday I hope to be as strong as you are. I'm weak, and always have been. A slave to my emotions."

Sophie pressed her lips together to hold back a sharp comment. She was also under siege from emotion, her feelings were beyond description. Her husband could be dead, or dying, he was far away and she had callously abandoned him to his fate.

Guilt about his deception, not the murder, must be the reason he was using opium. Why had he delayed his explanations? All this time he'd kept her in the dark, thwarting her efforts to understand him.

Bein seux, she reminded herself, she'd kept a secret from him. And if it had also contributed to his dependence on the drug, the damage she'd done could be irreparable.

"I'm going now," she said, freeing her hand from Cecelia's grateful clasp.

The only living creatures she spied in the woodland were the shy deer and the cheeky red squirrels darting from tree to tree. She heard the birds singing high above, and saw the iridescent blue flash as the kingfisher dove for his choice fishing place along the stream.

"Daniel!" she called, at every twist in the path.

She stopped at Andrew Searle's cottage to find out whether he'd noticed the child passing by. The door was hanging open, and she peeked inside.

The tattered curtains were drawn, shutting out the light, but not enough to hide the disarray. A blanket lay upon the floor, and the bedsheets were rumpled. A jumble of scattered papers and stacks of books covered the table. Sophie spied the snuff-box amidst the clutter.

Thinking he might be in the loft above, she went inside and called up the stairway, "Mr. Searle, are you there?"

There was no reply, so she turned to go. Again her gaze swept across the table. A small bottle of blue glass anchored several loose papers.

Into her head popped the words Andrew Searle had written: *Last night Cass produced a vial of Bristol glass, assuring me that its contents would soothe my pains....* Did the poet also rely on laudanum to relieve the symptoms of consumption?

She tried to restore order to the pages strewn about. Drafts of poems, mostly, all produced by a gloomy mind, but none were familiar to her or finished. She found the memorandum book filled with extracts from his diary. Beside it was a similar volume. It might, she hoped, give her a more complete picture of her husband's malady.

The initial entry described a woman who visited Searle by night. She lived in the castle, and had dark hair and brown eyes. She came to his bed, naked and willing. He felt alive only when his rigid flesh entered her soft body—

She was breaching his privacy—no matter that he'd apparently been writing about her. But curiosity about his unsuspected passion won out over her scruples, and she read on. Beneath the last paragraph he'd scrawled a notation: *This dream followed a dose of two hundred grains of opium.*

Turning the page, she found an account of another imagined sexual encounter, with an identical footnote. This, she realized, was his dream diary. Even more alarming than the poet's obsession with her was the discovery of his regular and extravagant use of opium.

Sophie sorted through the other books on the table. Some she recognized—his well-thumbed edition of Milton, his philosophical essay, *Sonnets by Various Authors*, with Andrew Searle included among them. With a shaking hand she seized a calf-bound volume that turned out to be exactly what she wanted, and dreaded: a genuine diary.

Luis had disappeared late in March. Swiftly she scanned the entries for that month, turning the pages so carelessly that she nearly tore them.

An accident. It wasn't supposed to happen. At dusk, on my way back from the village apothecary, I found him among the roses. The cake of opium was in my pocket. He babbled to me about Cass,

*frightened about some act of disobedience con-
nected to that grim Welshman. In my eagerness to
pursue the experiment, I offered to share my treasure. I repeated what Cass always told me, that it
soothes all suffering. With my penknife I divided
the sublime morsel. I licked off the few grains
clinging to the metal, and gave him a sizeable
lump.*

*He remained sensible for a time. After he col-
lapsed, his breathing slowed. He felt no pain. His
pulse stilled.*

*I could not leave him there, to be found. I took
a shovel from the stables, unseen, and chose a place
where the ground was soft enough to dig deep. It
took me half the night. I laid him in the ditch and
filled it in.*

*When I sat down to write this, I was drenched
in sweat.*

*And still I know not exactly how much pure
opium can safely be consumed.*

Sophie read on, hoping to learn precisely when
Searle had decided to fabricate evidence against the
earl to deflect suspicion from himself.

"Sophie! You've come back to me."

She looked up. The man responsible for Luis
Costa's death was standing in the doorway, watching her. Her joy at her husband's innocence was
crowded out by dread.

"This castle you've inherited lies at a most inconvenient distance from town."

Cass transferred his gaze from the carriage window to the scarred face across from him. "I do not
find it so. One hundred and fifteen miles is as close
to London as I care to live."

Sir Michael Tait raised his brows. "Unfathomable. And how does Cecelia feel about it?"

"You'll have to ask her. Country living is new to her, and I suspect she misses the shops of Clifton."

"You've seen Oakes Court, do you think she'd like it? There are shops in Guildford. But of course, she'd be near enough to town, she could take the carriage to Piccadilly whenever she pleased."

Cass frowned. "You forget, to Cecelia you're the enemy."

At the outset of their journey to Gloucestershire, Cass had doubted that he and the baronet could ever resume their friendship of old. But after a long night on the road, and part of another day, he rather thought they'd made good progress. Together they had attacked and solved the problem of when and how to inform Daniel that his father was living. They agreed that he was too young to comprehend his parents' tormented history, and decided the announcement must wait until he was older.

Tait's excitement at his impending introduction to his six-year-old son was almost endearing. Throughout the final leg of the trip he pelted Cass with questions that he'd answered at the outset: how tall was Daniel, was he really so clever, did he look like his mother?

"I told you, he has her black hair, and blue eyes. But he's cursed with your nose and jaw."

"Cursed with—you are a hard-hearted devil." But he smiled, as if aware that the teasing was proof that a particle of affection had survived years of hatred and mistrust.

On their arrival at the castle, they received the news of Daniel's long absence—and the circumstances of his return. Leading them through the warren of upstairs rooms, Bitton told them Emrys Jones had discovered the missing child.

"All curled up inside that cave in the wall, he was," the butler said. "Jones thought to look for him there, and a good thing. Dr. Jenner is examining the boy now."

"Is Daniel injured?" asked Cass.

"He's not in his right mind. Best I let the doctor tell you about it, my lord."

Cass entered the sickroom, the baronet following closely. His wife's aunt was bathing the patient's legs with a damp cloth. The doctor, spectacles perched on his nose, consulted a reference book.

Cecelia sat at the head of the small bed, gripping her son's hand, with his puppy curled in her lap. Her expression changed from worry to amazement to fear, and she whispered, "Michael."

"Be easy," Cass said soothingly. "He comes in friendship, to see the child."

Dr. Jenner came forward. "Lord Bevington, although the case is serious I do not despair of pulling him through. The difficulty is not knowing what brought on this strange and sudden illness."

Daniel's black head moved back and forth on the pillow, and he mumbled incoherently.

"All we've got out of him so far is that your friend Mr. Searle gave him something to drink."

Cass went to the bed and gazed down at his nephew. "The drink must have contained laudanum."

The doctor looked up, frowning. "An opiate? But why would Searle dispense it?"

"I mean to find out, you may be sure."

"Laudanum, you say? Interesting."

"Drew has been taking it for years."

The physician addressed the butler, hovering outside, "My good man, tell the kitchenmaid to brew a pot of strong coffee, and fetch it here as quick as you can."

"Very good, sir—at once, sir."

"I gather that's for Daniel. I could use a cup my-self," Cass said.

"This child needs a dose of nettle tea," Tante Douce insisted. "On Jersey, *thé d'orti* is the sover-eign remedy for purifying the blood."

Sir Michael Tait was pensively studying a rock-ing horse. He pressed down on the painted head, setting it in motion.

Cecelia laid the pup on her son's bed and ap-proached his father. "Your face," she said softly. "Cass told me you were changed."

"Only my looks, Cecelia. Never my heart."

"Oh, Michael. Don't—not now. If my son should die—"

"He's not going to die," Dr. Jenner declared, bending over the small figure writhing beneath the sheet.

"He is so precious to me," Cecelia said through her tears. "More than I could ever express."

"I'm glad," the baronet told her. "Precious to me also—both of you."

Cass averted his eyes from the affecting reunion scene.

He puzzled over why this crowded room should seem so very empty. When he found the answer, he jumped to his feet, startling everyone.

"Where is Sophie?"

She closed the diary.

"You came back to me," Andrew Searle re-peated. "I knew you would. This is the day I've dreamed of." He slurred his words.

"I came here looking for Daniel," she told him.

"Isn't here. Took him away."

"*You* took him? Where?"

He shook his head. "Not the heir. He can't be.

Had to get rid of him—to make sure."

His senses were so addled by the drug that she wouldn't be able to reason with him. "Please take me to Daniel. I want to see him."

"No. All is as it should be. You're with me now. I shall pour my seed into you, to swell and grow. My son will inherit the castle—he will be a lord. I've seen him in my visions."

"Mr. Searle," she said as calmly as she could, "you are unwell. I shall fetch Dr. Jenner from Berkeley."

When she moved away he came toward her, taking hold of her arm. "We will lie together now, Sophie. Me on top and you underneath." As she struggled against him, he said, "You will kiss and touch me, as you do in the night, every night. I'll make you see—I can give you a dream." He reached for the blue bottle.

"*Nânnîn!*" she cried, realizing what he meant to do. "I won't drink it!"

"You must," he insisted. "And you shall receive it from my own lips." He poured the laudanum into his mouth, and bent his head to kiss her.

To regions where, in spite of sin and woe,
Traces of Eden are still seen below.

WILLIAM COWPER

Chapter 23

Failing to find Sophie in her rooms, or any sign that she'd returned to them, Cass rushed down the spiral stair and emerged beneath the gatehouse. He saw her little leather trunk lying on the cobbles. Then, with rising panic, he trod every inch of the long terraces.

Emrys Jones was the only person in the gardens. He stood on his ladder, applying mortar to a gap in the wall. "To keep that weasel out," he explained. "How fares the little lad?"

"The doctor is confident of a recovery." Cass felt as awkward as ever in the man's presence, but gratitude outweighed prejudice. "I thank you for what you did, Jones. If you hadn't found him—" He hoped he'd said enough to convey his feelings. After explaining that Andrew Searle had drugged Daniel, he added, "I don't know whether he was taken to his hiding place and left there, or crawled inside on his own. Have you seen her ladyship?"

"Nay, my lord." The Welshman's thin lips stretched in a smile. "Ne'er say she's gone missing too."

"So it appears. She isn't in the house. She must be searching for Daniel still. Can I enlist your aid? You know these grounds better than I. We need to find her—immediately."

The gardener promptly descended from his perch. "Perhaps we ought to seek the countess in the same place I found your nephew."

They hurried along the laburnum arch, and passed the stone stag Sophie had rescued, standing at the entrance to the bowling green. Cass waited impatiently outside the cavern while the nimble Welshman climbed inside.

"Empty," Jones reported as he emerged, wiping his soiled hands on his breeches.

"According to my sister, she spoke of going into the wooded park. Whether she went there first or last, I don't know."

Together they returned to the shrubbery walk and sped through the rose garden, where the long-tailed white peacock paraded across the grass, pausing occasionally to preen. Cass decided that if he could only find his wife, she could keep the aggravating bird, and its hen, and all those damned chicks.

Jones was the first to reach the iron gate at the back of the pavilion. Opening it, he held back so Cass could precede him into the wilderness.

Sophie turned her head to avoid Andrew Searle's lips. When she felt liquid coursing down her cheek, she knew she'd foiled his attempt to subdue her.

Groaning, he held the bottle to her mouth. "Drink—you will. For me!"

Wrenching herself out of his partial embrace, she raced for the door.

Several narrow tracks wound through the wood, and she chose the one that would take her directly to the garden gate. Her long skirts were a disadvantage, and the ground was rough—she had to be careful, she couldn't trip and fall. Searle was in pursuit, she heard him gasping and stumbling behind her.

"Sophie, come back to me!"

Miraculously, the gate stood open. Looking over her shoulder, she saw Searle behind her, his face contorted in agony. She doubted he had enough strength for a protracted chase.

Briefly she paused under the porch of the pavilion, and considered seeking refuge within. Unwise, she warned herself, he could trap her. She plunged past the knot gardens and through the rose bower, frightening the white peafowl, desperate to reach the terrace steps before her pursuer caught up with her.

He was only a few paces away. She paused among the shielding hedges of the shrubbery walk and tried to gather her wits together. Perhaps, she thought wildly, the intricate landscape she'd preserved would be her salvation. Spying a ladder against the wall, she scrambled up.

The ledge at the top was a foot wide, narrower where the stones had fallen away. She crouched down and moved slowly forward, impeded by the gaps and her voluminous skirts. She lacked the breath to shout for help, the only sound she could produce was a whimper of pain when she cut her palm on a protruding flint.

Surely someone would notice her—Emrys Jones had to be around, or the Parham boys. Or any servant gazing out of a window.

"Sophie!"

He hadn't found her yet, he was searching among the topiaries. She couldn't see him, either, because of the tall hedge.

Awkwardly she climbed to her feet. Her view of the gardens was panoramic. What a grand vantage for making a picture, she marveled.

"Sophie, be careful! Don't fall!"

That warning came from Cassian—alive, and safely home again!

Searle was crawling up the ladder after her. Her husband pulled him off, prying his hands from the rungs.

"Damn you, she's mine!" raved Searle. "You stole her from me, you bastard!"

"Drew, I mean you no harm—I never did."

With a powerful lunge, the poet freed himself and limped across to the bridge. Turning back, he called, "If I cannot have her, I do not want to live."

He leaped into the canal. Instantly his tawny head sank beneath the surface.

Cass flung off his coat and dove in after his friend.

"Step you down, my lady."

The Welshman's quiet, insistent voice distracted Sophie from the violent struggle taking place in the water. Holding the ladder steady, he helped her to descend.

"Daniel," she gasped, "drugged."

"The lad is safe," he assured her. "The doctor says he'll recover."

If Cassian hadn't already possessed Sophie's heart, he could have won it with his effort to rescue his treacherous friend. Her heart jumped into her throat as she watched him risk his life for a man who had killed his valet, drugged his nephew, and tried to rape his wife.

Searle flailed his arms wildly, hampering Cassian's effort to tow him to the side. "I must die," he sputtered, "damn you, let me go!"

"We'll both drown, if you don't stop fighting me."

Suddenly Searle relaxed. His face fell slack, losing its mad expression, and his eyelids drooped.

Sophie stood out of the way while Cassian and Emrys Jones hoisted the limp body out of the water and laid it on the grass. She tested Searle's breathing and pulse. "He's unconscious," she reported. "Emrys, let me have your apron to wrap him in, for we must keep him warm. Find the doctor, and be sure he brings smelling salts."

Cassian, dripping wet, helped her lay the green woollen fabric over his friend's inert body. Then he held out his arms to her.

Sophie pressed her cheek against his soaked shirt, telling him, "He killed Luis—by accident. But he was deliberately trying to murder Daniel." She looked into his face. "He persuaded me that you were addicted to laudanum. And worse, that you got rid of Luis so I wouldn't find out Daniel was your son."

"Good God." He stared at her blankly. "You believed him?"

"Until today."

"You believed him," he repeated. "And yet you stayed with me, and shared my bed. Here and at Chiswick. Even though you thought me responsible for a murder?"

"I knew I could help you. I planned to take you away to Jersey, to make you stop taking the drug. And when I realized I had to bring you to your senses first, I came back to Bevington."

"You succeeded."

The lips that touched hers were so cold. Worried, she said, "Cassian, you must get out of these clothes."

Andrew Searle twitched, and he gave a great cough.

"Water in his lungs," said Cassian, kneeling down. "Poor fellow, Jenner is bound to send him to the Bristol asylum. Fearsome as that is, it's better than hanging."

When the physician arrived on the scene, he agreed with this assessment.

"The gentleman faces many trials, my lord, if opium has turned him mad. But iron bars and a straight-waistcoat are preferable to a noose."

A crowd had gathered—gardeners, grooms, and servants. The doctor sent someone to the house to fetch scissors and a sheet, which he cut into long strips.

"Must you tie him?" asked Cassian.

"He may become uncontrollable again, and it could take some time for my nephew Henry to arrive. I'll take him to the kitchen and sit him down by the fire."

Sophie gripped her husband's hand while Dr. Jenner wound the bands of linen around the poet's body.

"Should've let me die," Searle moaned, as the doctor led him away.

Looking down at Sophie, Cassian said gently, "Don't cry, for my handkerchief is as damp as the rest of me. We've done all we can for Drew, but we shall do more later. I may not be able to save him from the asylum, but I won't have him mistreated."

On their way to the house, he told her about Cecelia's reunion with the father of her son.

"Tait cares for her still. Her hatred, I gather, was actually love soured by circumstance. He is determined to sweeten it again."

When they reached their dressing room, Sophie

helped him remove his soggy garments. She struggled to unfasten the buckles at the knees of his breeches, then peeled them off. His small clothes posed no difficulty at all.

He handed her his silver watch. "Ruined. No matter, it has no sentimental value."

"I'll give you another," she offered. "A gold one."

"With your miniature fitted into the cover, so I can keep you by me always. After you fled Chiswick yesterday, I realized the sheer stupidity of my jealousy. Sophie, I should honor your Tobias for being such a fine husband. If he'd made you miserable, you would never have contemplated a second marriage. I am greatly in his debt."

"Cassian." She perched on the low chest, nervously threading his watch-chain through her fingers. "Now that your secrets have all come out, it's time to share my own. If I don't, they will forever impair true intimacy between us."

Cass very nearly asked her to wait until after they had enjoyed a bit of intimacy—desire for her was heating his blood. But he saw that this confession was necessary to her.

"My life with Tobias was no paradise. For him I had to become an Englishwoman, and leave off my Jèrriais expressions and island habits. That was but a small difficulty, for I was young and willingly adapted to please him. We were happy together. And then we learned about the condition of his heart. For the last years of his life we could not—" She halted. "His doctor warned us not to—" Again she paused. "He advised against being together as husband and wife. We both suffered. It made him feel less a man, and prevented me from bearing his child. To spare his feelings, and his pride, I pretended to be content with my painting and gardening and housekeeping.''

''That was a generous pretense, Sophie.''

''*Aussî*, I concealed my true opinions of his work. *Our* work. The plans I drew of rolling parks and serpentine rivers and clumps of trees led to the destruction of many fine gardens. I've never admitted to anyone how miserable I was. When I came here to be interviewed I needed the commission, it was such an important one, but I dreaded ruining what to me was well worth saving.''

''That's no great secret. After you accepted my proposal, with your very next breath you asked permission to preserve these castle gardens.'' He smiled. ''Your sins are not so great. Not in the eyes of a man who fought a duel, and made his sister out to be a widow when she'd never been a wife.''

Lifting her head, she said, ''I'm not finished. A number of the landscapes attributed to Tobias Pinnock were actually mine. We had always collaborated to some extent, but as he became weaker I took over all of his design work. He signed his name to my drawings. Together—with Fingal Moncrieff's compliance—we deceived our clients.''

He sat down beside her. ''I'm not shocked by that, either. You acted out of loyalty.''

''Cassian, I am loyal to you now. My love for you has grown so very strong. It is unique, unaffected by what I felt for another man at a different time in my life. There are aspects of my character that you understand far better than Tobias. And qualities that he appreciated more than you ever will.''

''Such as?'' he probed, quite certain that he appreciated everything about her.

''My ability to use a sepia wash over pen and ink.''

Well, he would have to concede that point.

"You're right. I admire your artistry as an observer, not a practitioner. But Sophie, it really isn't your skill for pen and ink work that interests me at this precise moment."

"No?"

"Not much. I'm far more concerned about your other talents. Kiss me, Lady Bevington."

"Do you command it?"

Ah, there was the saucy smile he adored!

"*Oui-dgia*, as you might say yourself. Remember, you vowed to obey."

"*Bein seux*, I shall do it," she said with spirit, "but only because I want to." Framing his face in her little hands, she pulled it down toward her smiling mouth.

He did not resist. Her lips were soft and sweet. He felt the fullness of her breasts rising and falling against his bare chest, more and more erratically. When he could no longer bear the delicious torture, he swept her up in his arms and carried her to their bed.

'Tis she that to these gardens gave
That wondrous beauty which they have.

ANDREW MARVELL

Epilogue

Sophie, her hands protected by thick leather gloves, set the thorny bush into the hole she had prepared. She spaded some dirt over the roots and pressed it down firmly to cover them. Reaching for the watering can, she poured water into the hole. While she filled it in with more earth, she envisioned the arching canes that would fill the gap and spread outward along the wall, a living memorial to Luis Costa.

Echo and Rosa, ever interested in digging, came over to investigate. Sophie warned them not to disturb her newly planted rose.

She twisted around to look for Cecelia and Sir Michael, who strolled among the arbors with their son. The baronet plucked a pink rose for his lady—*Quatre Saisons*, the fragrant damask famous for its repeated bloom. Now reconciled, the couple planned to wed at the end of the month.

Daniel came running over with a rose for Sophie, presenting it with a bow. "You can put this in your hair."

"You'll have to do it for me." She held up her gloved hands helplessly.

"Let me," her husband offered.

The child darted away as quickly as he'd come, and followed his parents into the knot garden. The dogs, bored and neglected, chased after him.

Cassian tucked the flower in among Sophie's braids. "Did I tell you what Daniel said when I announced he'll be getting a cousin next spring?"

She shook her head.

"He hoped that Parham's lurcher bitch would whelp again, so the baby could have its very own pup."

"Another dog!" Sophie laughed. *"Bein seux*, we do need help keeping that weasel away."

"What sort of rose have you planted here?"

"Rosa moschata plena. A late-blooming musk, a vigorous climber, and very ancient. Luis told me once he was fond of white roses." She removed her gloves and tossed them aside. As he helped her up, she added wistfully, "I wish he could see the gardens as they look now. He would be so pleased."

"As always, you've managed to achieve much in a brief time. How will you occupy yourself when this restoration project is complete?"

Sophie shook her head at him. *"J'avons hardi a faithe*—we've much more to do, Emrys and I. Gardens are never really finished."

Cassian laughed. "So I am discovering. Well, I once demanded that you make Bevington a showplace, and that is exactly what you've done. Do you know, Lady Bevington, I believe you could set a fashion."

"Nânnîn, nobody has ever heard of me. I never achieved the fame of Humphry Repton or Capability Brown. Or Tobias."

"Wherever a countess leads, society must follow. If we open our gardens to visitors, you could prevail upon other landowners to preserve the formal grandeur of the past."

"You think I could?"

"My dearest Sophie," he answered tenderly, "I am confident that you can accomplish anything."

She rose on tiptoe to press a loving and grateful kiss upon his cheek.

"A paltry reward for my great faith in you," he teased. "We may be old married folk, with a child on the way, but I think we can show my sister and her betrothed the proper mode of courtship in a rose bower. It was here, you know, that you pledged to become my wife. Sophie?"

Lost in reverie, she asked, "Don't you think it would be pleasant to have a bench under each of the arbors?"

"Yes, yes, you may have as many damned benches as you want. And statues. And rosebushes. I'm learning to accept your obsession with this glorious garden," he said, taking her firmly in his arms. "But you must always be aware of the man standing with you in the garden. Loving you."

"*Tréjous*," she assured him. "Always," she repeated, discarding vague plans for benches and arbors, and concentrating all her attention and talents on the man who was kissing her.

Author's Note

While writing *The Proposal* I became acquainted, through my research, with a famous Romantic poet, a celebrated landscape gardener, and a renowned Gloucestershire physician.

It is true that Samuel Taylor Coleridge was inspired to write his epic poem "The Rime of the Ancient Mariner" after a friend told him about a disturbing nightmare. During his "honeymoon period" with laudanum he produced some of his finest verses, but in later years addiction wrecked his marriage and his health.

Debate about garden styles raged throughout the final decade of the 18th century, when painters, essayists, and poets publicized rival theories through their works. Others shared my heroine's prejudice against Humphry Repton, although this was a minority opinion. Various accounts of his life and his own writings indicate that he was well-intentioned and not deliberately controversial. His transition from naturalistic to more formal designs did indeed occur in the late 1790s.

Dr. Edward Jenner's experiments and eventual success with his cowpox vaccine eventually eradicated the dreaded smallpox. Visitors to his residence at Berkeley, now the Jenner Museum, will learn how actively and selflessly he worked to develop and promote his procedure.

I should also add that all the historic roses referred to in this story thrive in my own garden—tending them was undoubtedly my favorite type of "research"! The varieties known and preferred by my heroine are unsurpassed in beauty, color, fragrance, and hardiness.

Avon Romances—
the best in exceptional authors and unforgettable novels!

Avon Romantic Treasures

*Unforgettable, enthralling love stories,
sparkling with passion and adventure
from Romance's bestselling authors*